ANiMUS

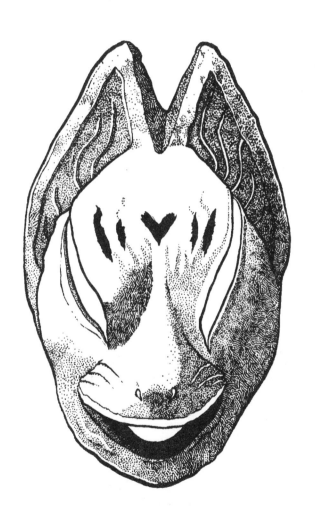

MAY   2018

J-GN REVOY

FOR DOMINIQUE
AND AIMÉE REVOY

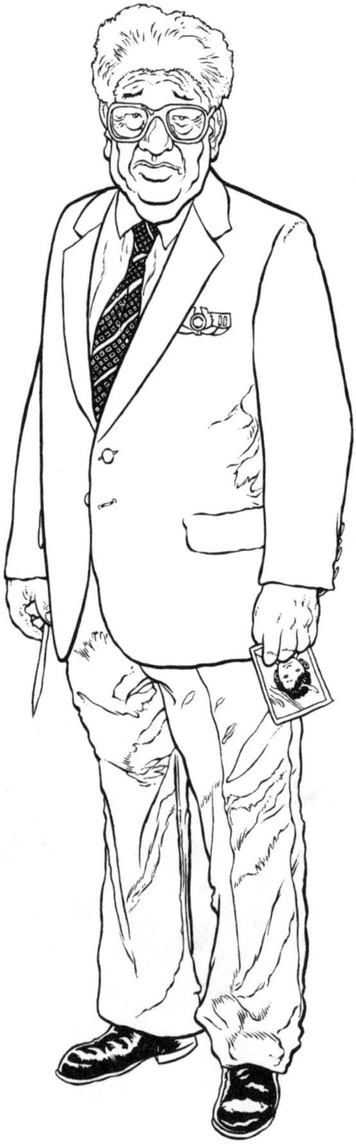

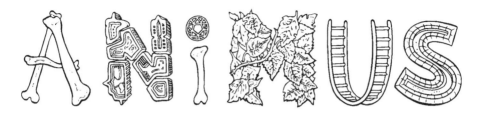

ANTOINE REVOY

:01

First Second
New York

Prologue:
Find me

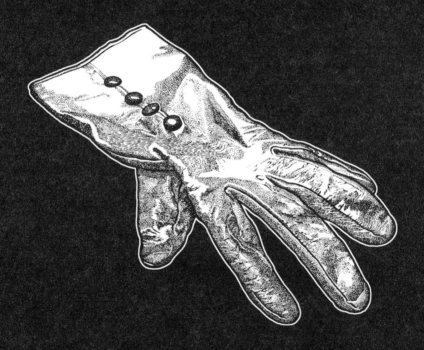

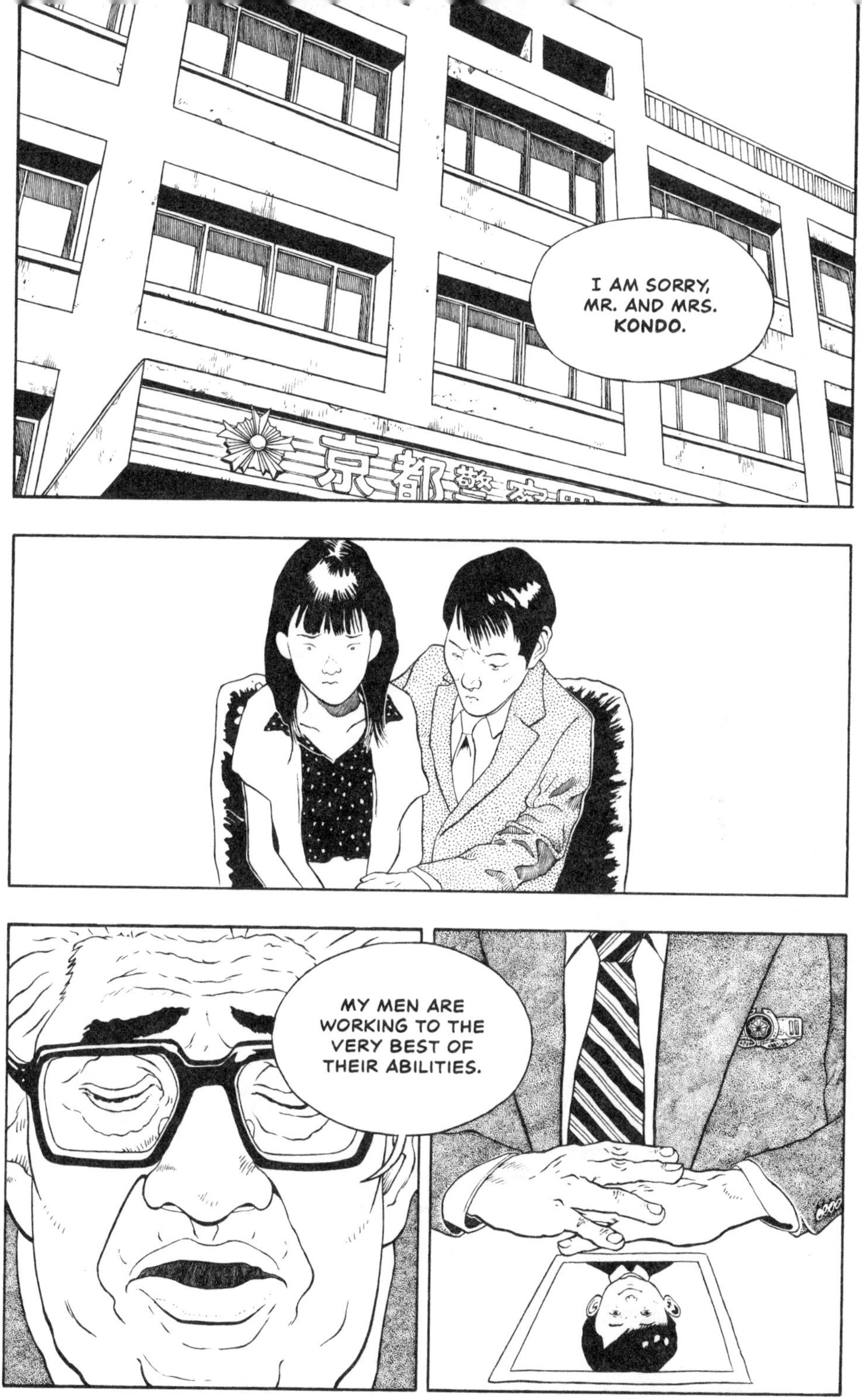
I AM SORRY, MR. AND MRS. KONDO.
京都
MY MEN ARE WORKING TO THE VERY BEST OF THEIR ABILITIES.

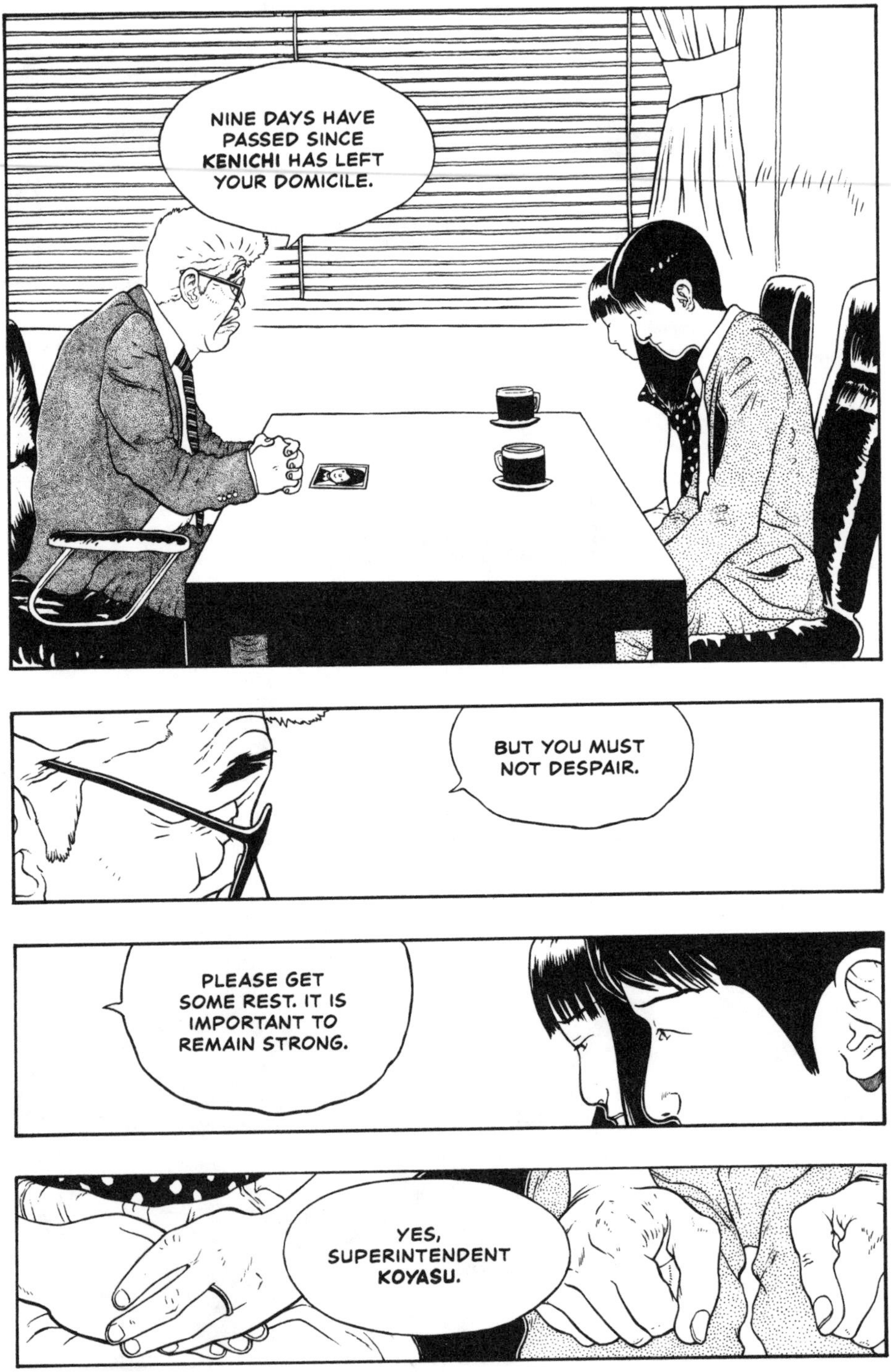
NINE DAYS HAVE PASSED SINCE KENICHI HAS LEFT YOUR DOMICILE.
BUT YOU MUST NOT DESPAIR.
PLEASE GET SOME REST. IT IS IMPORTANT TO REMAIN STRONG.
YES, SUPERINTENDENT KOYASU.

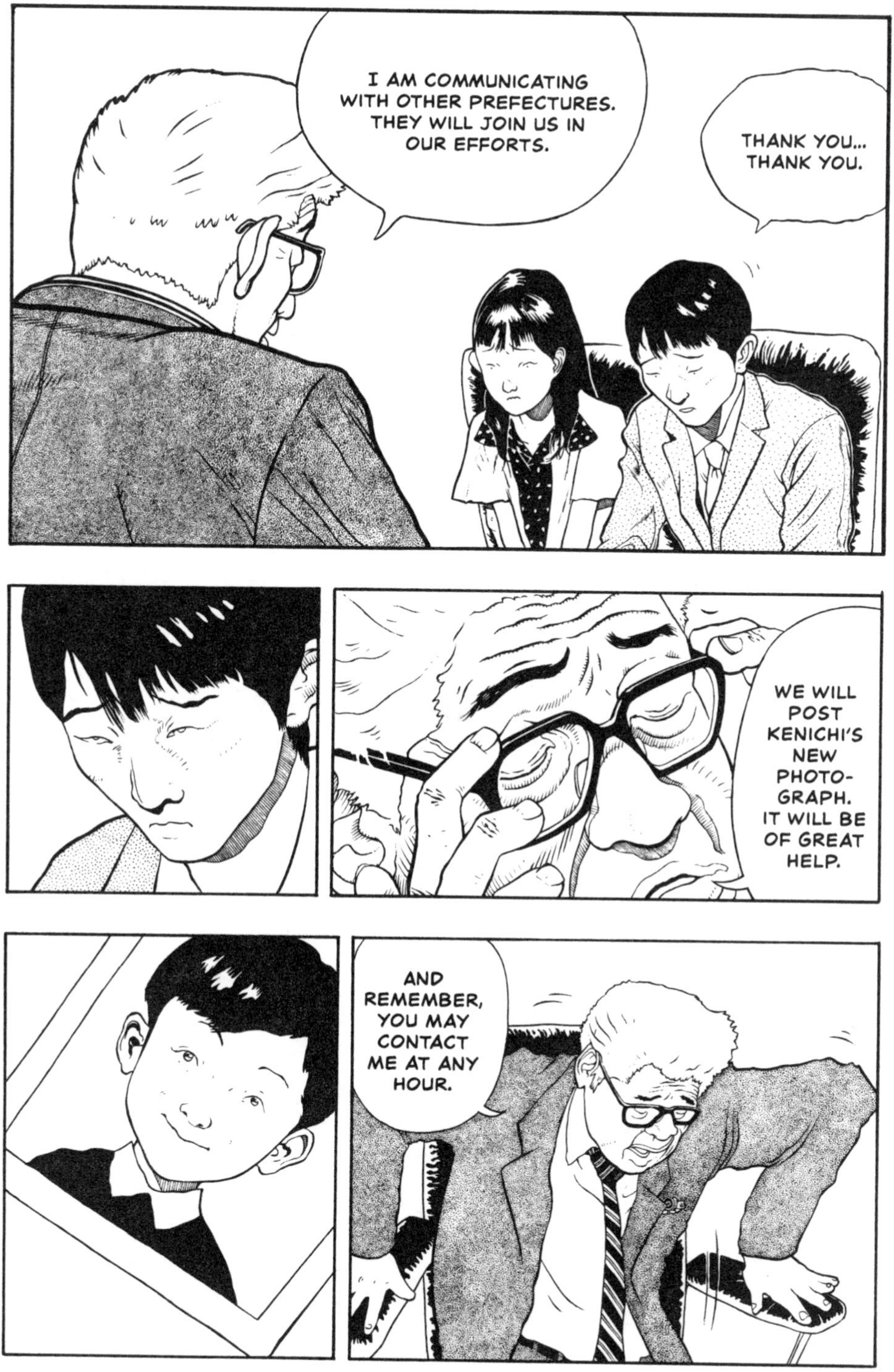
I AM COMMUNICATING WITH OTHER PREFECTURES. THEY WILL JOIN US IN OUR EFFORTS.
THANK YOU... THANK YOU.
WE WILL POST KENICHI'S NEW PHOTO-GRAPH. IT WILL BE OF GREAT HELP.
AND REMEMBER, YOU MAY CONTACT ME AT ANY HOUR.

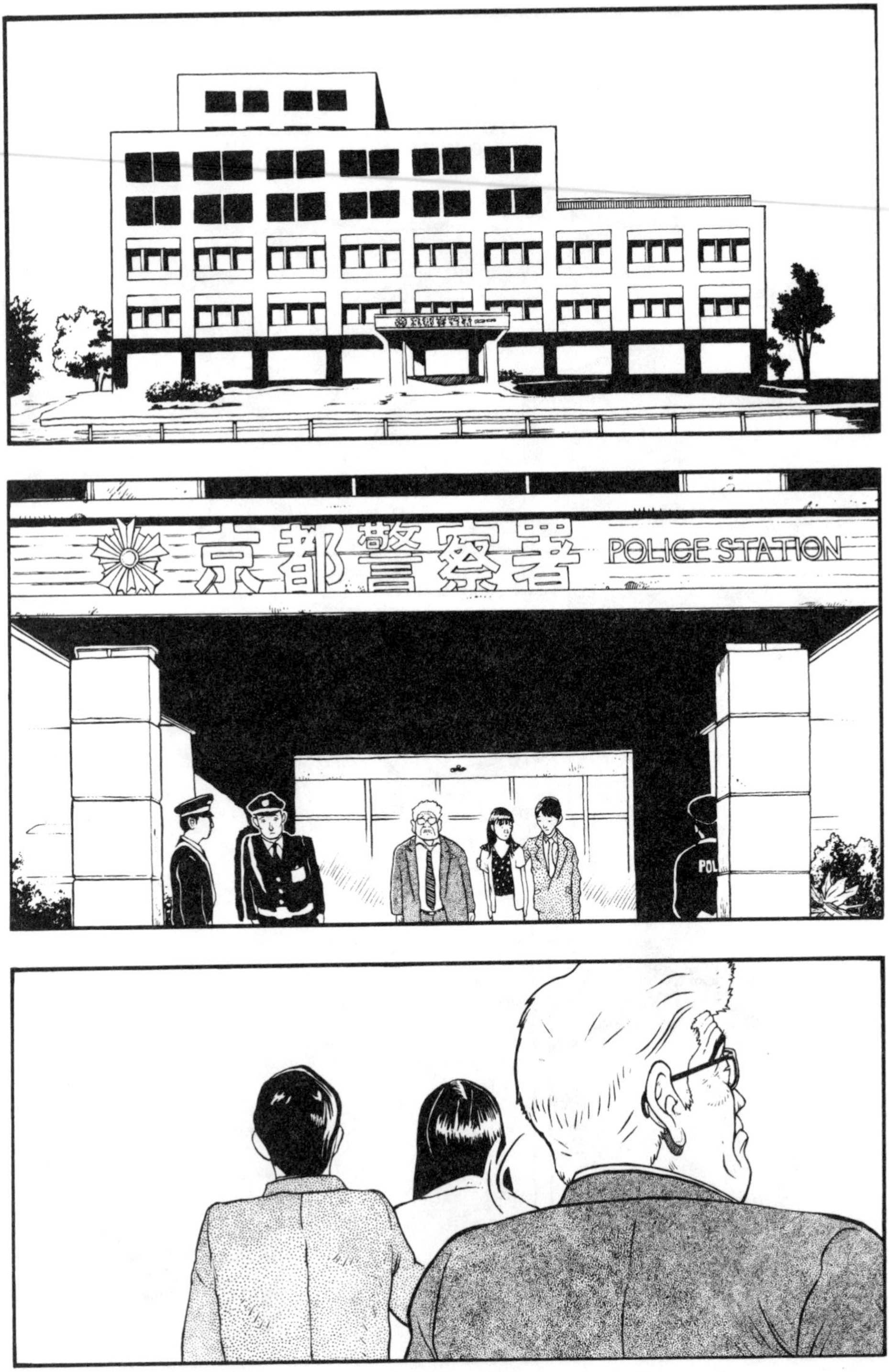
京都警察署
POLICE STATION
POL

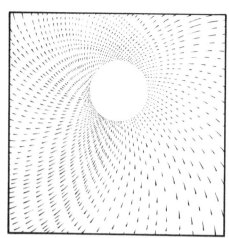

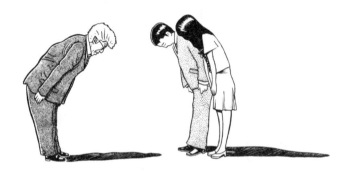

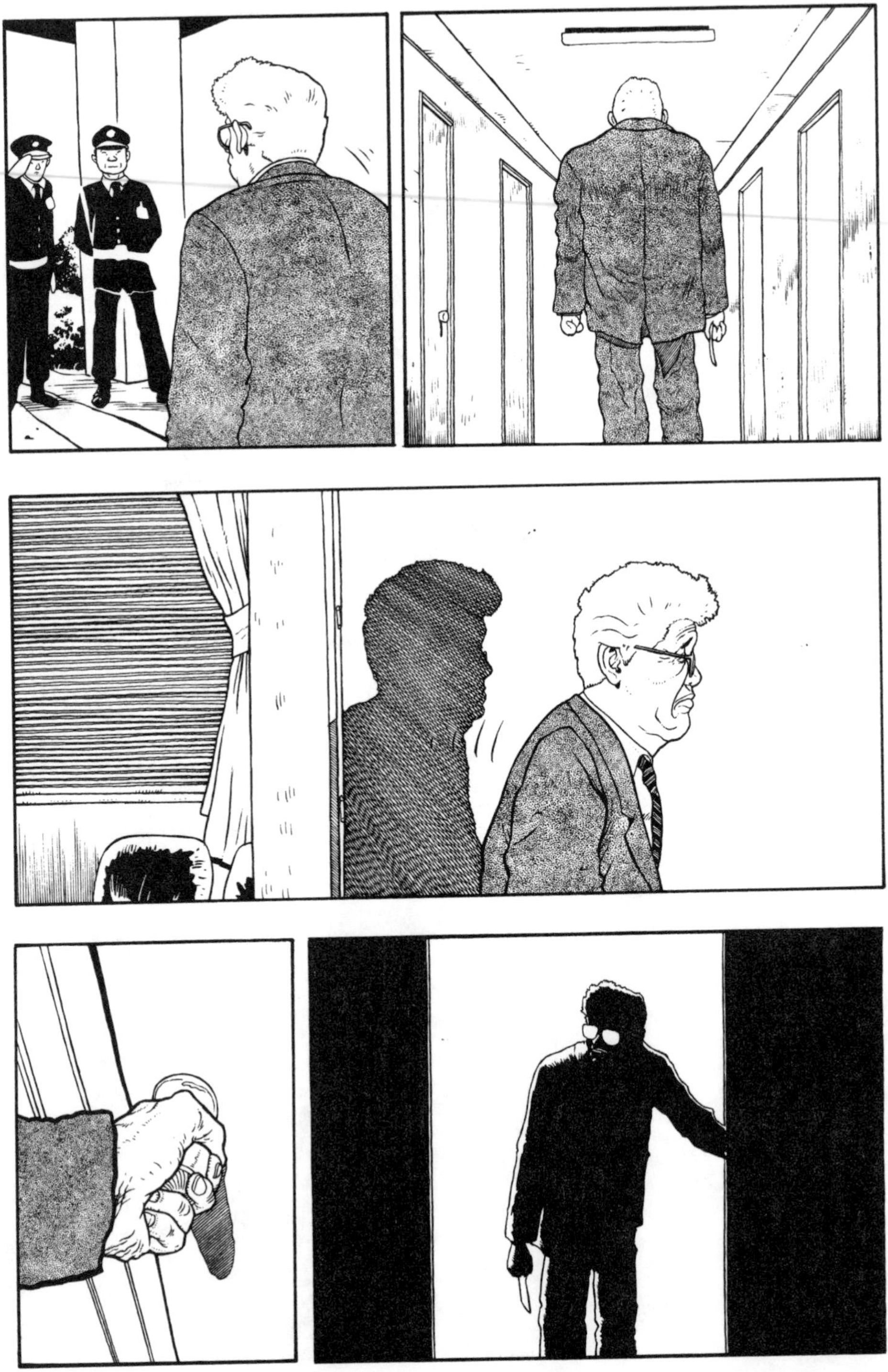

CLICK

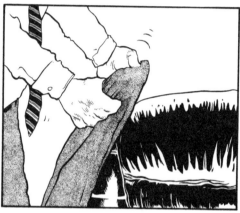

...

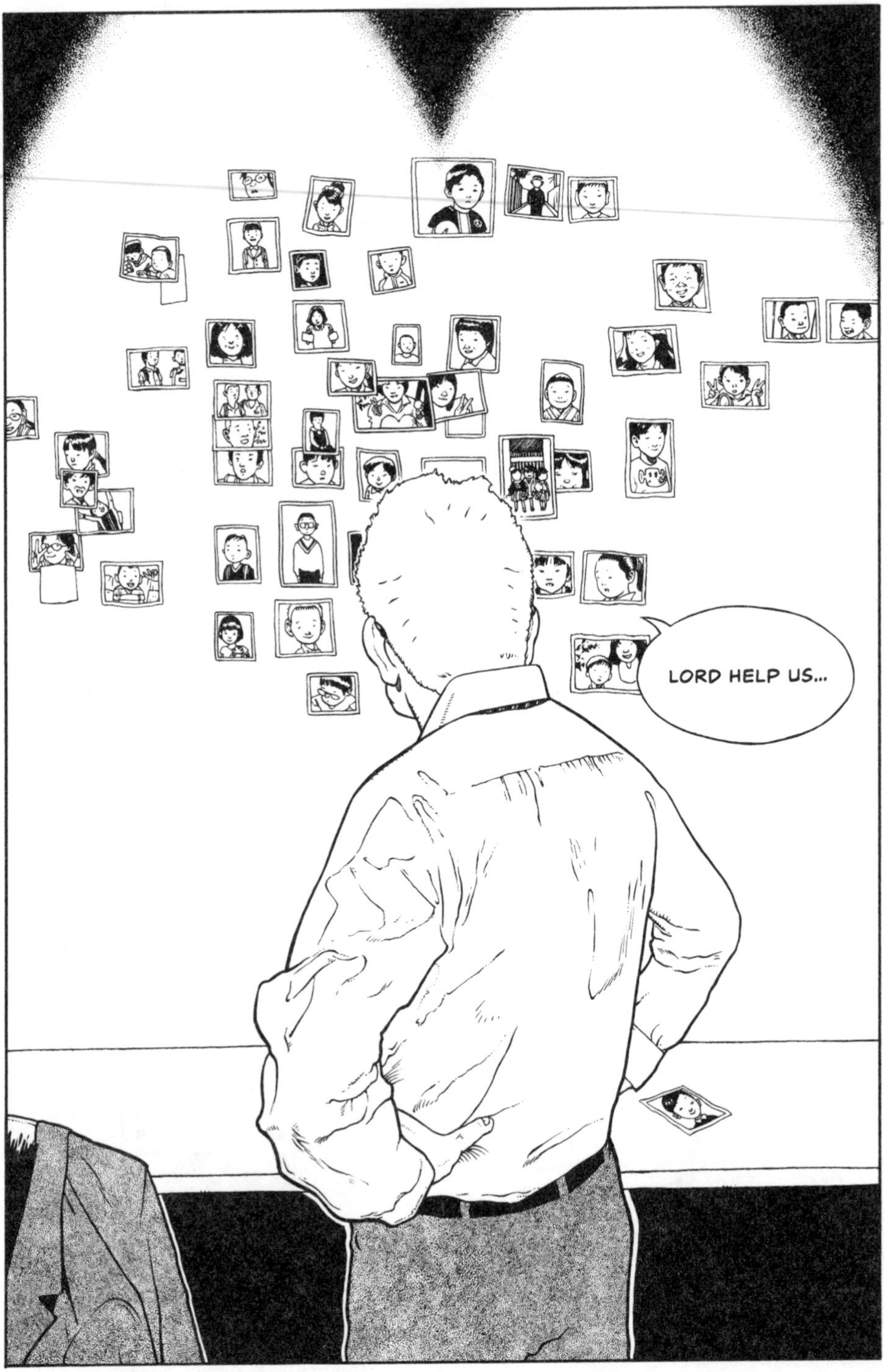
LORD HELP US...

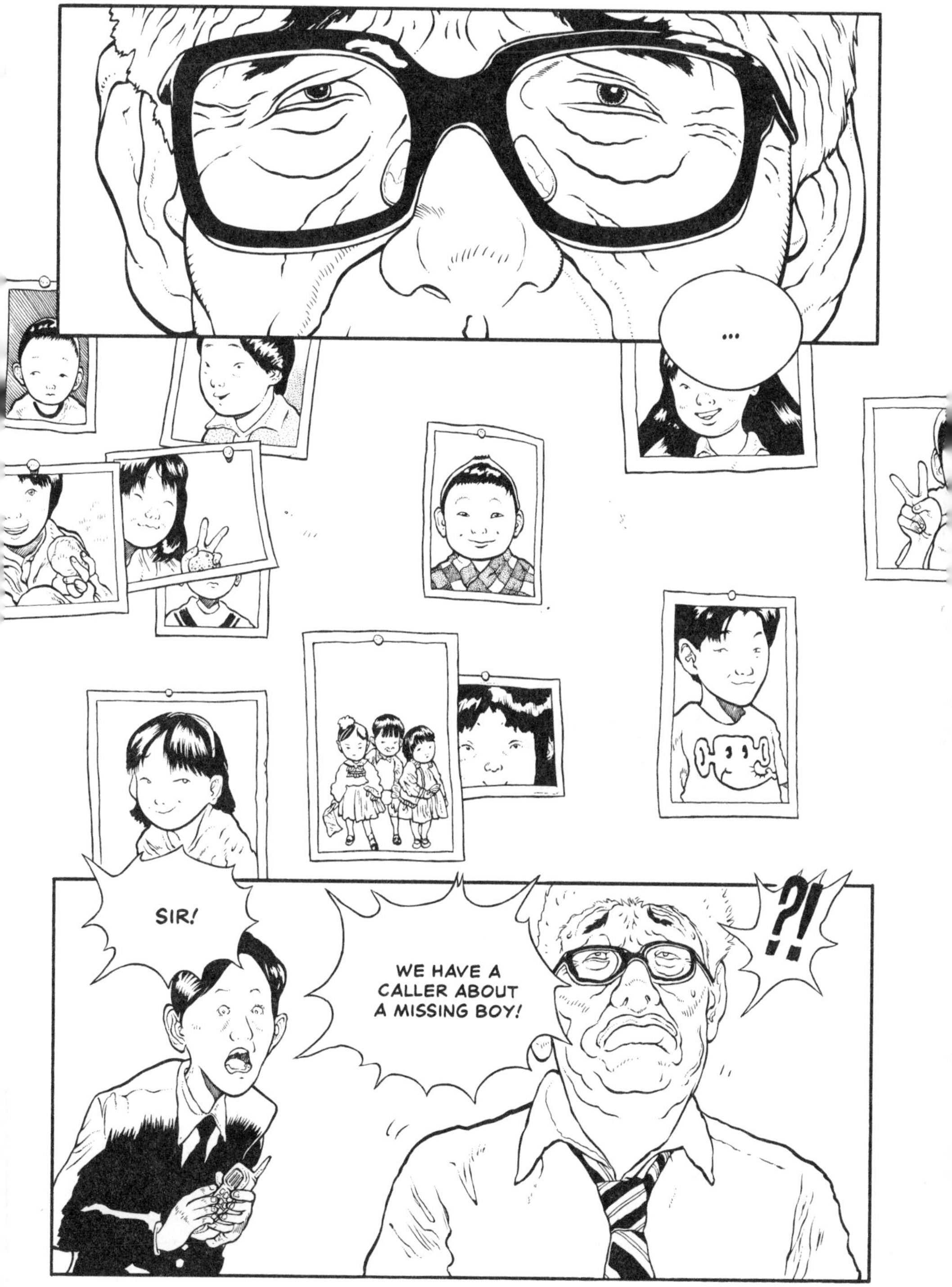
...
SIR!
WE HAVE A CALLER ABOUT A MISSING BOY!
?!

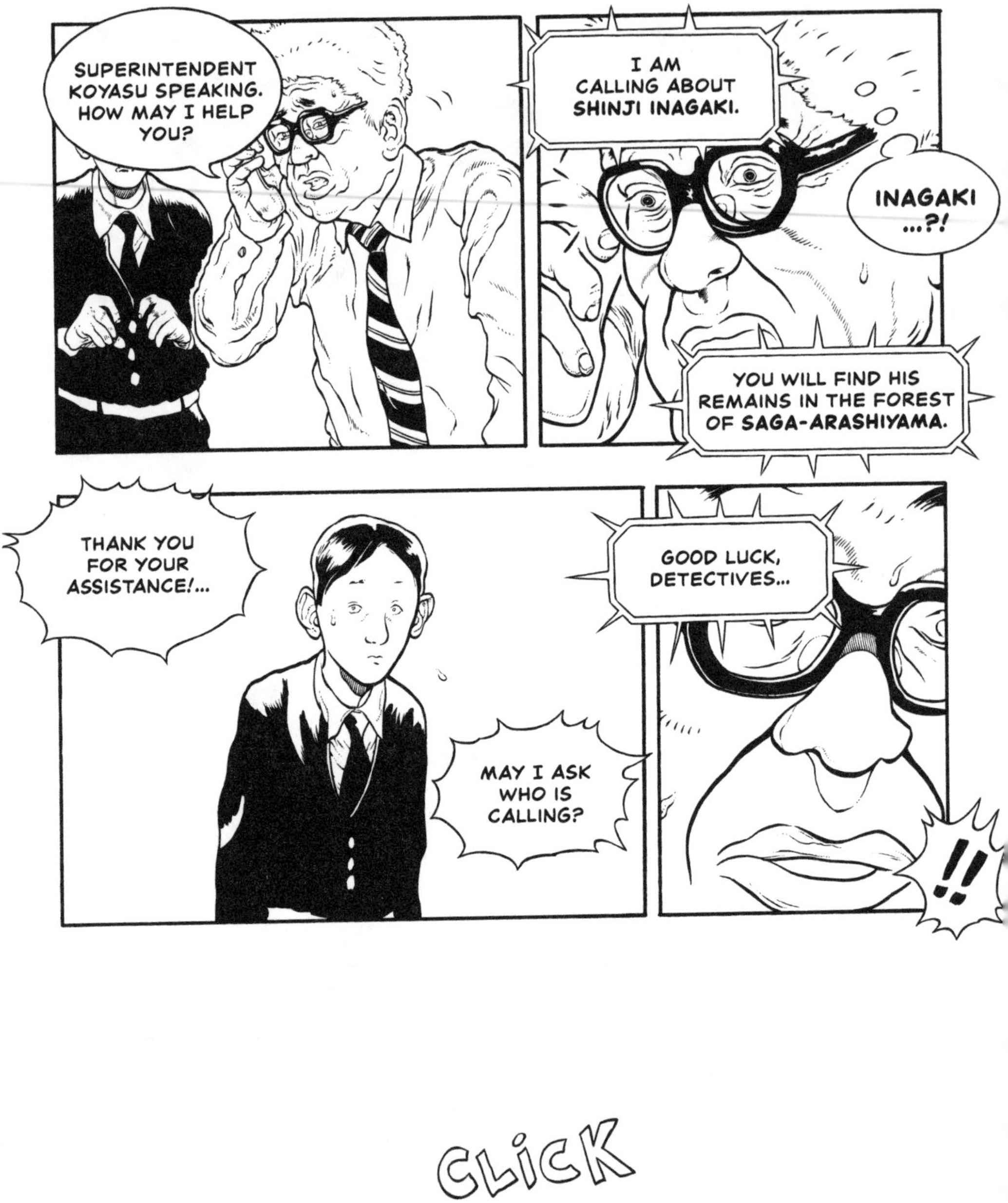
SUPERINTENDENT KOYASU SPEAKING. HOW MAY I HELP YOU?
I AM CALLING ABOUT SHINJI INAGAKI.
INAGAKI ...?!
YOU WILL FIND HIS REMAINS IN THE FOREST OF SAGA-ARASHIYAMA.
THANK YOU FOR YOUR ASSISTANCE!...
MAY I ASK WHO IS CALLING?
GOOD LUCK, DETECTIVES...
!!
CLICK

Chapter 1:
The Playground

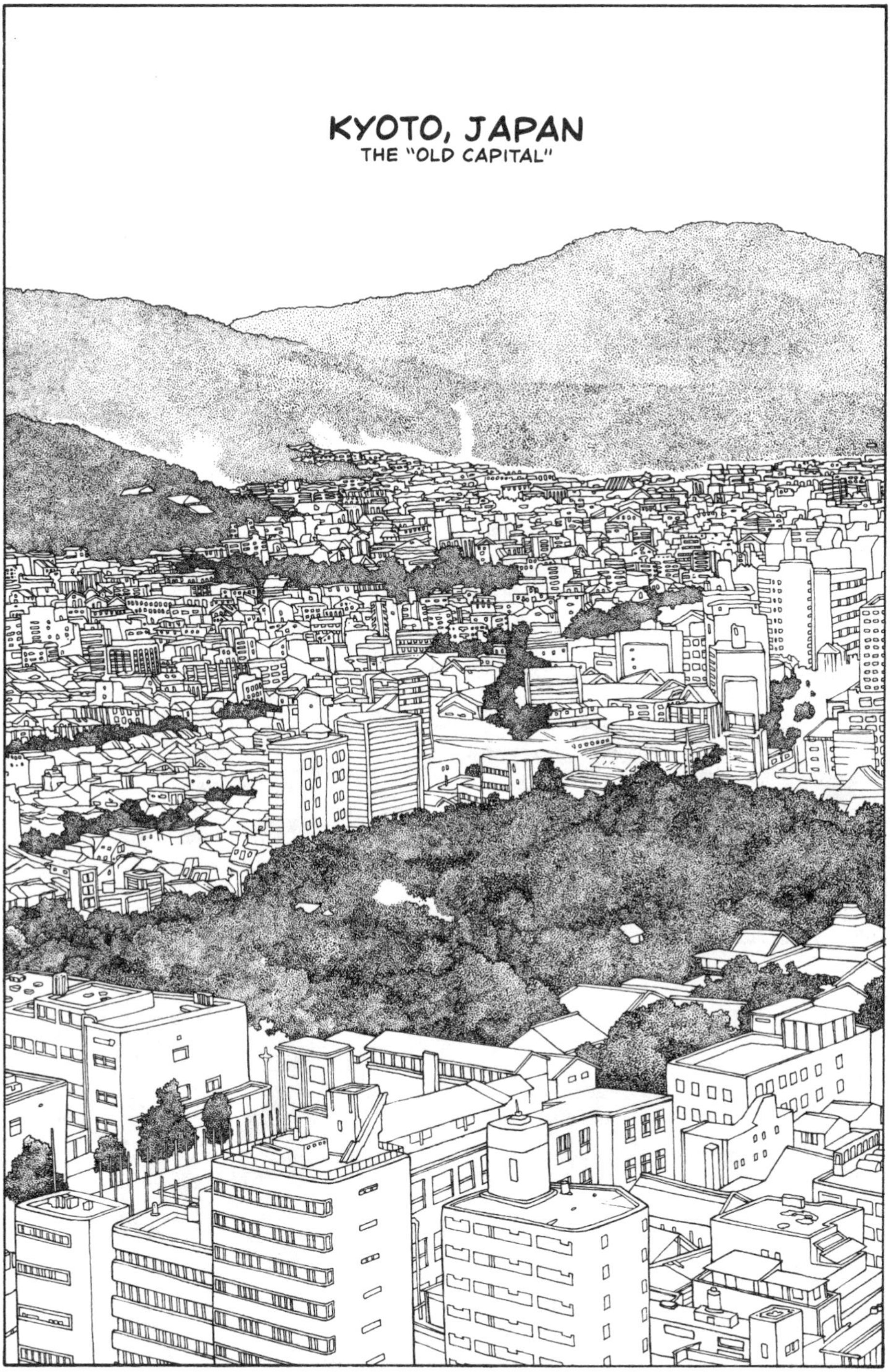
KYOTO, JAPAN
THE "OLD CAPITAL"

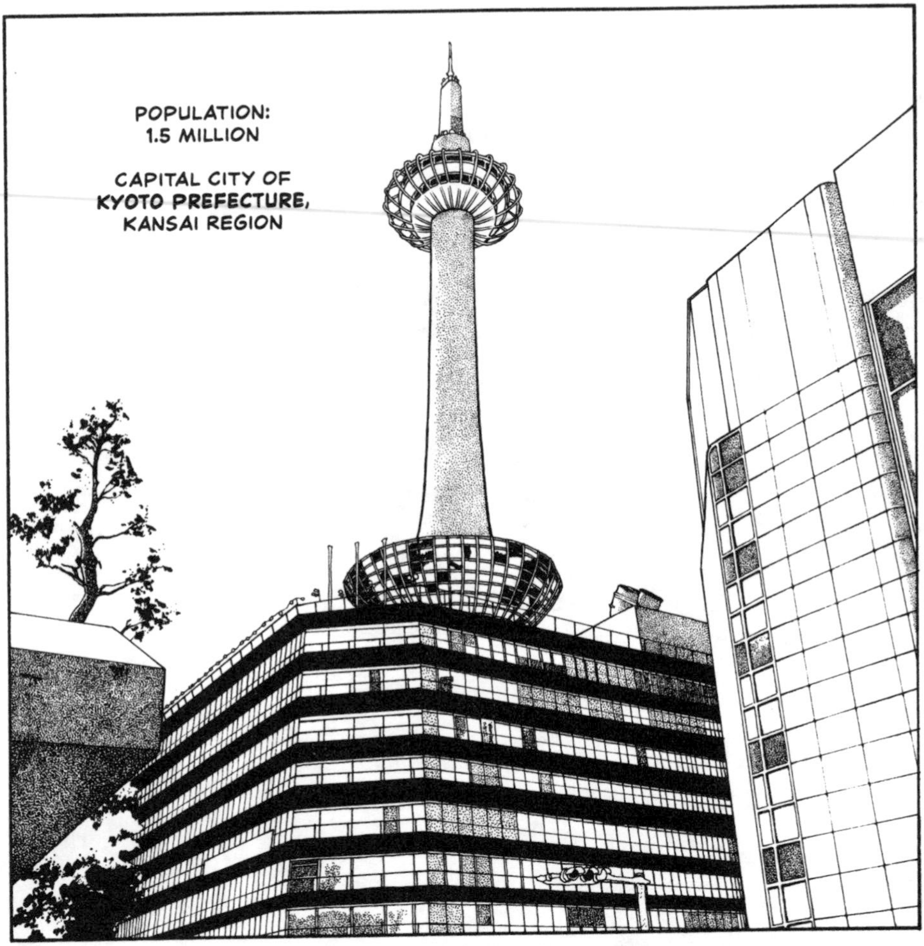
POPULATION:
1.5 MILLION
CAPITAL CITY OF
KYOTO PREFECTURE,
KANSAI REGION

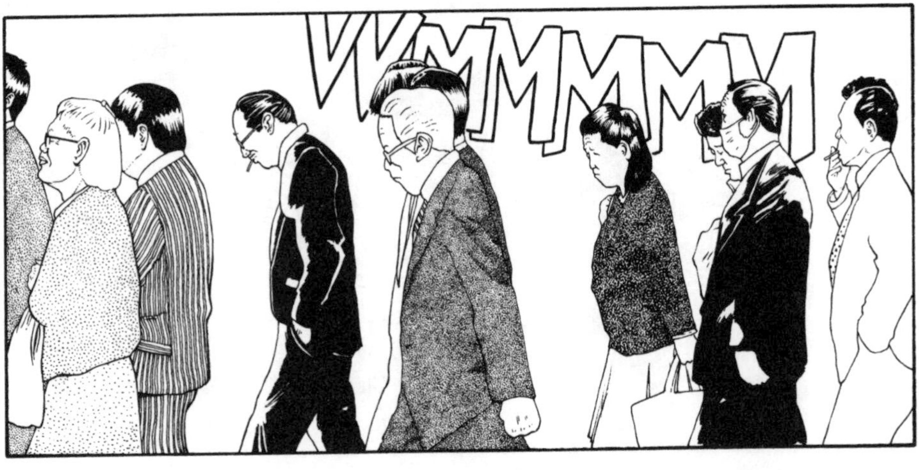
VVMMMMMM

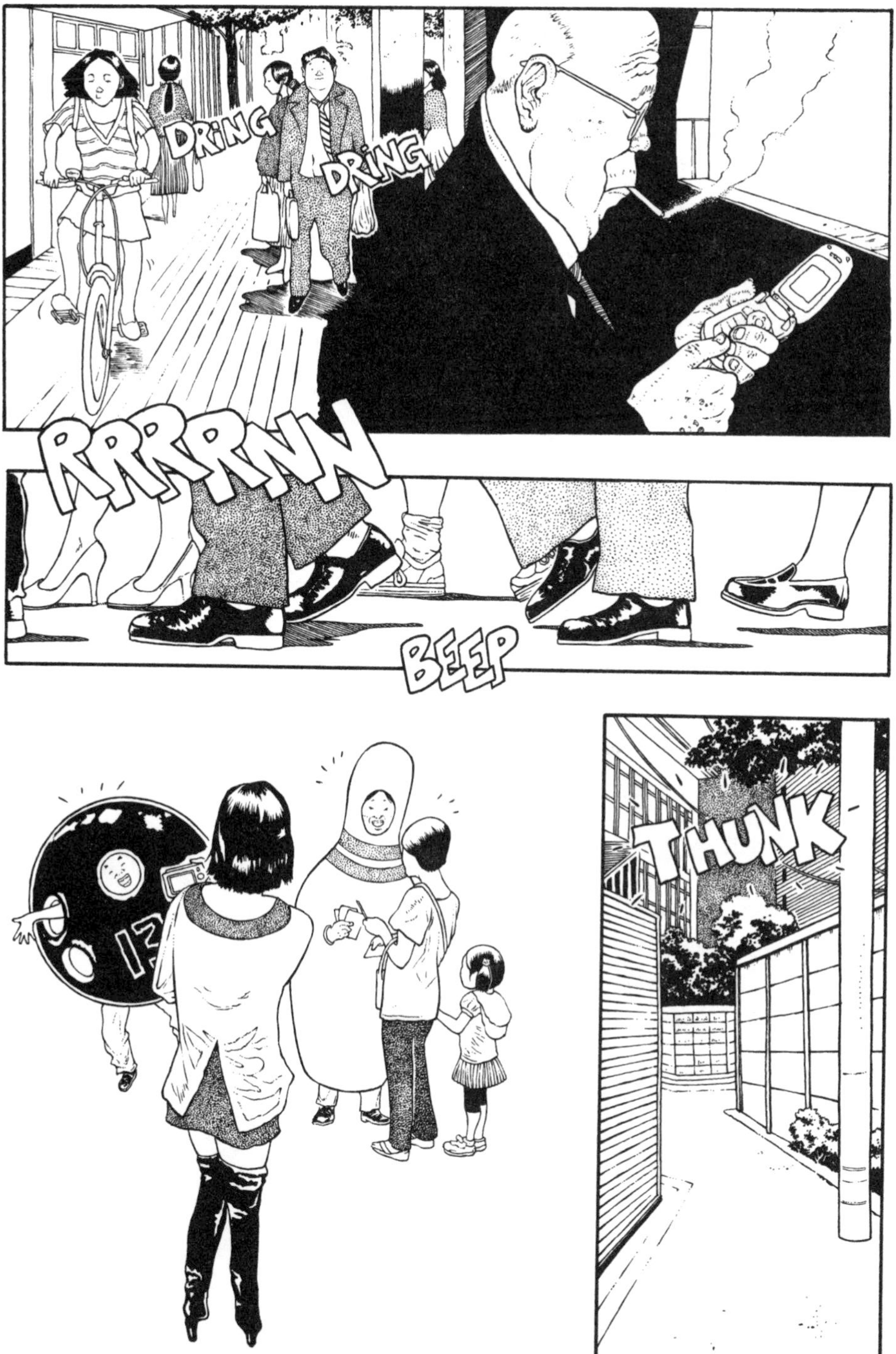
DRiNG
DRiNG
RRRRNN
BEEP
THUNK

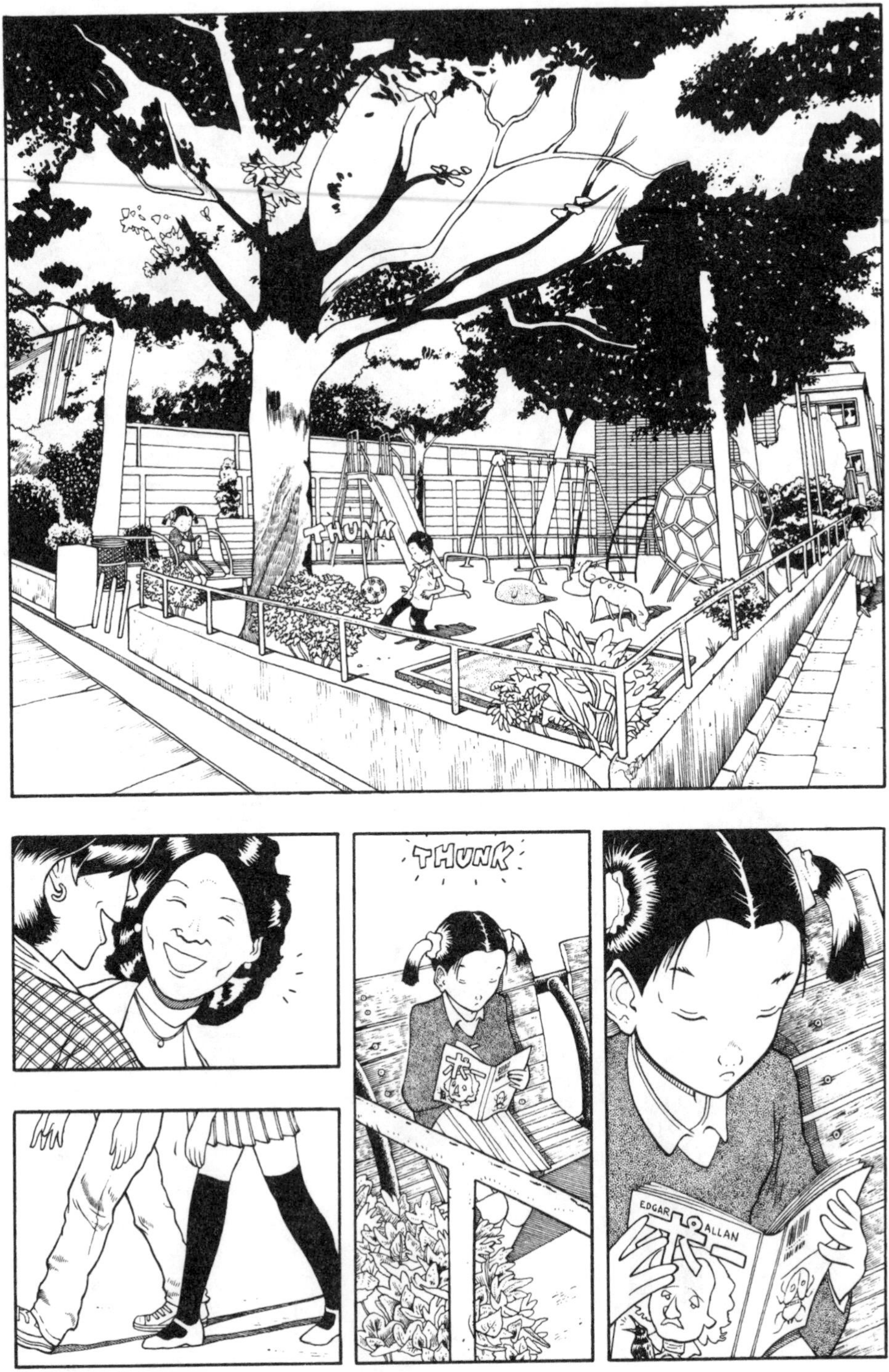
THUNK
THUNK
EDGAR
ALLAN

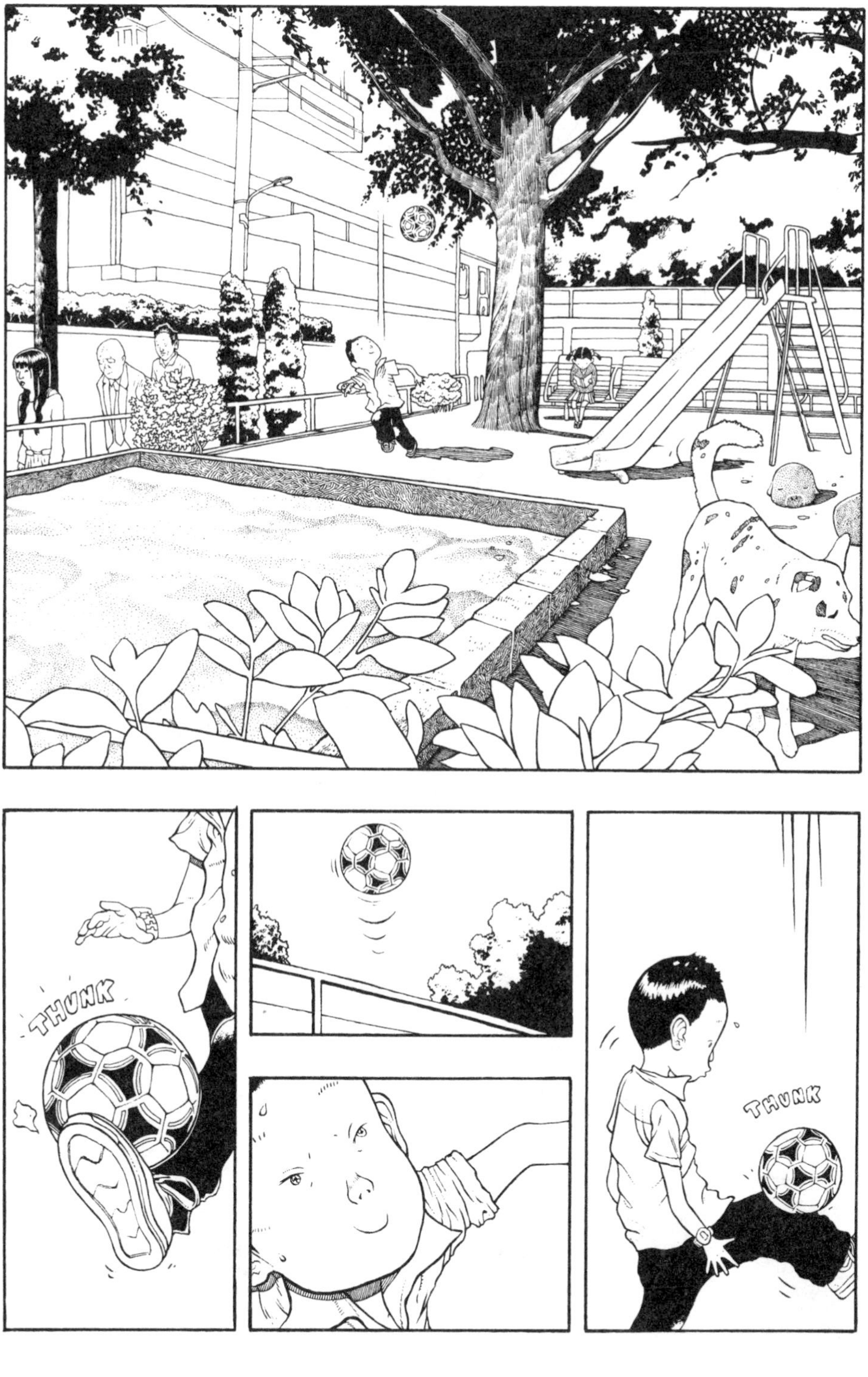
THUNK
THUNK

YOU SHOULDN'T PLAY WITH YOUR SOCCER BALL ON THE TAR, HISAO.

YOU'RE GONNA RUIN ITS LEATHER.

HE-HE, WHATEVER, SAYURI.

YOU KNOW...

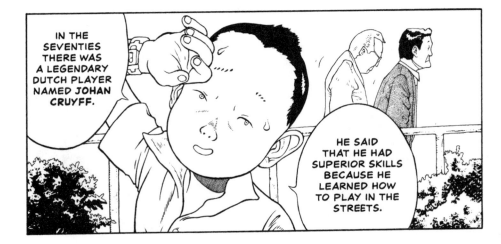

IN THE SEVENTIES THERE WAS A LEGENDARY DUTCH PLAYER NAMED JOHAN CRUYFF.

HE SAID THAT HE HAD SUPERIOR SKILLS BECAUSE HE LEARNED HOW TO PLAY IN THE STREETS.

22

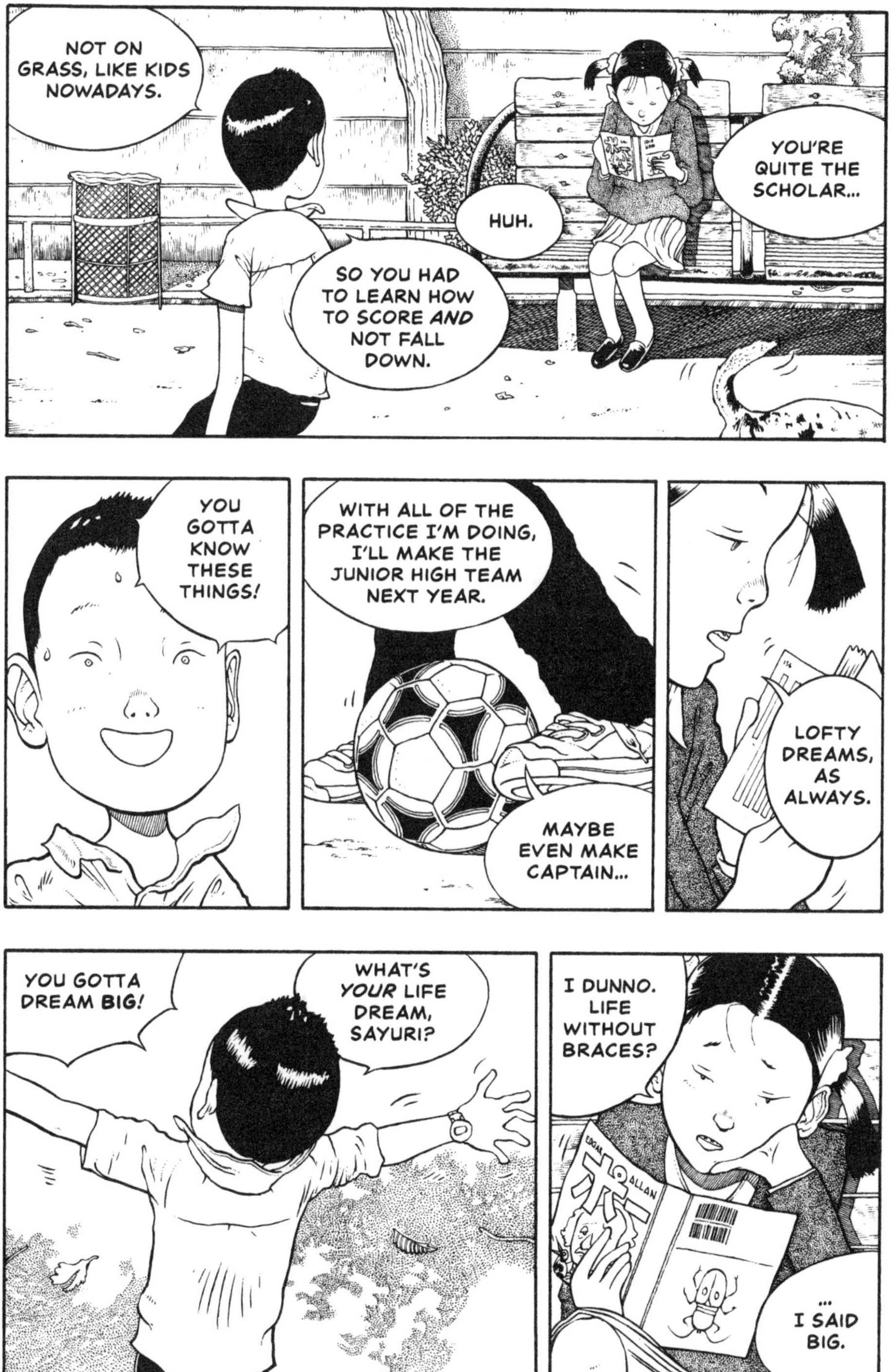
NOT ON GRASS, LIKE KIDS NOWADAYS.
HUH.
SO YOU HAD TO LEARN HOW TO SCORE *AND* NOT FALL DOWN.
YOU'RE QUITE THE SCHOLAR...
YOU GOTTA KNOW THESE THINGS!
WITH ALL OF THE PRACTICE I'M DOING, I'LL MAKE THE JUNIOR HIGH TEAM NEXT YEAR.
MAYBE EVEN MAKE CAPTAIN...
LOFTY DREAMS, AS ALWAYS.
YOU GOTTA DREAM BIG!
WHAT'S *YOUR* LIFE DREAM, SAYURI?
I DUNNO. LIFE WITHOUT BRACES?
... I SAID BIG.

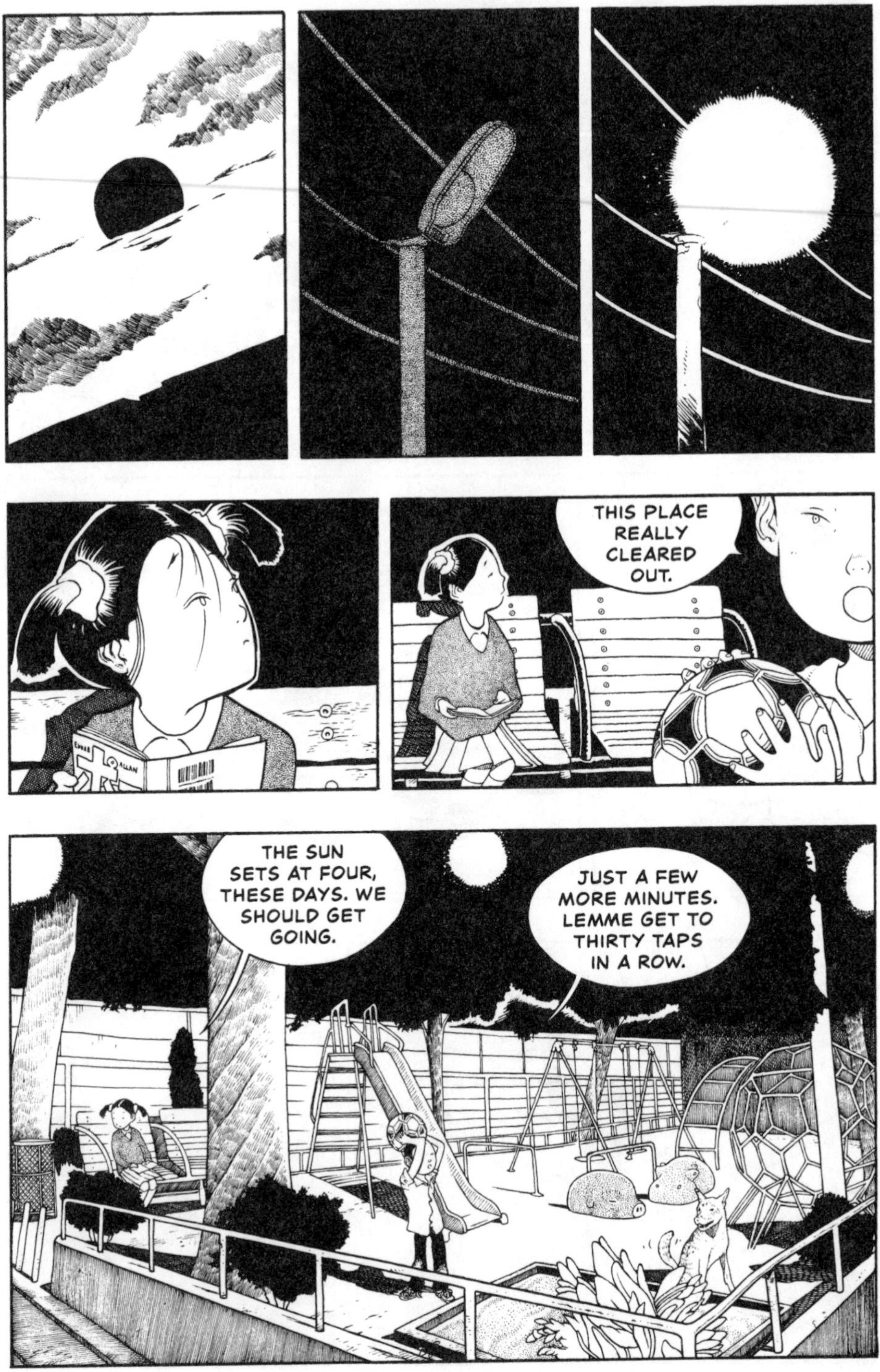
THIS PLACE REALLY CLEARED OUT.
THE SUN SETS AT FOUR, THESE DAYS. WE SHOULD GET GOING.
JUST A FEW MORE MINUTES. LEMME GET TO THIRTY TAPS IN A ROW.

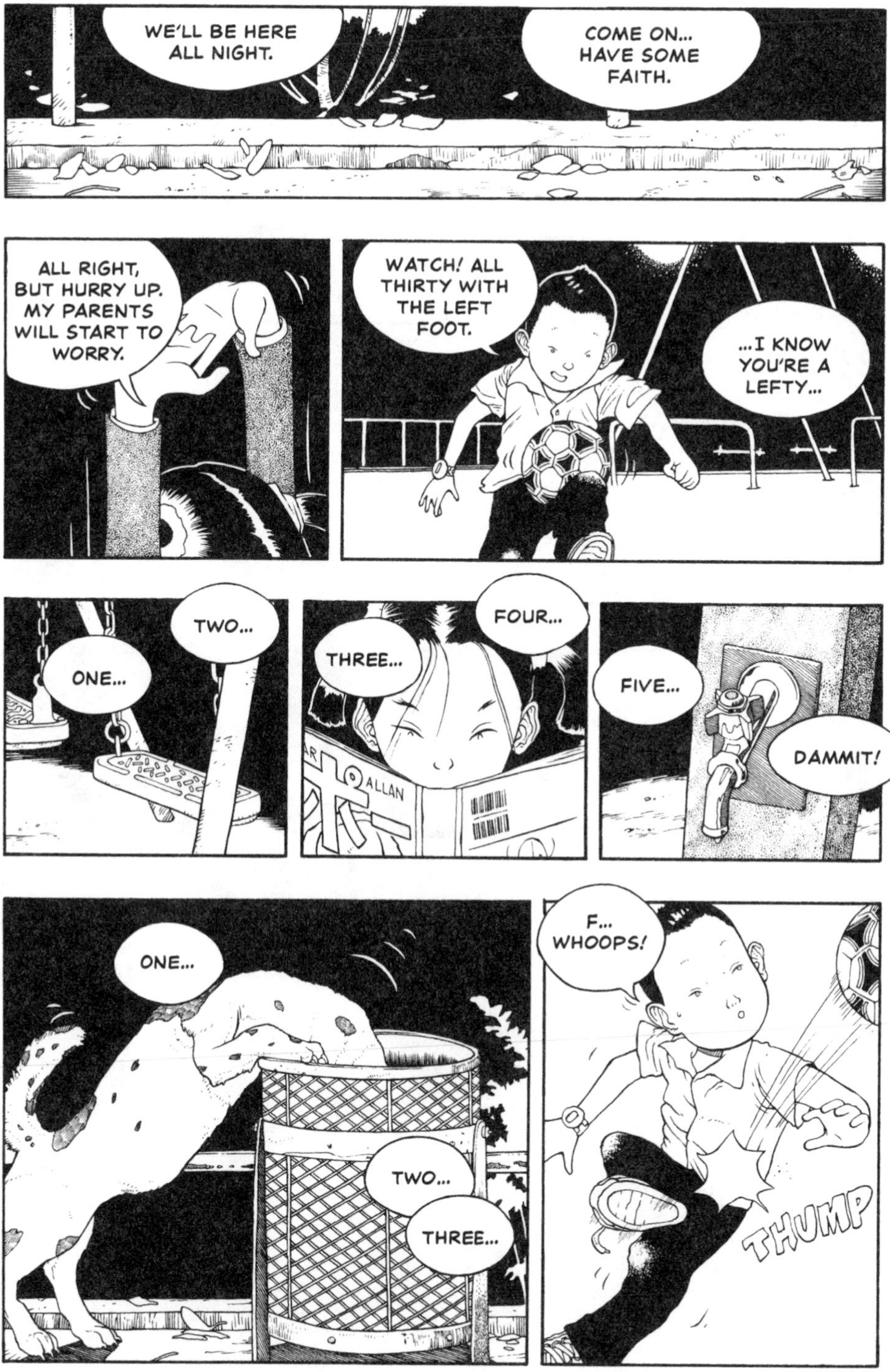
WE'LL BE HERE ALL NIGHT.
COME ON... HAVE SOME FAITH.
ALL RIGHT, BUT HURRY UP. MY PARENTS WILL START TO WORRY.
WATCH! ALL THIRTY WITH THE LEFT FOOT.
...I KNOW YOU'RE A LEFTY...
ONE...
TWO...
THREE...
FOUR...
FIVE...
DAMMIT!
ONE...
TWO...
THREE...
F... WHOOPS!
THUMP

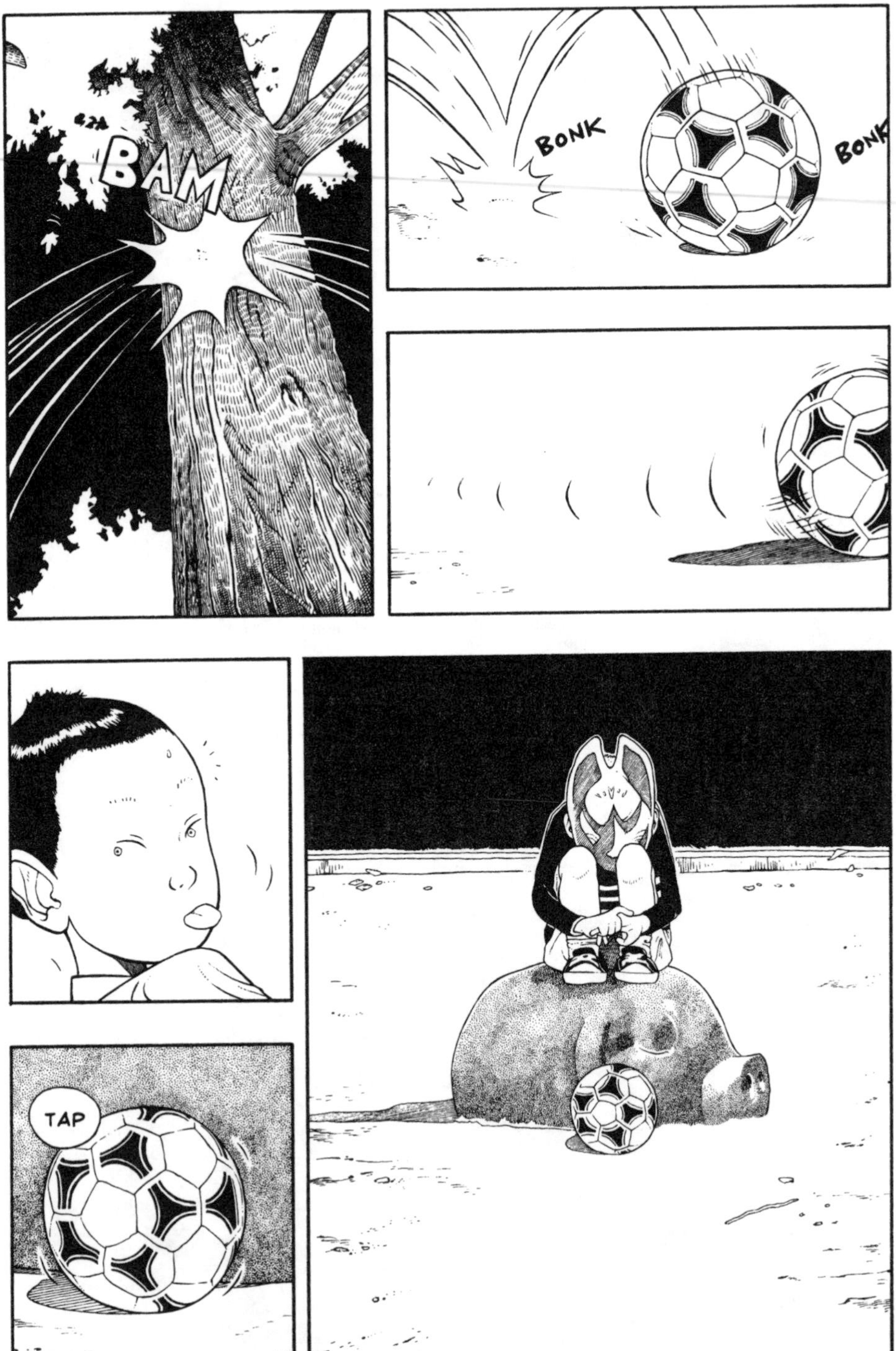
BAM
BONK
BONK
TAP

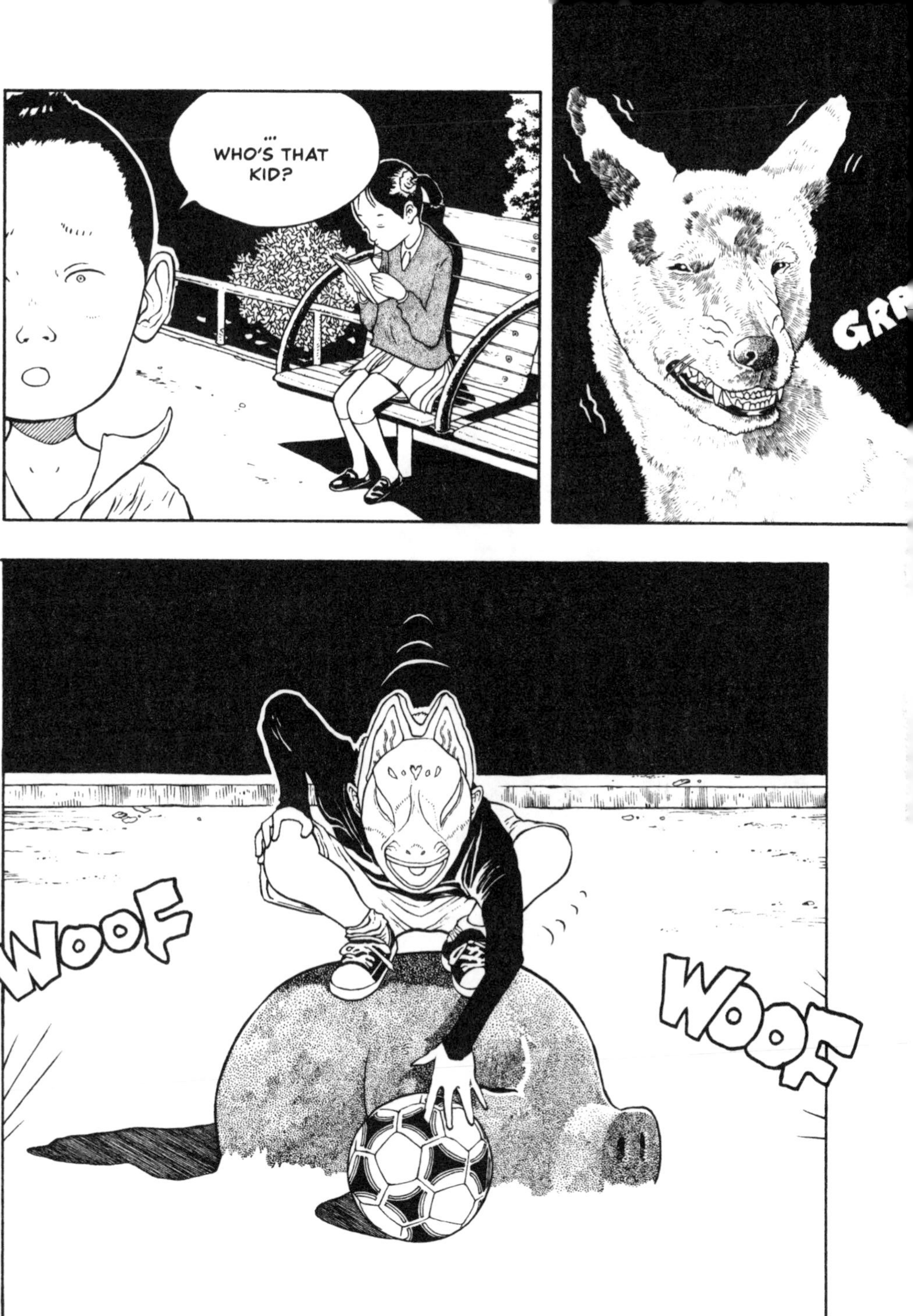
... WHO'S THAT KID?
GRR
WOOF
WOOF

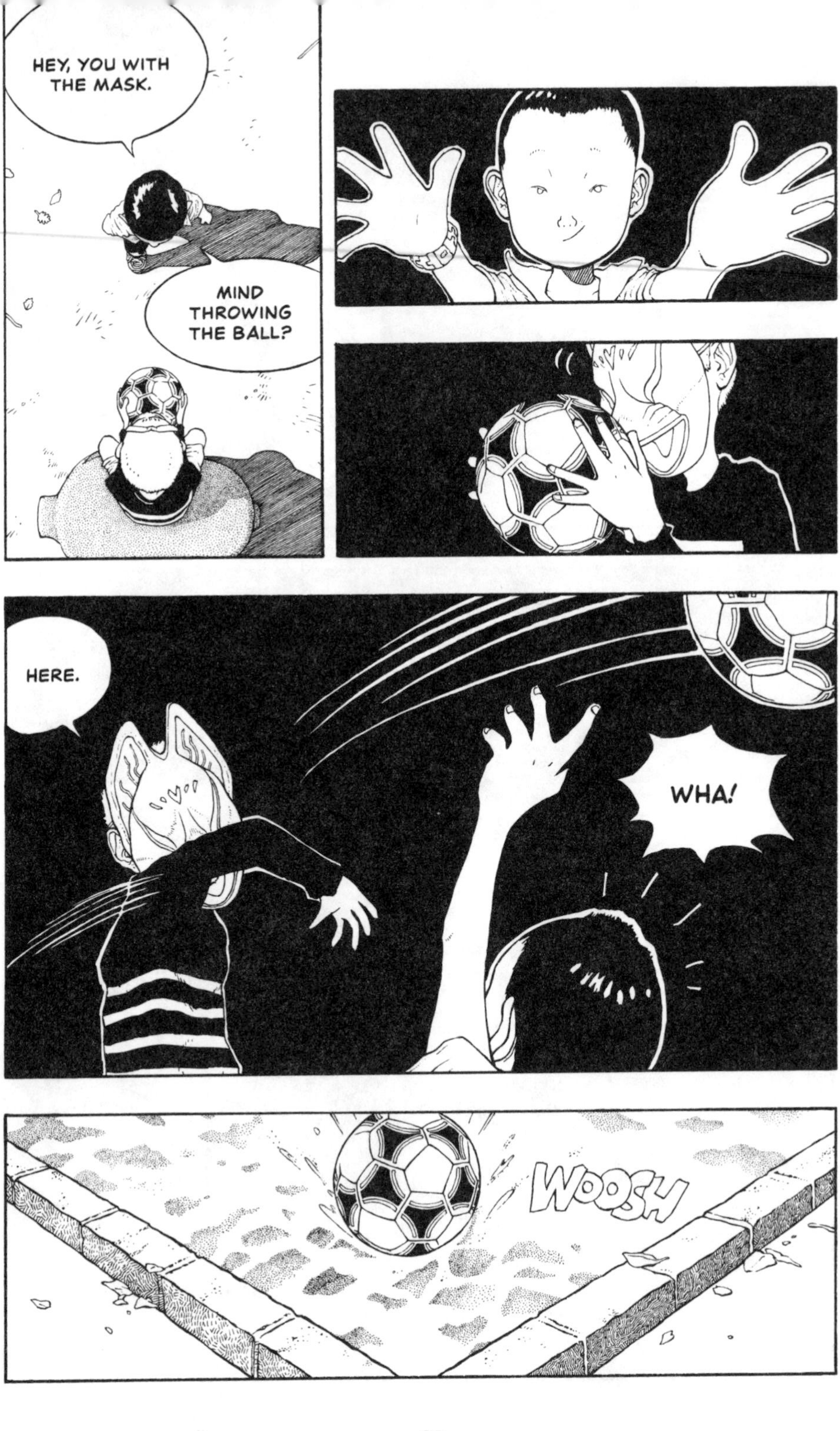
HEY, YOU WITH THE MASK.
MIND THROWING THE BALL?
HERE.
WHA!
WOOSH

VERY MATURE...

WHAT THE HELL IS YOUR PROBLEM?!

SERIOUSLY
...

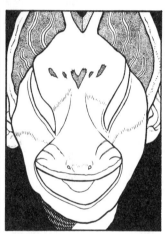

WOOF

WOOF

AND THAT'S ENOUGH OUT OF YOU, TOO, STRAY MUTT!

!!!

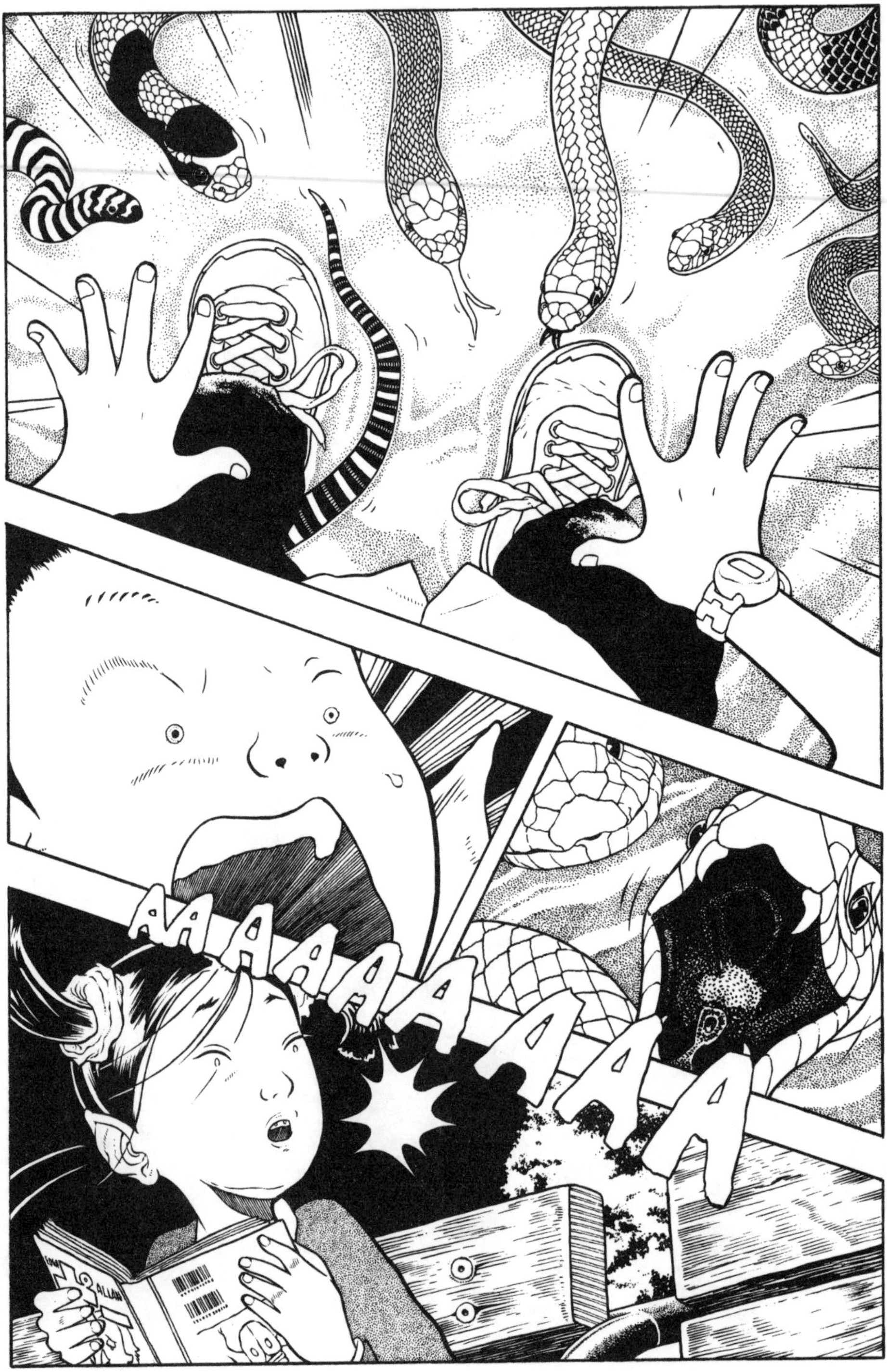
AAAAAAAAAAA

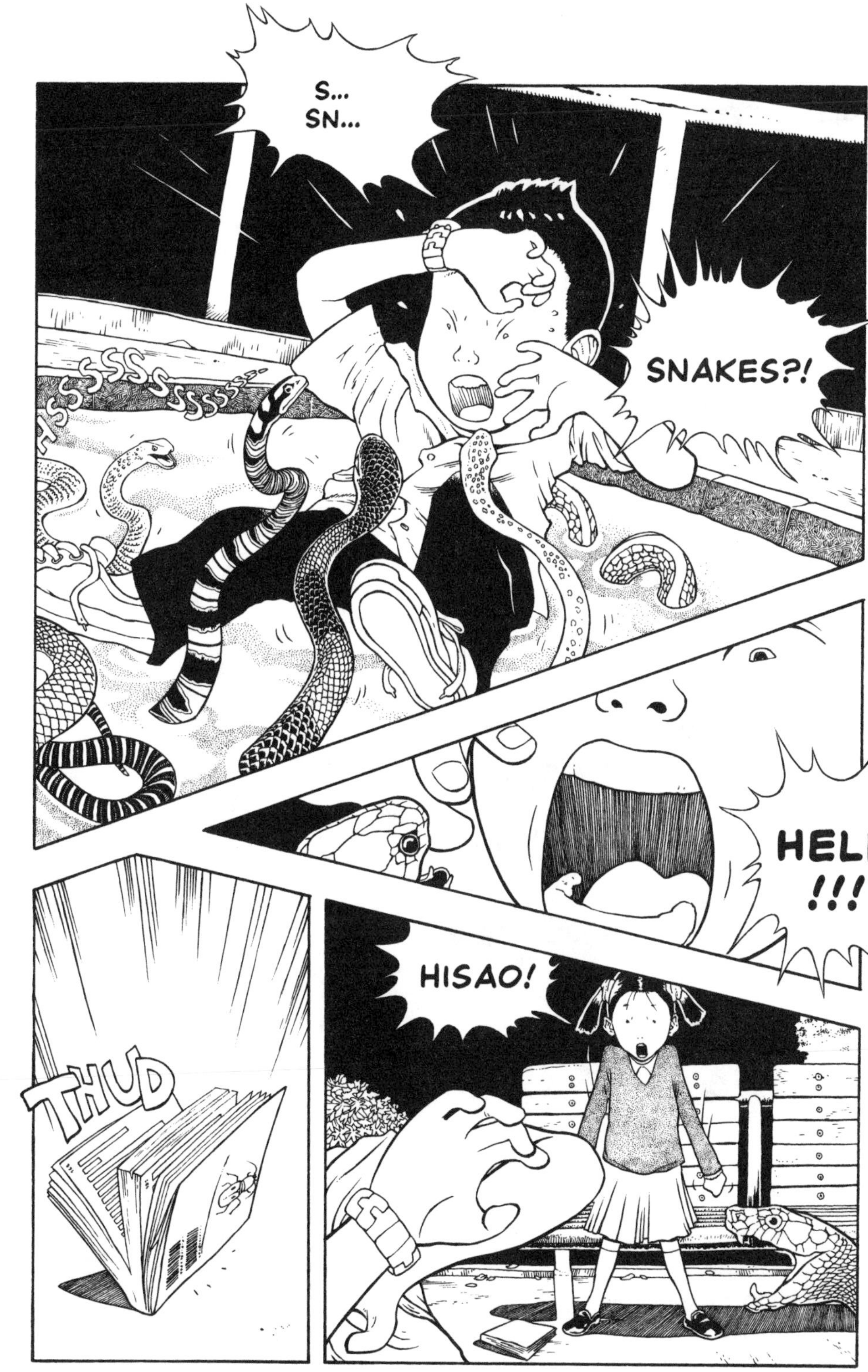
S...
SN...
SSSSSSSSS
SNAKES?!
HELP
!!!
THUD
HISAO!

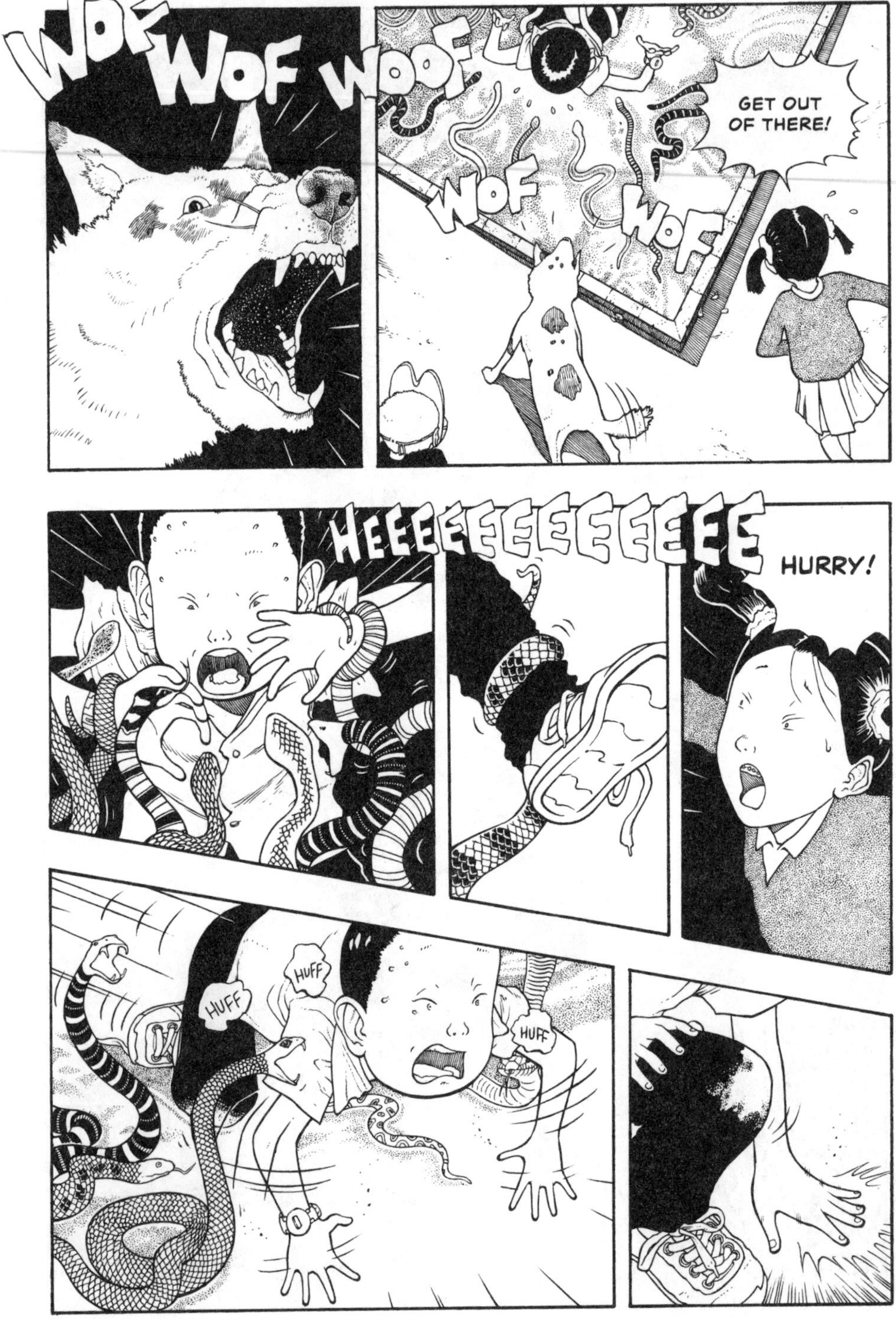
WOF WOF WOOF
WOF
WOF
GET OUT OF THERE!
HEEEEEEEEEEEE
HURRY!
HUFF
HUFF
HUFF

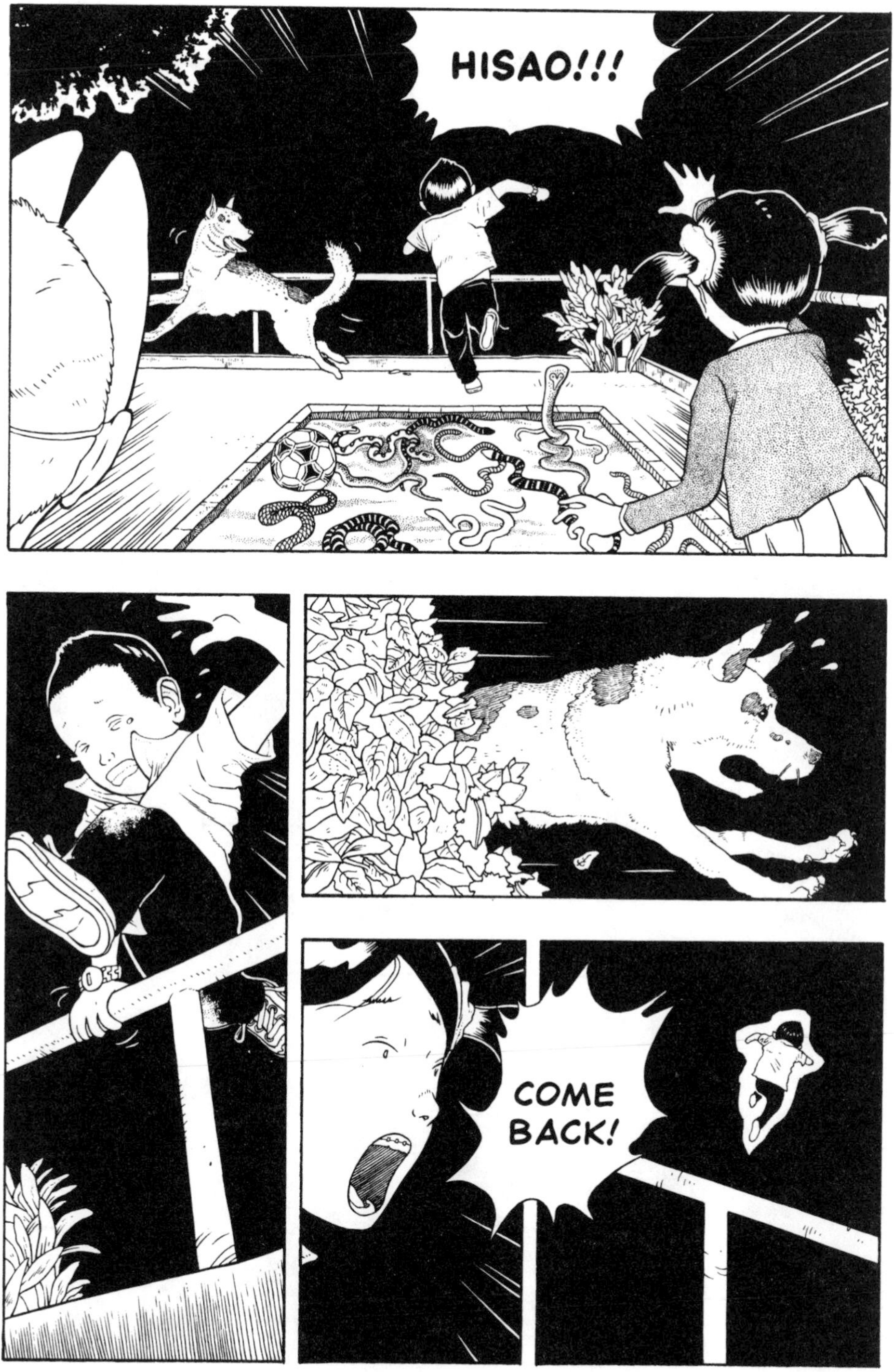
HISAO!!!
COME BACK!

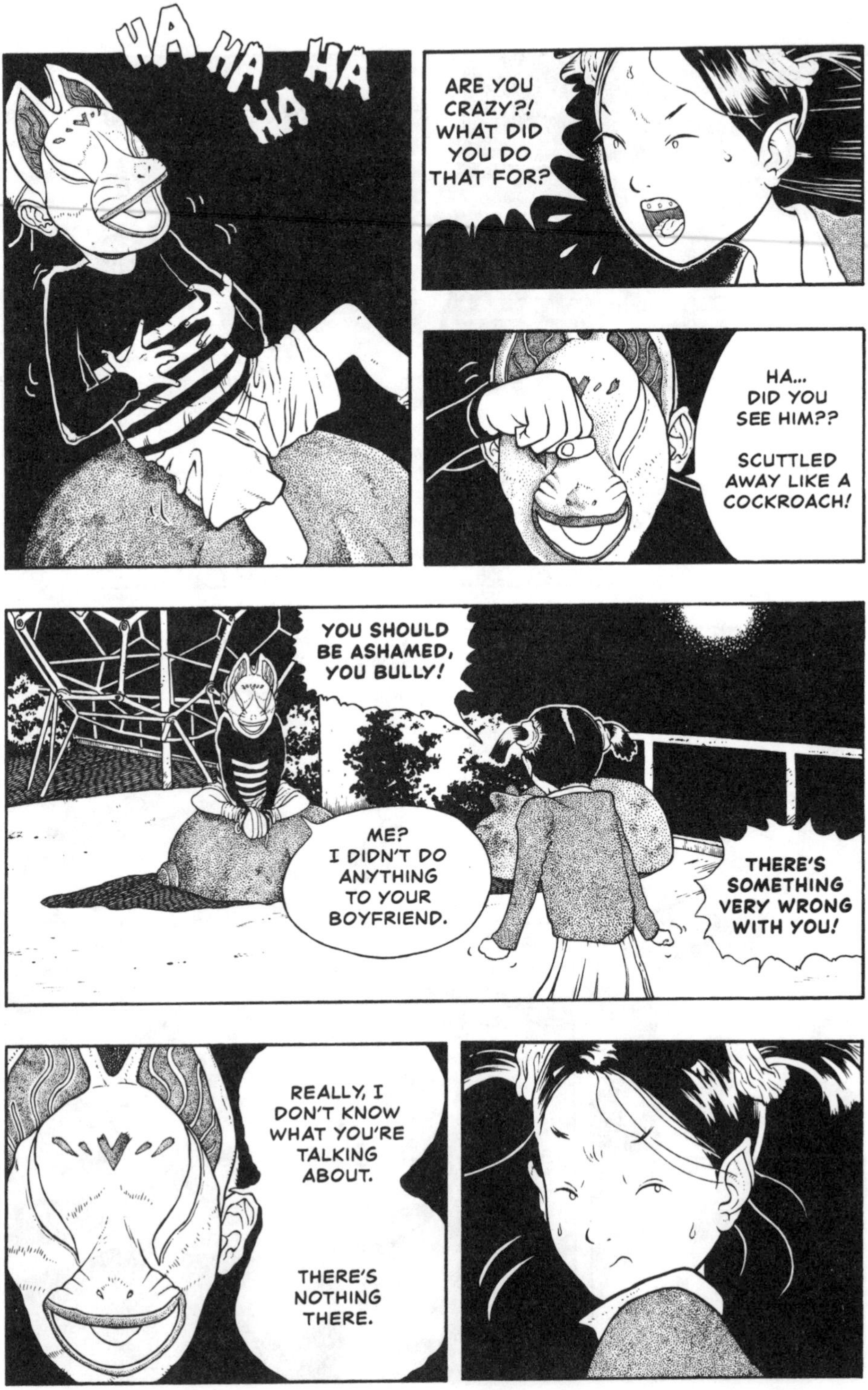
HA HA HA HA
ARE YOU CRAZY?! WHAT DID YOU DO THAT FOR?
HA... DID YOU SEE HIM??
SCUTTLED AWAY LIKE A COCKROACH!
YOU SHOULD BE ASHAMED, YOU BULLY!
ME? I DIDN'T DO ANYTHING TO YOUR BOYFRIEND.
THERE'S SOMETHING VERY WRONG WITH YOU!
REALLY, I DON'T KNOW WHAT YOU'RE TALKING ABOUT.
THERE'S NOTHING THERE.

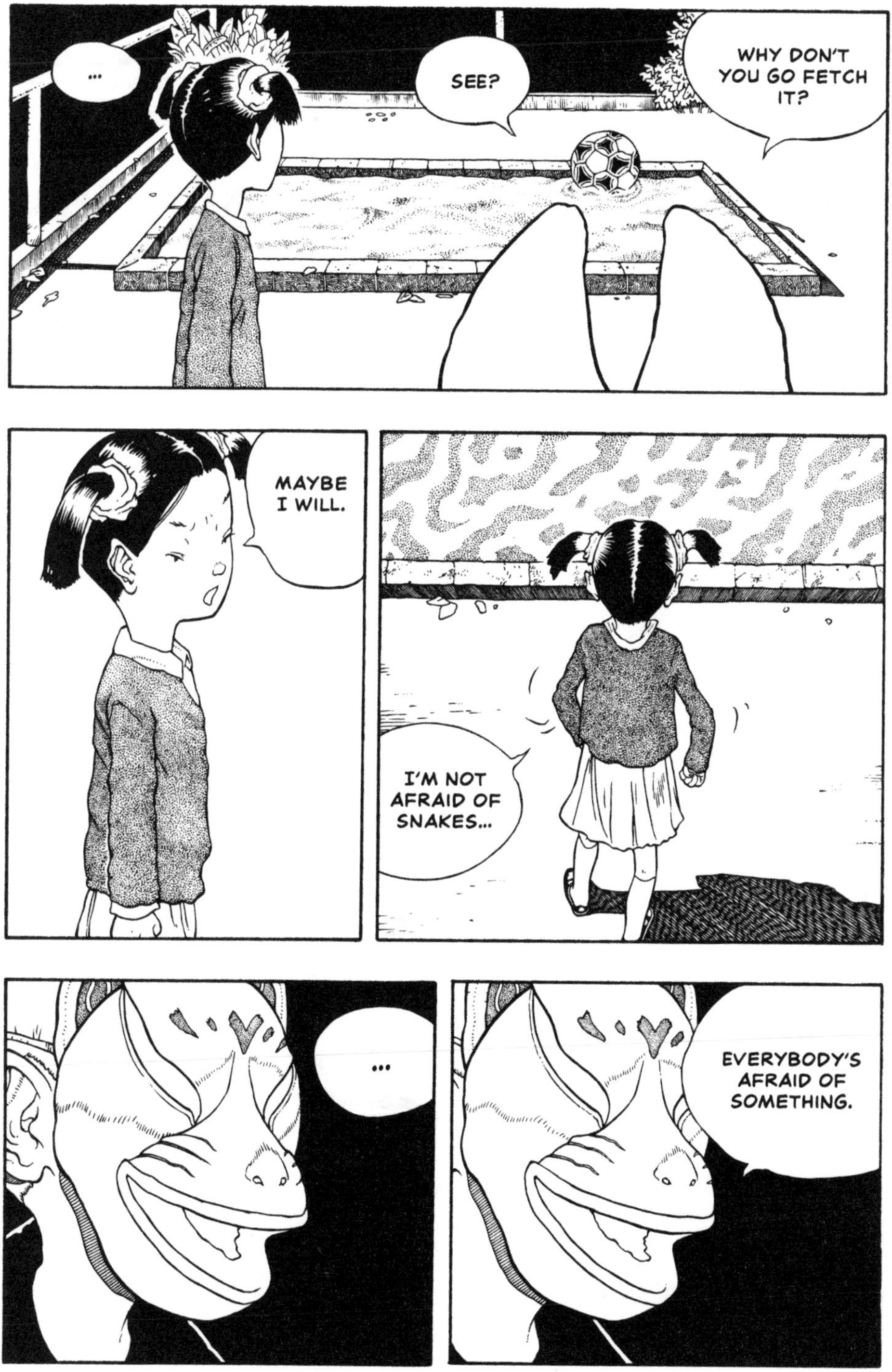
...
SEE?
WHY DON'T YOU GO FETCH IT?
MAYBE I WILL.
I'M NOT AFRAID OF SNAKES...
...
EVERYBODY'S AFRAID OF SOMETHING.

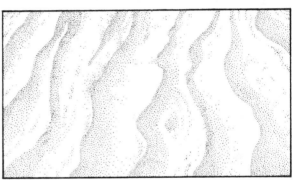

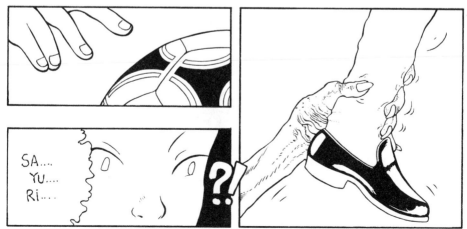

SA....
YU....
RI....

?!

37

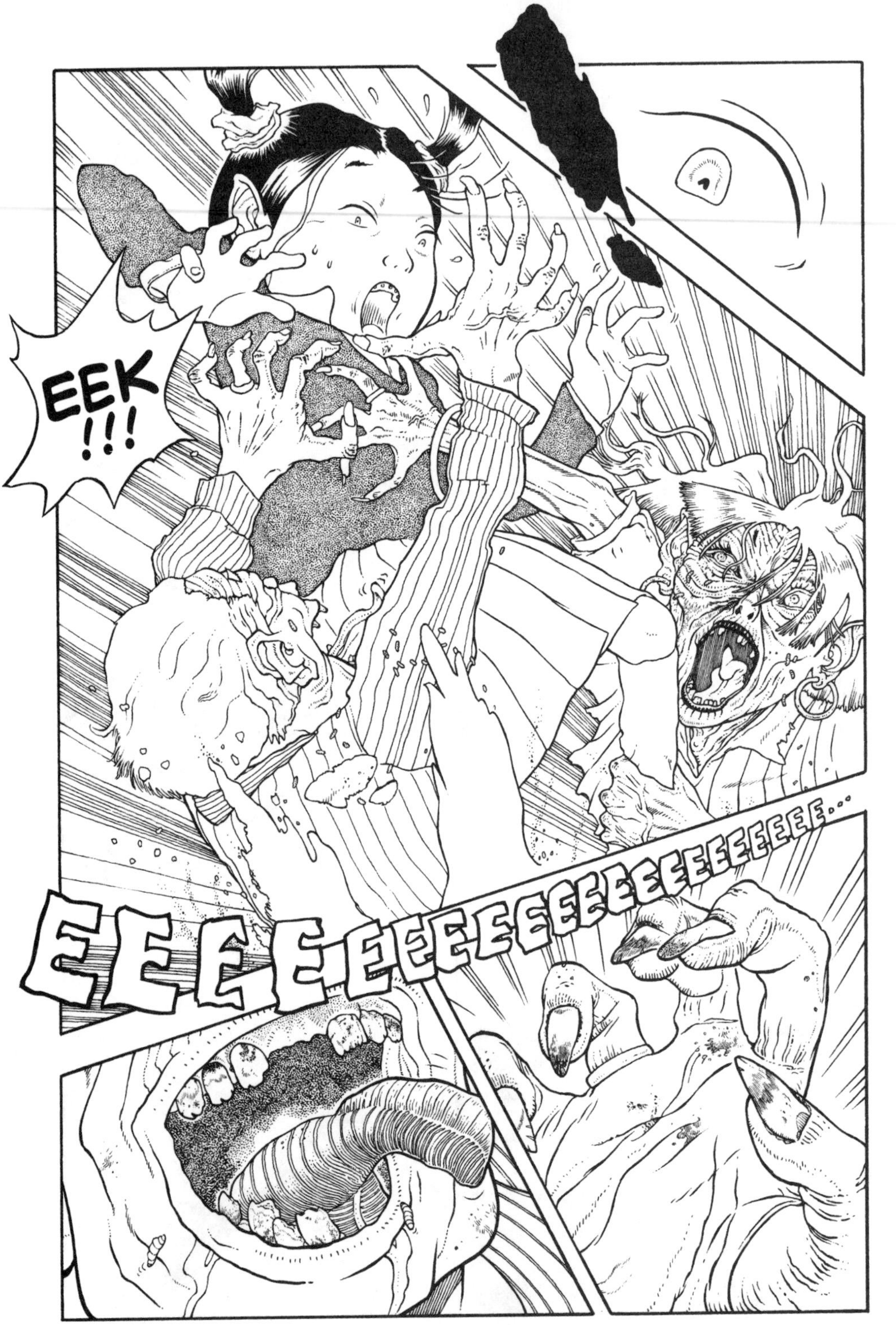
EEK !!!
EEEEEEEEEEEEEEEEEEEEEEE...

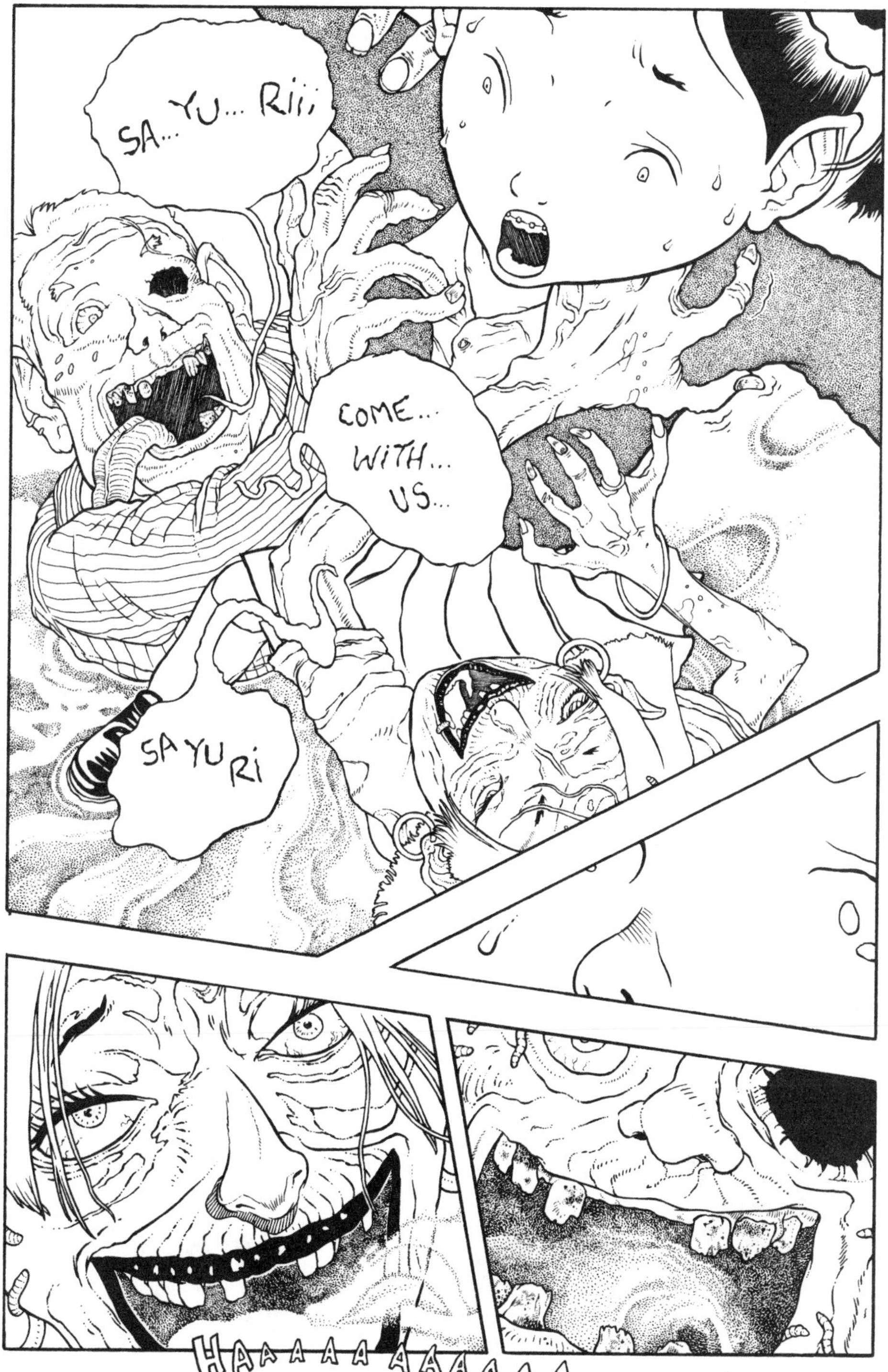
SA... YU... Riii
COME... WITH... US...
SA YU Ri
HAAAAA AAAAAA.....

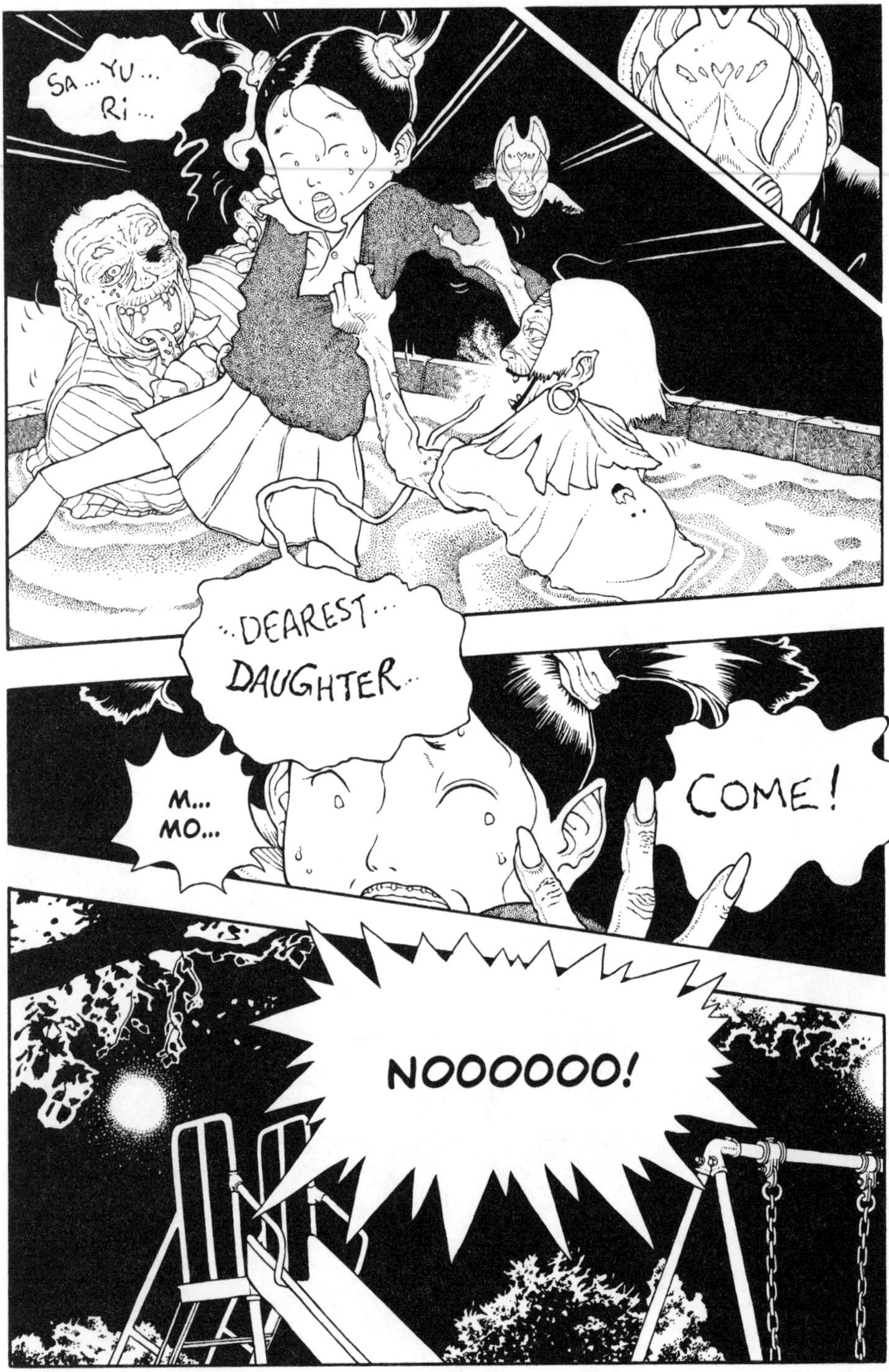
SA... YU... Ri...
...DEAREST... DAUGHTER...
M... MO...
COME!
NOOOOOO!

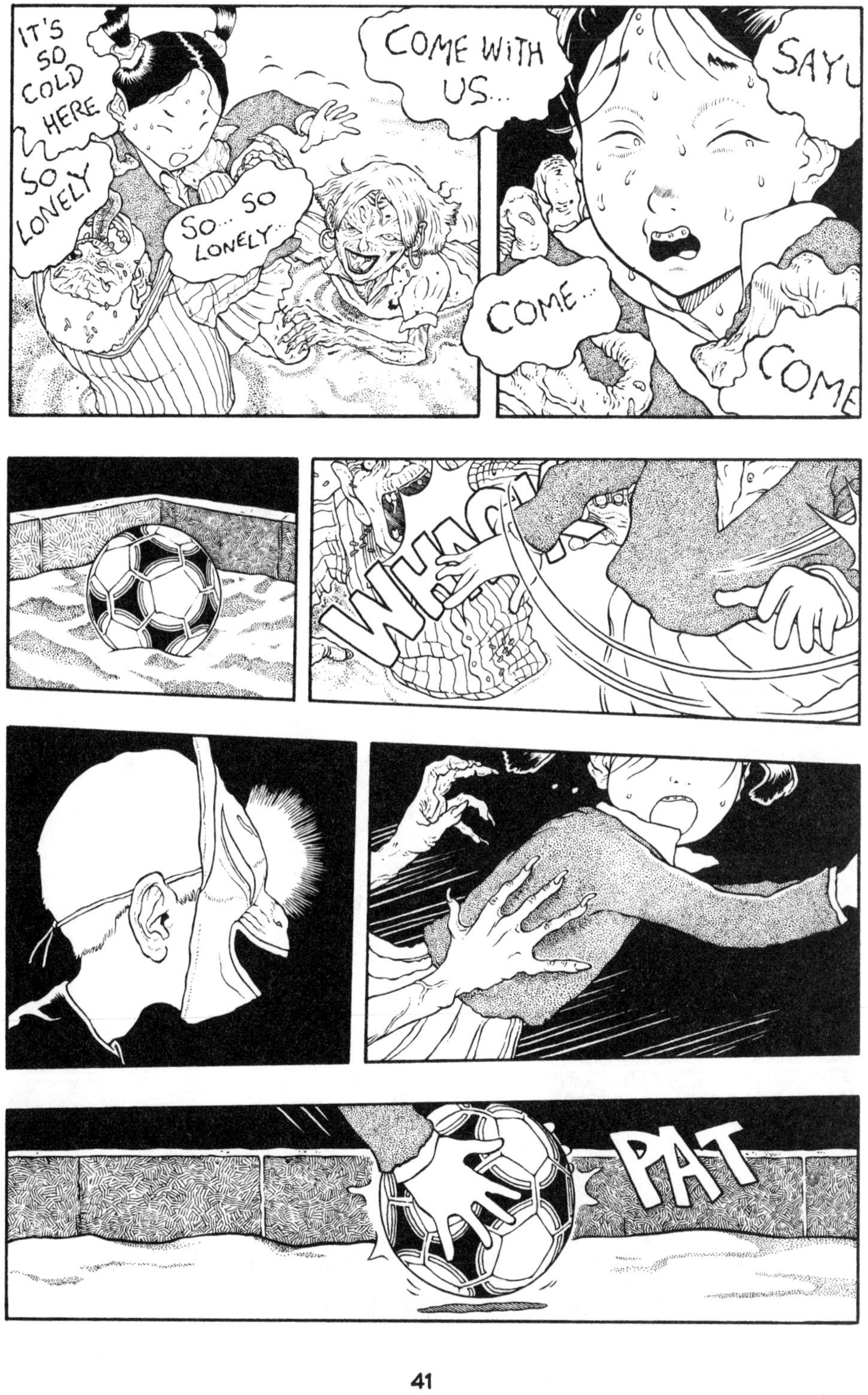
IT'S SO COLD HERE
SO LONELY
SO... SO LONELY...
COME WITH US...
SAYU
COME...
COME
WHAC
PAT

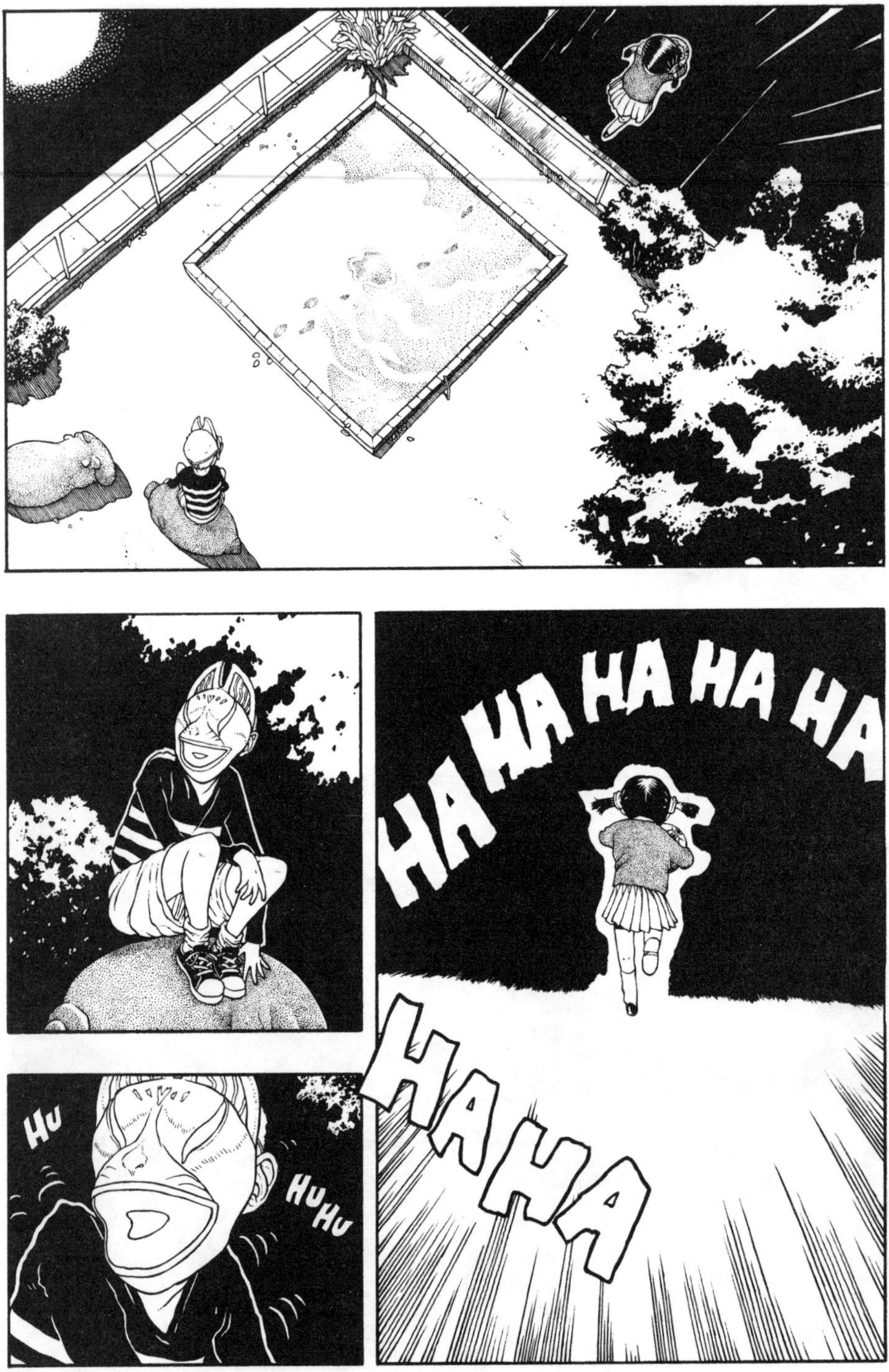
HA HA HA HA HA HA
HA HA HA
HU
HU HU

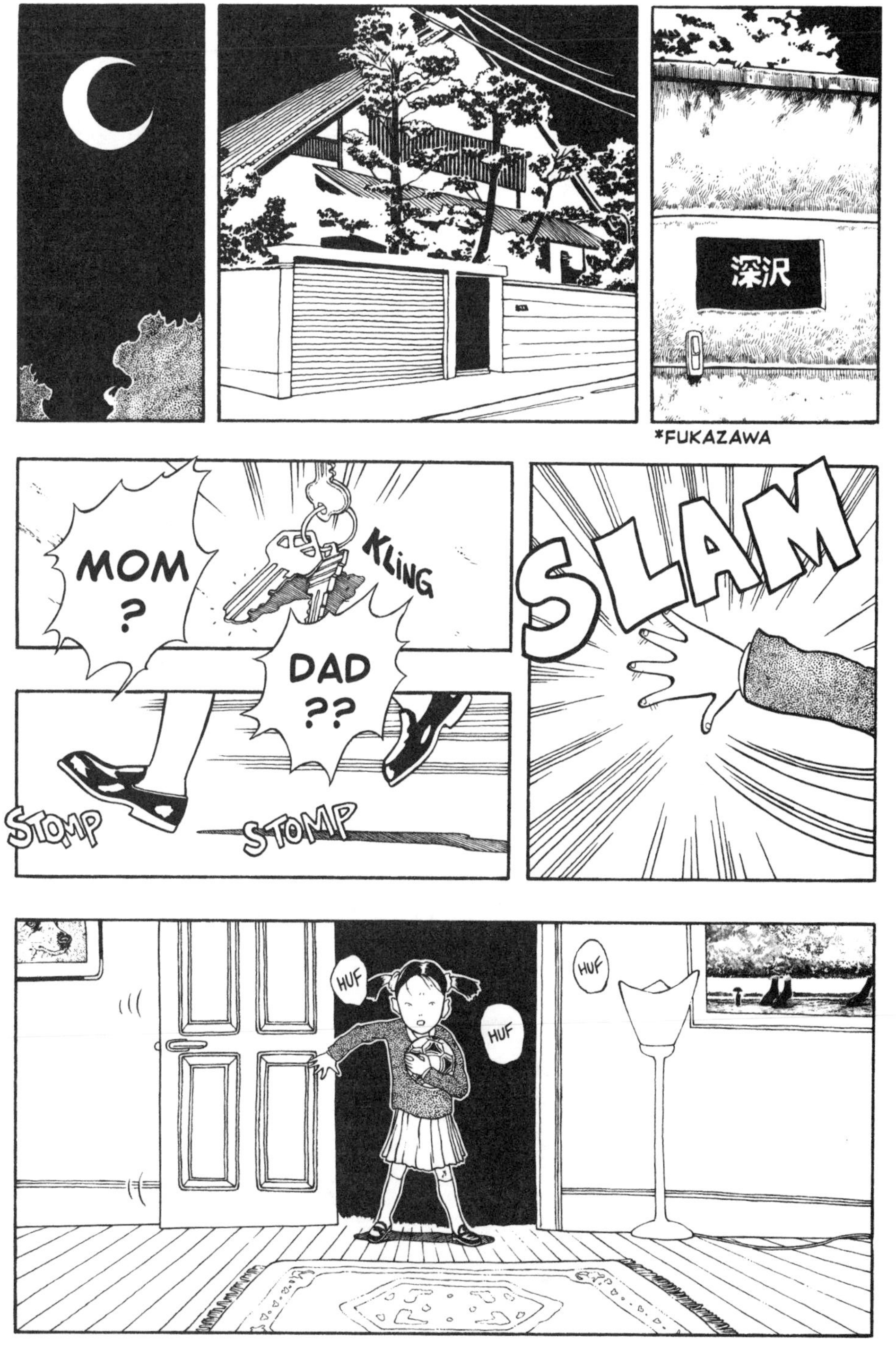
深沢
*FUKAZAWA
MOM ?
KLING
DAD ??
STOMP
STOMP
SLAM
HUF
HUF
HUF

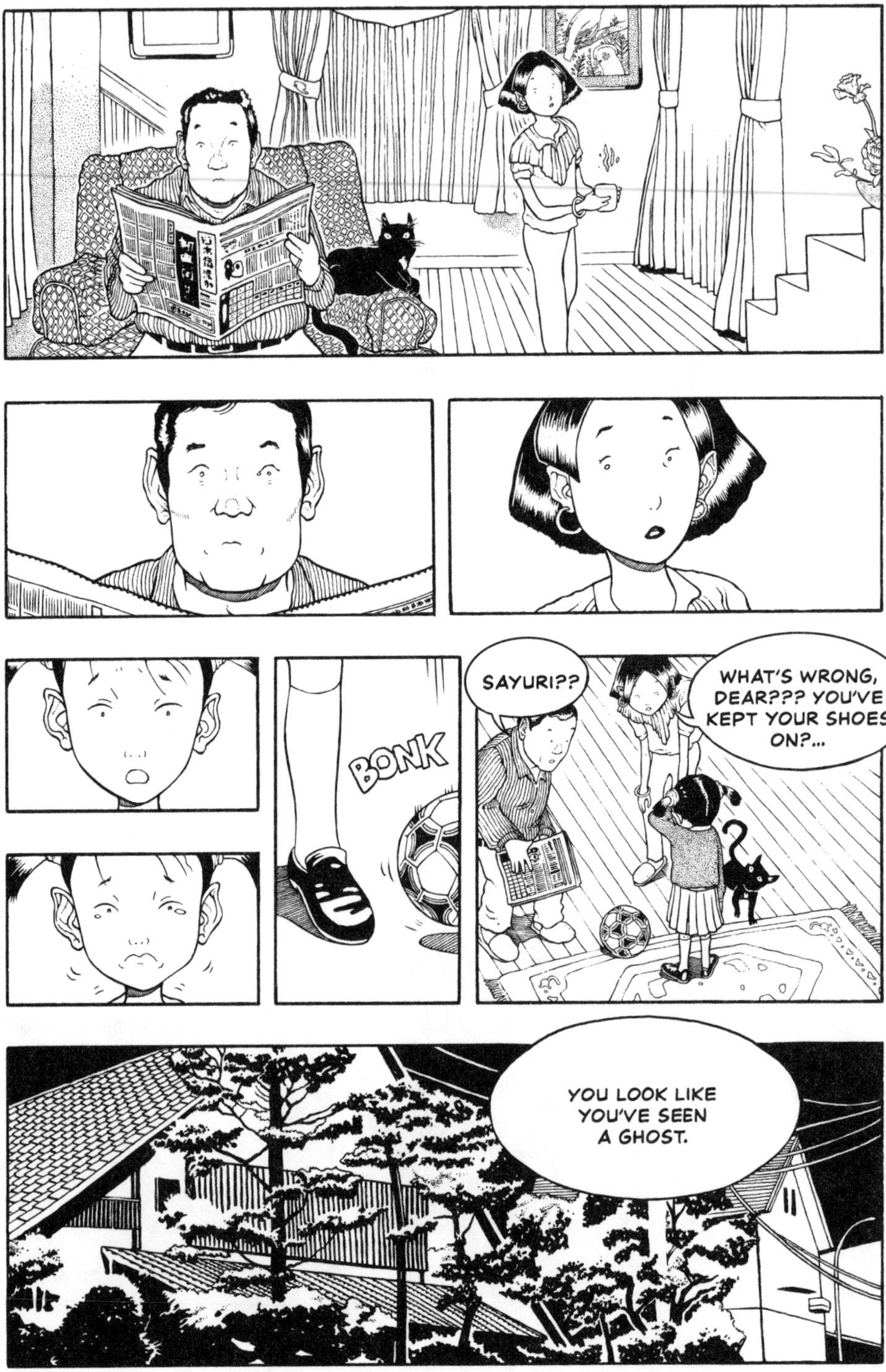

BONK
SAYURI??
WHAT'S WRONG, DEAR??? YOU'VE KEPT YOUR SHOES ON?...
YOU LOOK LIKE YOU'VE SEEN A GHOST.

Chapter 2:
Snakes

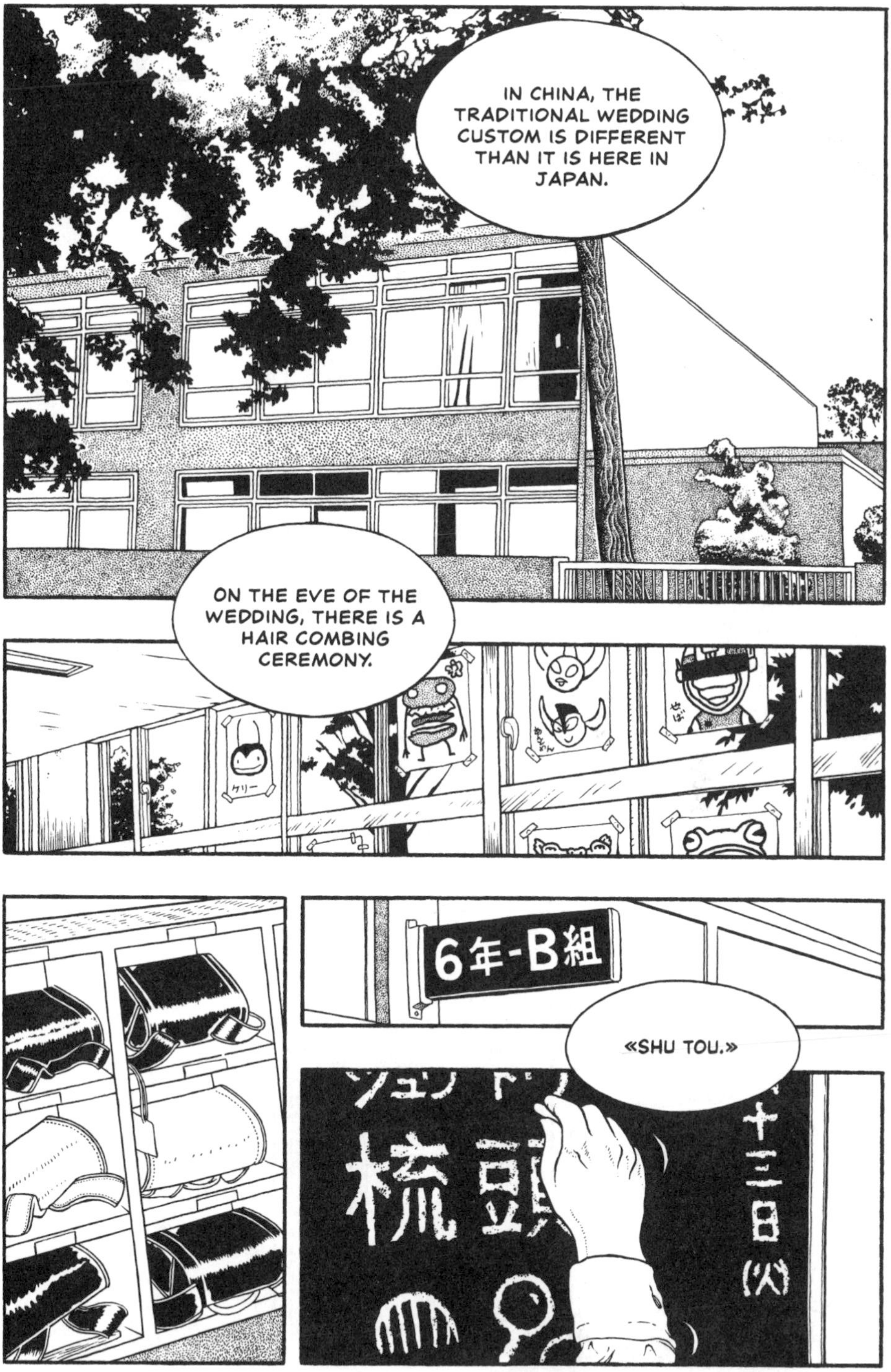
IN CHINA, THE TRADITIONAL WEDDING CUSTOM IS DIFFERENT THAN IT IS HERE IN JAPAN.
ON THE EVE OF THE WEDDING, THERE IS A HAIR COMBING CEREMONY.
6年-B組
«SHU TOU.»

THE BRIDE AND GROOM ARE BLESSED ALOUD, IN FRONT OF A MIRROR OR BY A WINDOW GAZING UPON THE MOON.

THERE ARE **FOUR SACRED** BLESSINGS:

FIRST COMBING, "MAY YOU BE BLESSED TO BE TOGETHER TO THE END."

SECOND COMBING, "BLESSINGS FOR A HUNDRED YEARS OF HARMONY."

THIRD COMBING, "MAY YOU BE BLESSED WITH A HOUSEFUL OF CHILDREN AND GRAND-CHILDREN."

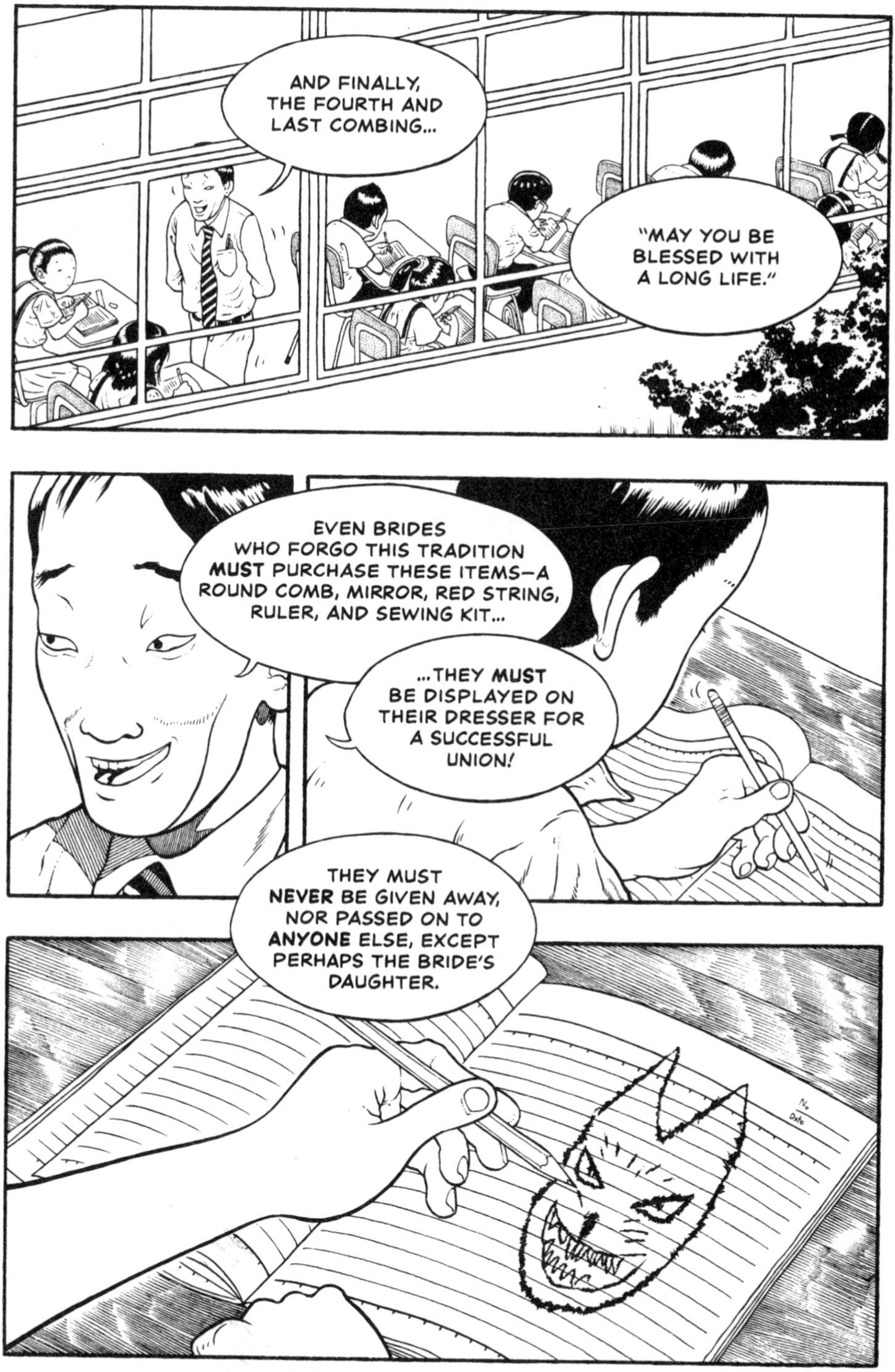
AND FINALLY, THE FOURTH AND LAST COMBING...
"MAY YOU BE BLESSED WITH A LONG LIFE."
EVEN BRIDES WHO FORGO THIS TRADITION **MUST** PURCHASE THESE ITEMS—A ROUND COMB, MIRROR, RED STRING, RULER, AND SEWING KIT...
...THEY **MUST** BE DISPLAYED ON THEIR DRESSER FOR A SUCCESSFUL UNION!
THEY MUST **NEVER** BE GIVEN AWAY, NOR PASSED ON TO **ANYONE** ELSE, EXCEPT PERHAPS THE BRIDE'S DAUGHTER.

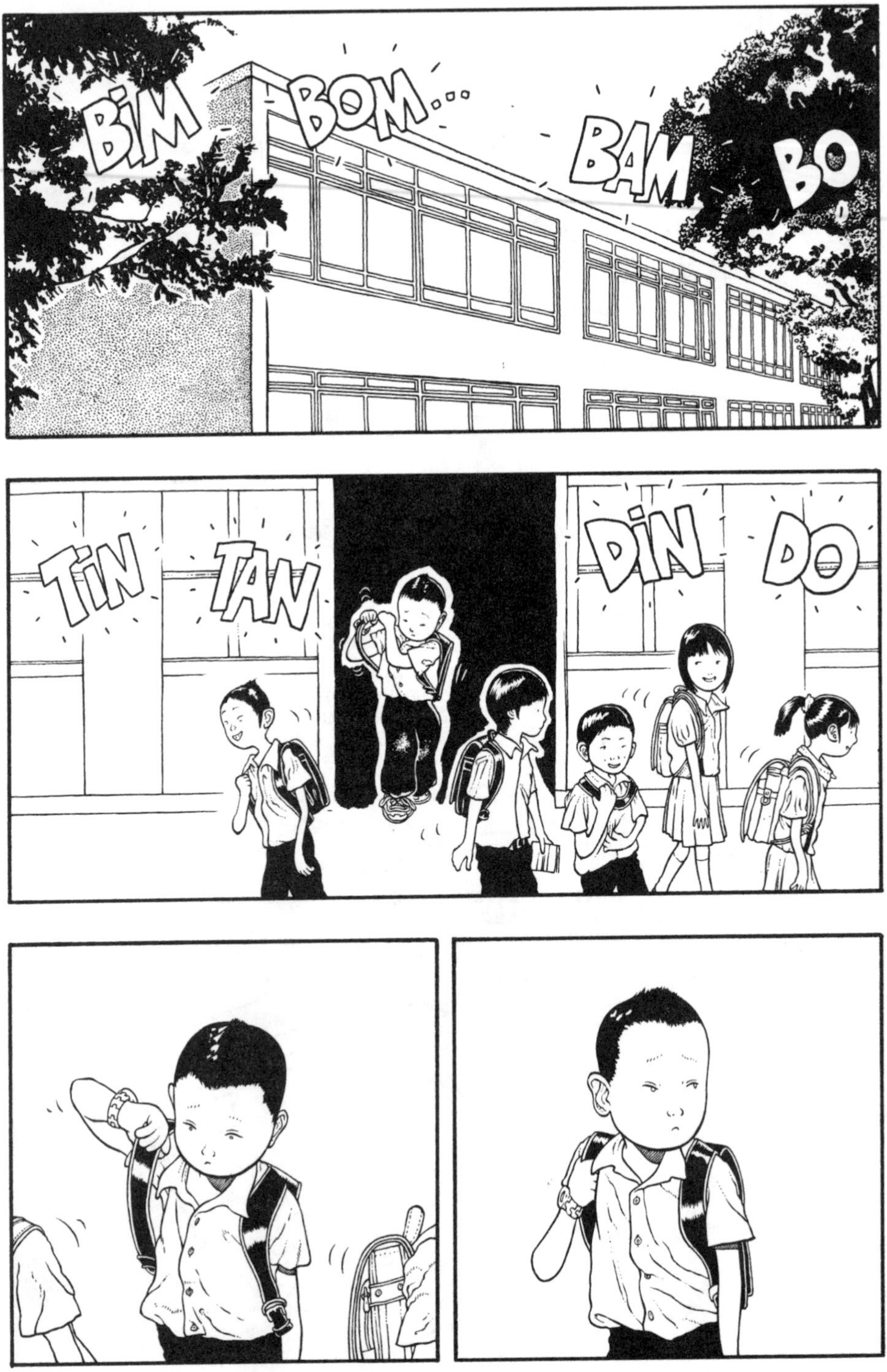
BIM
BOM...
BAM
BO
TIN
TAN
DIN
DO

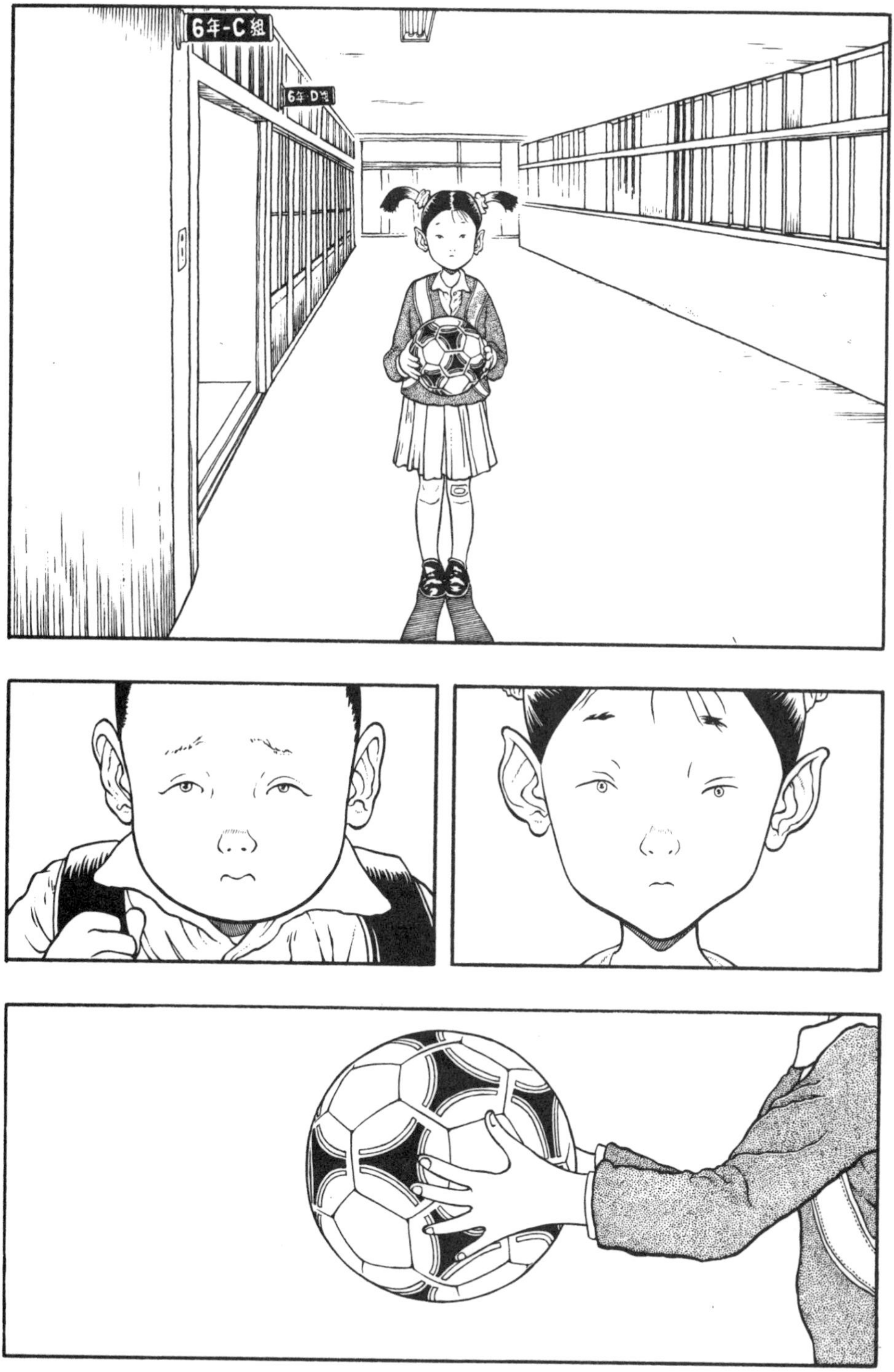
6年-C組
6年-D組

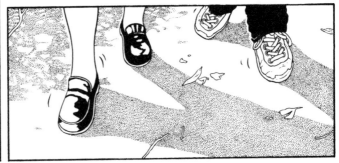

SO.

YOU'RE BACK.

52

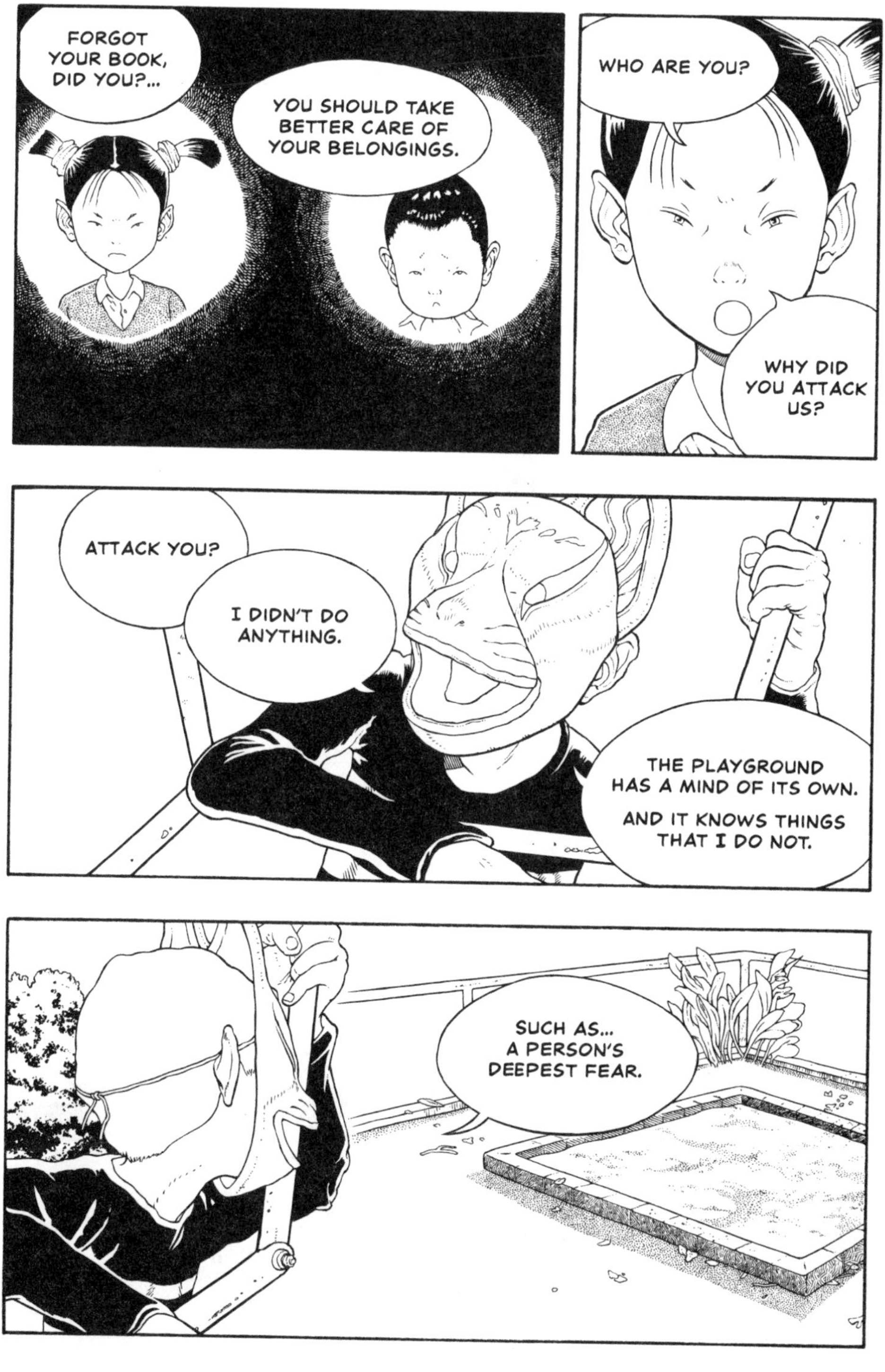
FORGOT YOUR BOOK, DID YOU?...
YOU SHOULD TAKE BETTER CARE OF YOUR BELONGINGS.
WHO ARE YOU?
WHY DID YOU ATTACK US?
ATTACK YOU?
I DIDN'T DO ANYTHING.
THE PLAYGROUND HAS A MIND OF ITS OWN.
AND IT KNOWS THINGS THAT I DO NOT.
SUCH AS... A PERSON'S DEEPEST FEAR.

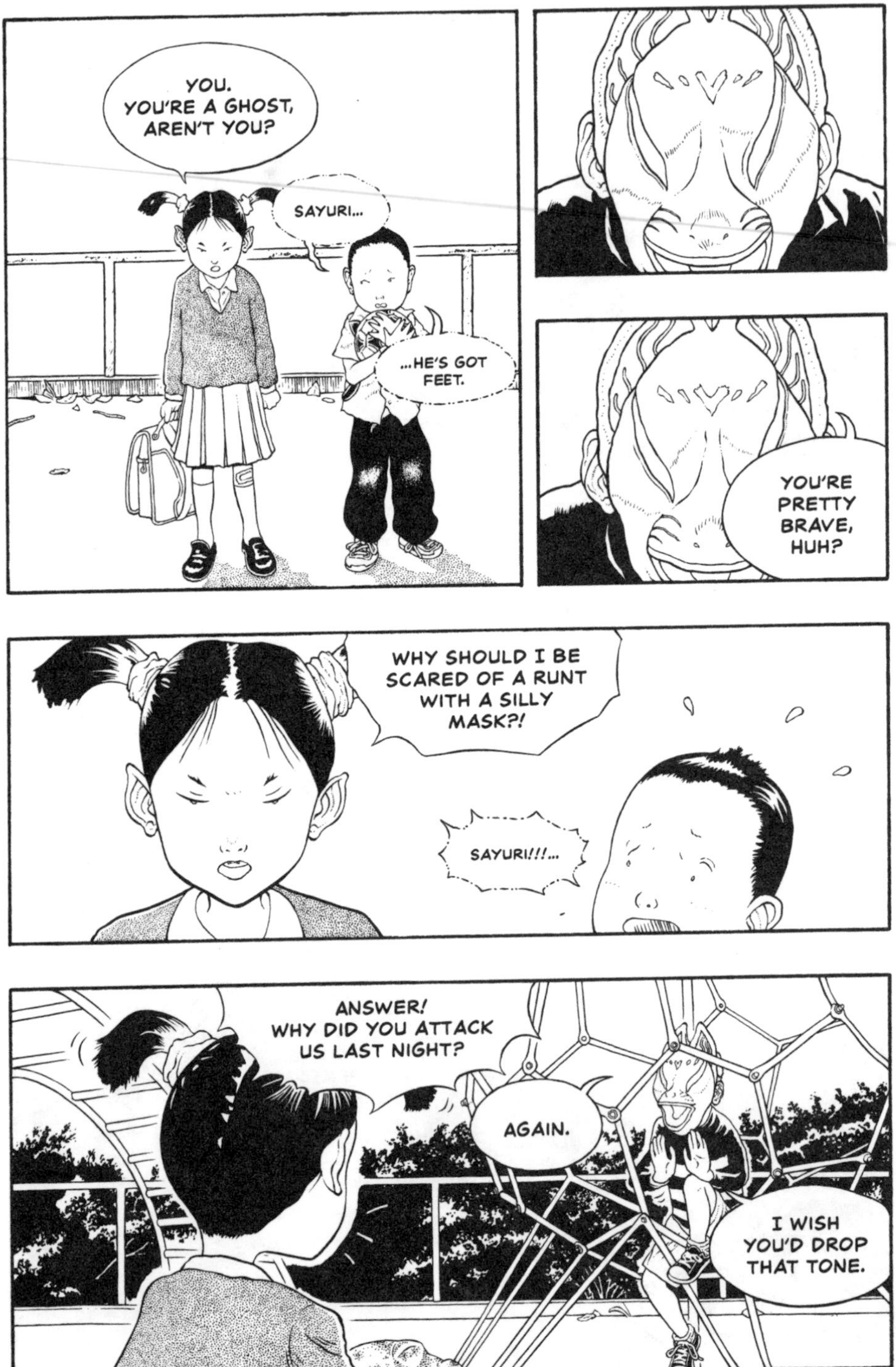
YOU.
YOU'RE A GHOST, AREN'T YOU?
SAYURI...
...HE'S GOT FEET.
YOU'RE PRETTY BRAVE, HUH?
WHY SHOULD I BE SCARED OF A RUNT WITH A SILLY MASK?!
SAYURI!!!...
ANSWER! WHY DID YOU ATTACK US LAST NIGHT?
AGAIN.
I WISH YOU'D DROP THAT TONE.

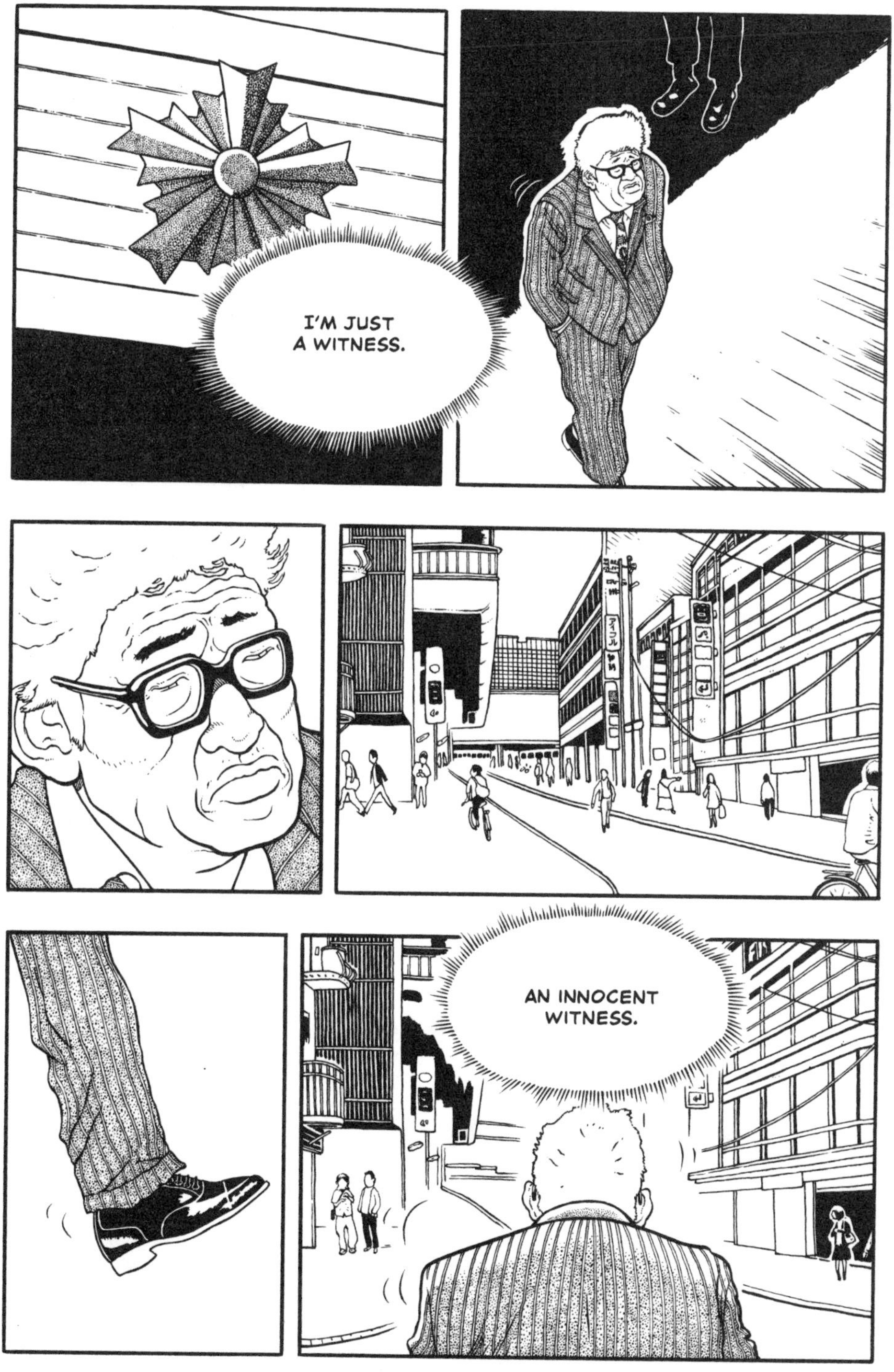
I'M JUST A WITNESS.
AN INNOCENT WITNESS.

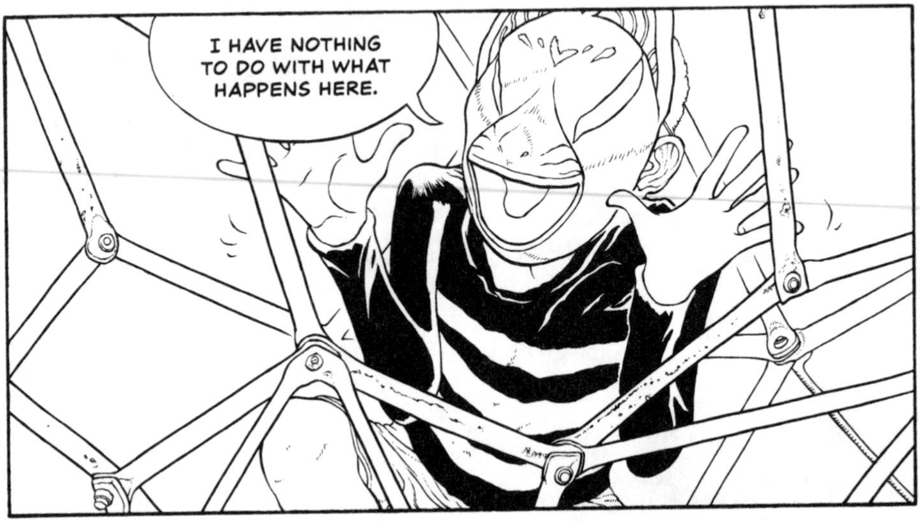
I HAVE NOTHING
TO DO WITH WHAT
HAPPENS HERE.

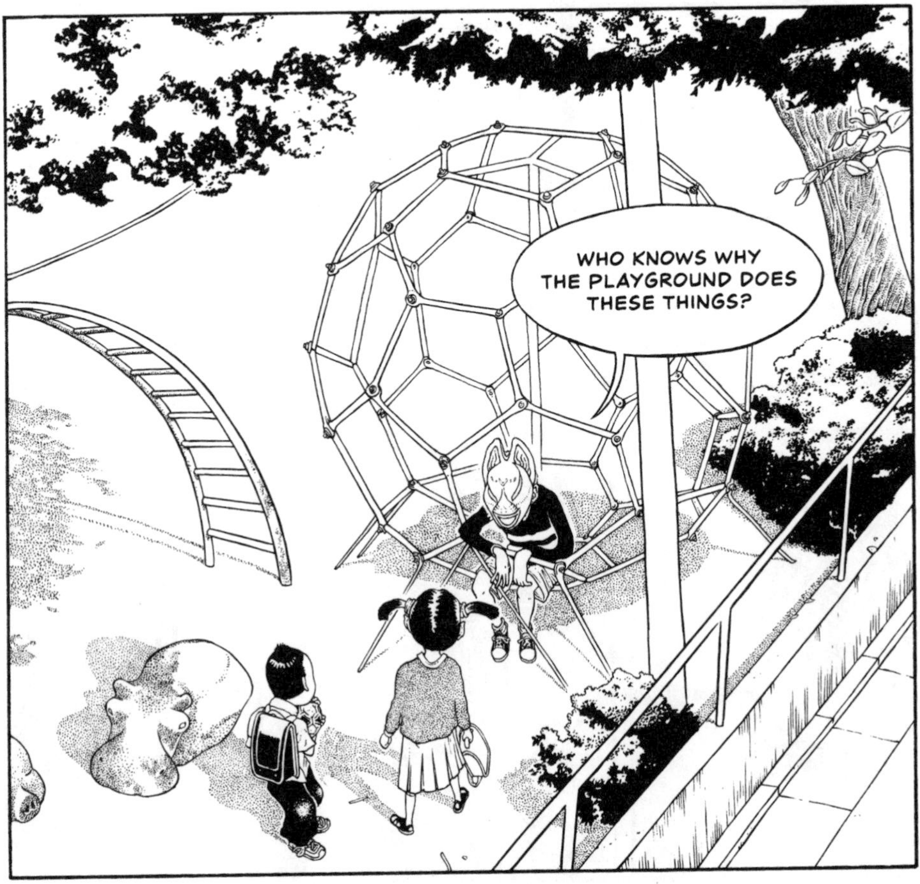
WHO KNOWS WHY
THE PLAYGROUND DOES
THESE THINGS?

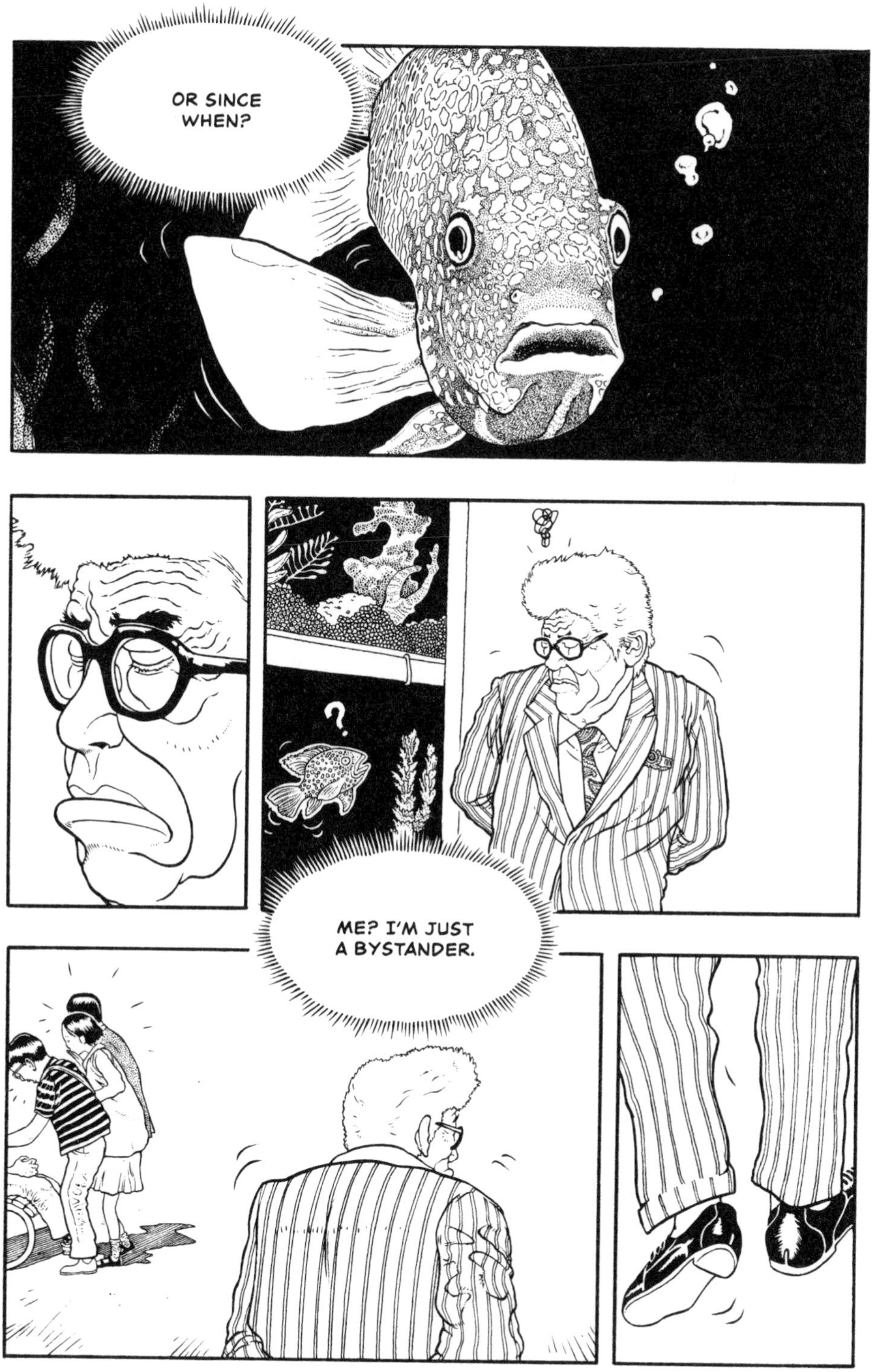
OR SINCE WHEN?
?
ME? I'M JUST A BYSTANDER.

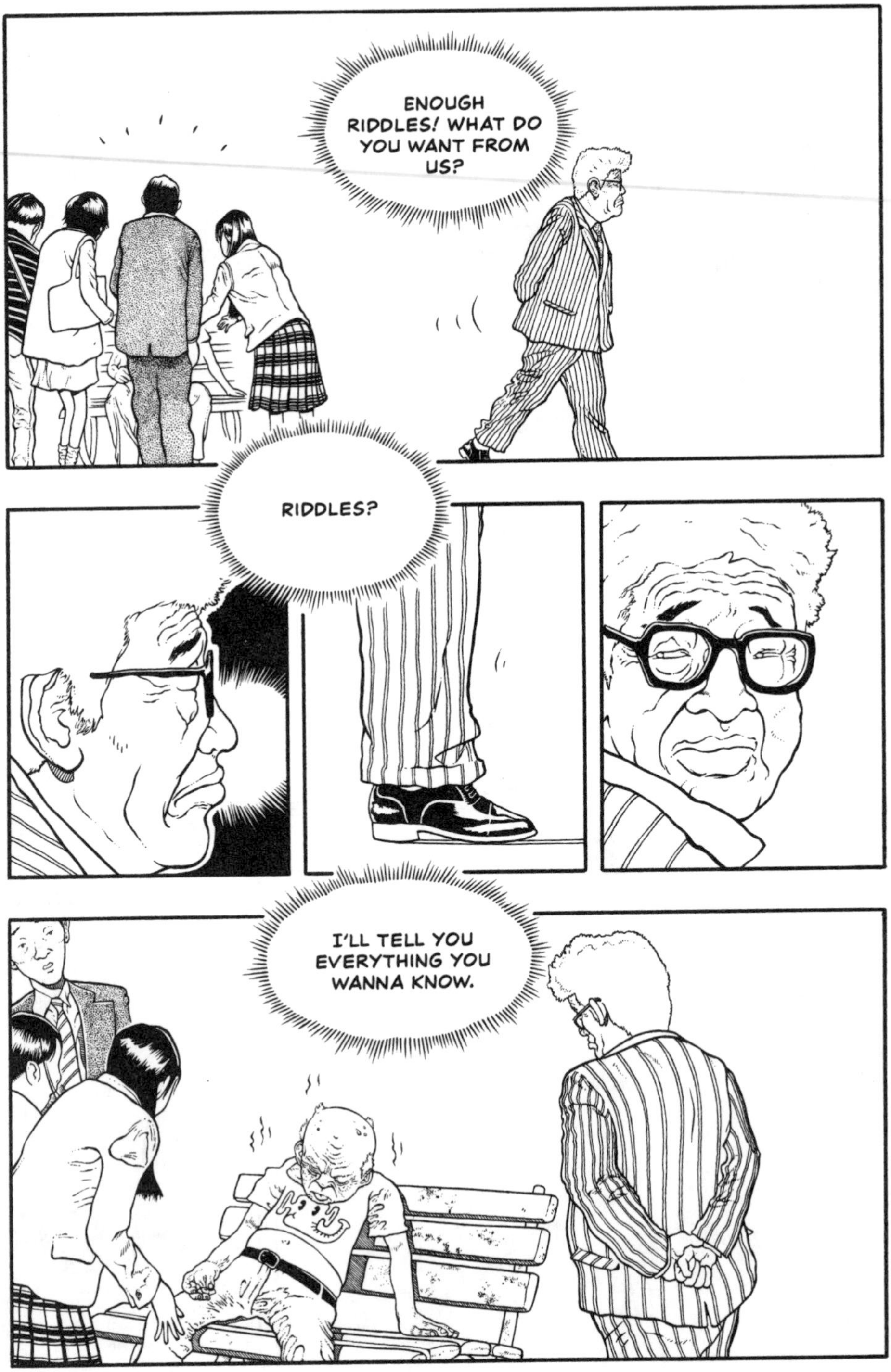
ENOUGH RIDDLES! WHAT DO YOU WANT FROM US?
RIDDLES?
I'LL TELL YOU EVERYTHING YOU WANNA KNOW.

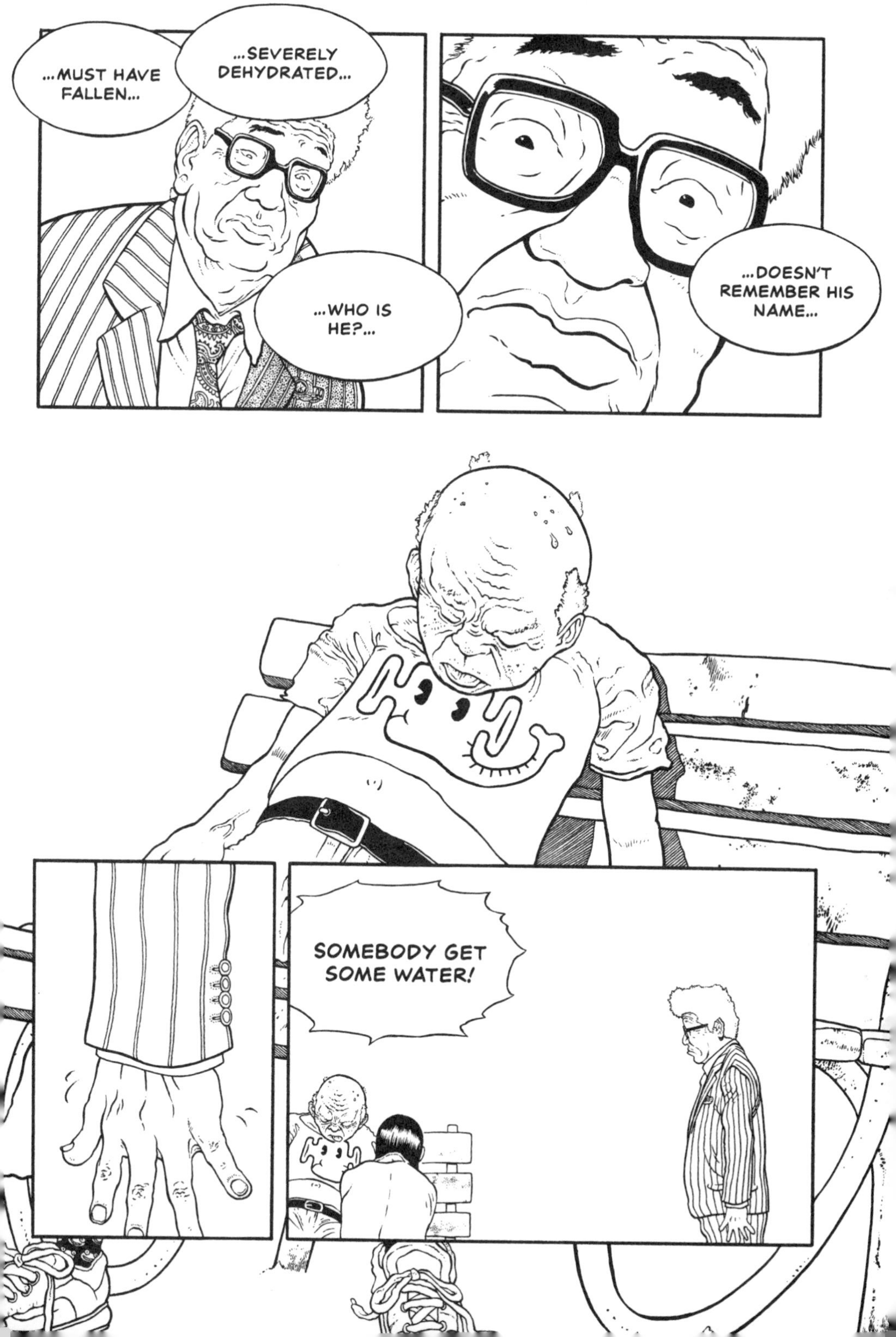
...MUST HAVE FALLEN...
...SEVERELY DEHYDRATED...
...WHO IS HE?...
...DOESN'T REMEMBER HIS NAME...
SOMEBODY GET SOME WATER!

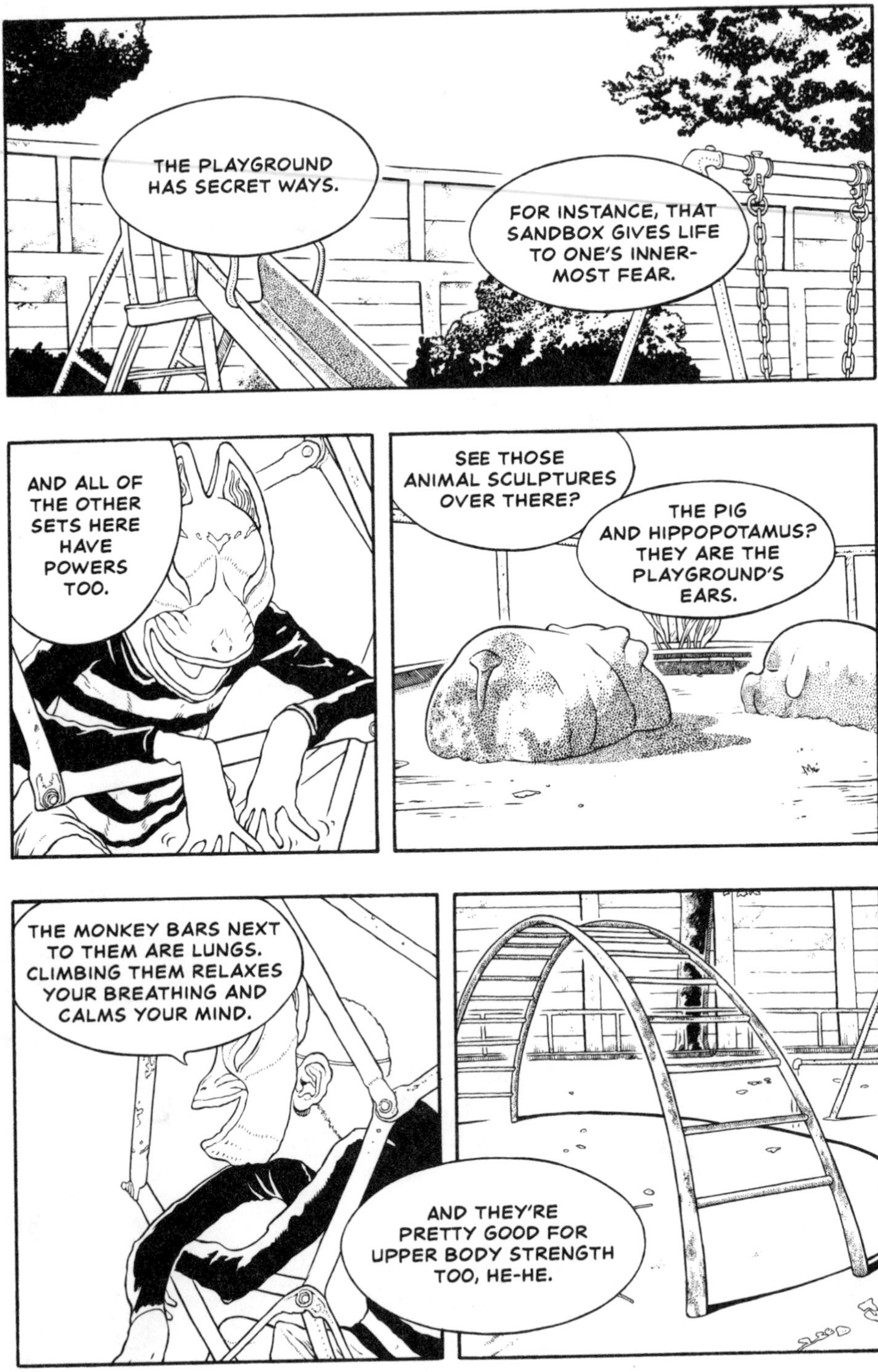
THE PLAYGROUND HAS SECRET WAYS.
FOR INSTANCE, THAT SANDBOX GIVES LIFE TO ONE'S INNER-MOST FEAR.
AND ALL OF THE OTHER SETS HERE HAVE POWERS TOO.
SEE THOSE ANIMAL SCULPTURES OVER THERE?
THE PIG AND HIPPOPOTAMUS? THEY ARE THE PLAYGROUND'S EARS.
THE MONKEY BARS NEXT TO THEM ARE LUNGS. CLIMBING THEM RELAXES YOUR BREATHING AND CALMS YOUR MIND.
AND THEY'RE PRETTY GOOD FOR UPPER BODY STRENGTH TOO, HE-HE.

THOSE SWINGS...

...THEY ARE DOORS TO OTHER PEOPLE'S DREAMS...

TAP

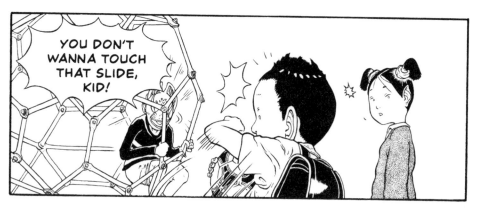

YOU DON'T WANNA TOUCH THAT SLIDE, KID!

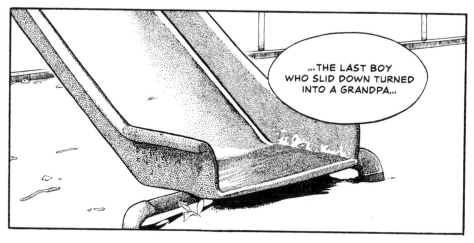

...THE LAST BOY WHO SLID DOWN TURNED INTO A GRANDPA...

CRAWL UP IT, YOU'RE BACK IN DIAPERS.

SLIDE DOWN, YOU TURN INTO A WRINKLED OLD MESS.

WOOSH

AS FOR THIS JUNGLE GYM...

WELL...

YOU DON'T WANNA KNOW WHAT THIS ONE DOES.

WHAT ARE *YOU* DOING HERE?

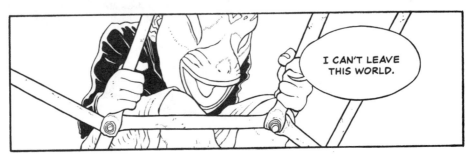

I CAN'T LEAVE THIS WORLD.

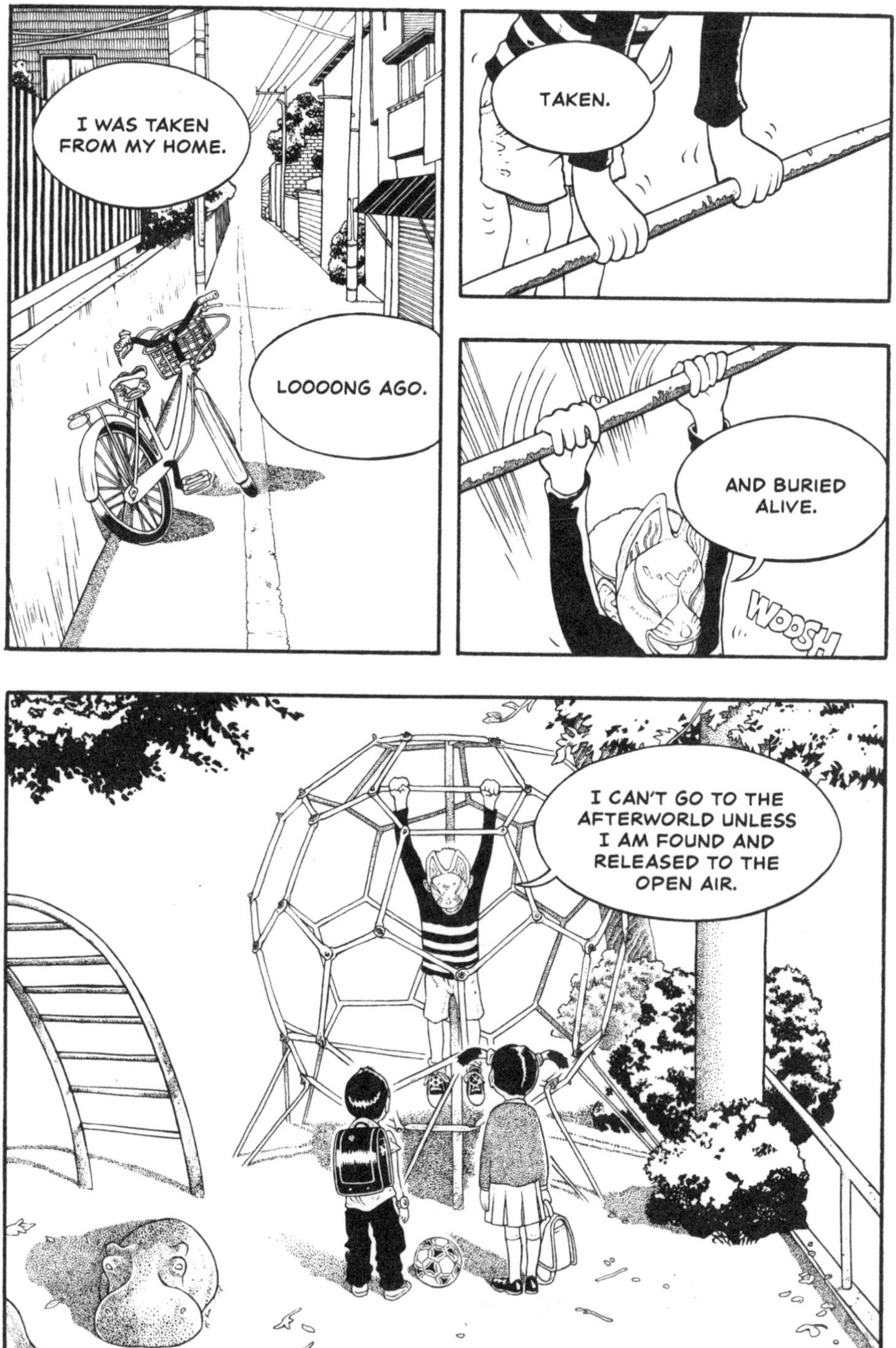
I WAS TAKEN FROM MY HOME.
LOOOONG AGO.
TAKEN.
AND BURIED ALIVE.
WOOSH
I CAN'T GO TO THE AFTERWORLD UNLESS I AM FOUND AND RELEASED TO THE OPEN AIR.

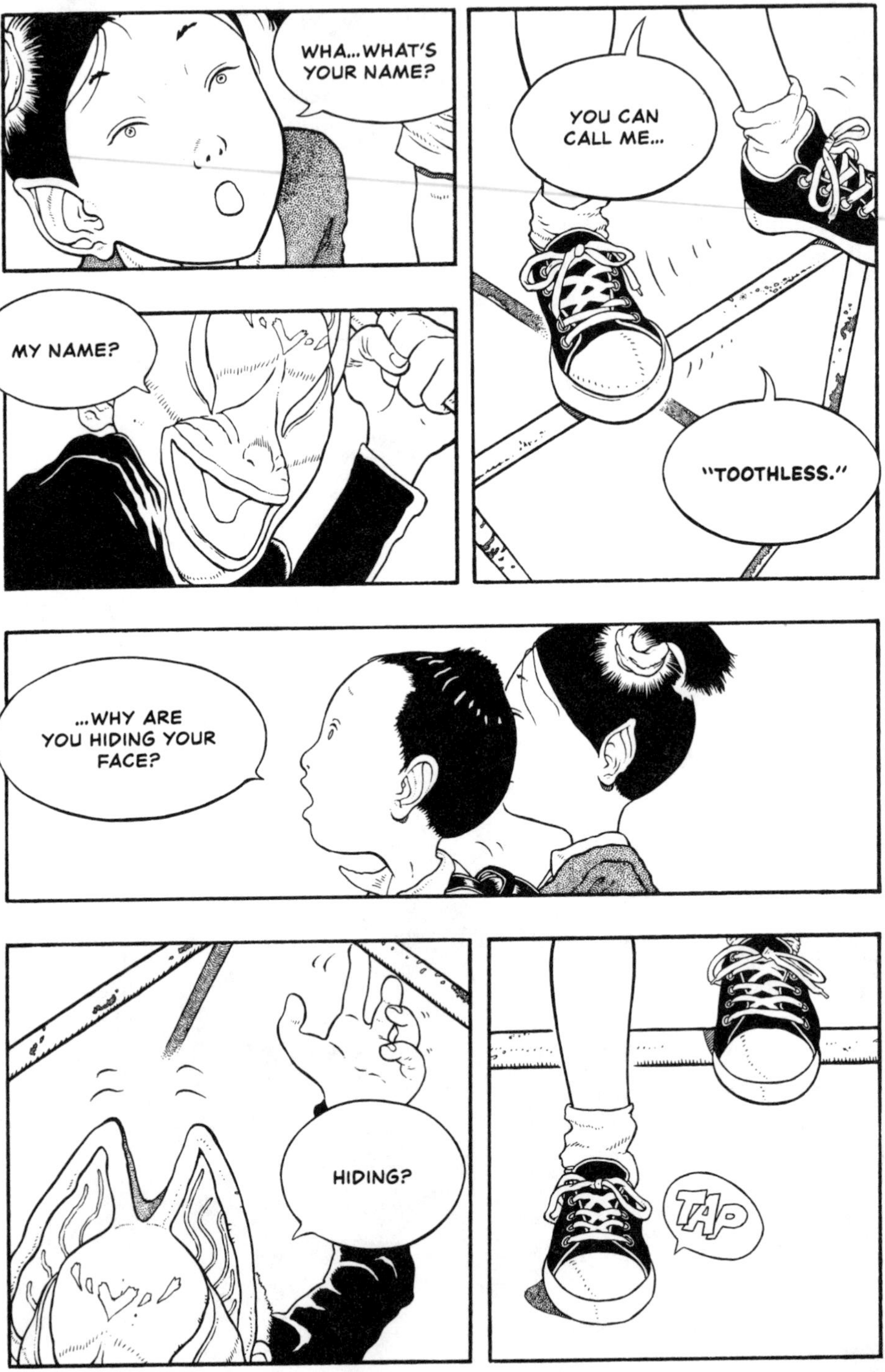
WHA...WHAT'S YOUR NAME?
YOU CAN CALL ME...
MY NAME?
"TOOTHLESS."
...WHY ARE YOU HIDING YOUR FACE?
HIDING?
TAP

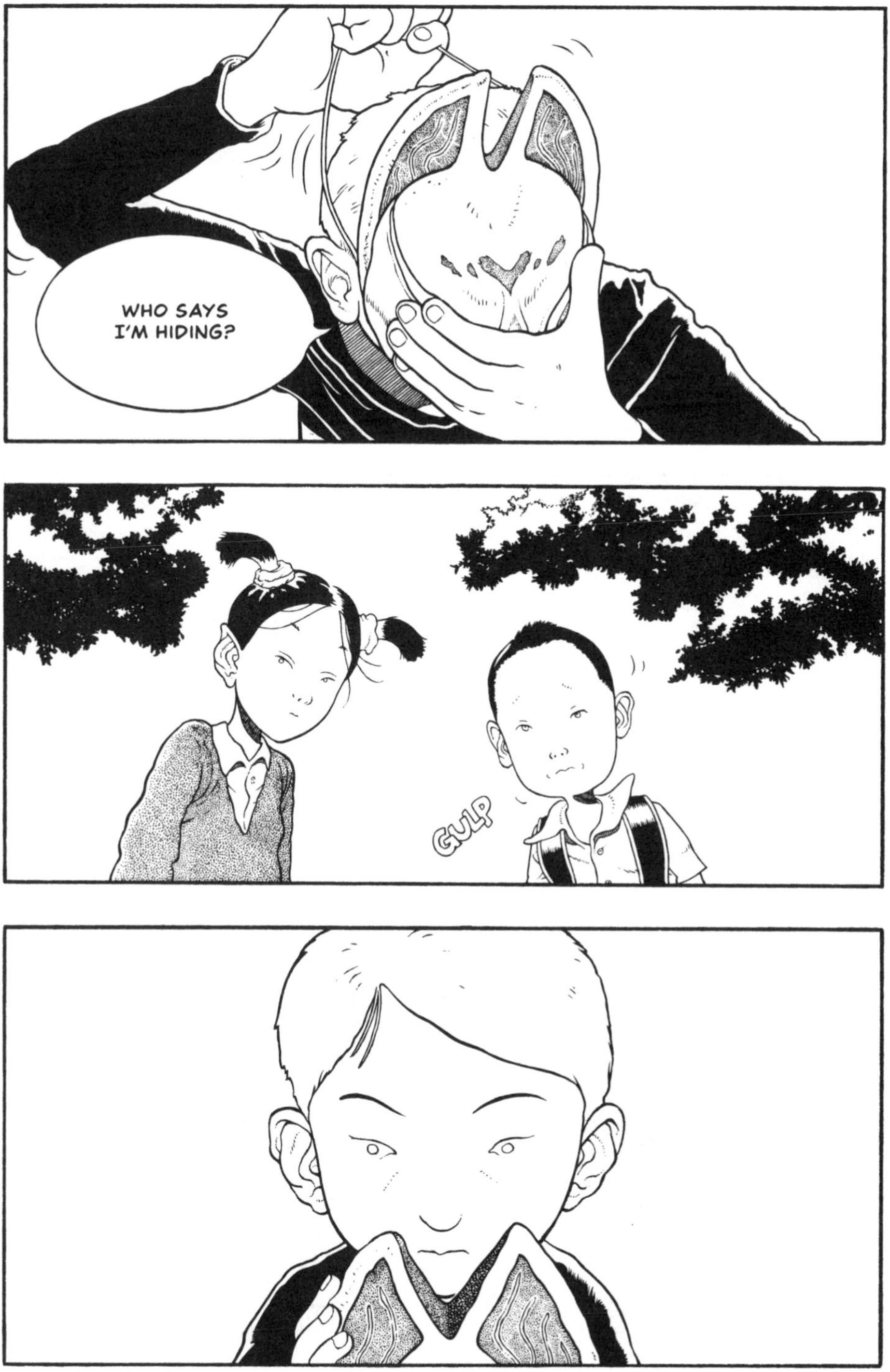
WHO SAYS
I'M HIDING?
GULP

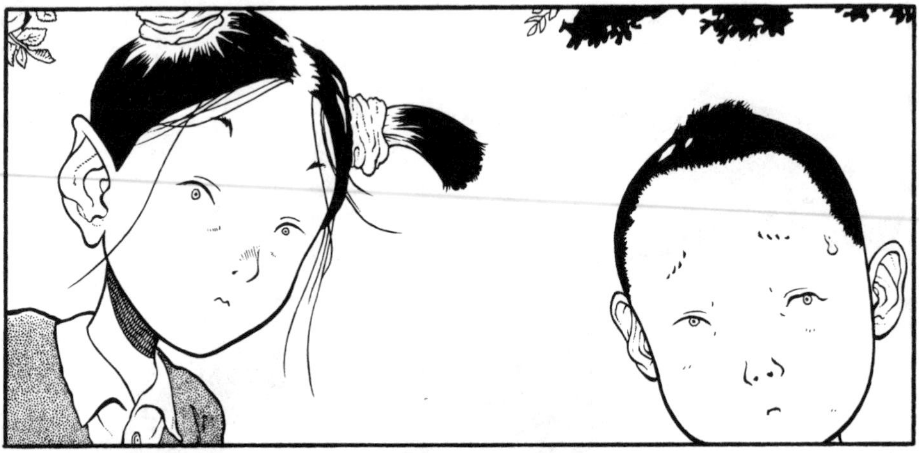

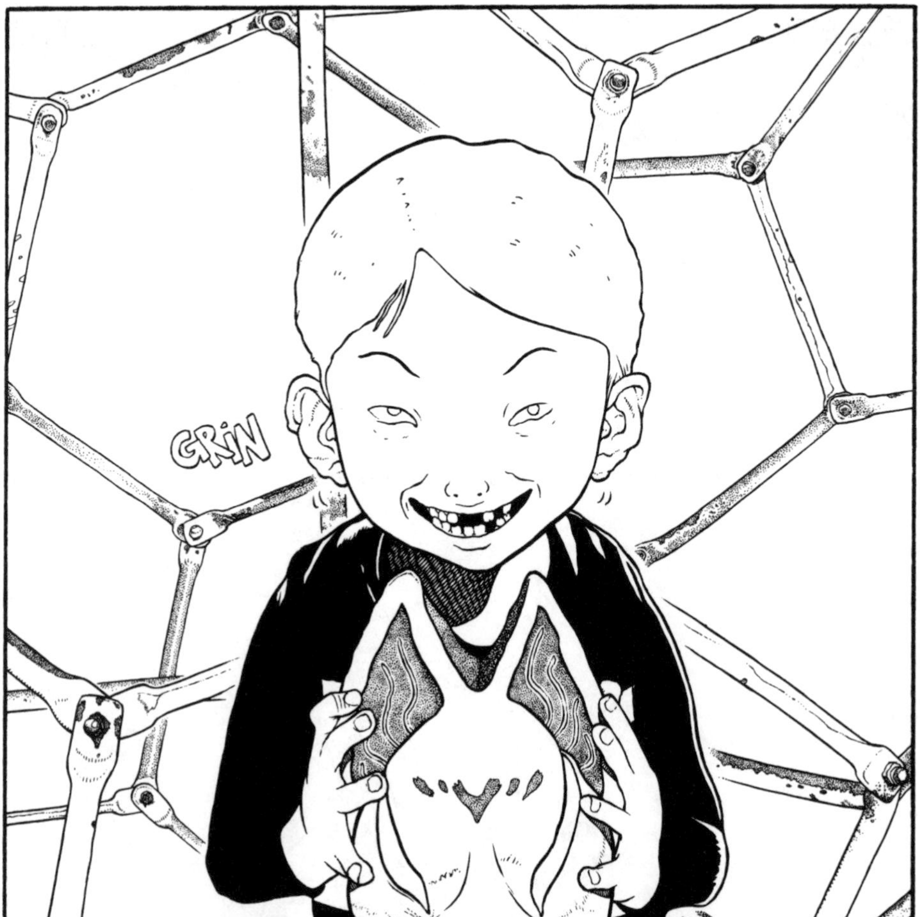
GRIN

Chapter 3:
Copycats

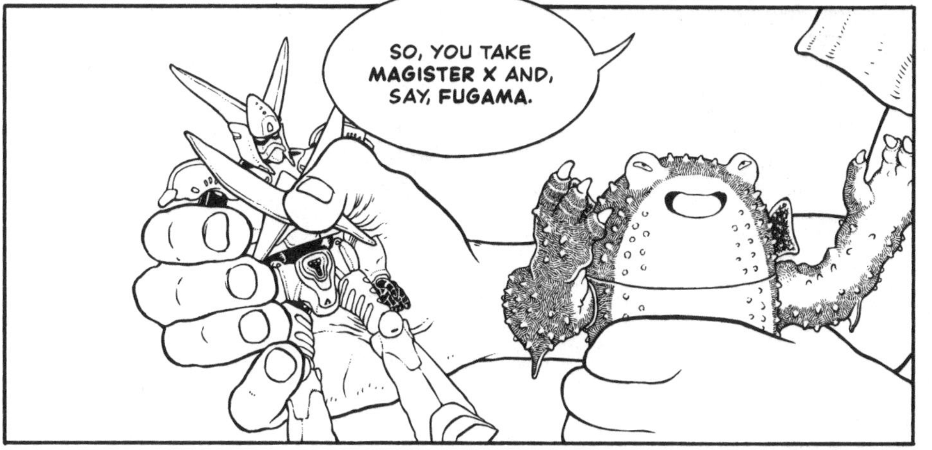
SO, YOU TAKE MAGISTER X AND, SAY, FUGAMA.

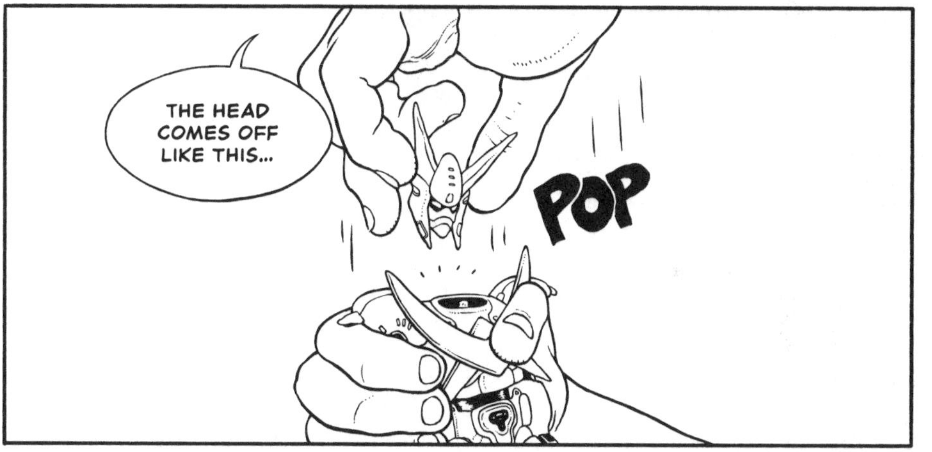
THE HEAD COMES OFF LIKE THIS...
POP

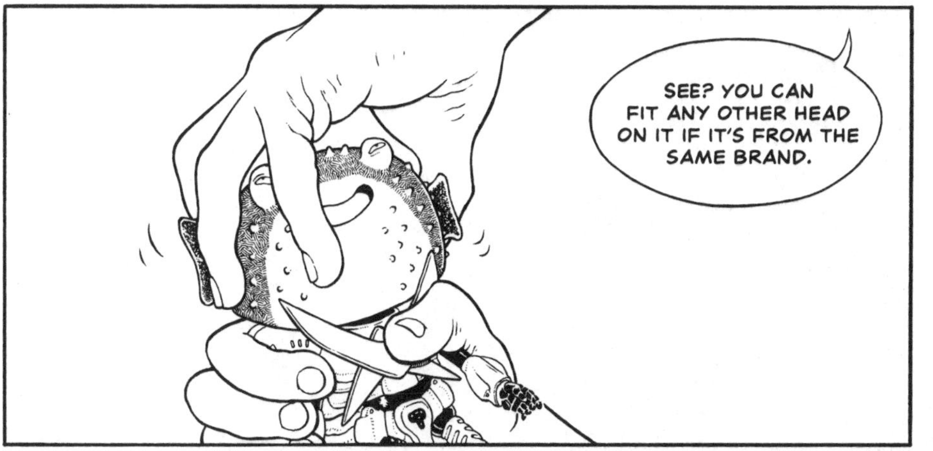
SEE? YOU CAN FIT ANY OTHER HEAD ON IT IF IT'S FROM THE SAME BRAND.

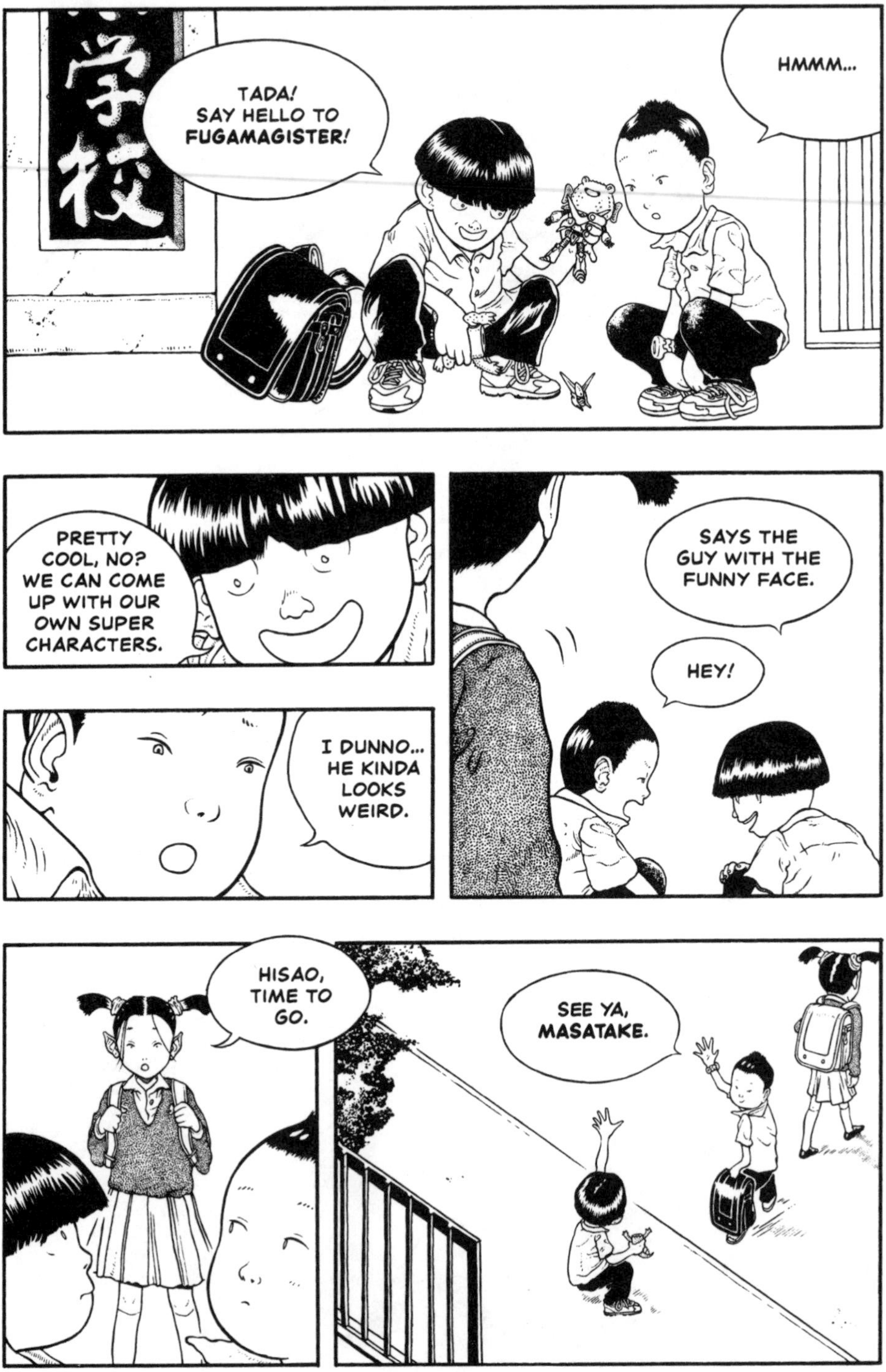
学校
TADA! SAY HELLO TO FUGAMAGISTER!
HMMM...
PRETTY COOL, NO? WE CAN COME UP WITH OUR OWN SUPER CHARACTERS.
I DUNNO... HE KINDA LOOKS WEIRD.
SAYS THE GUY WITH THE FUNNY FACE.
HEY!
HISAO, TIME TO GO.
SEE YA, MASATAKE.

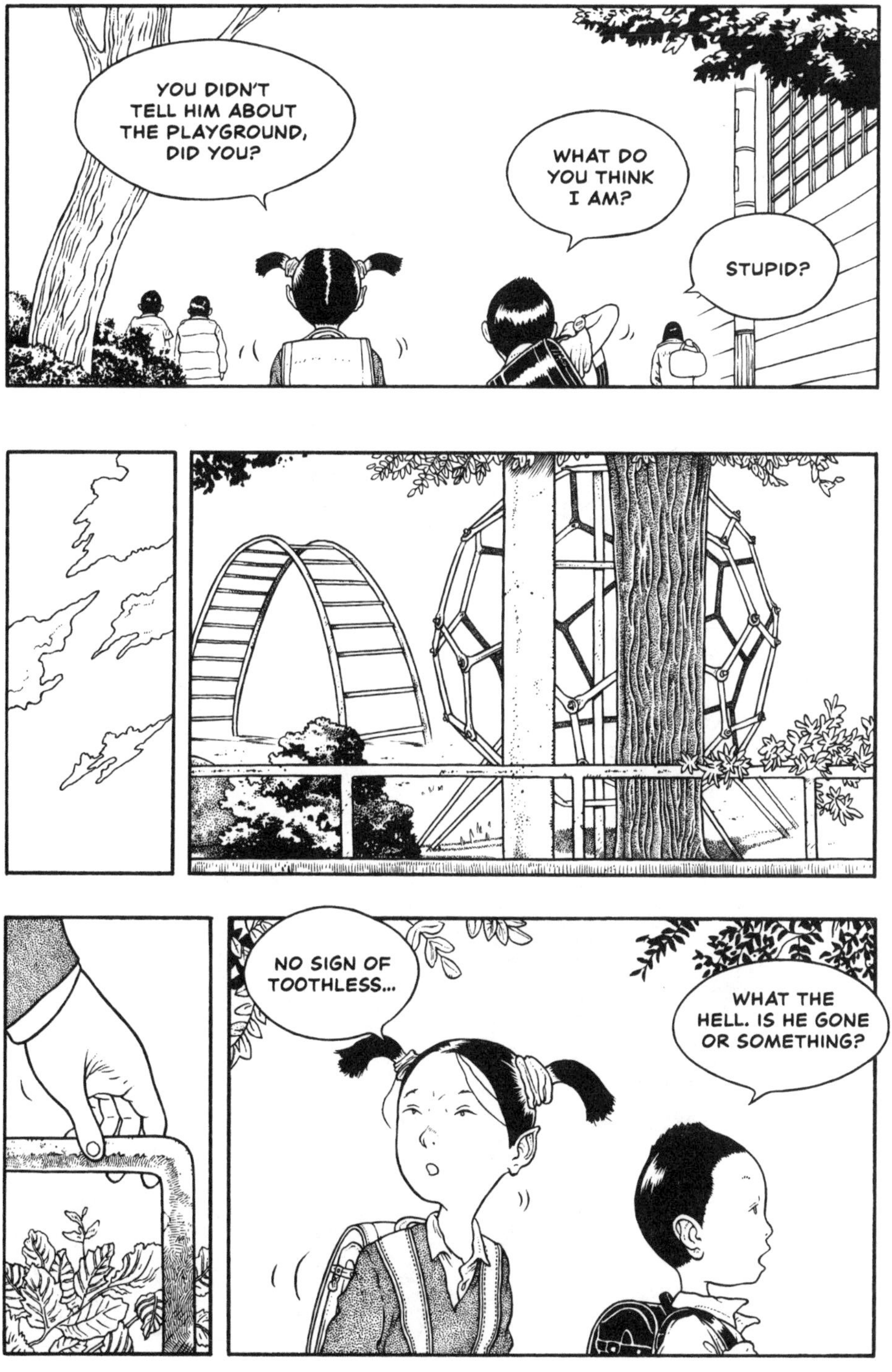
YOU DIDN'T TELL HIM ABOUT THE PLAYGROUND, DID YOU?
WHAT DO YOU THINK I AM?
STUPID?
NO SIGN OF TOOTHLESS...
WHAT THE HELL. IS HE GONE OR SOMETHING?

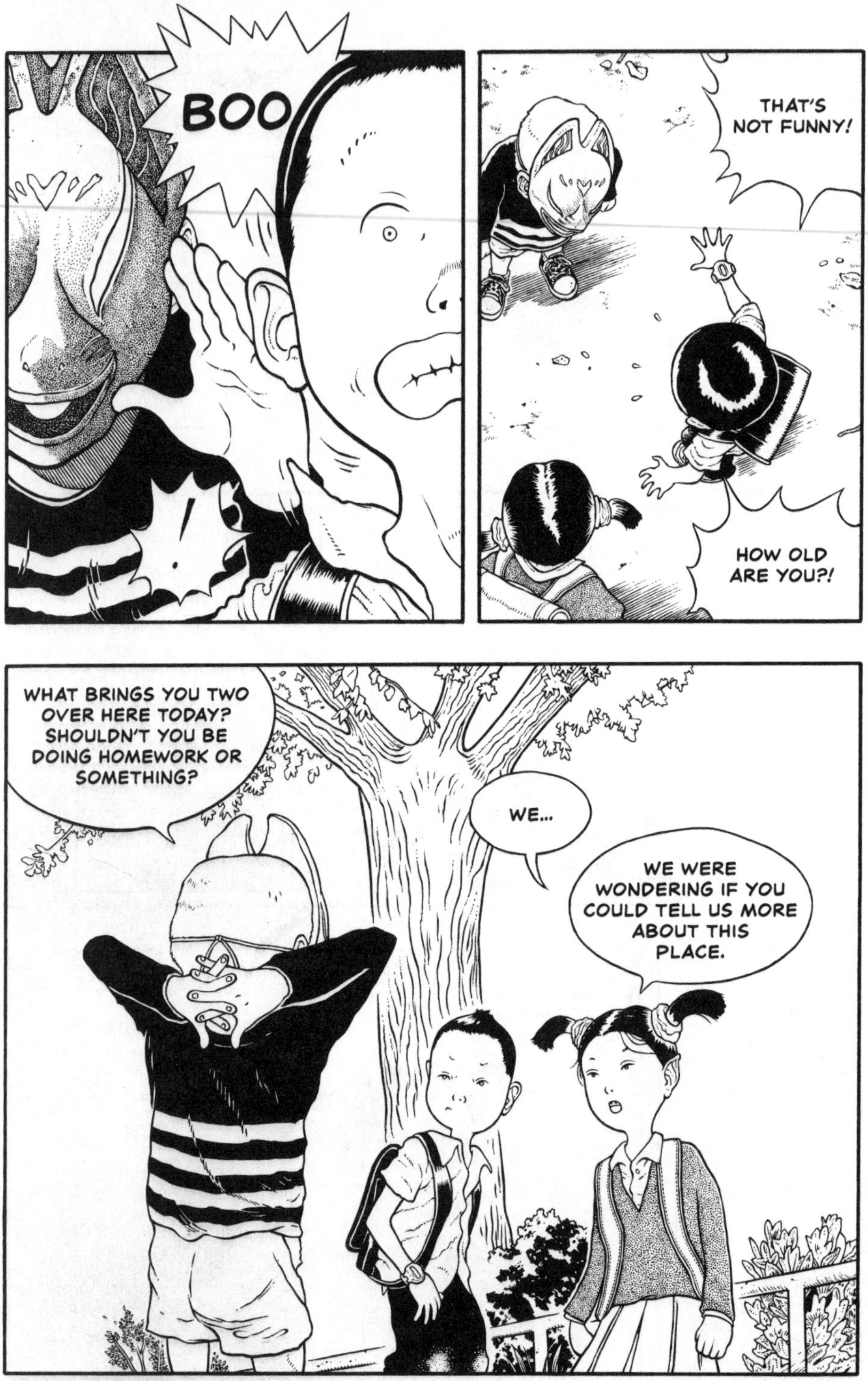
BOO
!
THAT'S NOT FUNNY!
HOW OLD ARE YOU?!
WHAT BRINGS YOU TWO OVER HERE TODAY? SHOULDN'T YOU BE DOING HOMEWORK OR SOMETHING?
WE...
WE WERE WONDERING IF YOU COULD TELL US MORE ABOUT THIS PLACE.

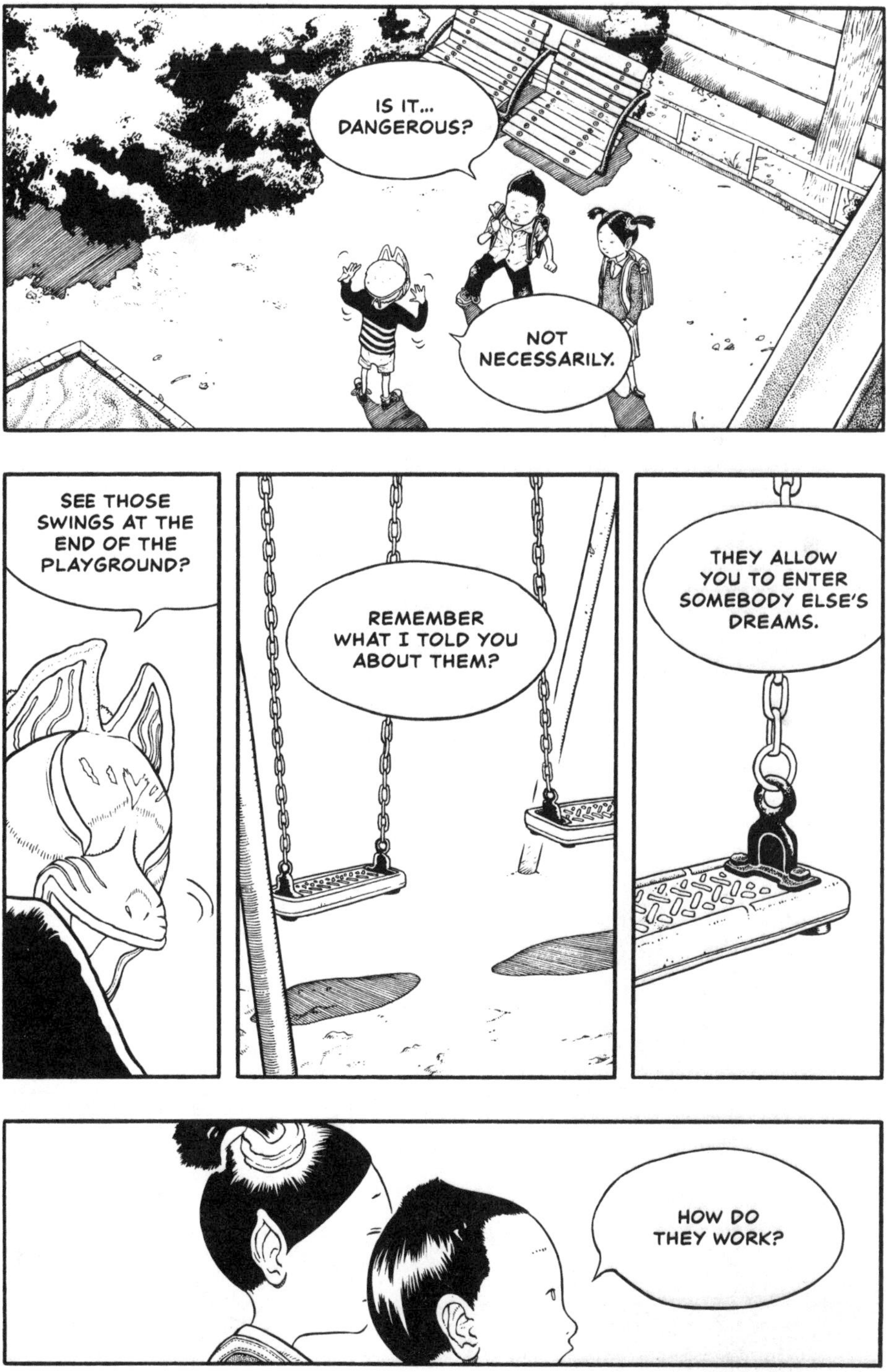
IS IT... DANGEROUS?
NOT NECESSARILY.
SEE THOSE SWINGS AT THE END OF THE PLAYGROUND?
REMEMBER WHAT I TOLD YOU ABOUT THEM?
THEY ALLOW YOU TO ENTER SOMEBODY ELSE'S DREAMS.
HOW DO THEY WORK?

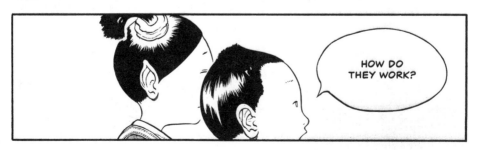

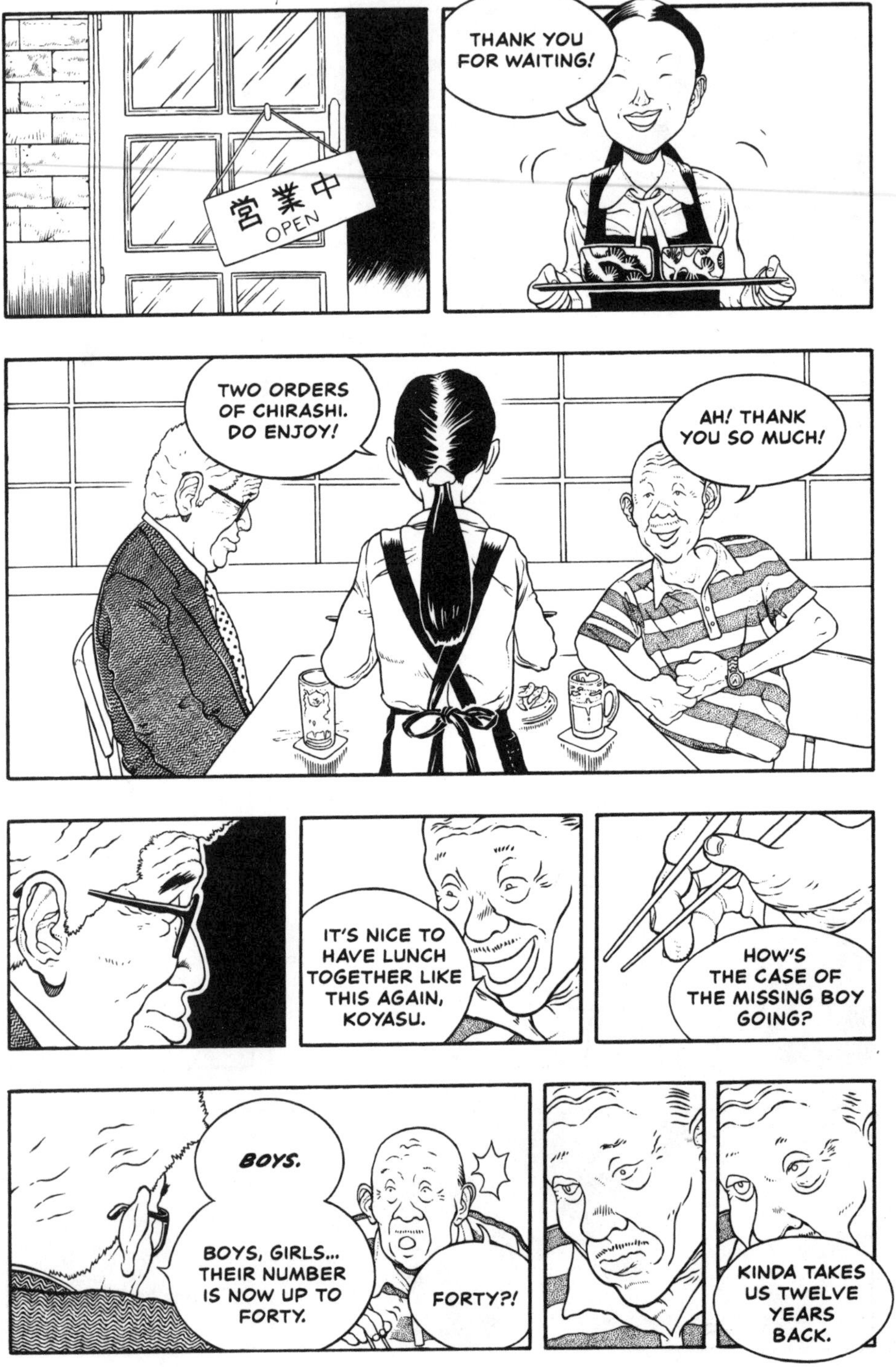

営業中
OPEN
THANK YOU FOR WAITING!
TWO ORDERS OF CHIRASHI. DO ENJOY!
AH! THANK YOU SO MUCH!
IT'S NICE TO HAVE LUNCH TOGETHER LIKE THIS AGAIN, KOYASU.
HOW'S THE CASE OF THE MISSING BOY GOING?
BOYS.
BOYS, GIRLS... THEIR NUMBER IS NOW UP TO FORTY.
FORTY?!
KINDA TAKES US TWELVE YEARS BACK.

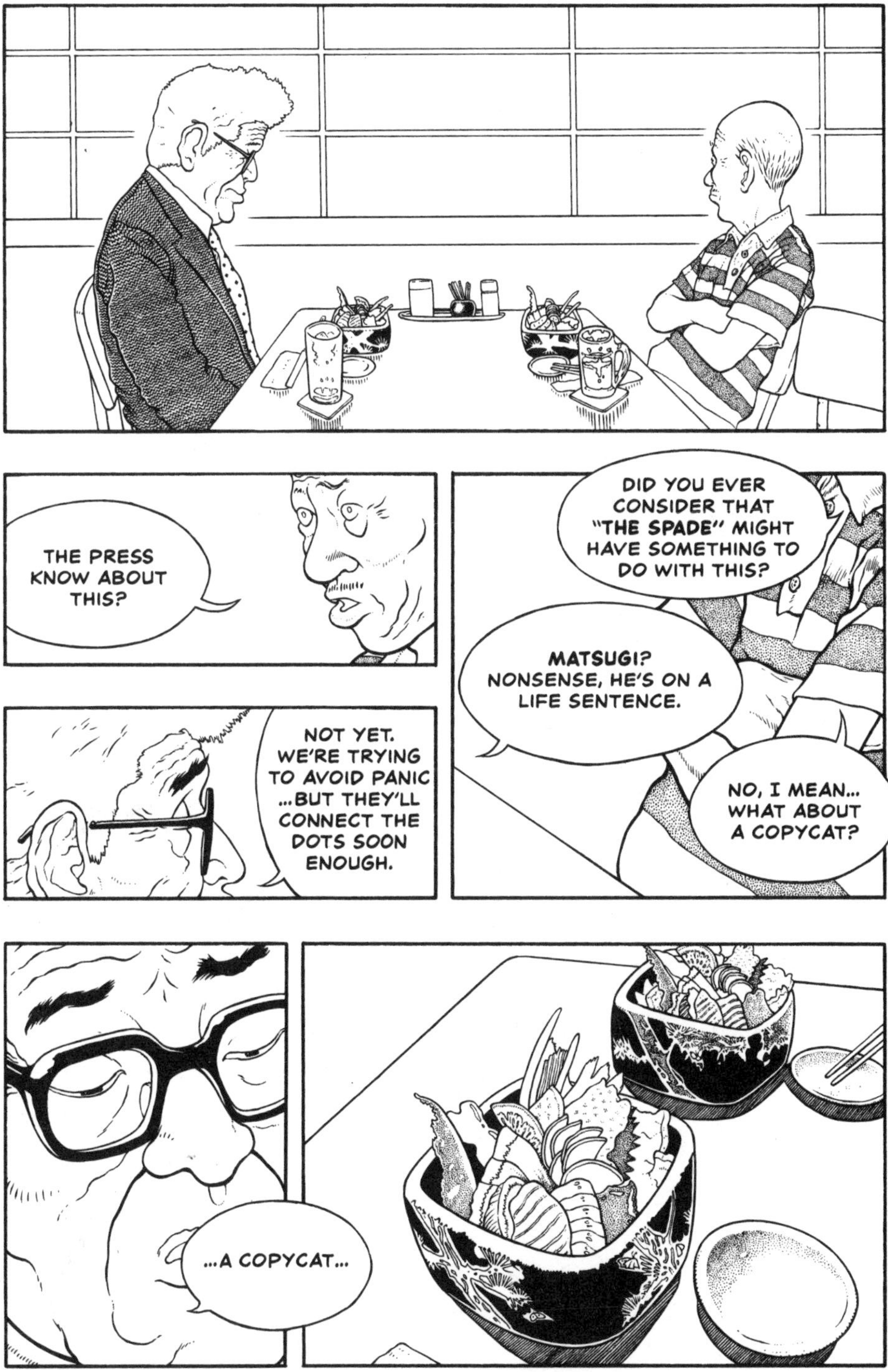
THE PRESS KNOW ABOUT THIS?
NOT YET. WE'RE TRYING TO AVOID PANIC ...BUT THEY'LL CONNECT THE DOTS SOON ENOUGH.
DID YOU EVER CONSIDER THAT "THE SPADE" MIGHT HAVE SOMETHING TO DO WITH THIS?
MATSUGI? NONSENSE, HE'S ON A LIFE SENTENCE.
NO, I MEAN... WHAT ABOUT A COPYCAT?
...A COPYCAT...

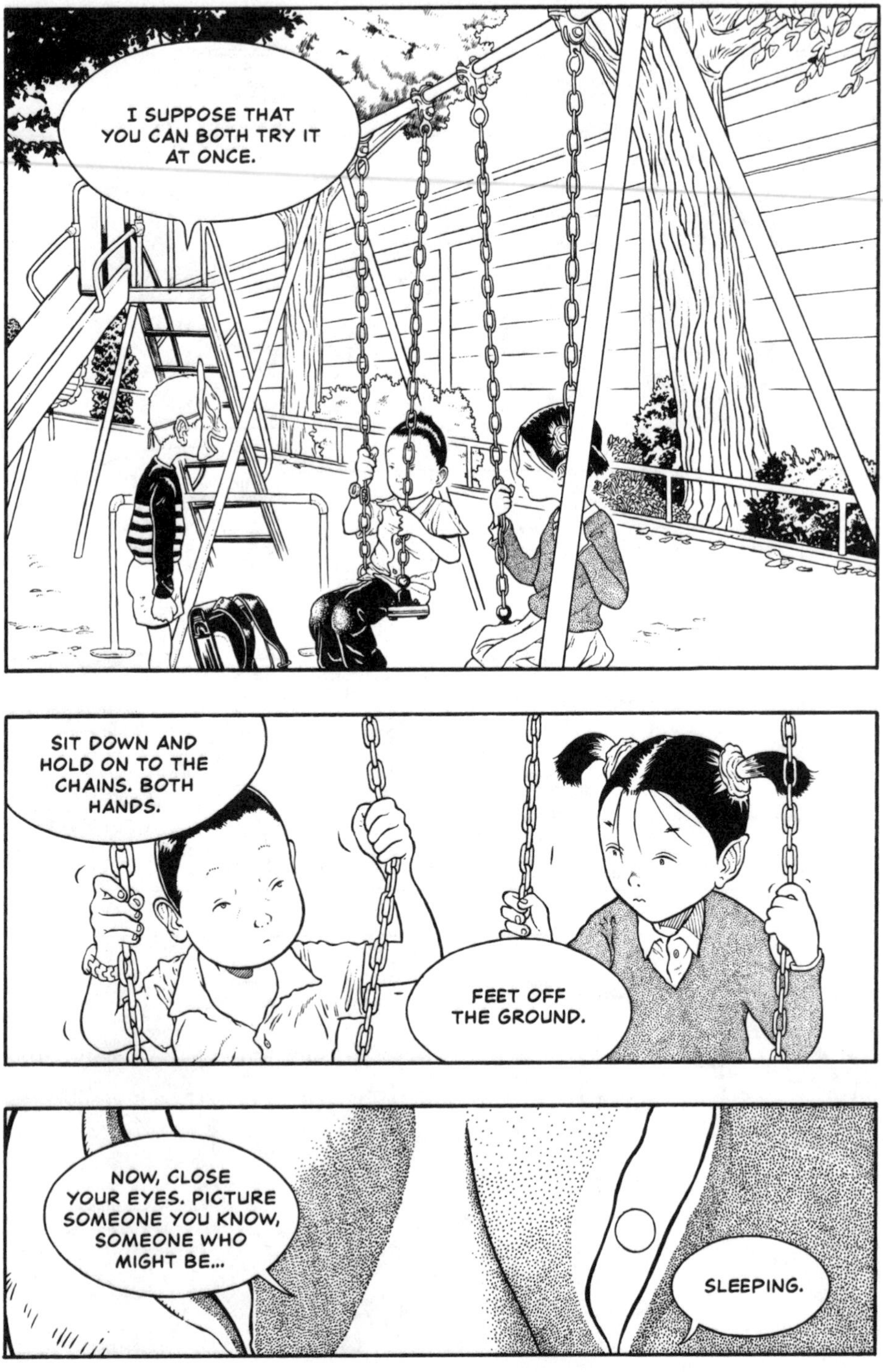
I SUPPOSE THAT YOU CAN BOTH TRY IT AT ONCE.
SIT DOWN AND HOLD ON TO THE CHAINS. BOTH HANDS.
FEET OFF THE GROUND.
NOW, CLOSE YOUR EYES. PICTURE SOMEONE YOU KNOW, SOMEONE WHO MIGHT BE...
SLEEPING.

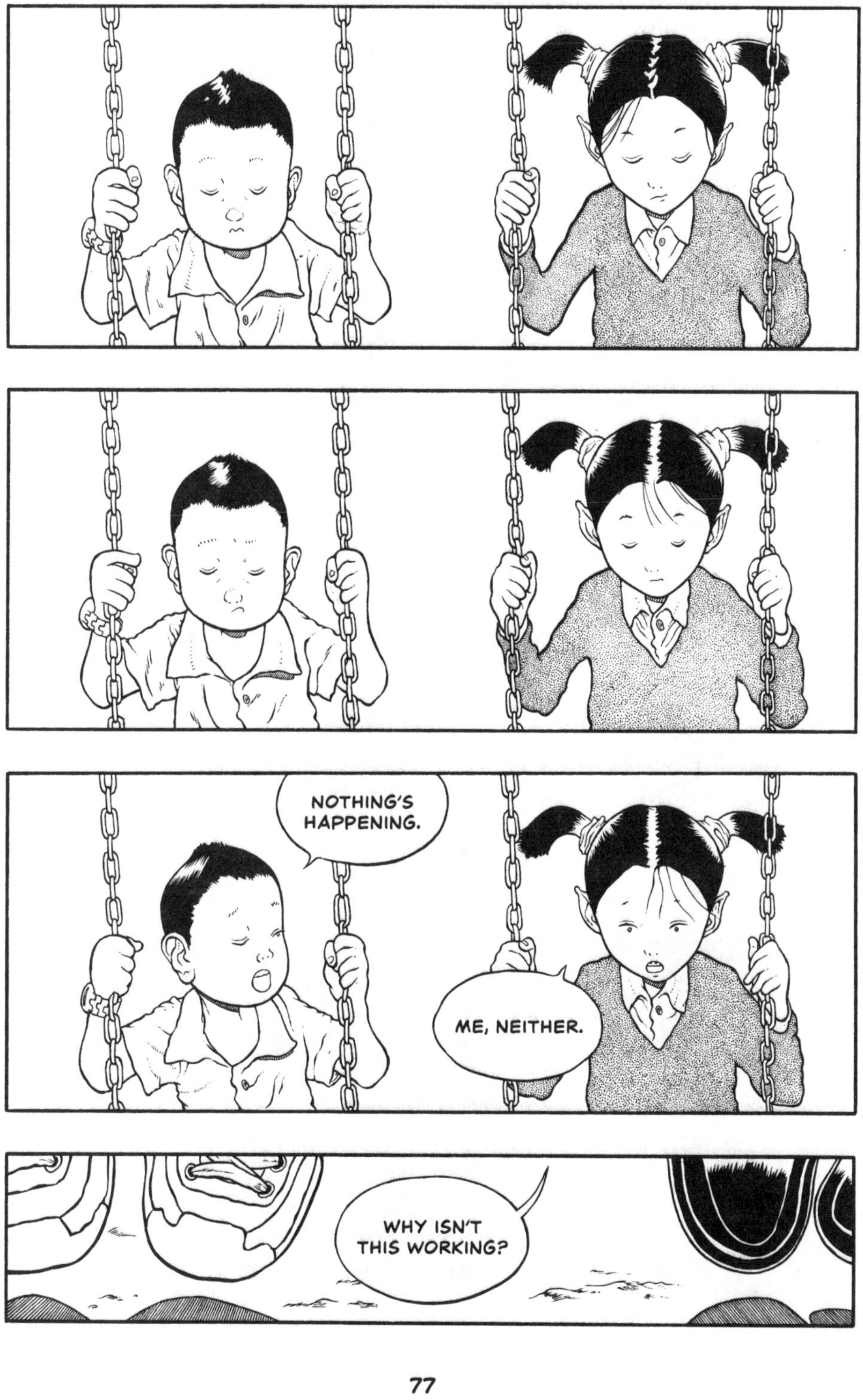
NOTHING'S HAPPENING.
ME, NEITHER.
WHY ISN'T THIS WORKING?

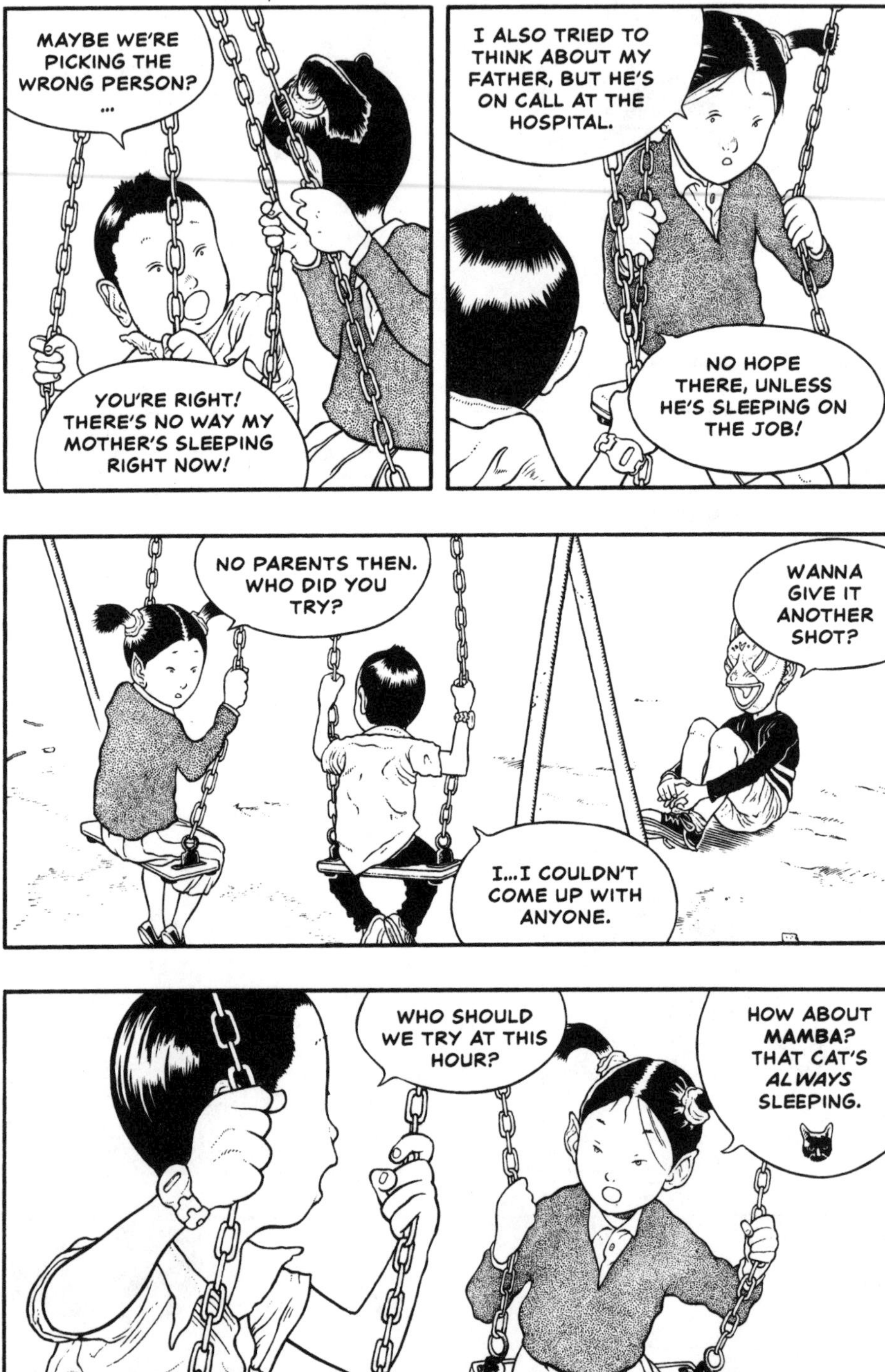
MAYBE WE'RE PICKING THE WRONG PERSON? ...
YOU'RE RIGHT! THERE'S NO WAY MY MOTHER'S SLEEPING RIGHT NOW!
I ALSO TRIED TO THINK ABOUT MY FATHER, BUT HE'S ON CALL AT THE HOSPITAL.
NO HOPE THERE, UNLESS HE'S SLEEPING ON THE JOB!
NO PARENTS THEN. WHO DID YOU TRY?
I...I COULDN'T COME UP WITH ANYONE.
WANNA GIVE IT ANOTHER SHOT?
WHO SHOULD WE TRY AT THIS HOUR?
HOW ABOUT MAMBA? THAT CAT'S *ALWAYS* SLEEPING.

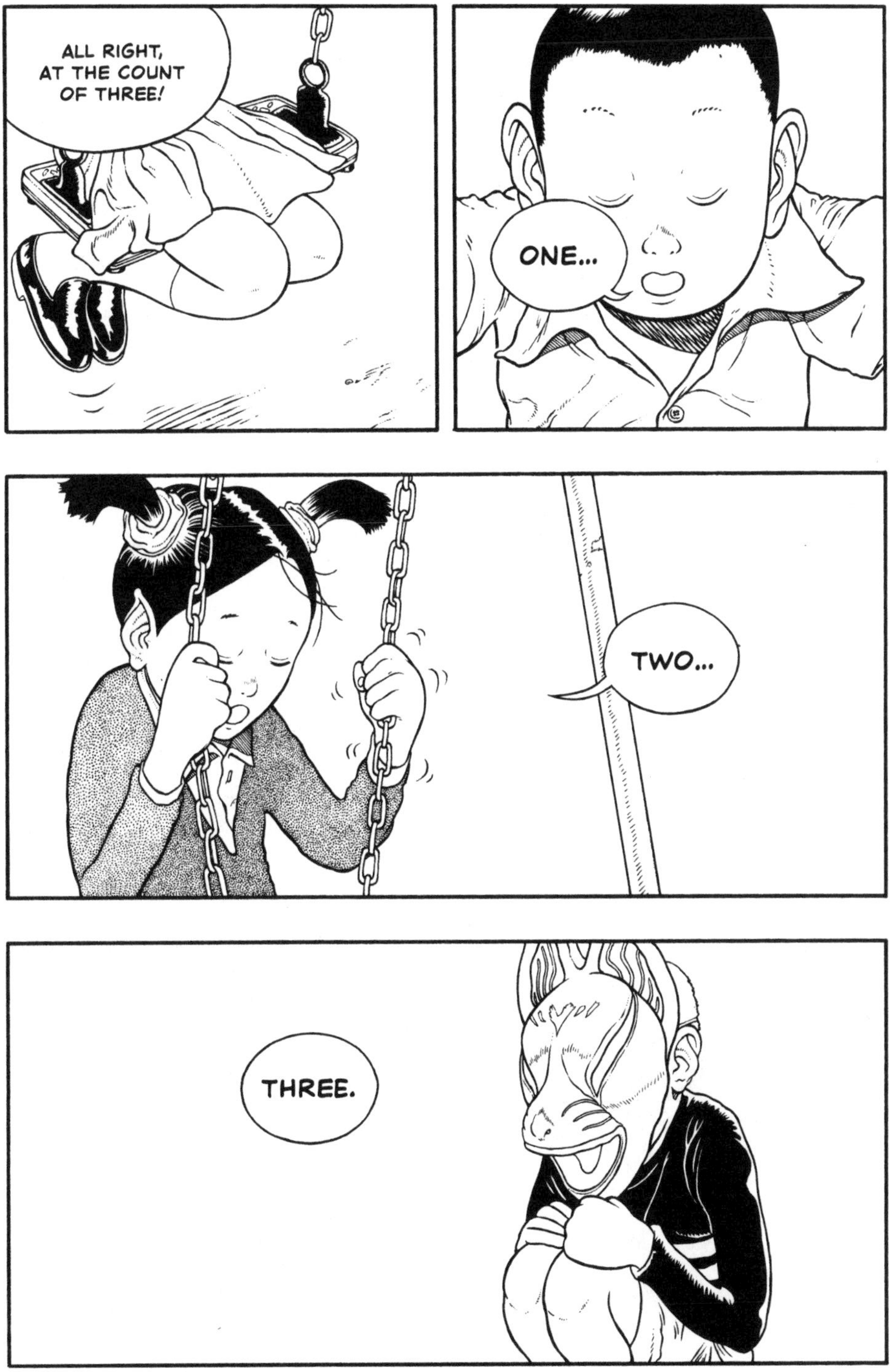
ALL RIGHT, AT THE COUNT OF THREE!
ONE...
TWO...
THREE.

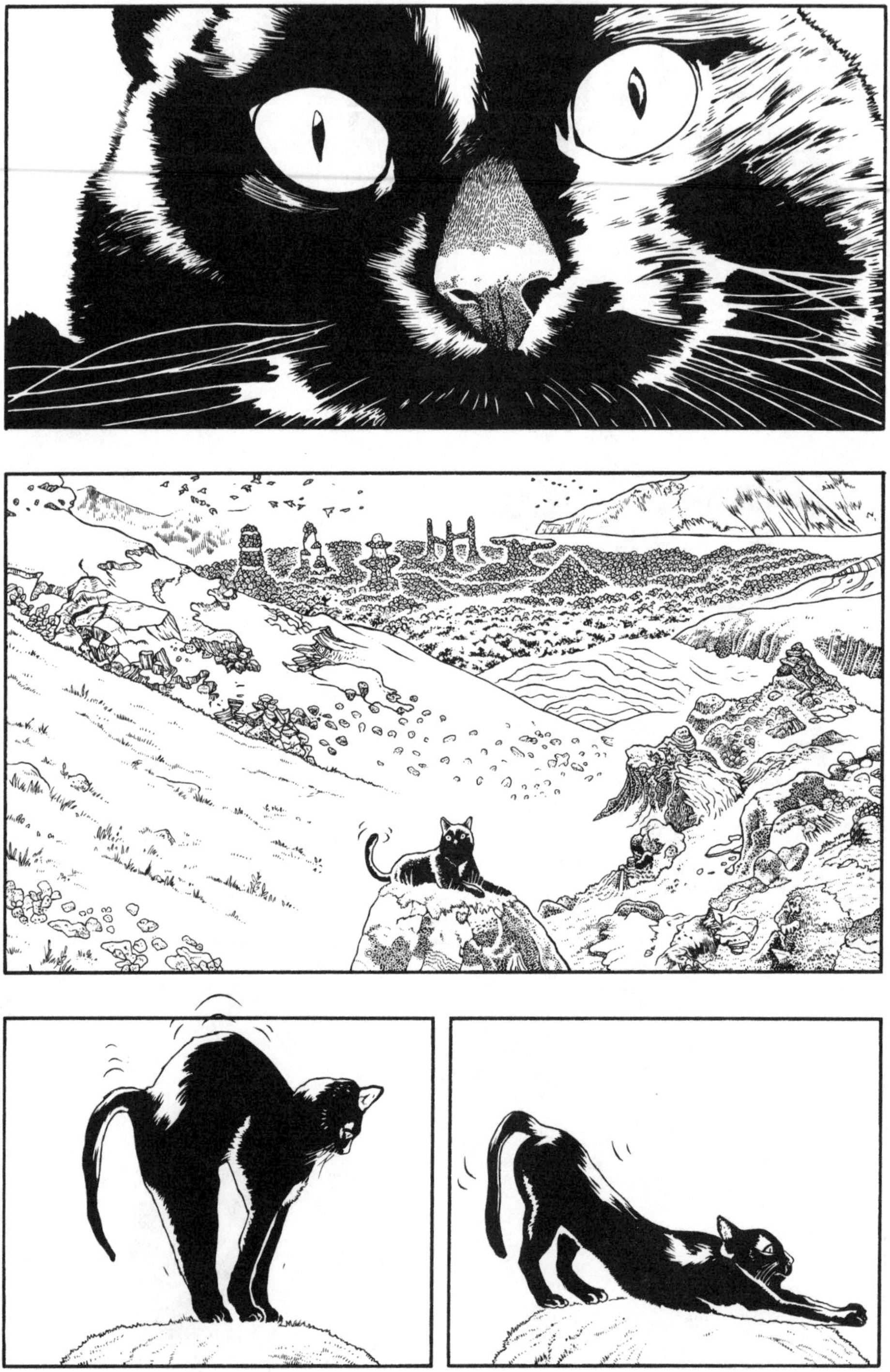

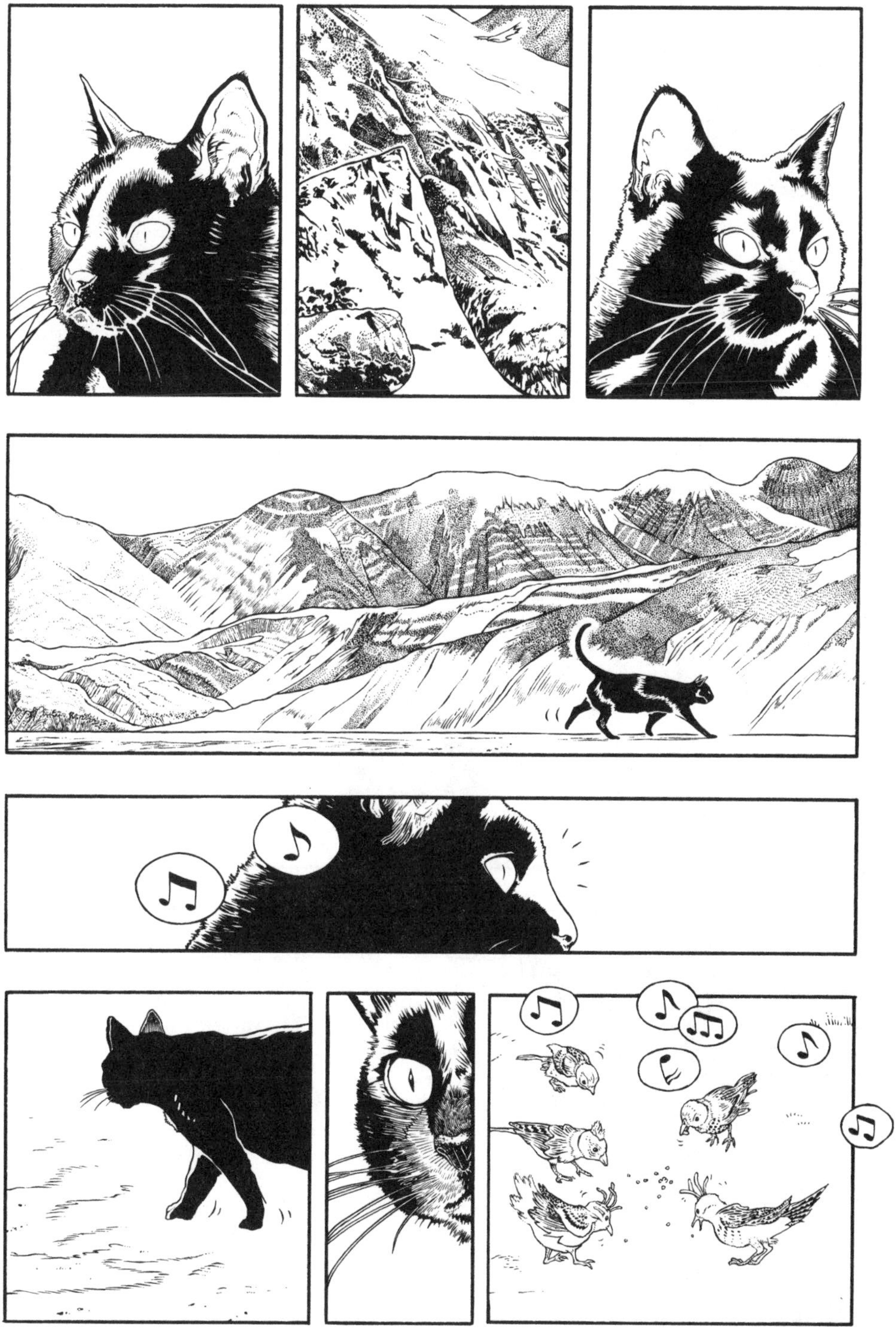

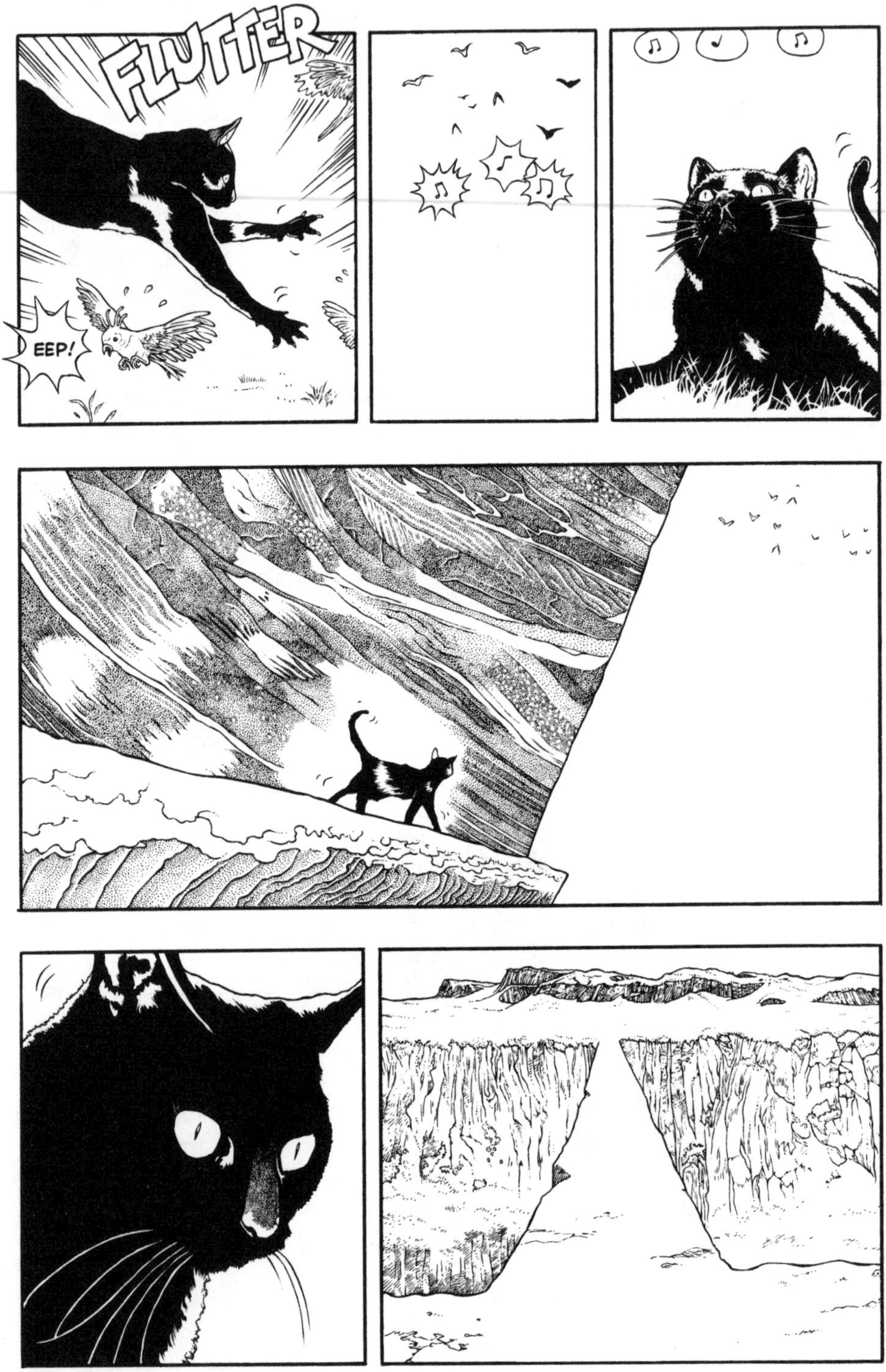
FLUTTER
EEP!

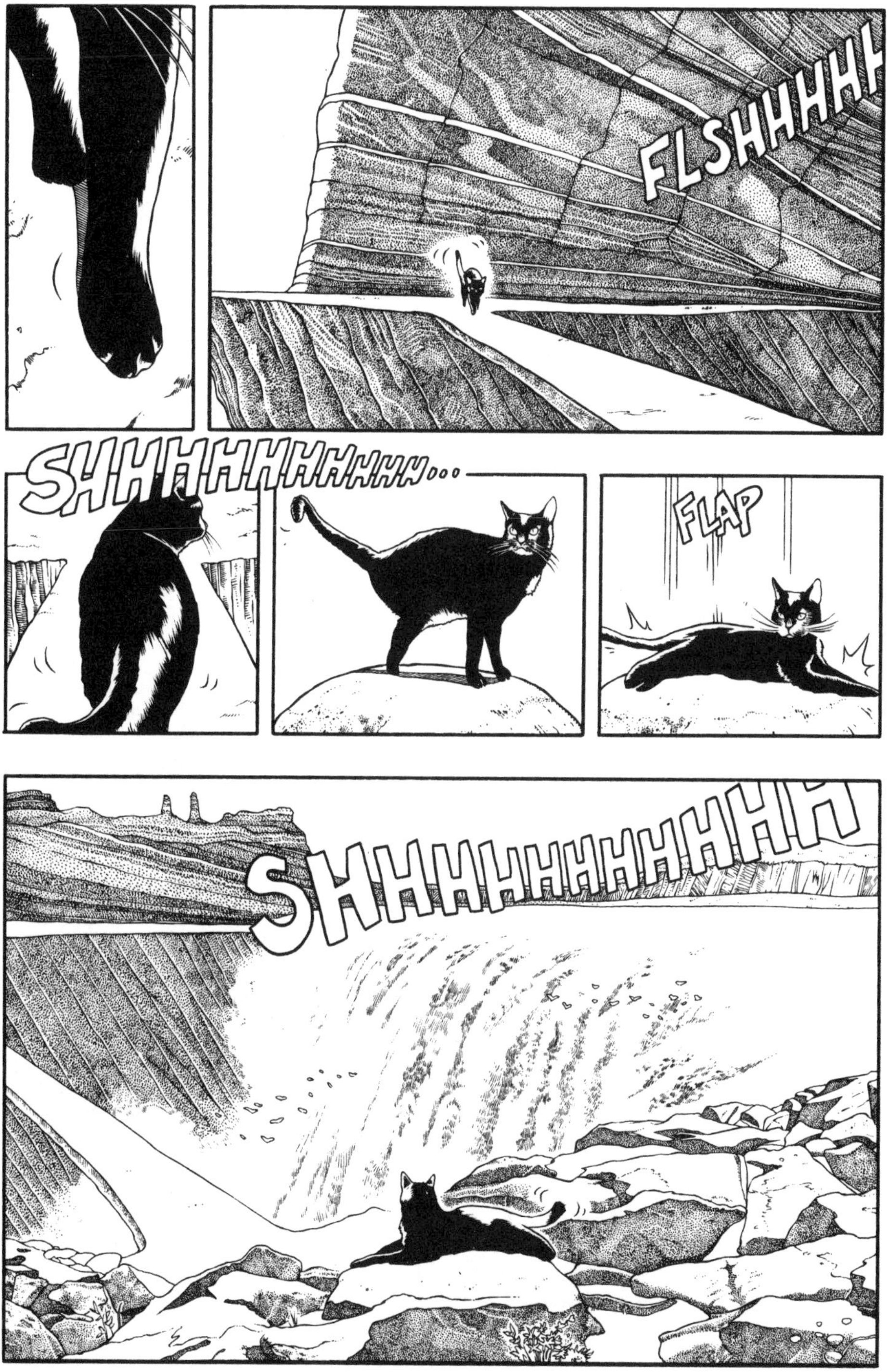

FLSHHHHH
SHHHHHHHHHH...
FLAP
SHHHHHHHHHHHHH

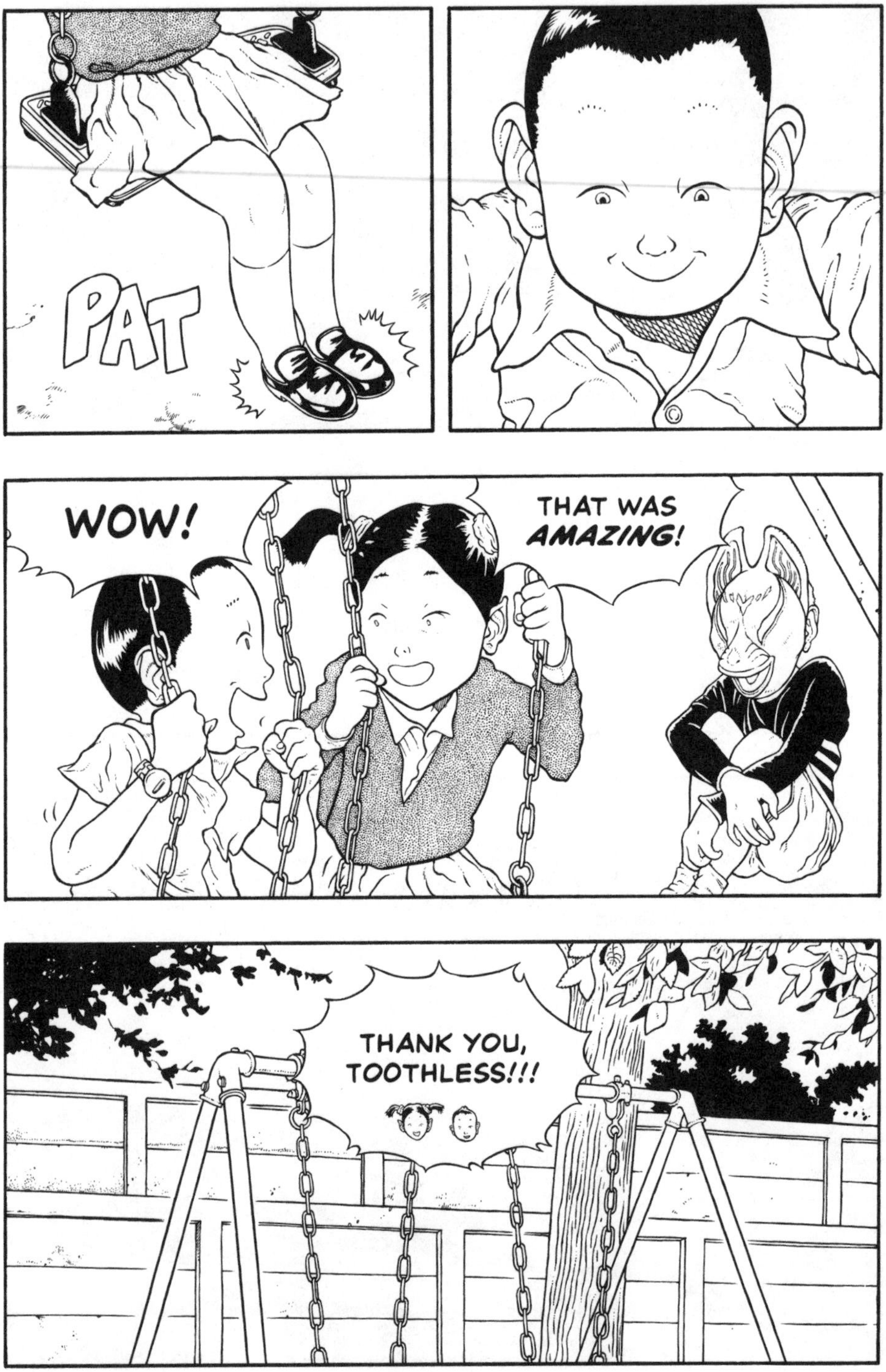
PAT
WOW!
THAT WAS *AMAZING*!
THANK YOU, TOOTHLESS!!!

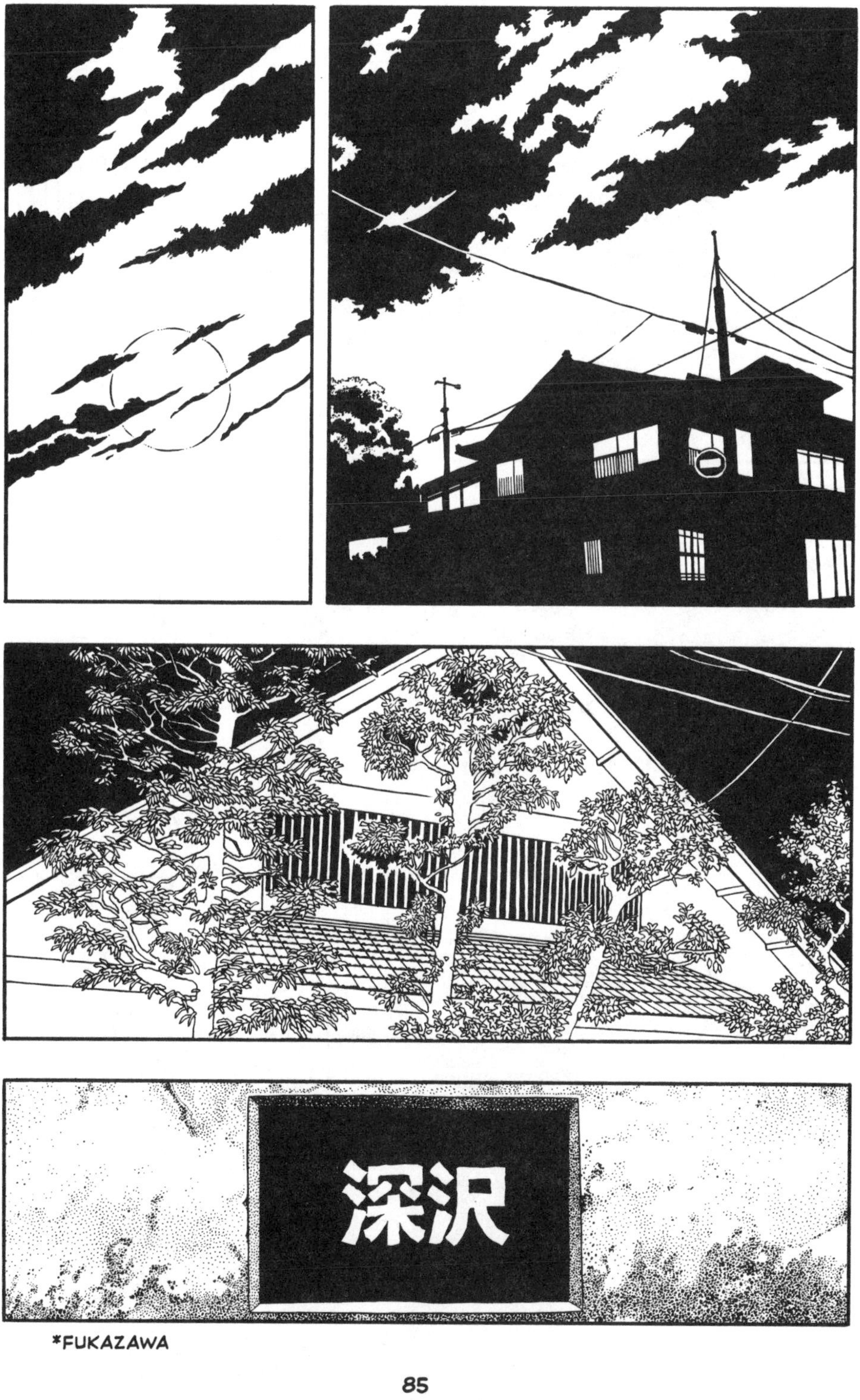
深沢

*FUKAZAWA

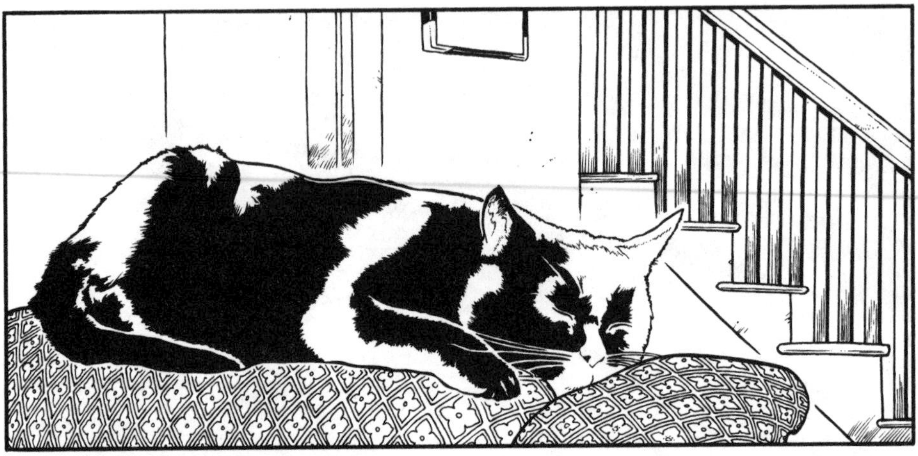

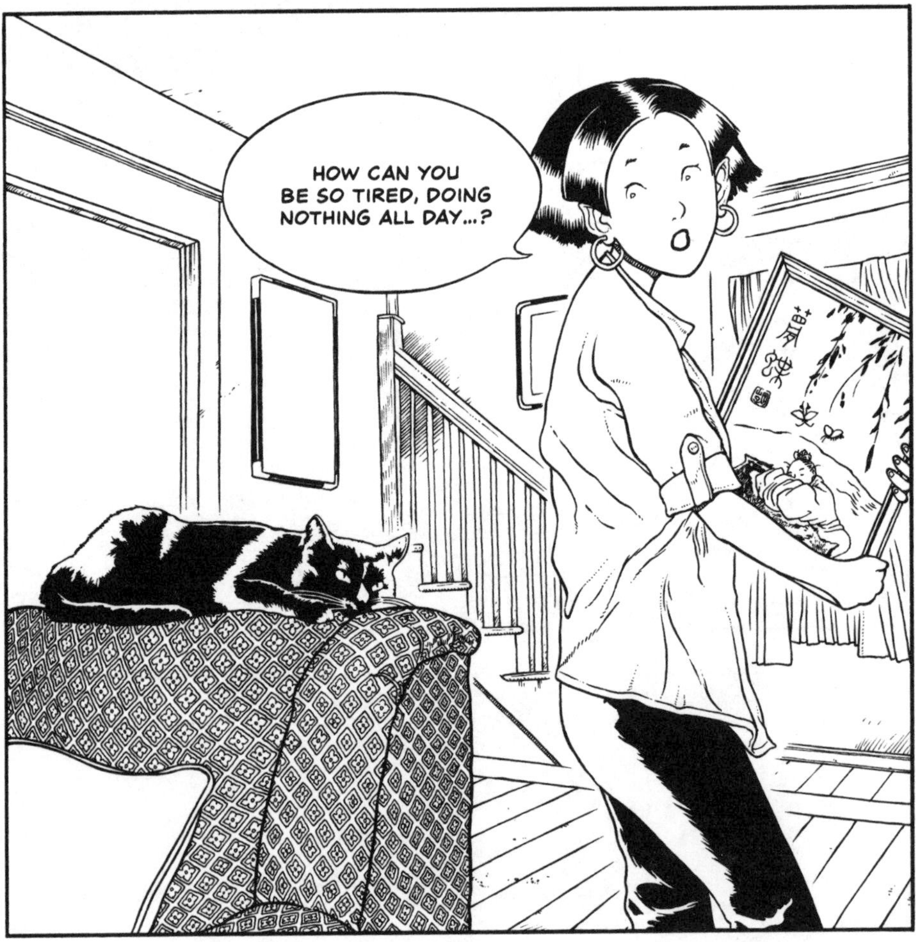
HOW CAN YOU BE SO TIRED, DOING NOTHING ALL DAY...?

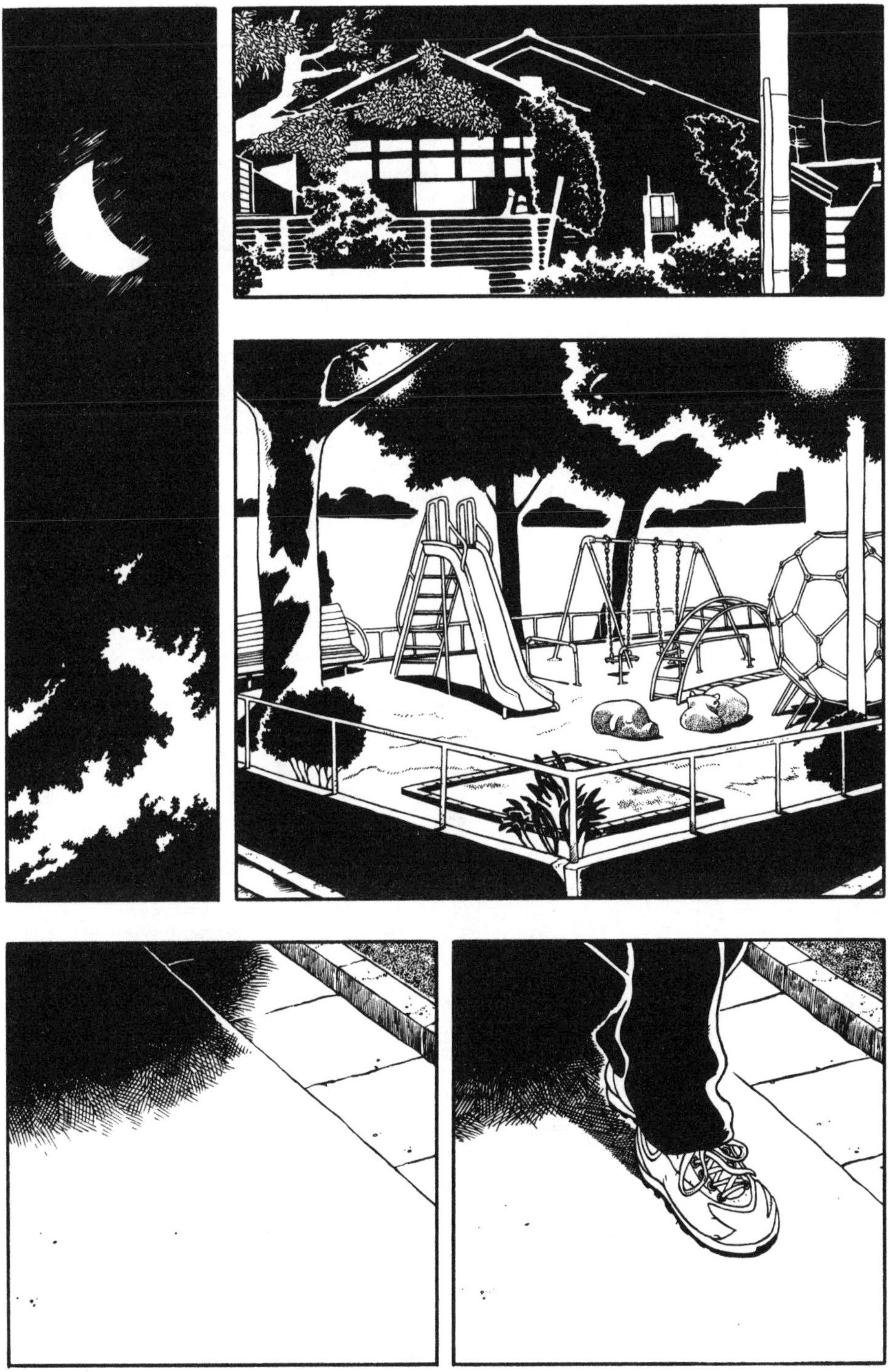

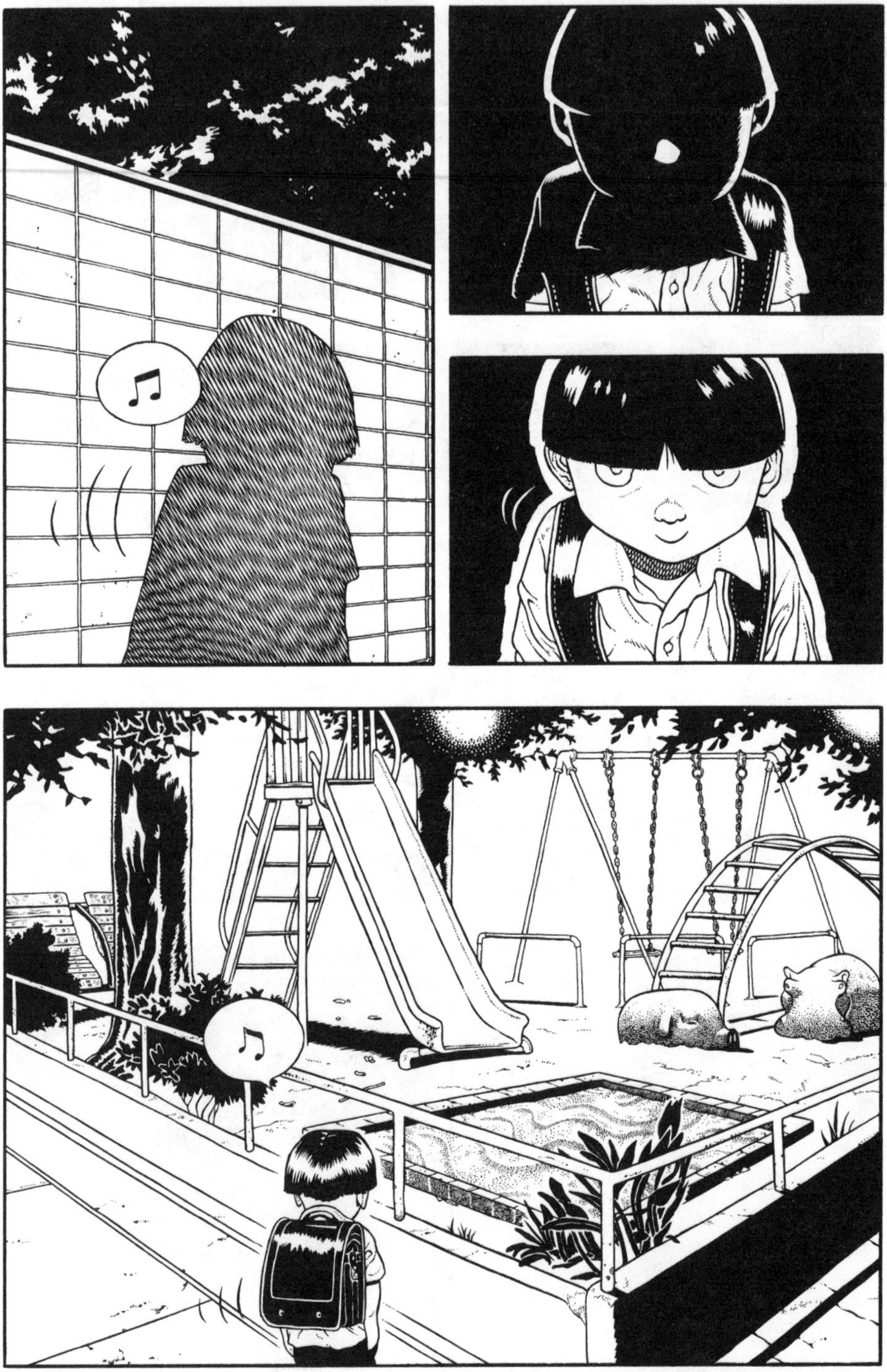

Chapter 4:
Animals

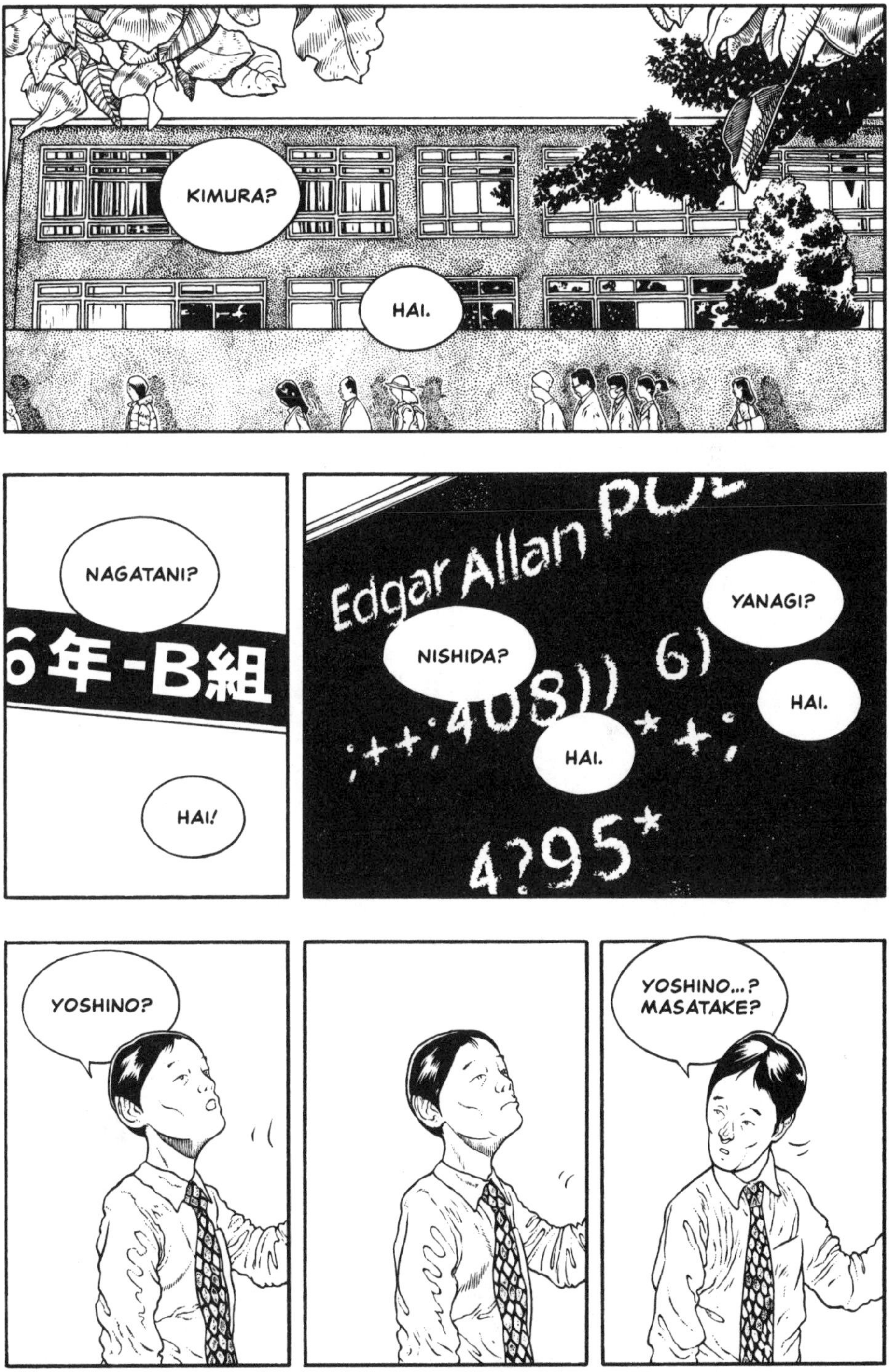
KIMURA?
HAI.
NAGATANI?
6年-B組
HAI!
Edgar Allan POE
;++;4081) 6)
*+;
4?95*
NISHIDA?
HAI.
YANAGI?
HAI.
YOSHINO?
YOSHINO...?
MASATAKE?

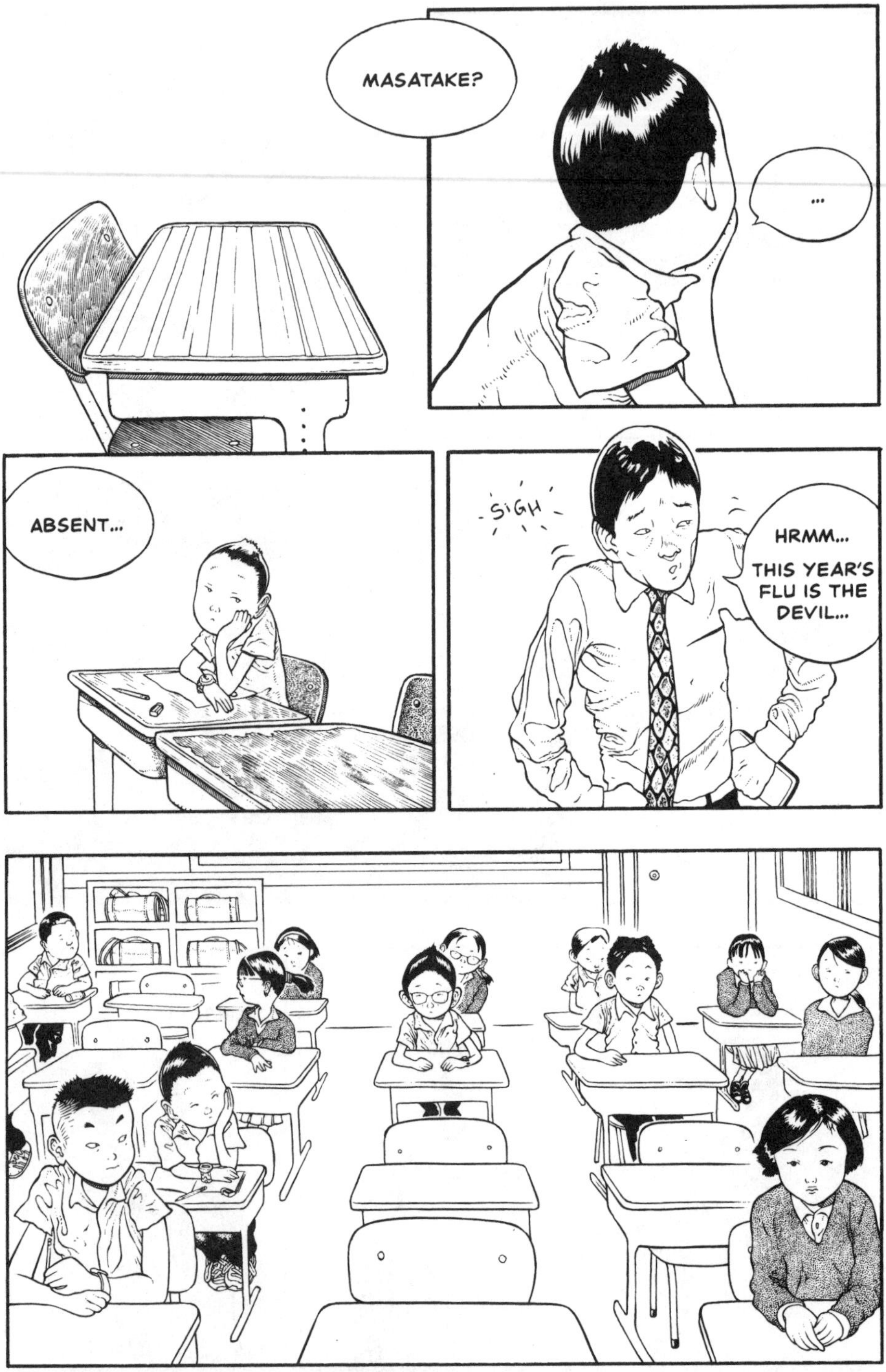
MASATAKE?
...
ABSENT...
SIGH
HRMM...
THIS YEAR'S FLU IS THE DEVIL...

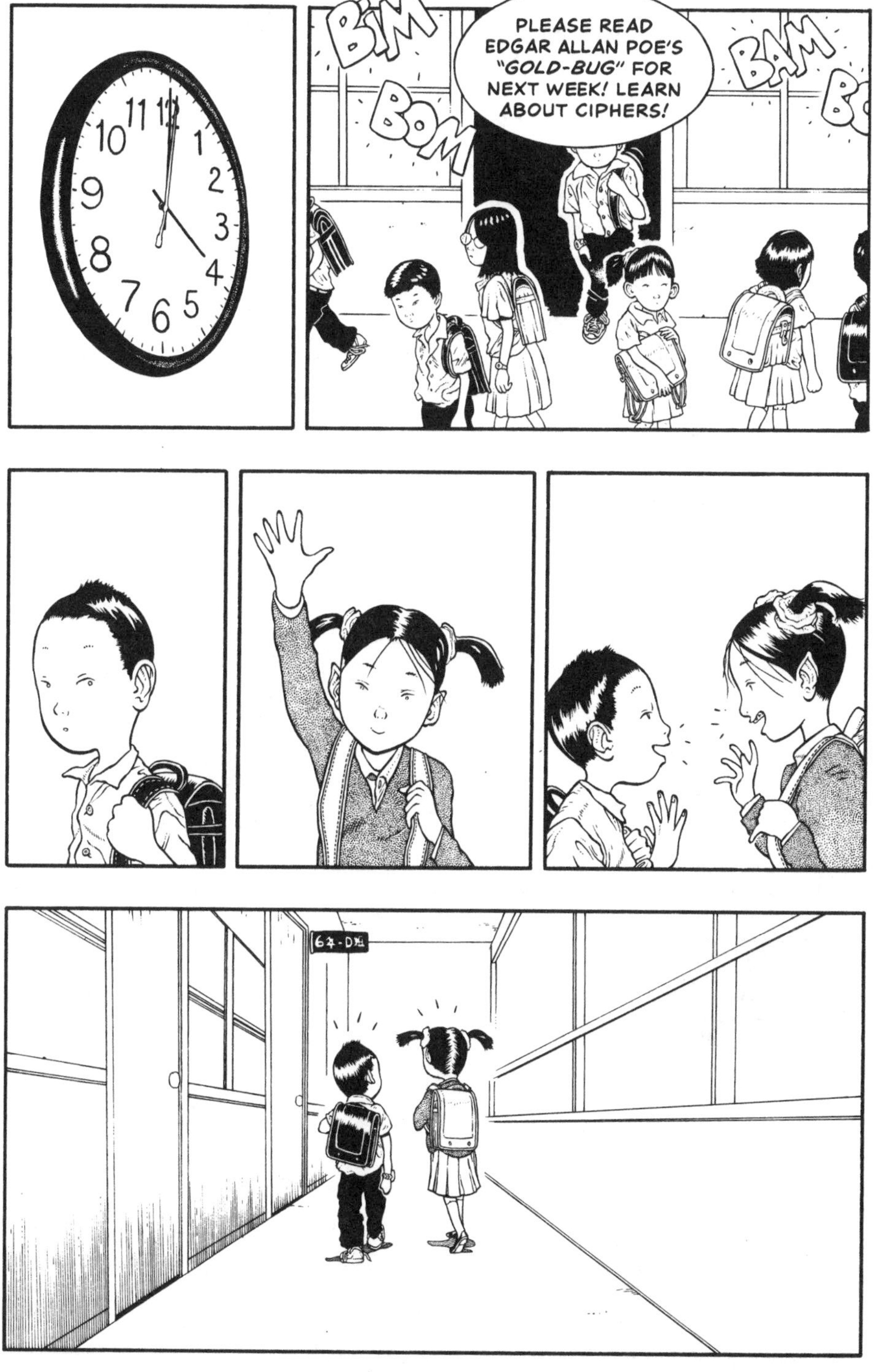
BIM
BOM
PLEASE READ EDGAR ALLAN POE'S *"GOLD-BUG"* FOR NEXT WEEK! LEARN ABOUT CIPHERS!
BAM

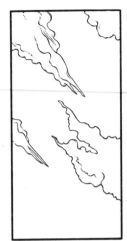

HI, TOOTHLESS.

HI, GUYS.

YOU'RE IN THE SANDBOX... WHY IS NOTHING HAPPENING?

HA.

THERE'S NOT MUCH LEFT TO FEAR IN MY POSITION, YOU KNOW.

NOTHING BUT LONELINESS. MAYBE.

SORRY...

TOOTHLESS, YOU SAID THESE SCULPTURES "ARE THE PLAYGROUND'S EARS."

WHAT DID YOU MEAN?

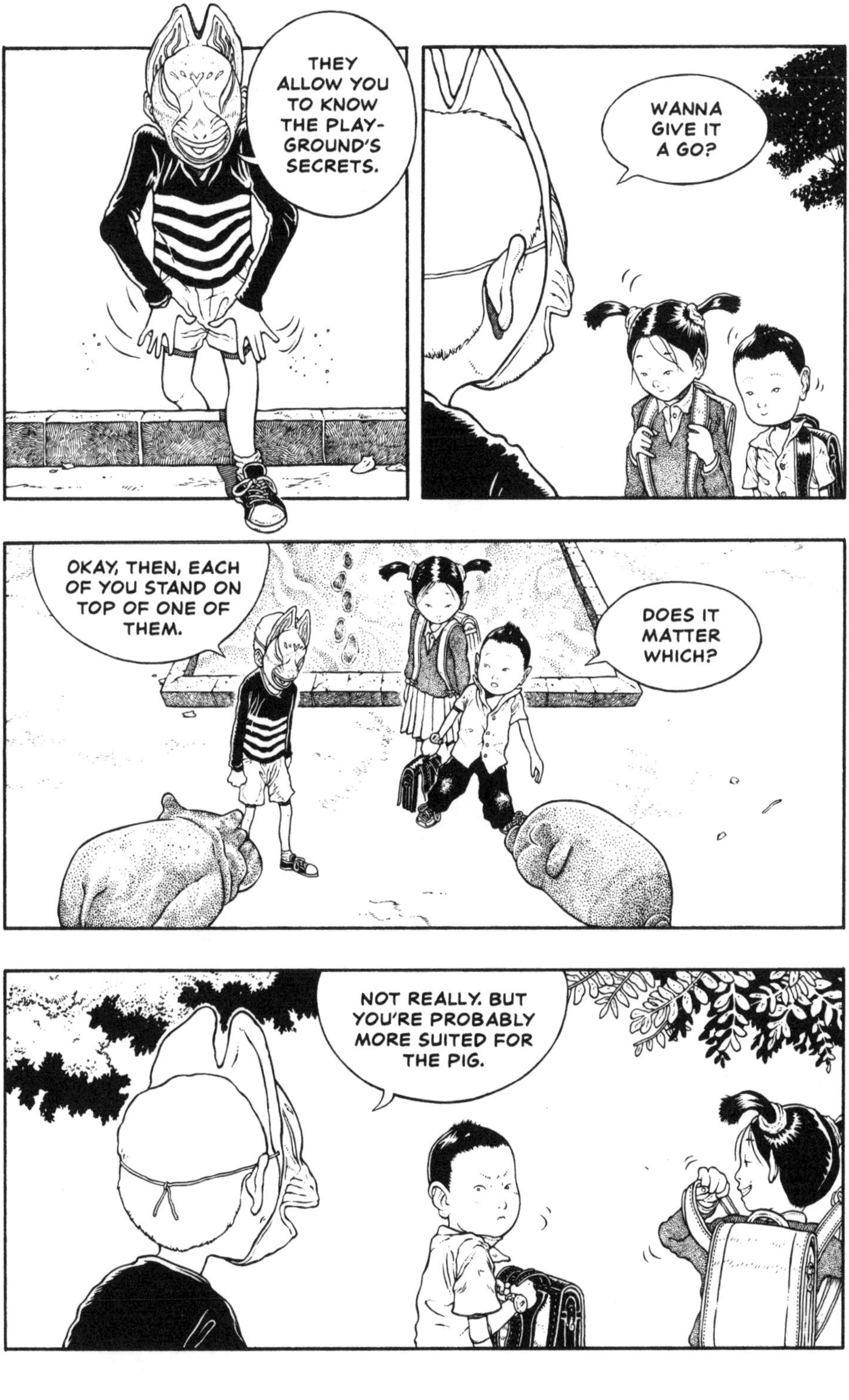
THEY ALLOW YOU TO KNOW THE PLAY-GROUND'S SECRETS.
WANNA GIVE IT A GO?
OKAY, THEN, EACH OF YOU STAND ON TOP OF ONE OF THEM.
DOES IT MATTER WHICH?
NOT REALLY. BUT YOU'RE PROBABLY MORE SUITED FOR THE PIG.

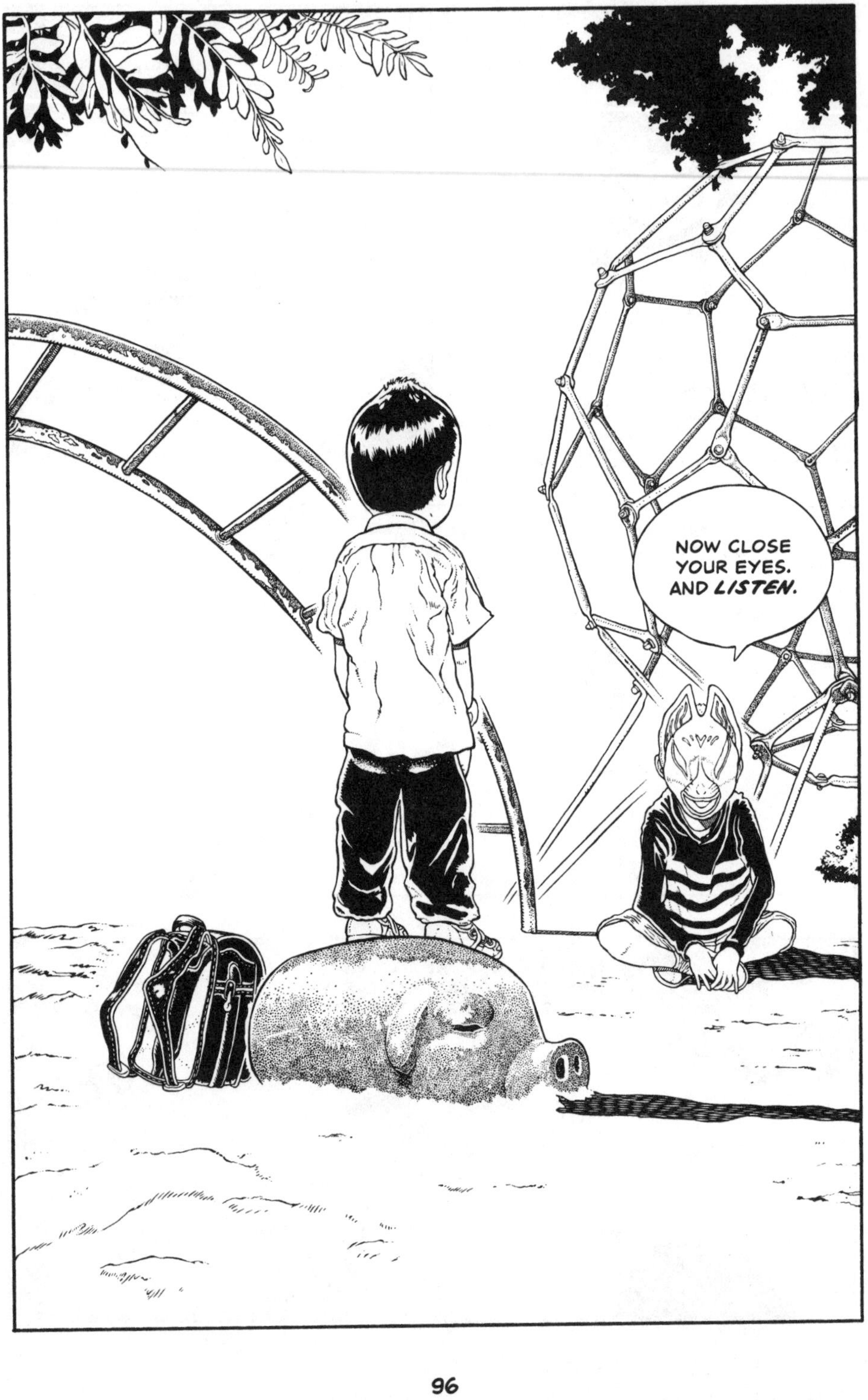
NOW CLOSE YOUR EYES. AND LISTEN.

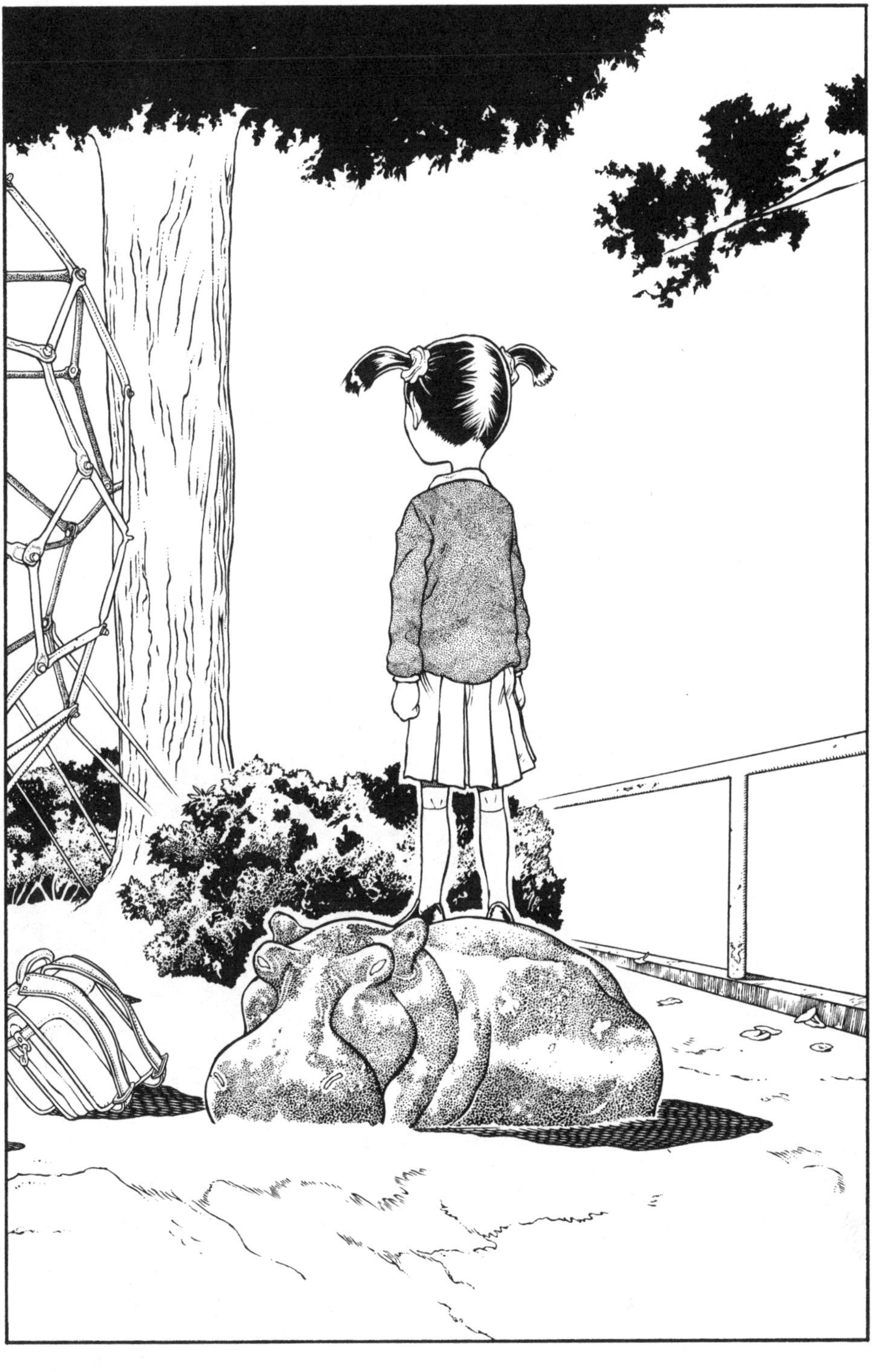

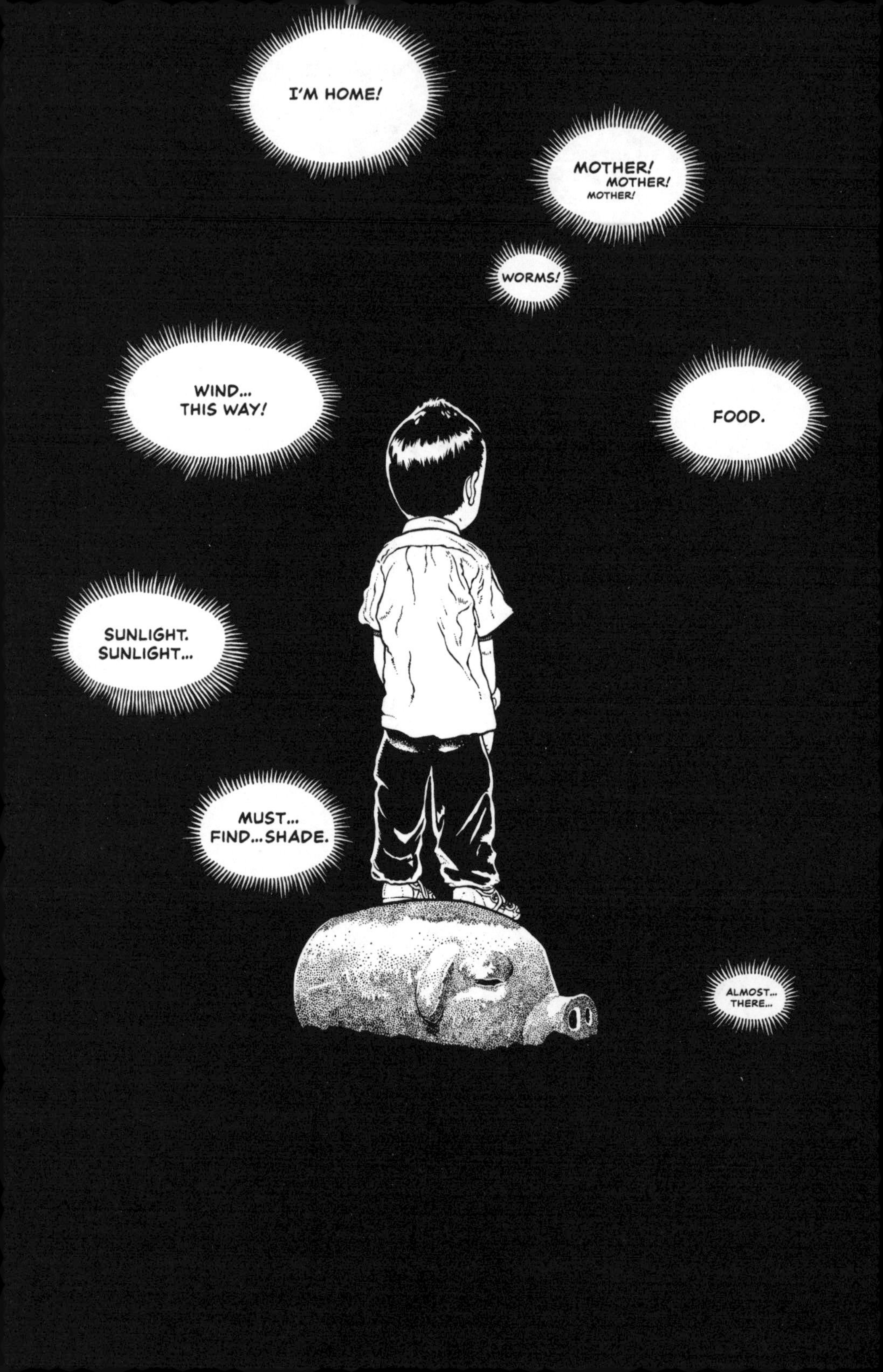
I'M HOME!
MOTHER! MOTHER! MOTHER!
WORMS!
WIND... THIS WAY!
FOOD.
SUNLIGHT. SUNLIGHT...
MUST... FIND...SHADE.
ALMOST... THERE...

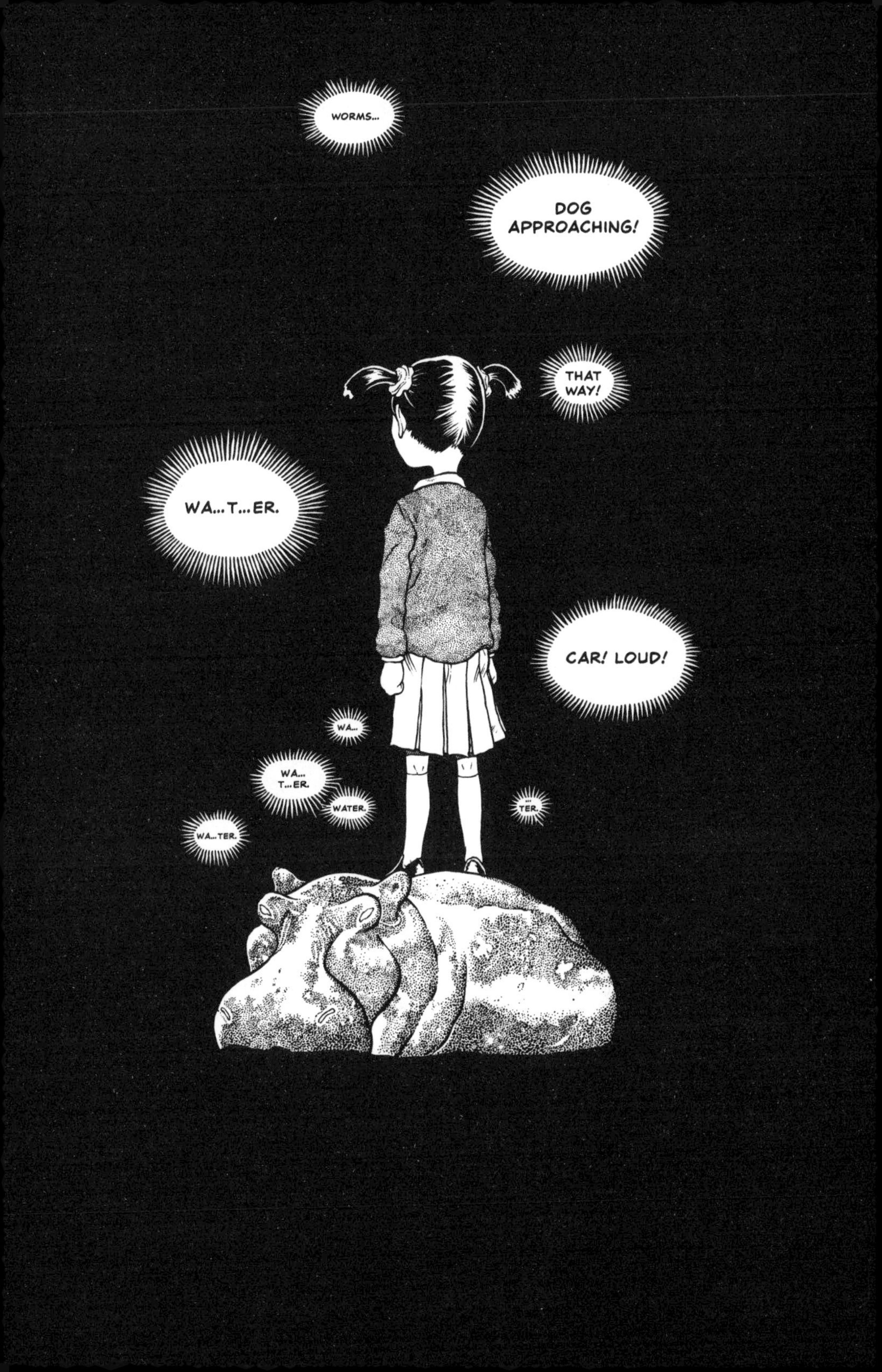
WORMS...
DOG APPROACHING!
THAT WAY!
WA...T...ER.
CAR! LOUD!
WA...
WA... T...ER.
WATER.
...TER.
WA...TER.

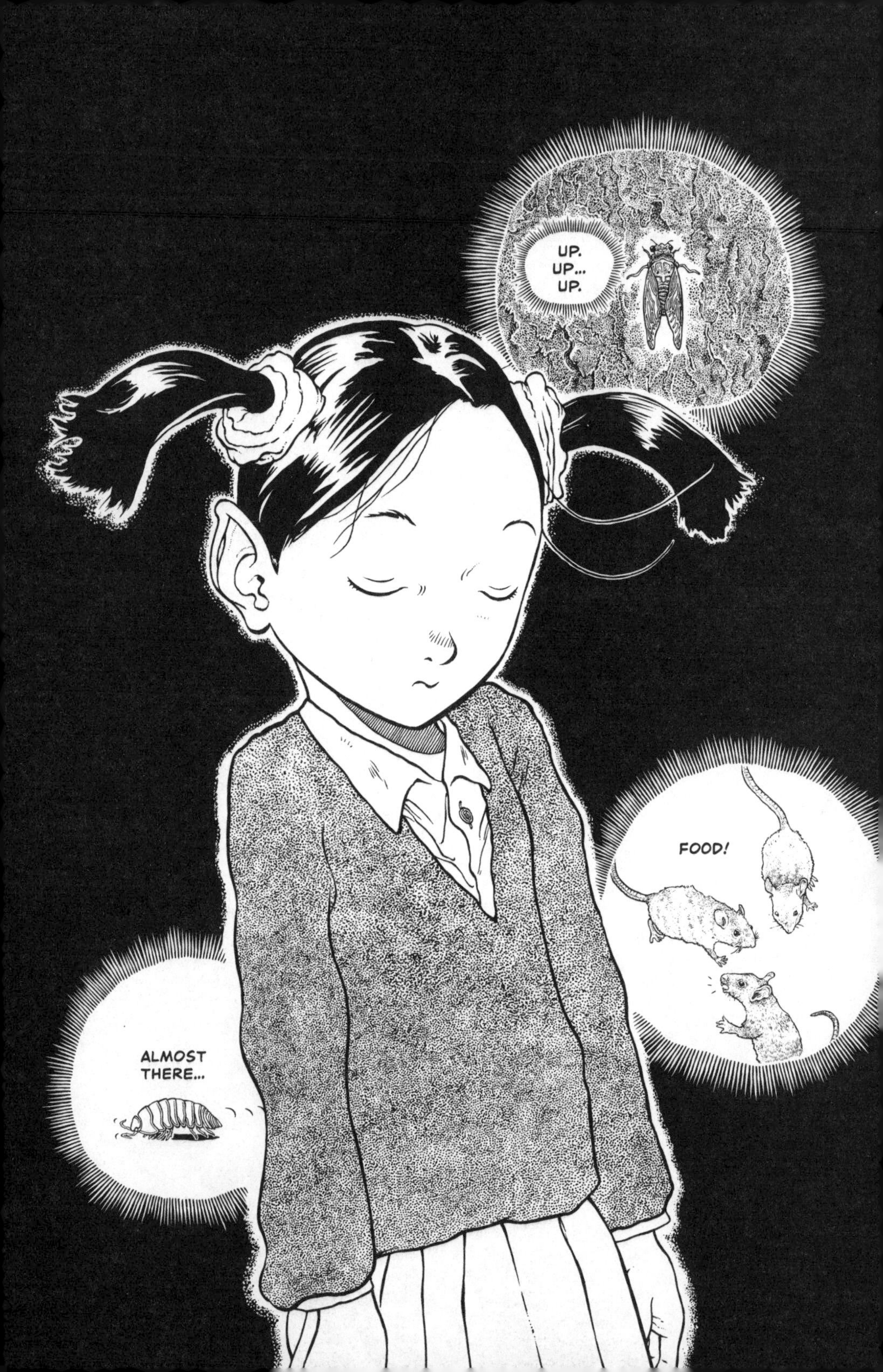
UP.
UP...
UP.
FOOD!
ALMOST
THERE...

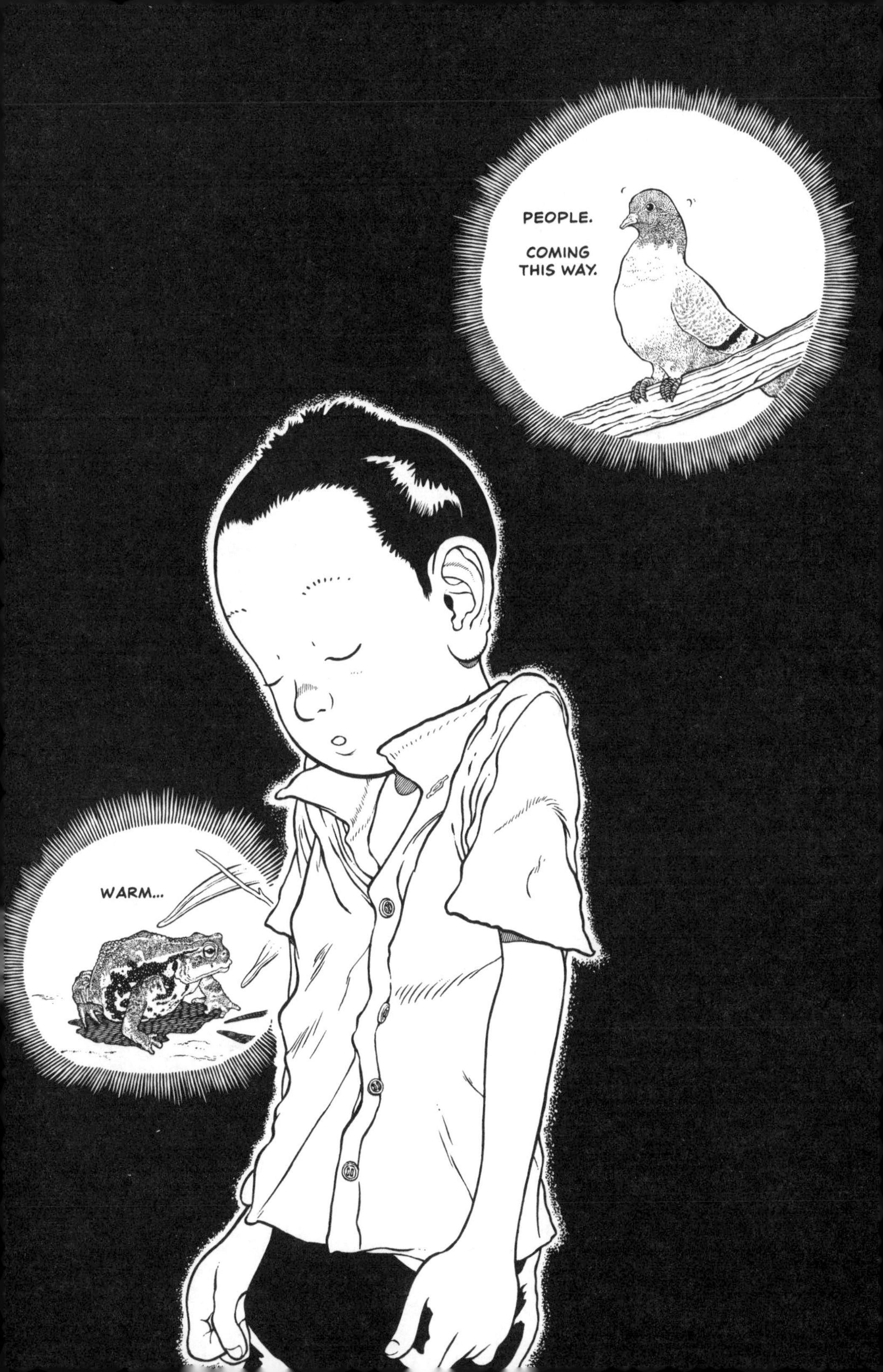
PEOPLE.
COMING THIS WAY.
WARM...

CAT—
WATCH OUT!
SUNLIGHT...
SUNLIGHT.
WA...T...ER.
THIS WAY,
EVERYONE.
NOW PULL!

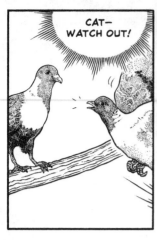

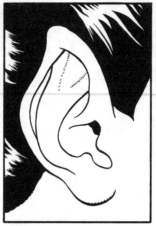

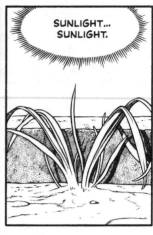

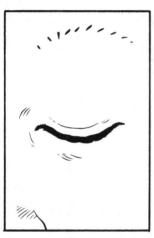

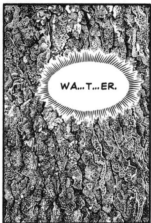

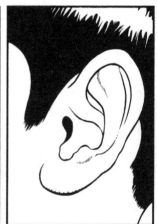

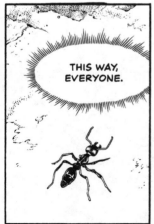

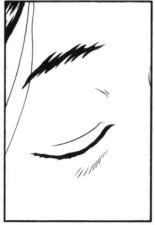

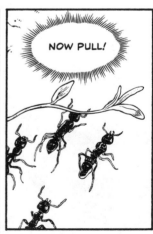

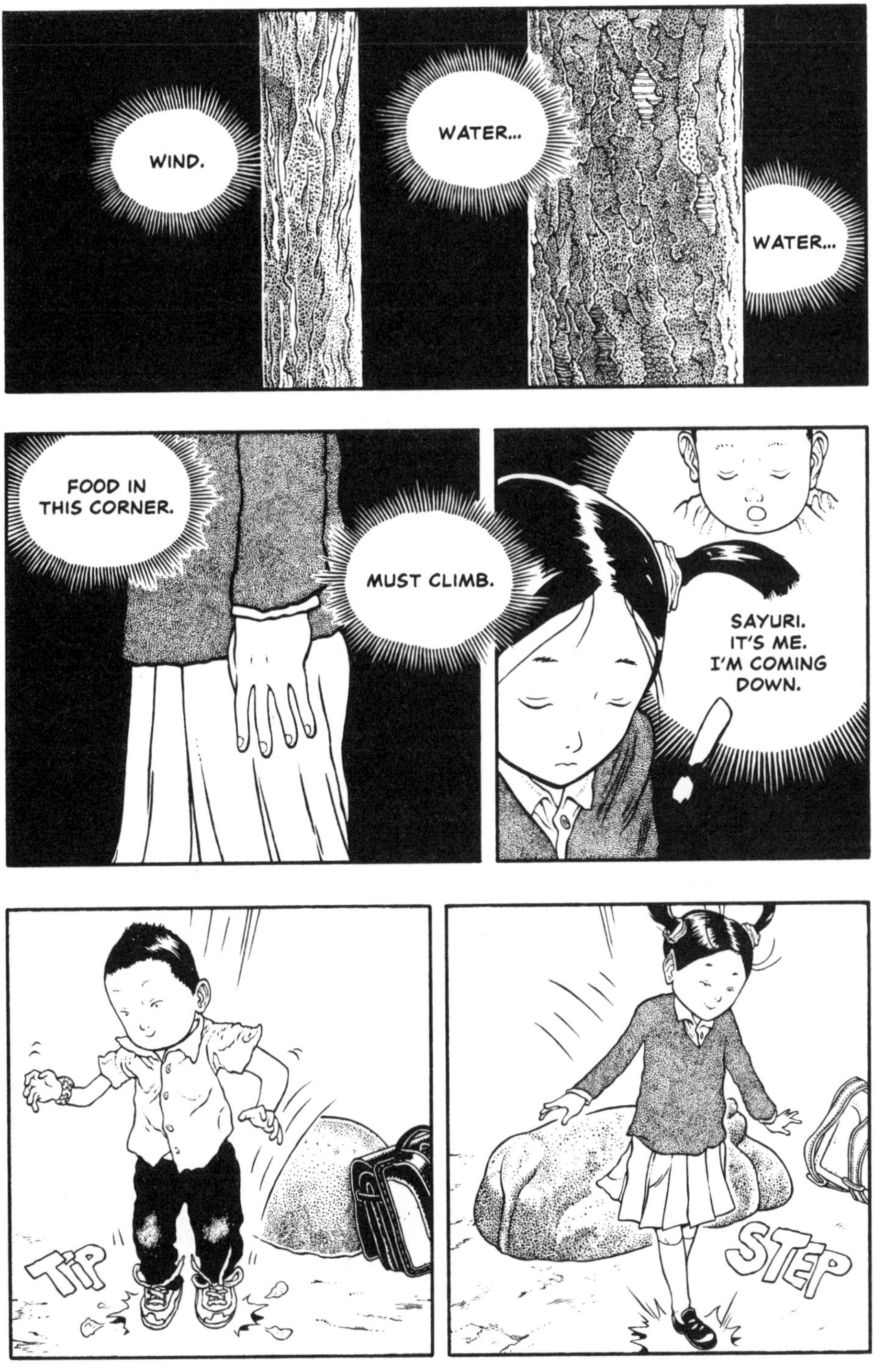
WIND.
WATER...
WATER...
FOOD IN THIS CORNER.
MUST CLIMB.
SAYURI. IT'S ME. I'M COMING DOWN.
TIP
STEP

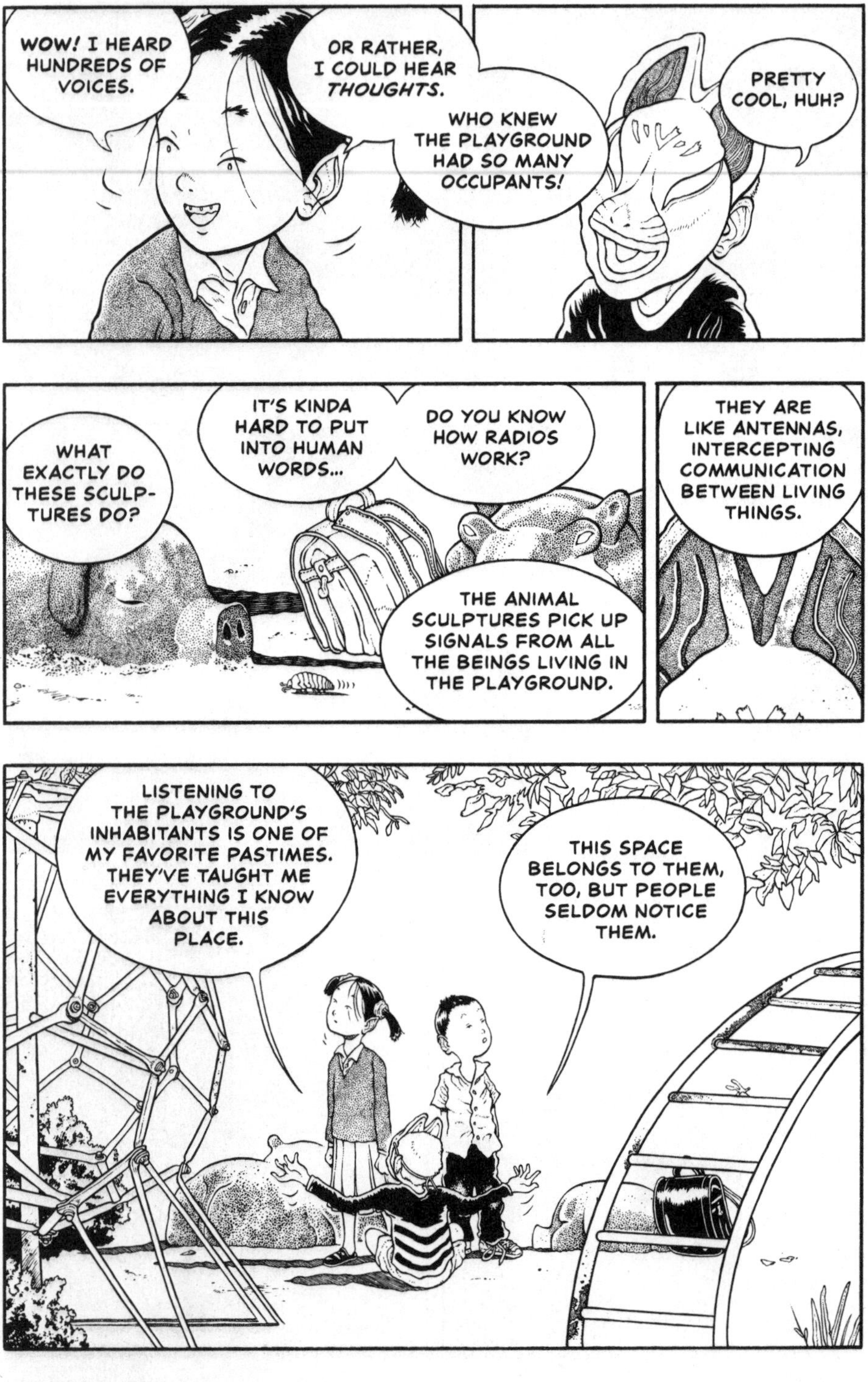
WOW! I HEARD HUNDREDS OF VOICES.
OR RATHER, I COULD HEAR *THOUGHTS*.
WHO KNEW THE PLAYGROUND HAD SO MANY OCCUPANTS!
PRETTY COOL, HUH?
WHAT EXACTLY DO THESE SCULPTURES DO?
IT'S KINDA HARD TO PUT INTO HUMAN WORDS...
DO YOU KNOW HOW RADIOS WORK?
THE ANIMAL SCULPTURES PICK UP SIGNALS FROM ALL THE BEINGS LIVING IN THE PLAYGROUND.
THEY ARE LIKE ANTENNAS, INTERCEPTING COMMUNICATION BETWEEN LIVING THINGS.
LISTENING TO THE PLAYGROUND'S INHABITANTS IS ONE OF MY FAVORITE PASTIMES. THEY'VE TAUGHT ME EVERYTHING I KNOW ABOUT THIS PLACE.
THIS SPACE BELONGS TO THEM, TOO, BUT PEOPLE SELDOM NOTICE THEM.

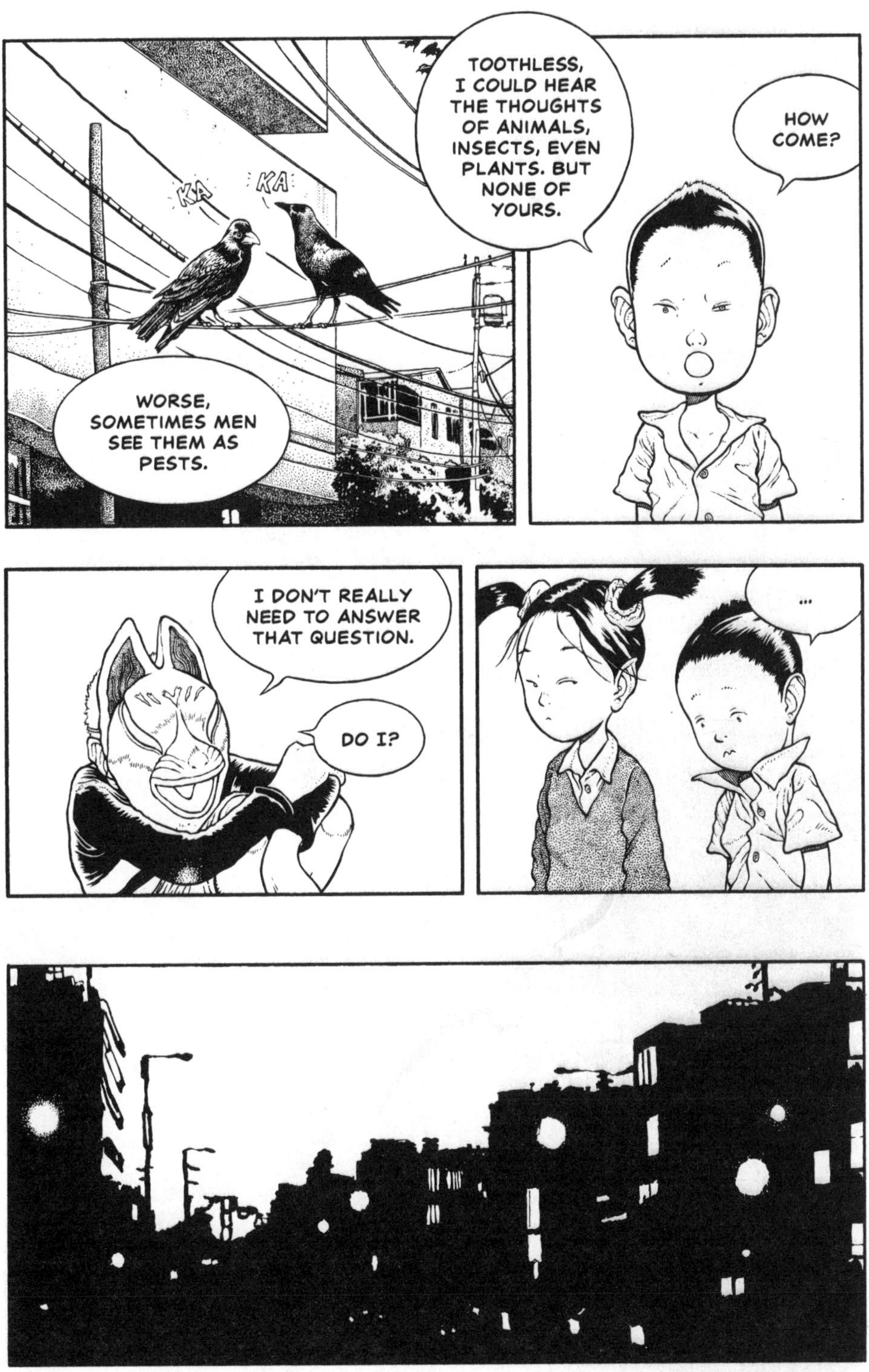
TOOTHLESS, I COULD HEAR THE THOUGHTS OF ANIMALS, INSECTS, EVEN PLANTS. BUT NONE OF YOURS.
KA
KA
WORSE, SOMETIMES MEN SEE THEM AS PESTS.
HOW COME?
I DON'T REALLY NEED TO ANSWER THAT QUESTION.
DO I?
...

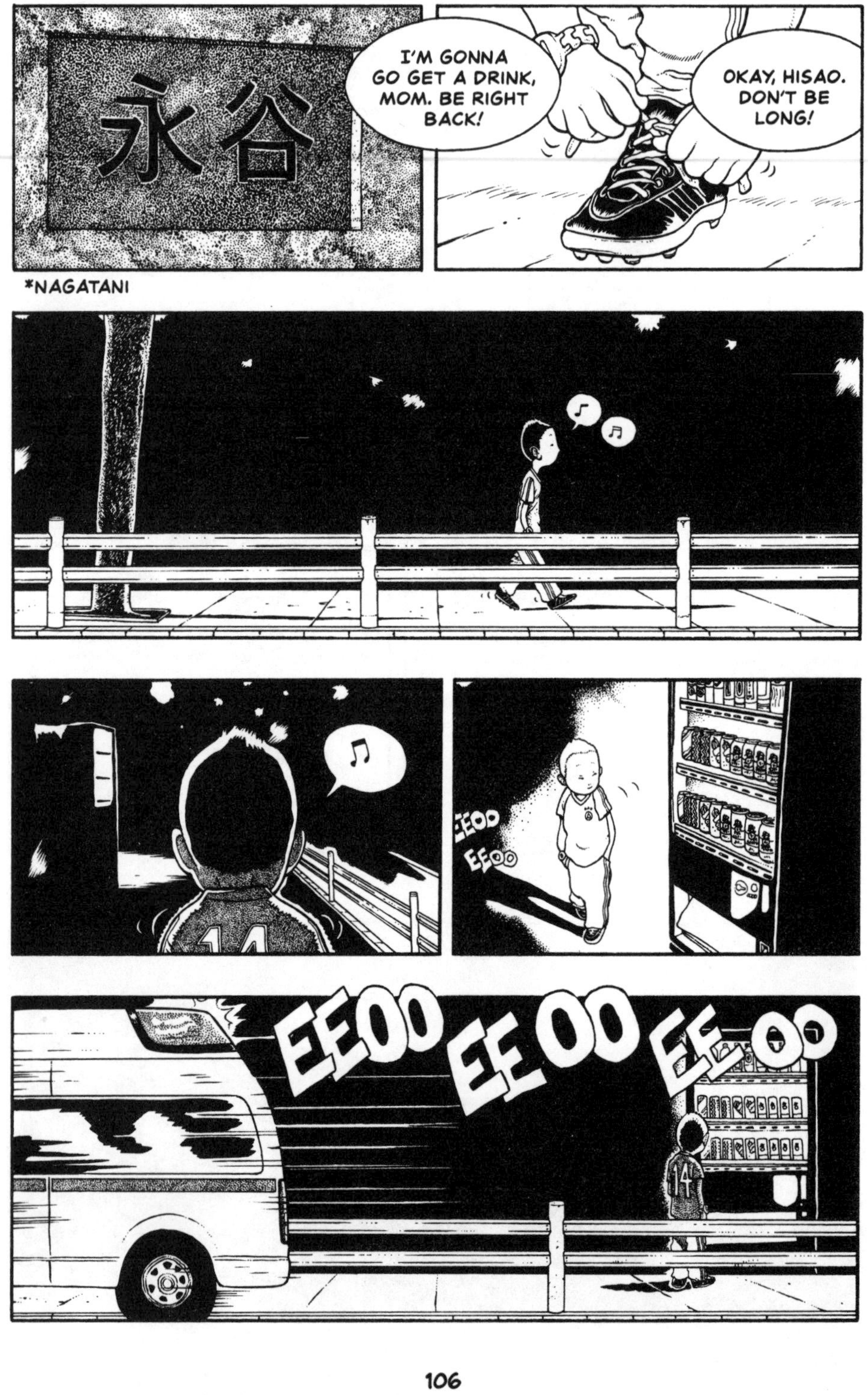
永谷
*NAGATANI
I'M GONNA GO GET A DRINK, MOM. BE RIGHT BACK!
OKAY, HISAO. DON'T BE LONG!
EEOO
EEOO
EEOO EE OO EE OO

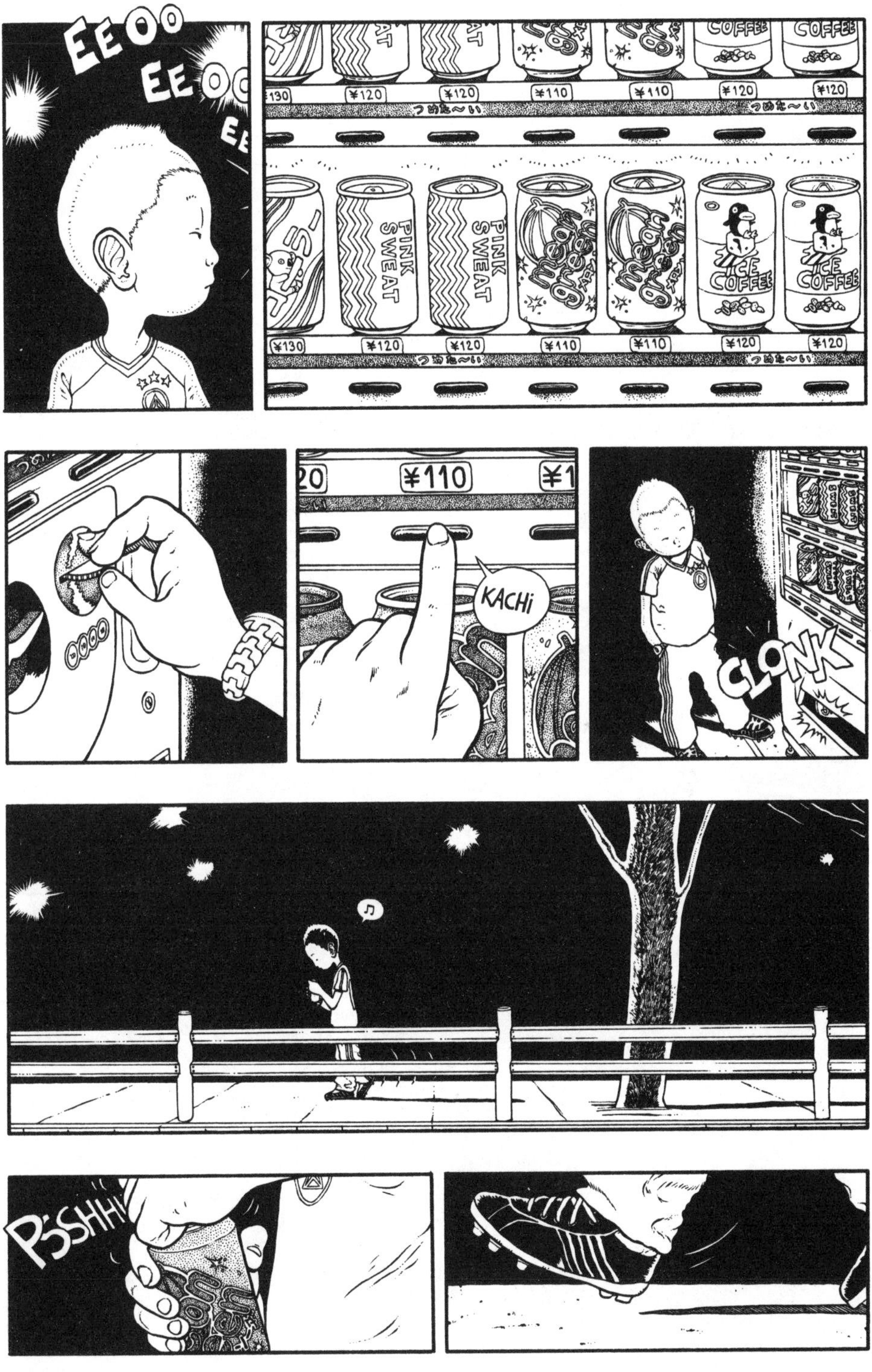
EEOO
EEOO
EE
COFFEE
COFFEE
¥130
¥120
¥120
¥110
¥110
¥120
¥120
つめた〜い
PINK SWEAT
PINK SWEAT
ICE COFFEE
ICE COFFEE
¥130
¥120
¥120
¥110
¥110
¥120
¥120
つめた〜い
¥110
KACHi
CLONK
♪
P'SSHH

IT'S A
FALL!

...POOR
THING...

...OUTSIDE
OVERNIGHT...
COULDN'T
GET UP...

GENTLE!

DEMENTIA?
...

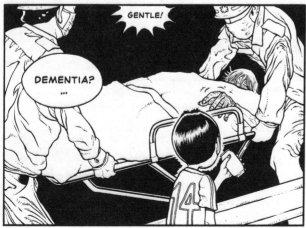

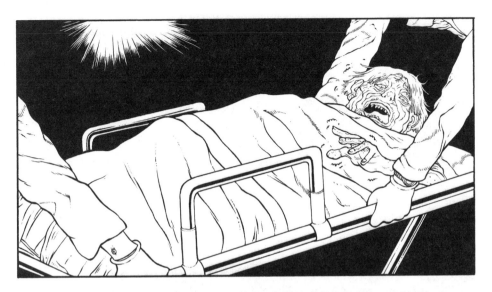

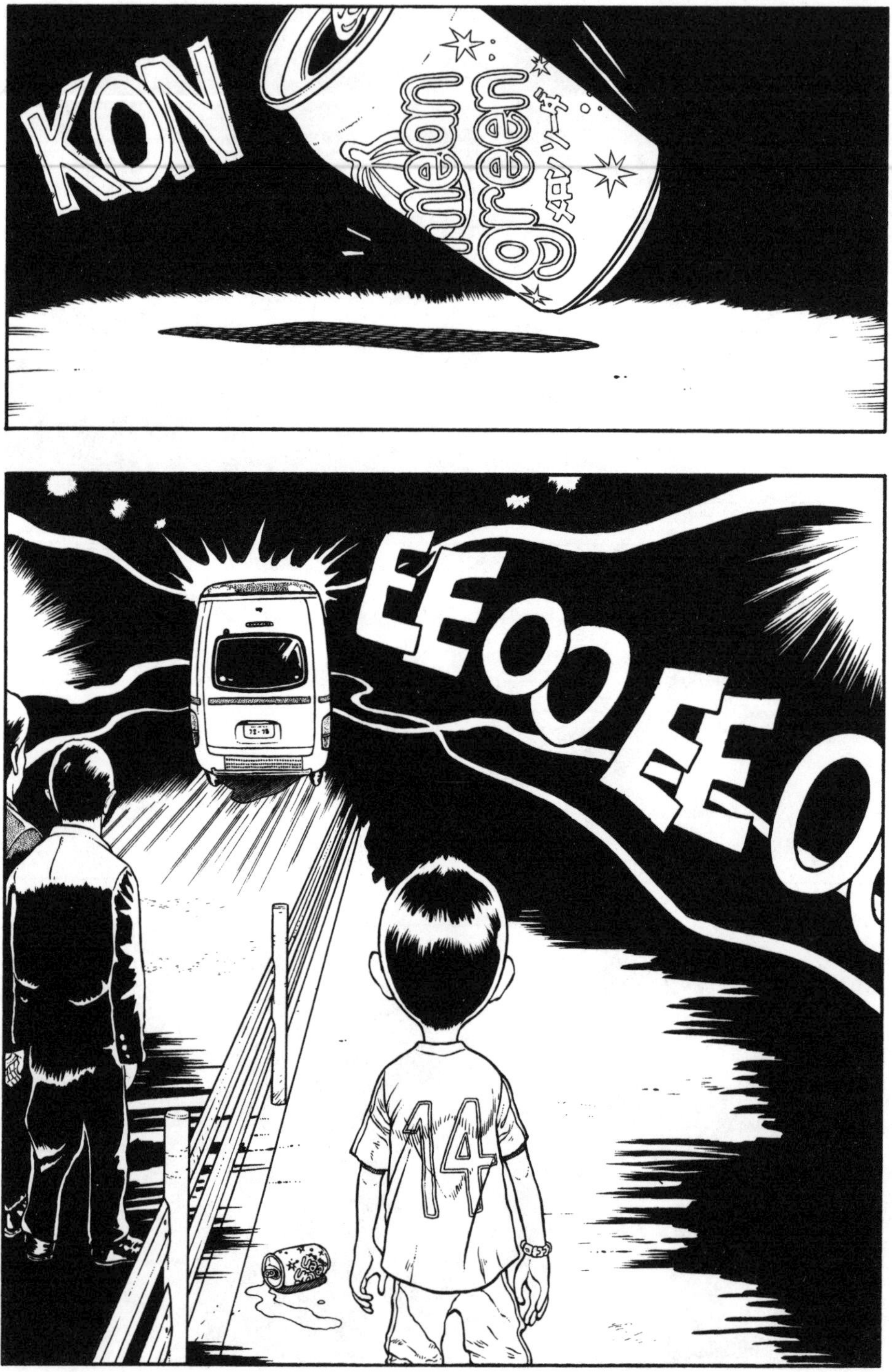
KON
EEOO EEOO

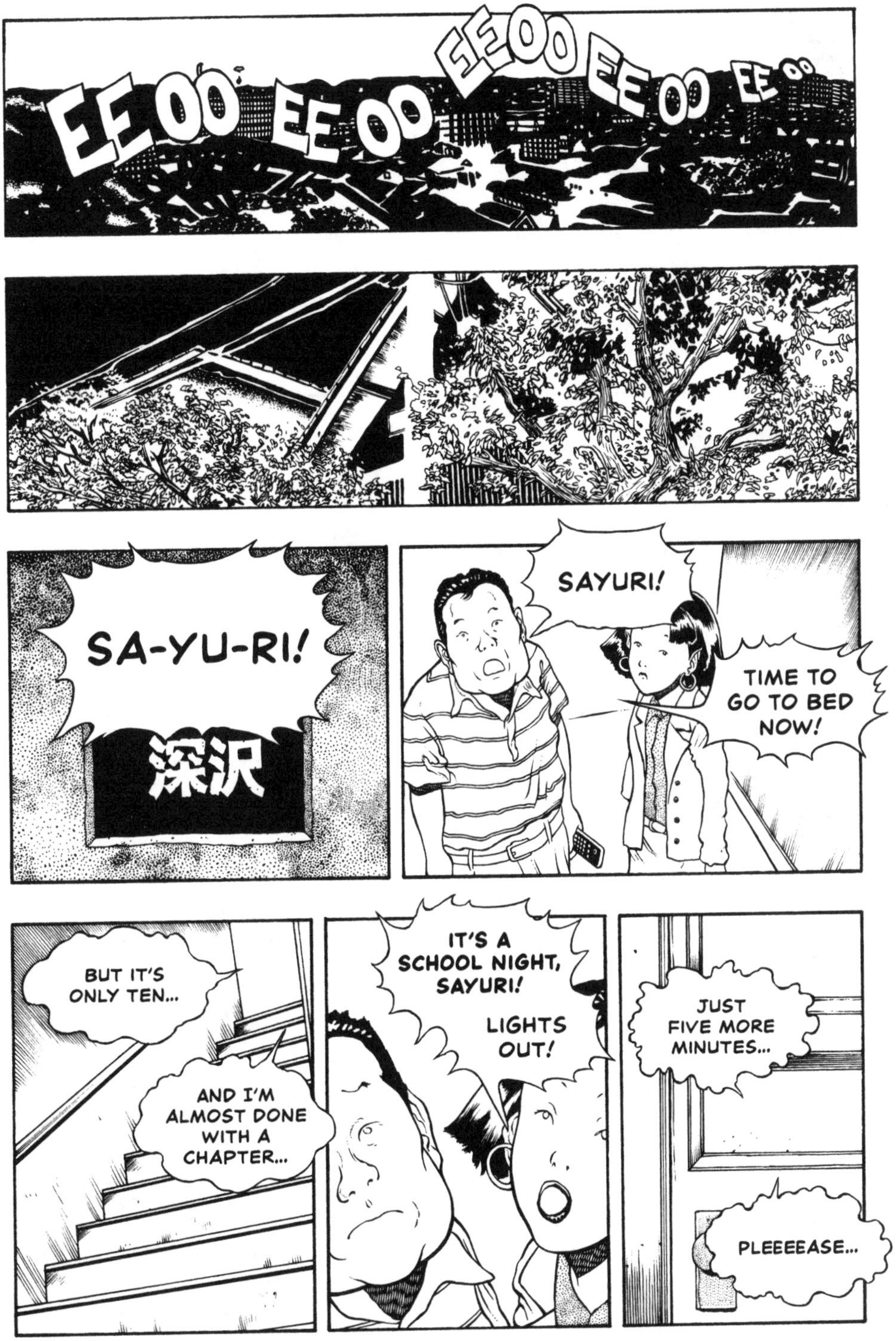
EE OO EE OO EE OO EE OO EE OO
SA-YU-RI!
深沢
SAYURI!
TIME TO GO TO BED NOW!
BUT IT'S ONLY TEN...
AND I'M ALMOST DONE WITH A CHAPTER...
IT'S A SCHOOL NIGHT, SAYURI!
LIGHTS OUT!
JUST FIVE MORE MINUTES...
PLEEEEASE...

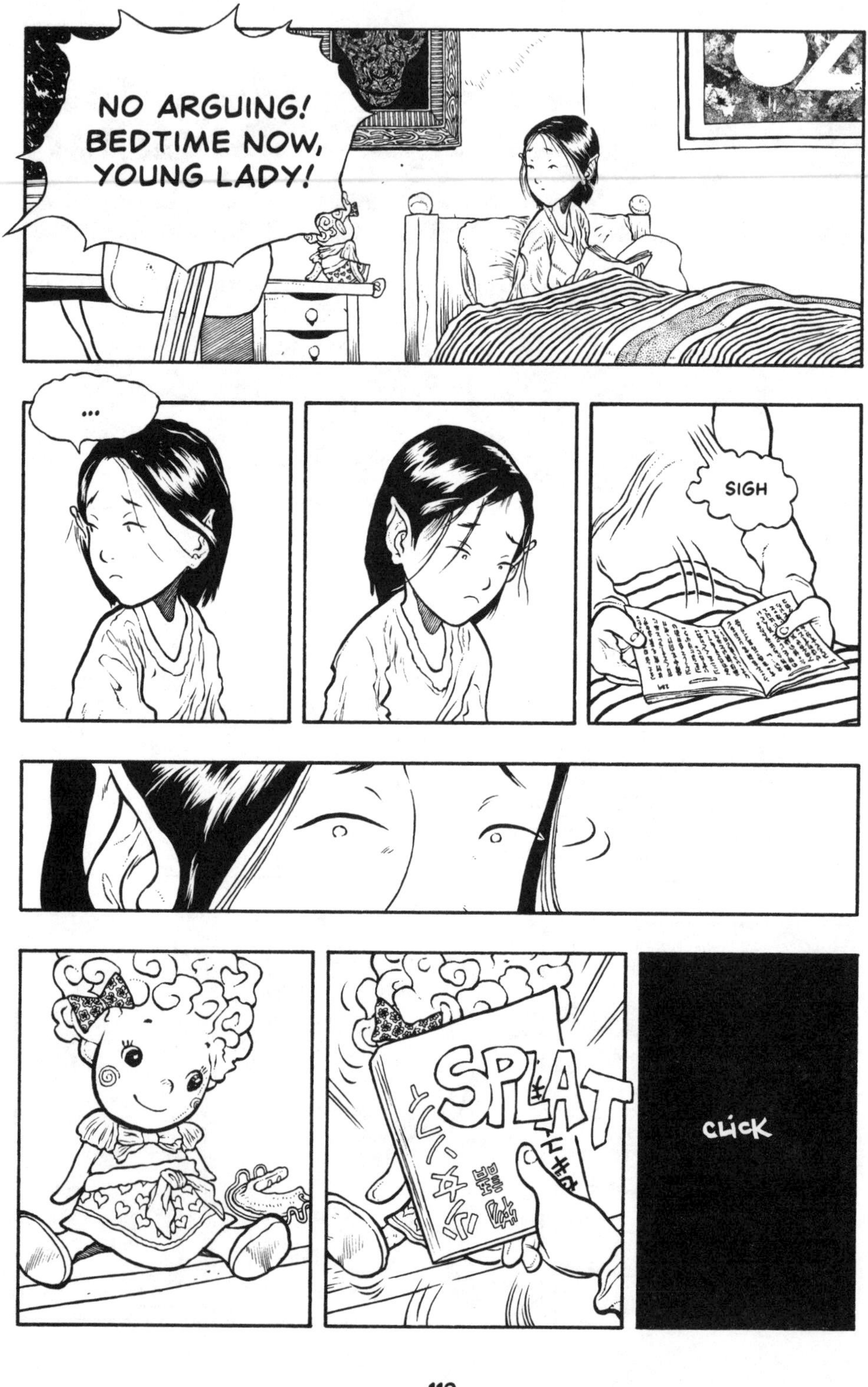
NO ARGUING! BEDTIME NOW, YOUNG LADY!
...
SIGH
SPLAT
CLICK

Chapter 5:
Digging Up the Past

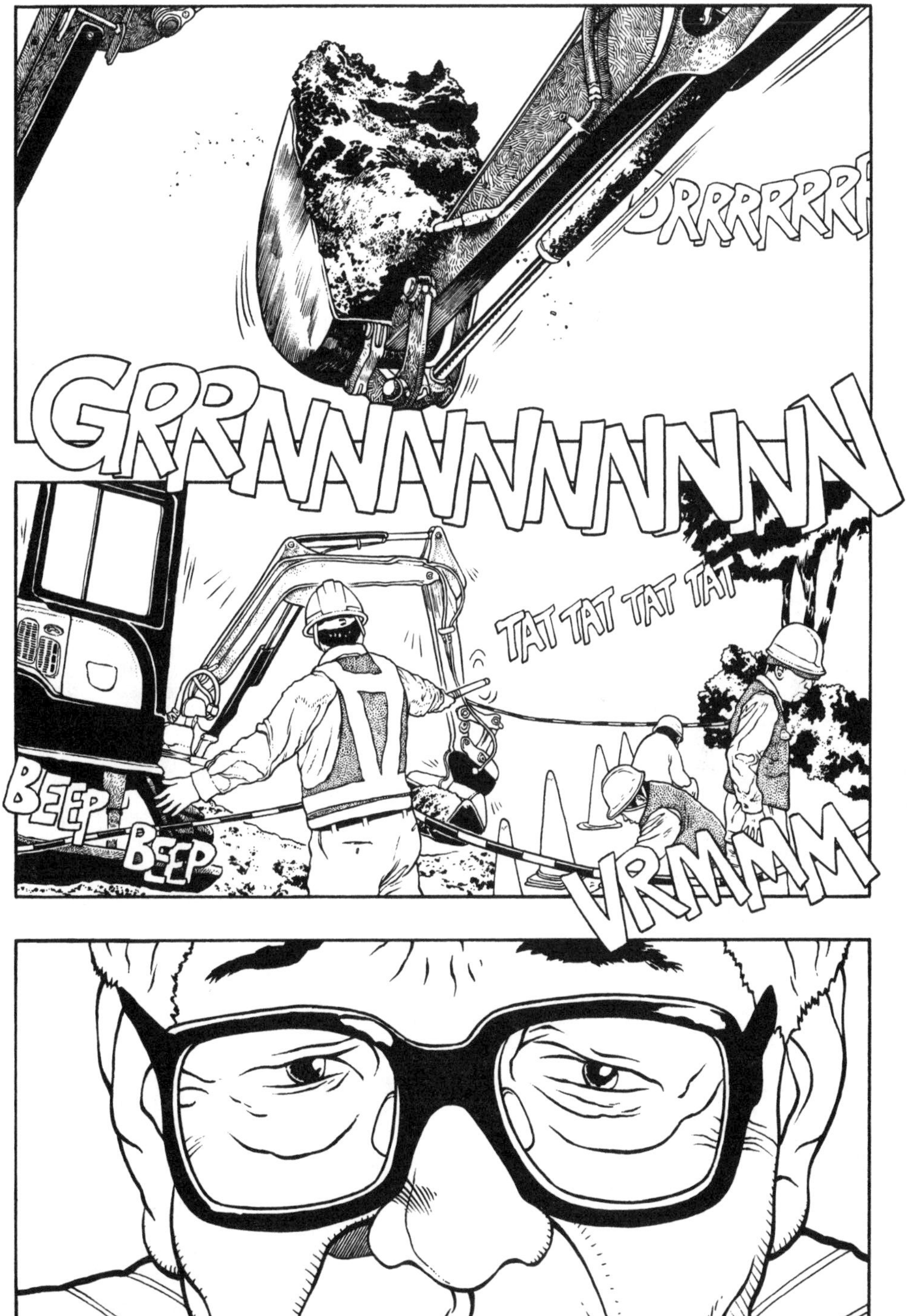

GRRRRRRR
GRRNNNNNNNNNN
TAT TAT TAT TAT
BEEP
BEEP
VRMMM

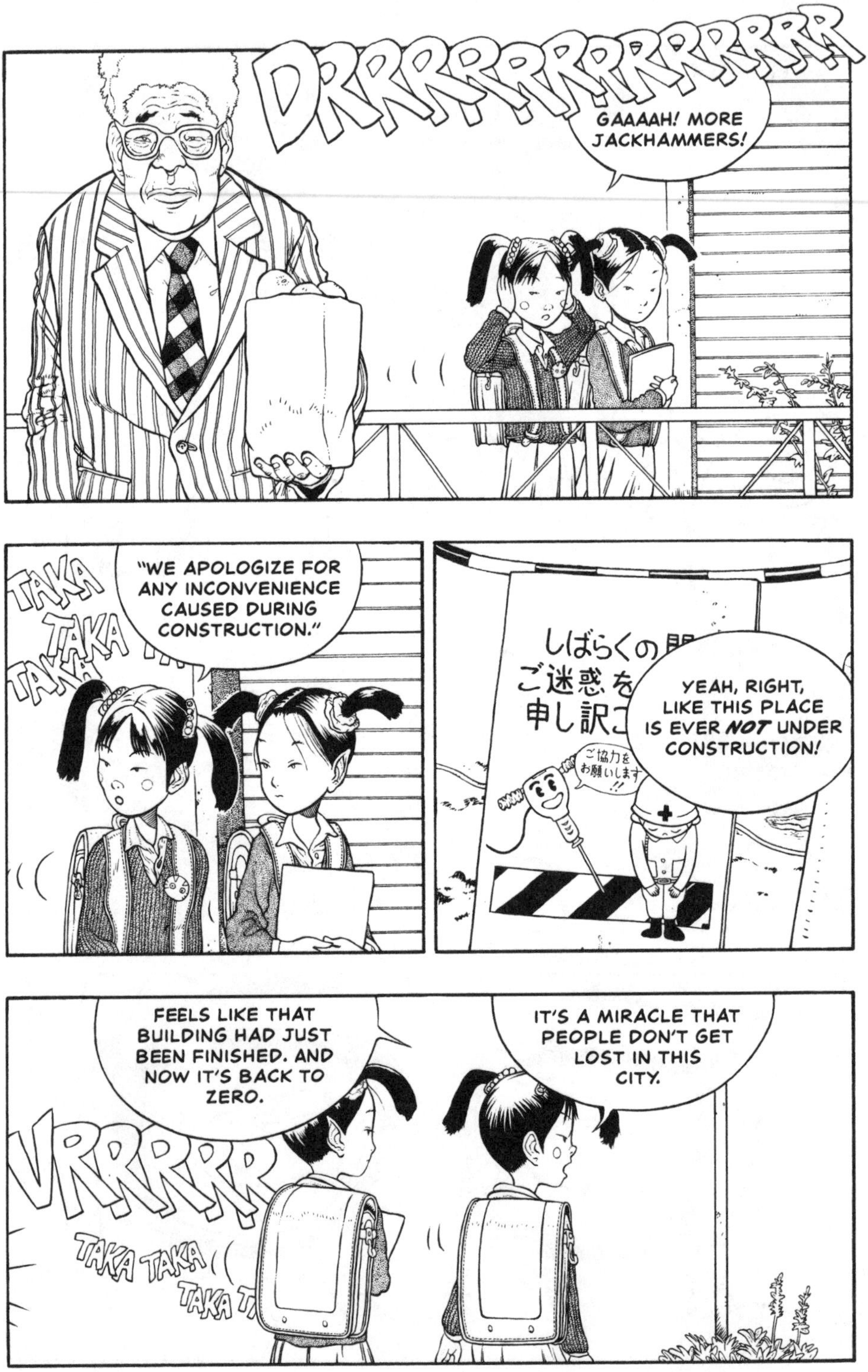
DRRRRRRRRRRRRR
GAAAAH! MORE JACKHAMMERS!
TAKA TAKA TAKA
"WE APOLOGIZE FOR ANY INCONVENIENCE CAUSED DURING CONSTRUCTION."
しばらくの
ご迷惑を
申し訳
ご協力を
お願いします
!!
YEAH, RIGHT, LIKE THIS PLACE IS EVER ***NOT*** UNDER CONSTRUCTION!
FEELS LIKE THAT BUILDING HAD JUST BEEN FINISHED. AND NOW IT'S BACK TO ZERO.
IT'S A MIRACLE THAT PEOPLE DON'T GET LOST IN THIS CITY.
VRRRRR
TAKA TAKA TAKA

ANYWAY, ABOUT **HIROMI**, HER PARENTS ARE TAKING HER TO TOKYO DURING GOLDEN WEEK.

THEY'RE GONNA GO TO DISNEYLAND.

SHE'S SO LUCKY... I'VE ALWAYS WANTED TO RIDE IN SPACE MOUNTAIN!

SAYURI?

WHERE ARE YOU GOING?

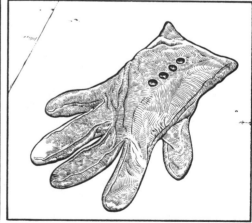

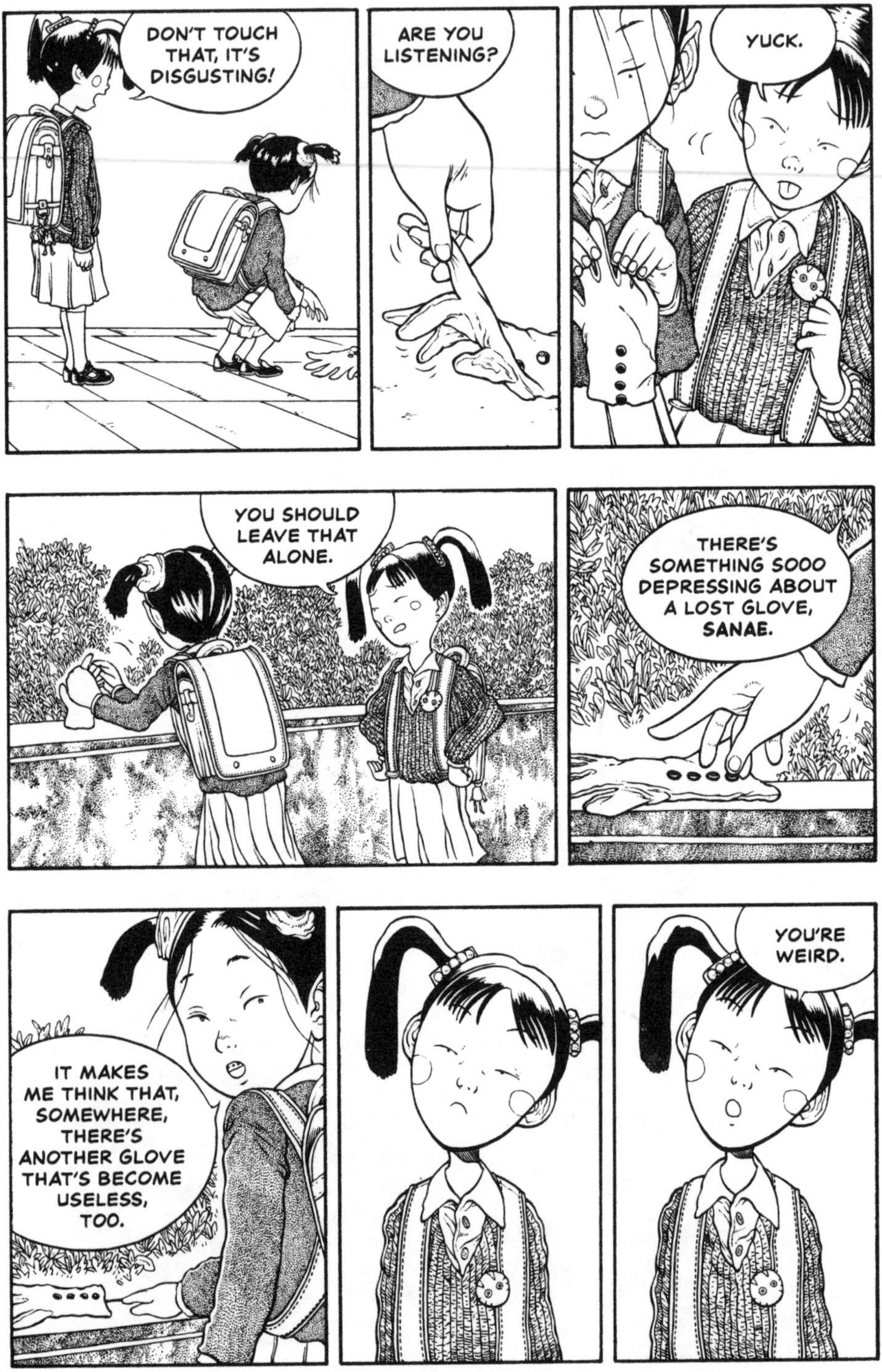
DON'T TOUCH THAT, IT'S DISGUSTING!
ARE YOU LISTENING?
YUCK.
YOU SHOULD LEAVE THAT ALONE.
THERE'S SOMETHING SOOO DEPRESSING ABOUT A LOST GLOVE, SANAE.
IT MAKES ME THINK THAT, SOMEWHERE, THERE'S ANOTHER GLOVE THAT'S BECOME USELESS, TOO.
YOU'RE WEIRD.

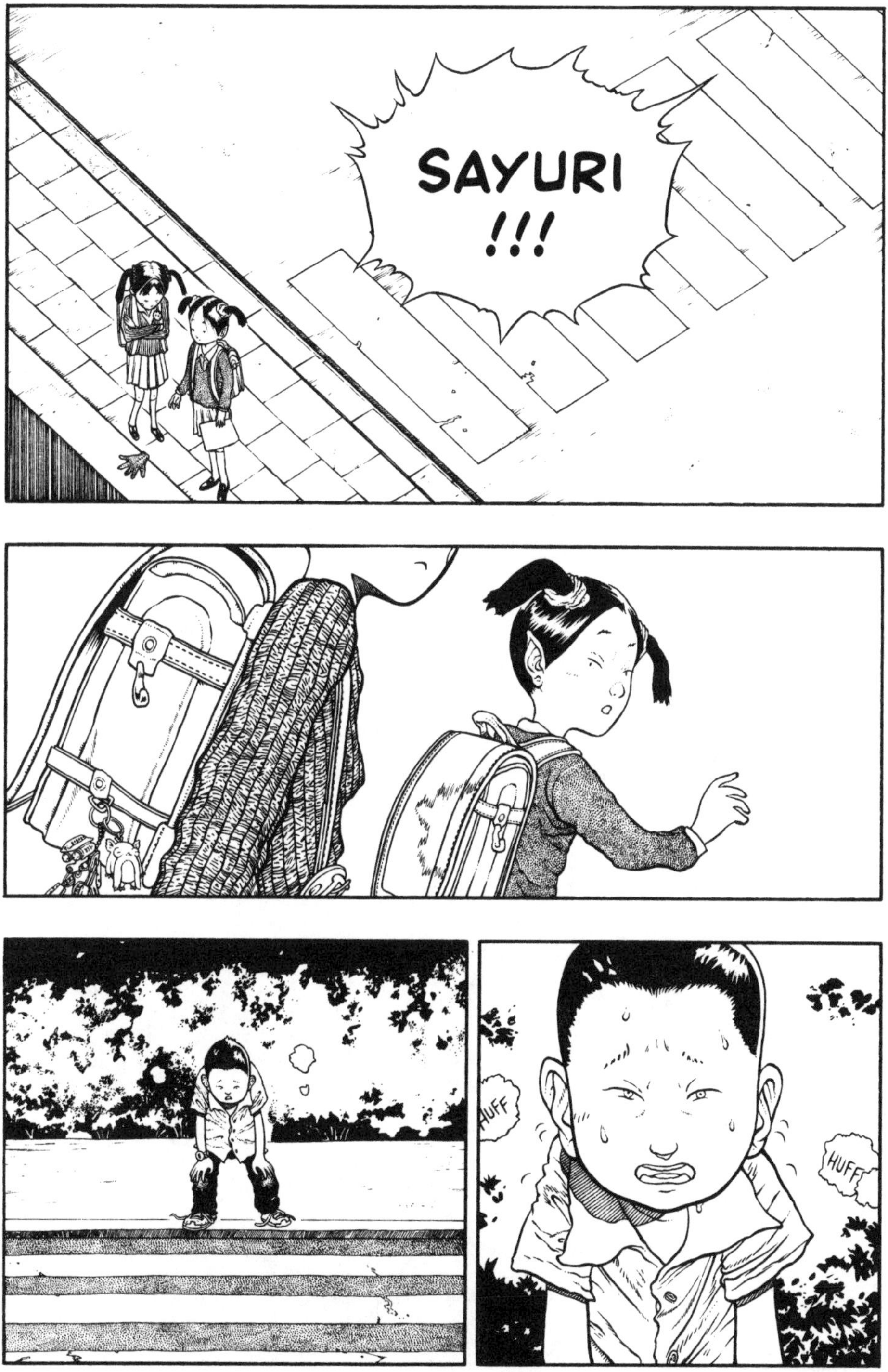
SAYURI
!!!
HUFF
HUFF

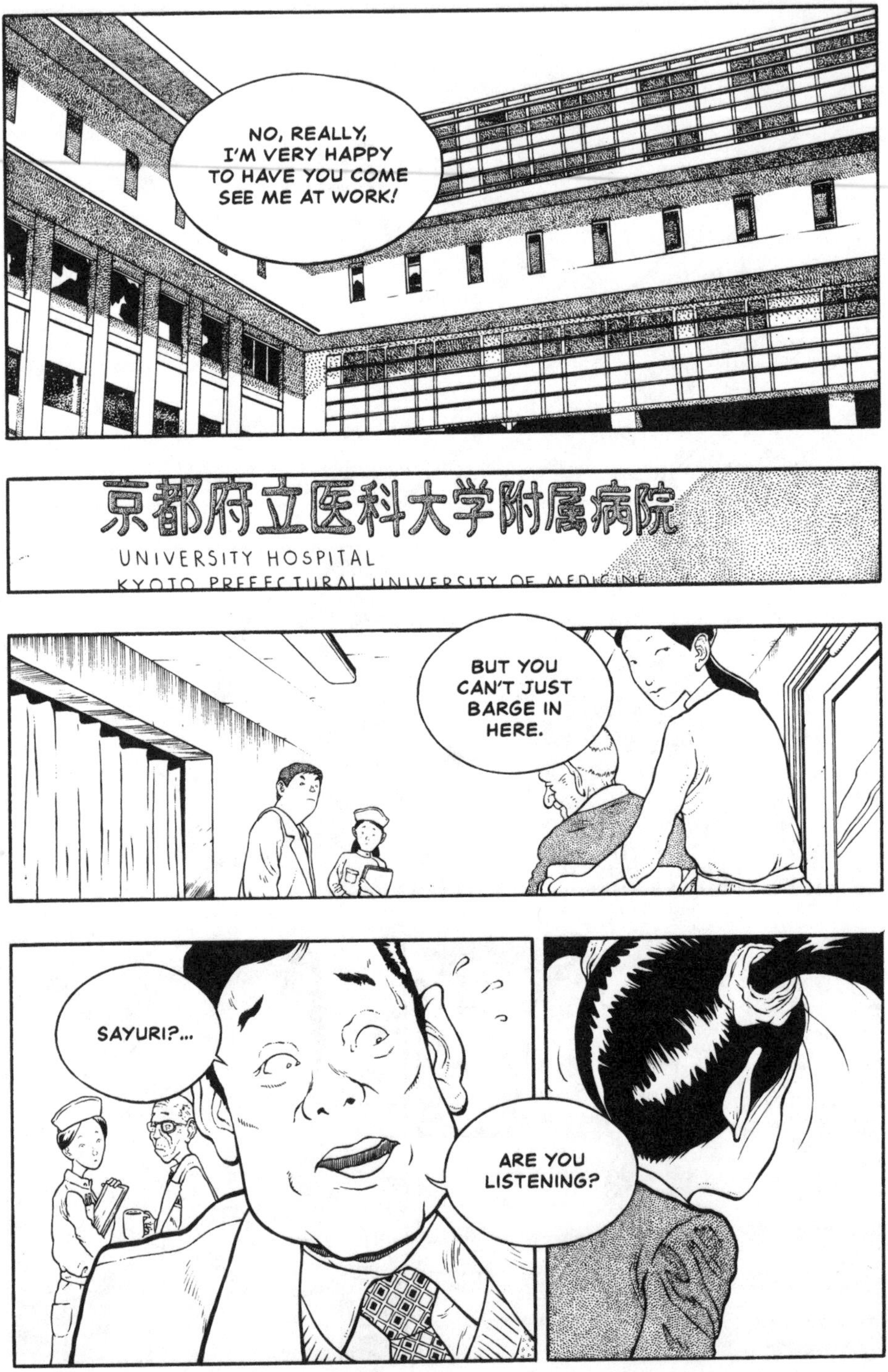
NO, REALLY, I'M VERY HAPPY TO HAVE YOU COME SEE ME AT WORK!
京都府立医科大学附属病院
UNIVERSITY HOSPITAL
KYOTO PREFECTURAL UNIVERSITY OF MEDICINE
BUT YOU CAN'T JUST BARGE IN HERE.
SAYURI?...
ARE YOU LISTENING?

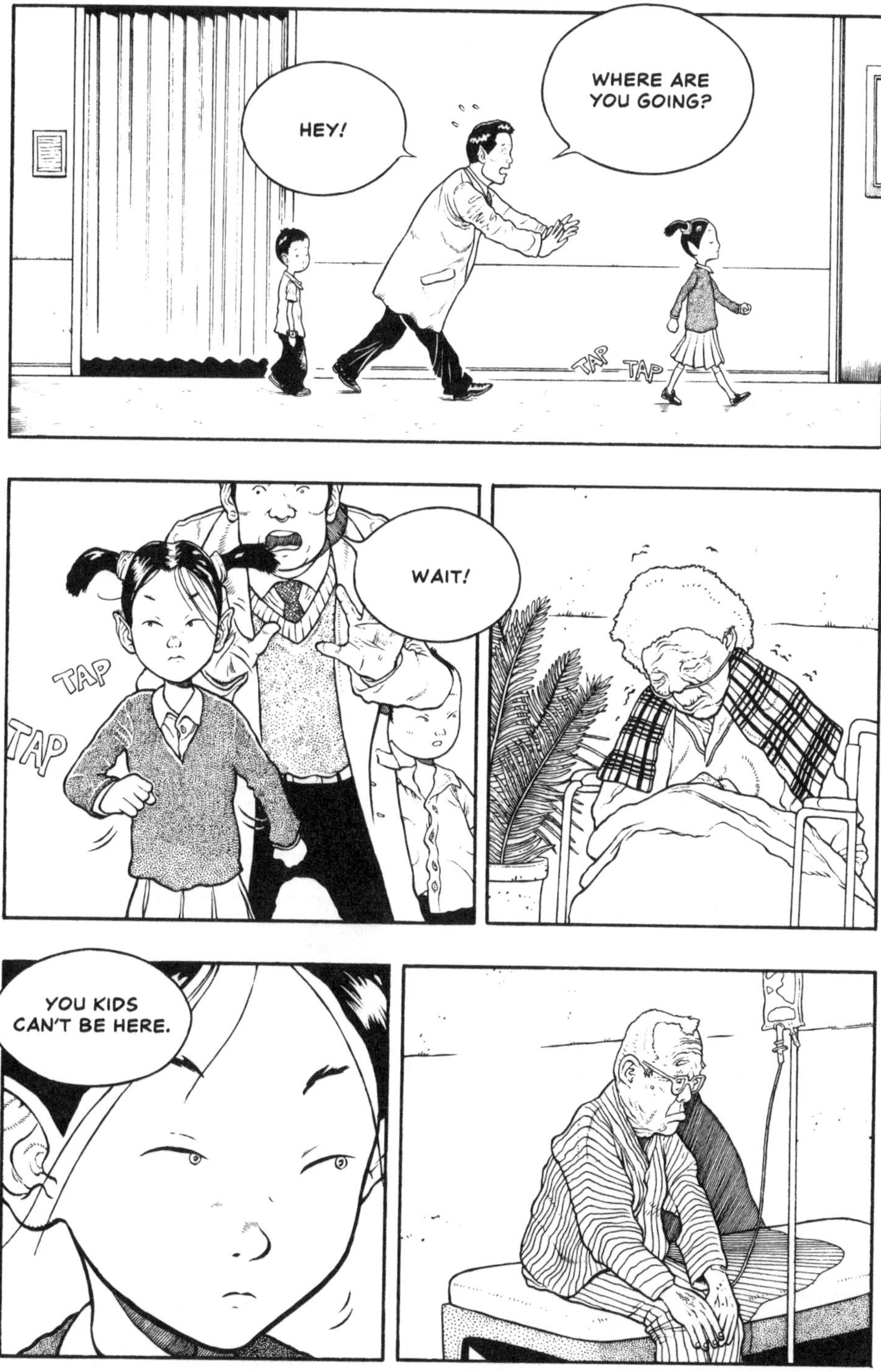
HEY!
WHERE ARE YOU GOING?
TAP TAP
WAIT!
TAP
TAP
YOU KIDS CAN'T BE HERE.

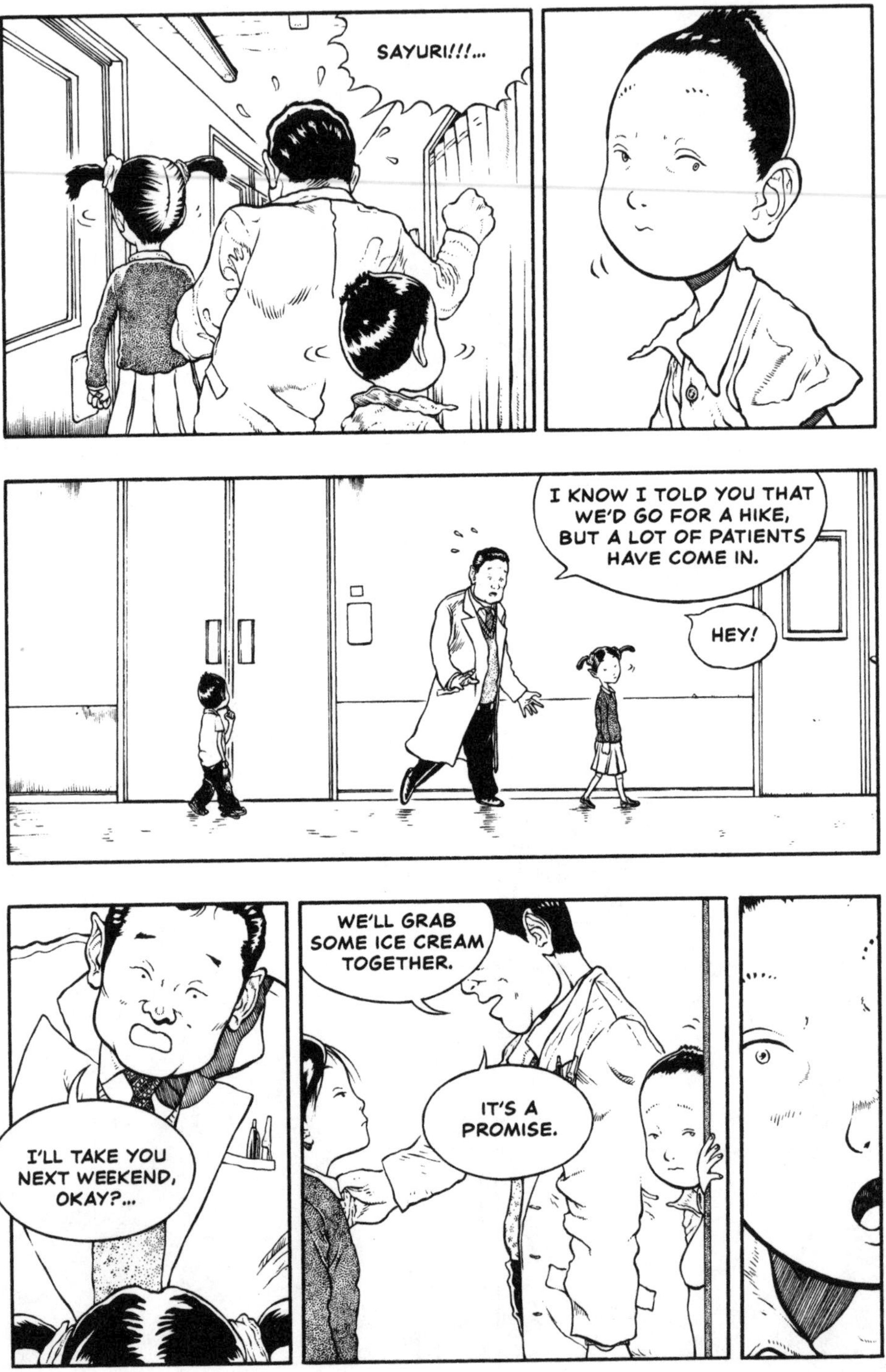
SAYURI!!!...
I KNOW I TOLD YOU THAT WE'D GO FOR A HIKE, BUT A LOT OF PATIENTS HAVE COME IN.
HEY!
I'LL TAKE YOU NEXT WEEKEND, OKAY?...
WE'LL GRAB SOME ICE CREAM TOGETHER.
IT'S A PROMISE.

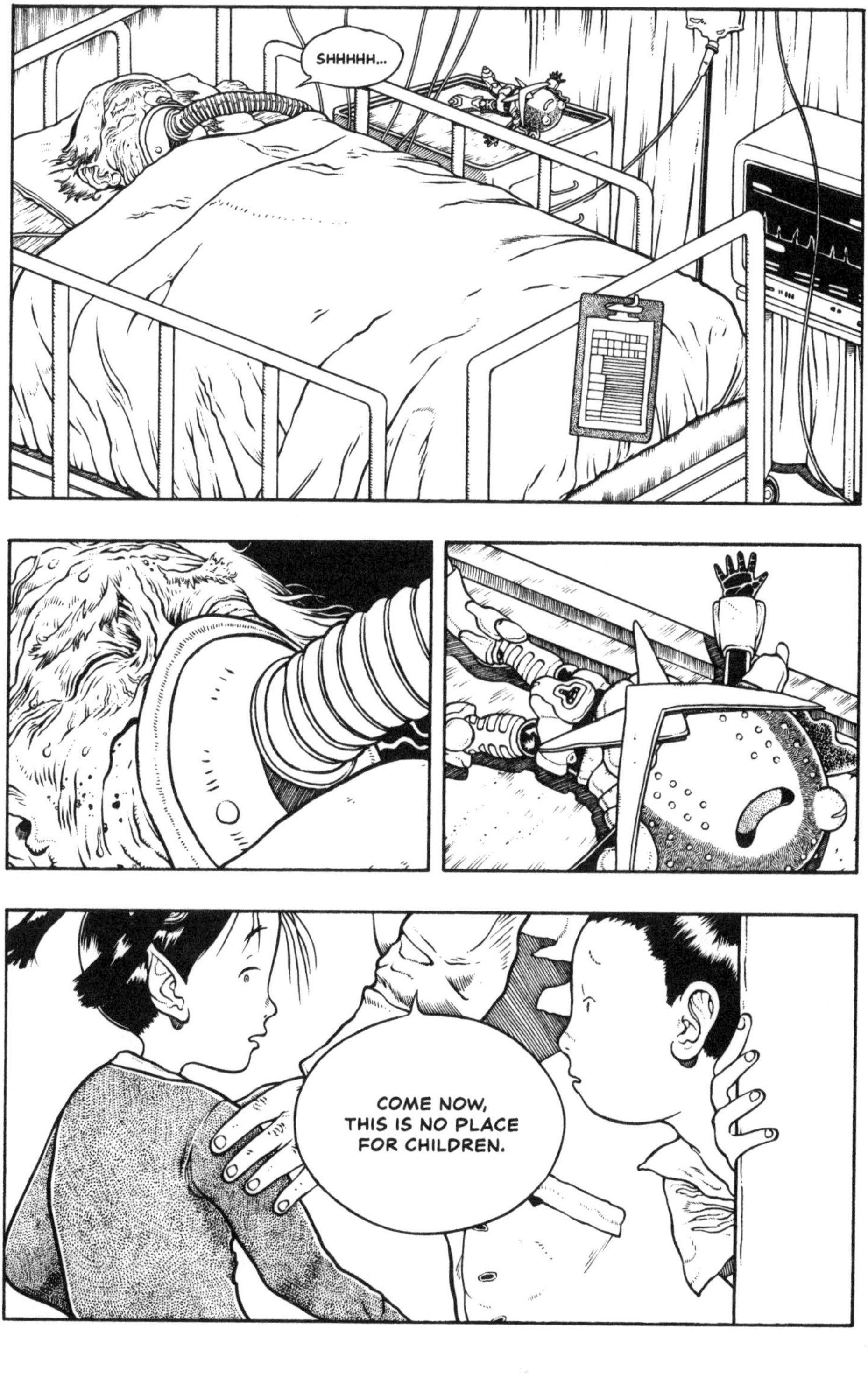
SHHHHH...
COME NOW, THIS IS NO PLACE FOR CHILDREN.

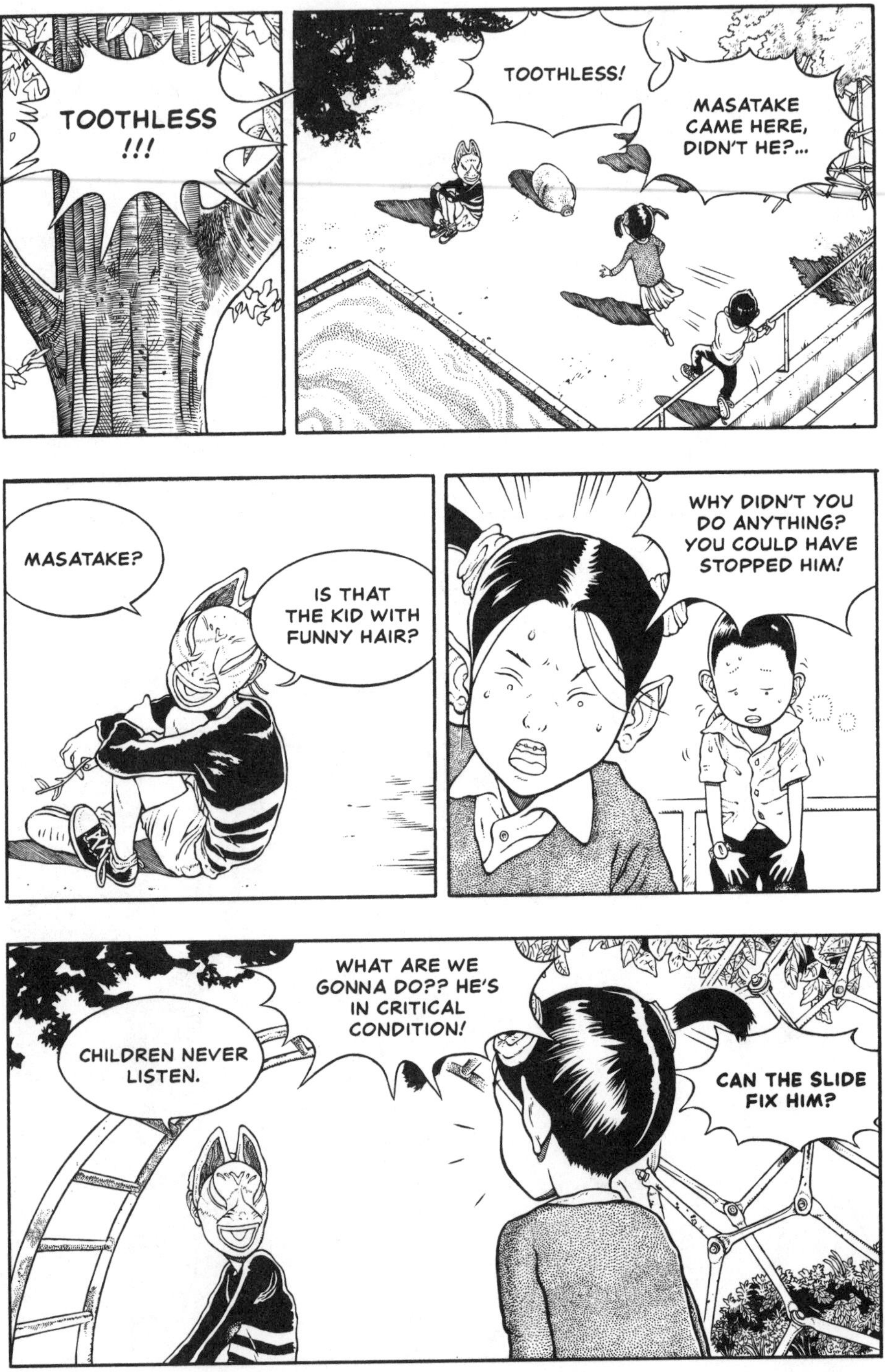
TOOTHLESS !!!
TOOTHLESS!
MASATAKE CAME HERE, DIDN'T HE?...
MASATAKE?
IS THAT THE KID WITH FUNNY HAIR?
WHY DIDN'T YOU DO ANYTHING? YOU COULD HAVE STOPPED HIM!
WHAT ARE WE GONNA DO?? HE'S IN CRITICAL CONDITION!
CHILDREN NEVER LISTEN.
CAN THE SLIDE FIX HIM?

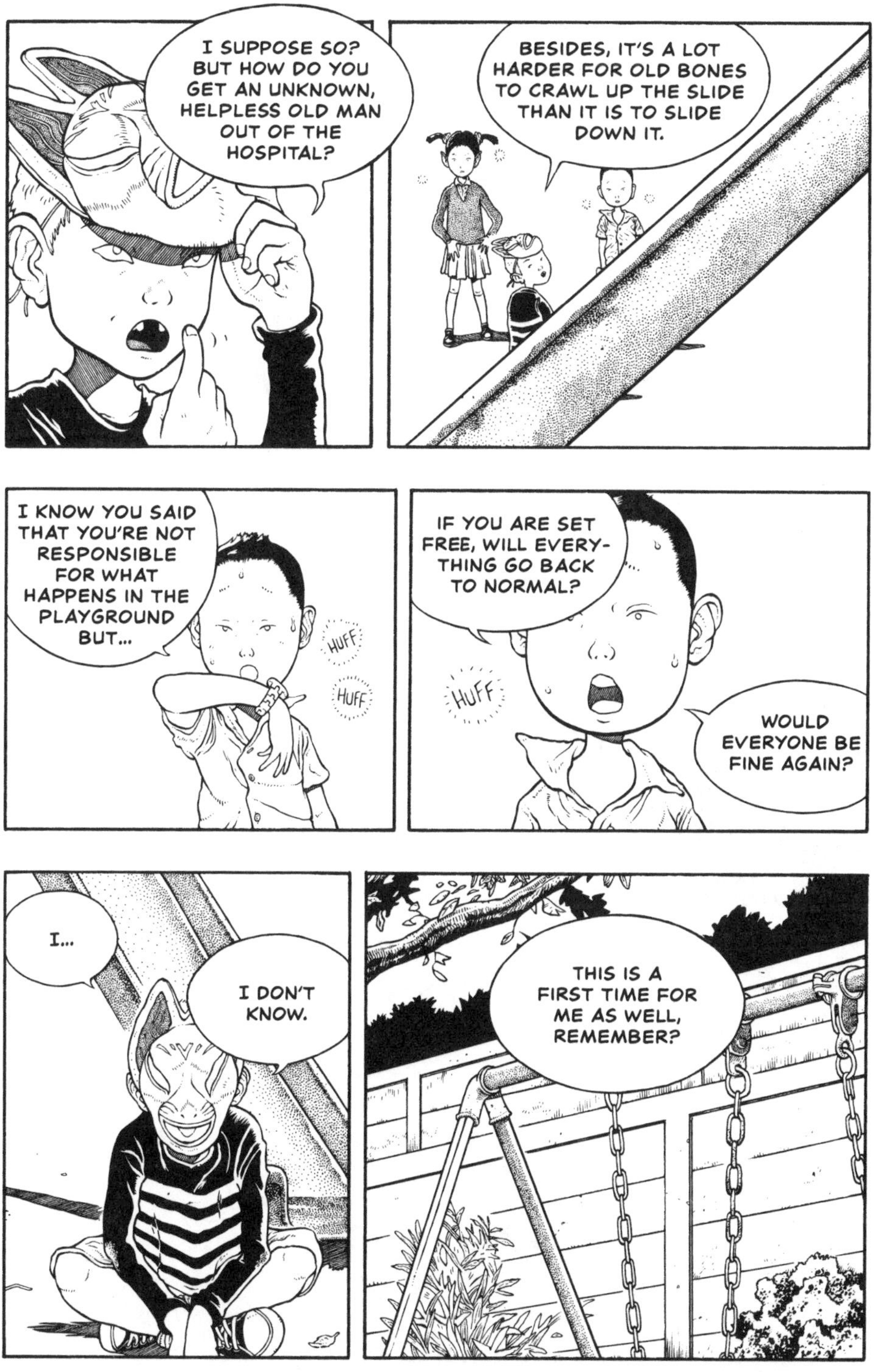
I SUPPOSE SO? BUT HOW DO YOU GET AN UNKNOWN, HELPLESS OLD MAN OUT OF THE HOSPITAL?
BESIDES, IT'S A LOT HARDER FOR OLD BONES TO CRAWL UP THE SLIDE THAN IT IS TO SLIDE DOWN IT.
I KNOW YOU SAID THAT YOU'RE NOT RESPONSIBLE FOR WHAT HAPPENS IN THE PLAYGROUND BUT...
HUFF
HUFF
IF YOU ARE SET FREE, WILL EVERY-THING GO BACK TO NORMAL?
HUFF
WOULD EVERYONE BE FINE AGAIN?
I...
I DON'T KNOW.
THIS IS A FIRST TIME FOR ME AS WELL, REMEMBER?

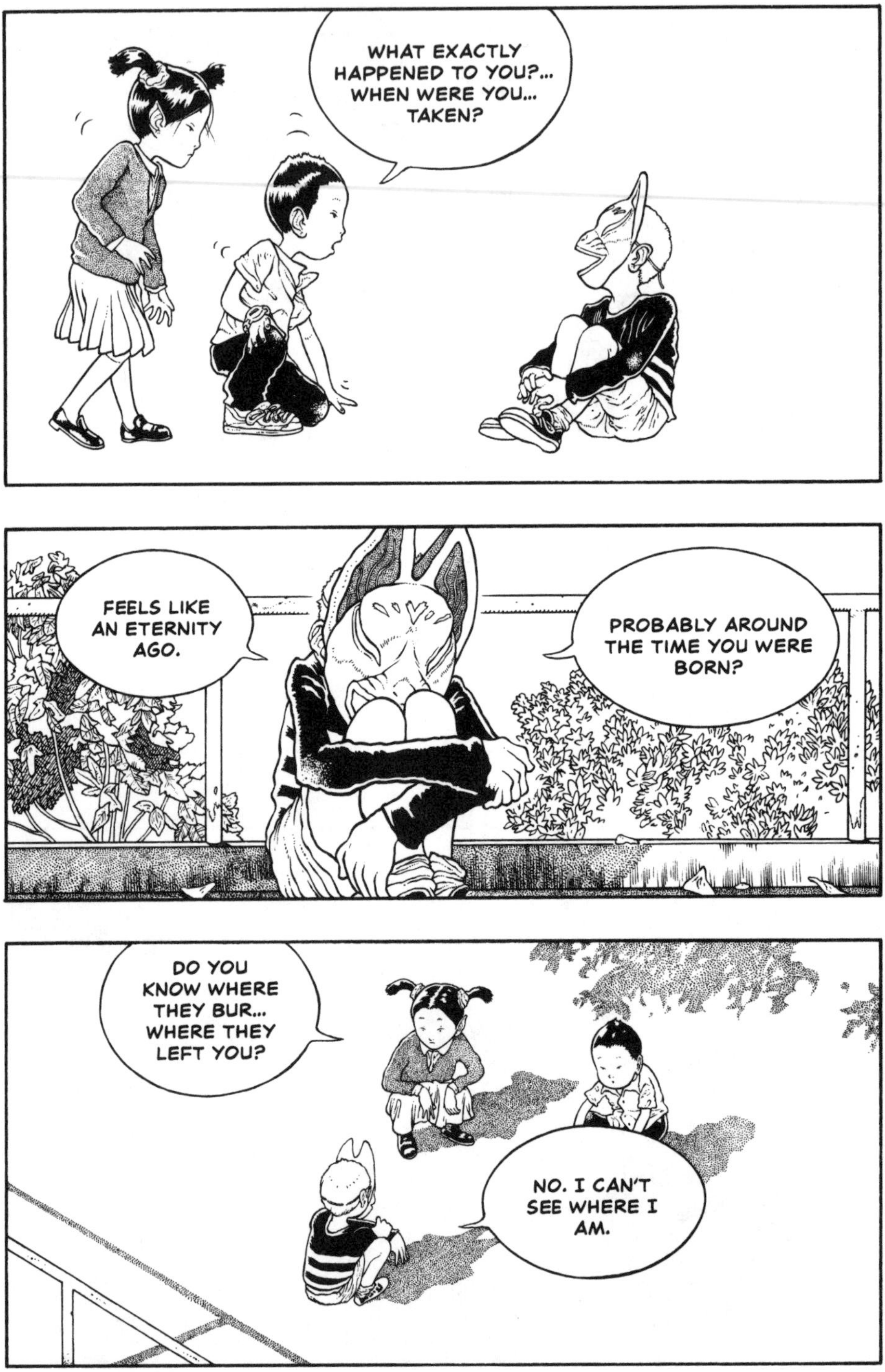
WHAT EXACTLY HAPPENED TO YOU?... WHEN WERE YOU... TAKEN?
FEELS LIKE AN ETERNITY AGO.
PROBABLY AROUND THE TIME YOU WERE BORN?
DO YOU KNOW WHERE THEY BUR... WHERE THEY LEFT YOU?
NO. I CAN'T SEE WHERE I AM.

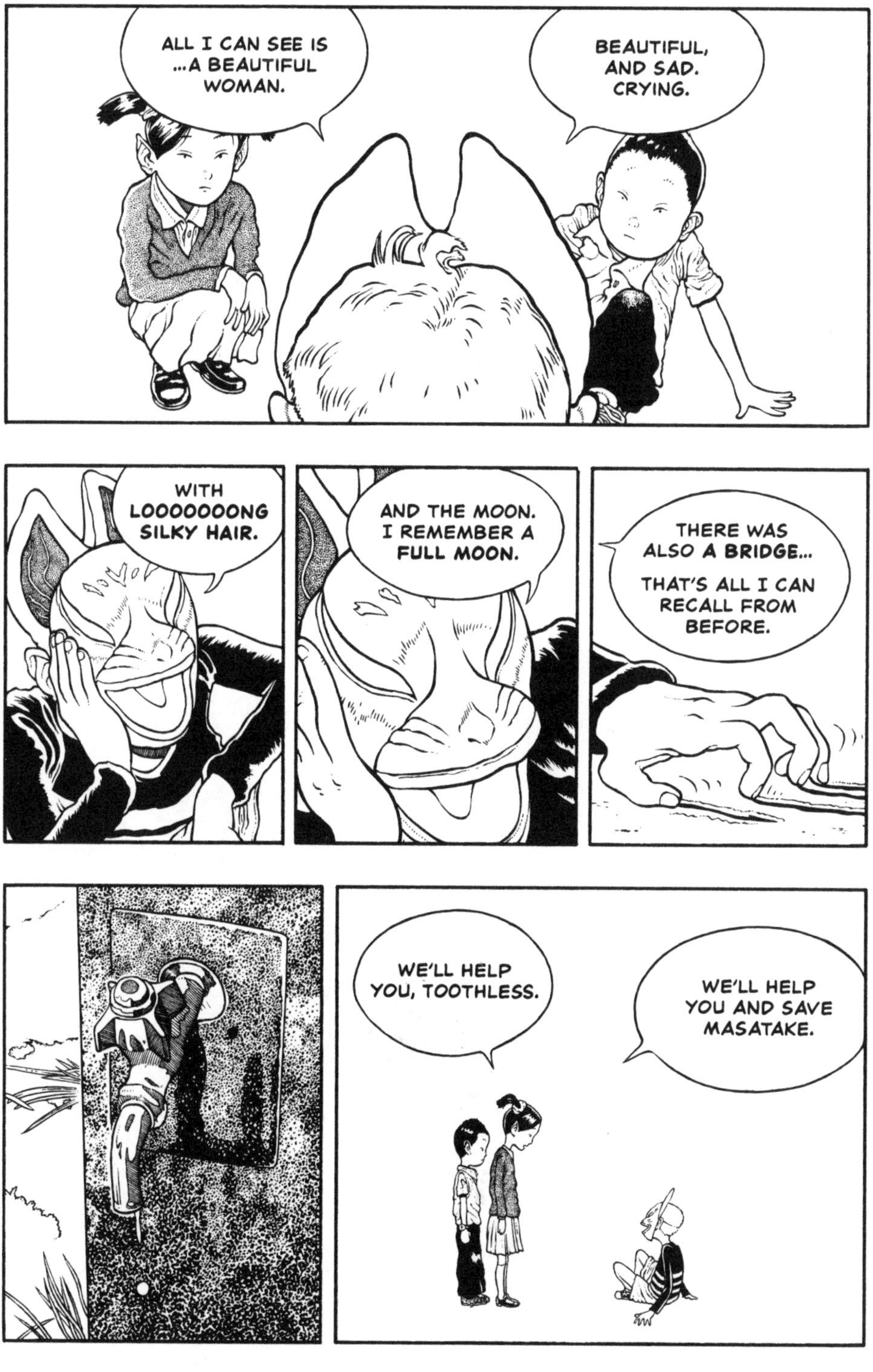
ALL I CAN SEE IS ...A BEAUTIFUL WOMAN.
BEAUTIFUL, AND SAD. CRYING.
WITH LOOOOOOONG SILKY HAIR.
AND THE MOON. I REMEMBER A FULL MOON.
THERE WAS ALSO A BRIDGE...
THAT'S ALL I CAN RECALL FROM BEFORE.
WE'LL HELP YOU, TOOTHLESS.
WE'LL HELP YOU AND SAVE MASATAKE.

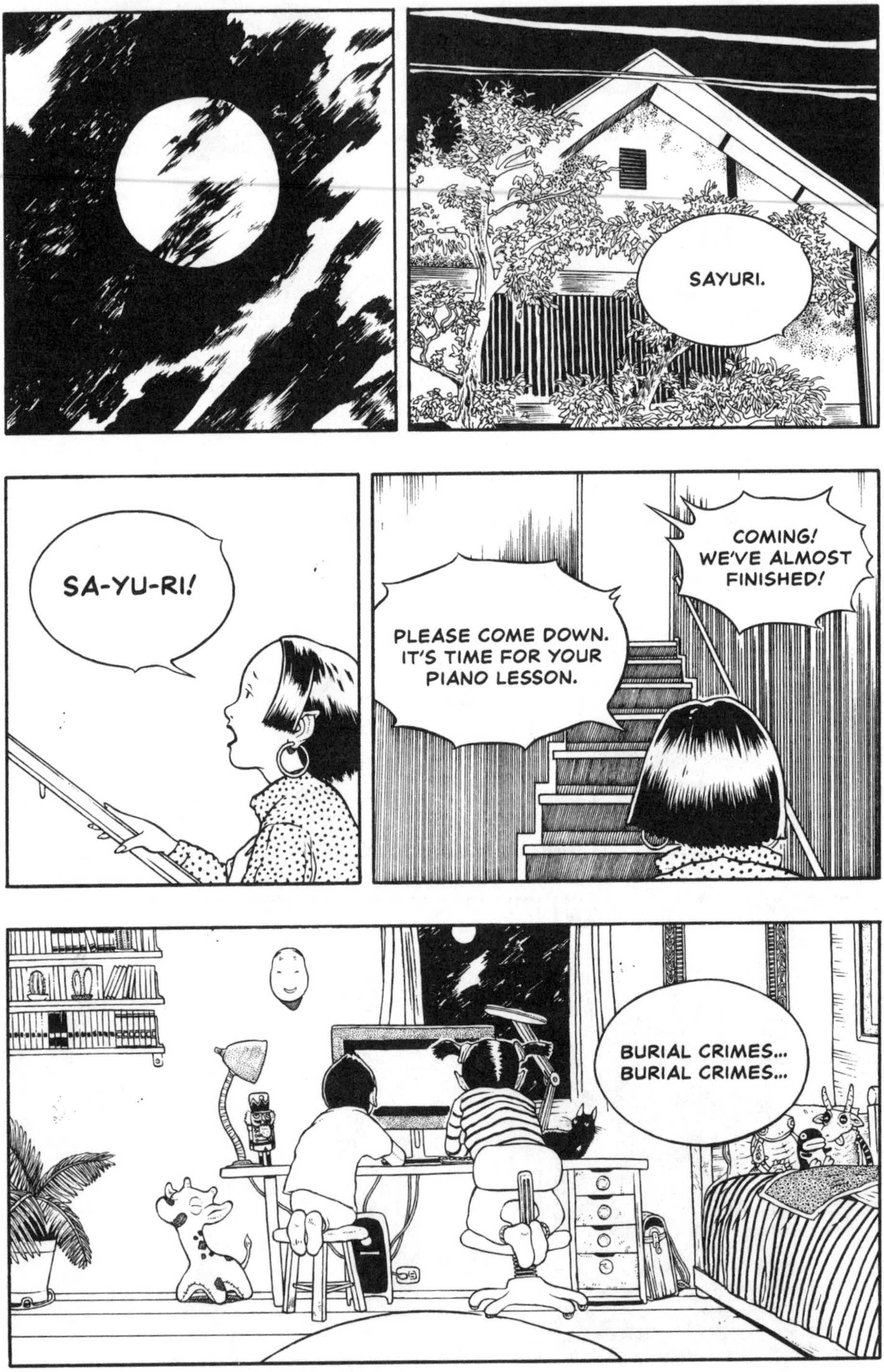
SAYURI.
SA-YU-RI!
COMING! WE'VE ALMOST FINISHED!
PLEASE COME DOWN. IT'S TIME FOR YOUR PIANO LESSON.
BURIAL CRIMES... BURIAL CRIMES...

WE SHOULD GET A MATCH... CRIMES THAT INVOLVE BURIALS ARE NOT VERY COMMON.
THANK GOD.
HERE WE GO...
"TWELVE YEARS LATER, THE CRIMES OF ISSEY MATSUGI REMAIN SHROUDED IN MYSTERY.
"SERIAL KILLER ISSEY MATSUGI (37) WAS ARRESTED ON CHARGES OF KIDNAPPING AND MURDER.
"MATSUGI, NICKNAMED 'THE SPADE' DUE TO HIS ANGULAR FEATURES, BURIED HIS FOURTEEN VICTIMS IN VARIOUS PARTS OF THE REGION, A SERIES OF CRIMES KNOWN AS THE CASE OF THE ARIJIGOKU."
ウェブ検索
サイト内
買い物
今週
大人は知らない。
子どもたちはイン
ターネットをこう使
う!
ARIJIGOKU?
IT'S AN INSECT, ALSO CALLED AN ANT-LION... ANT-LIONS ARE FAMOUS FOR CREATING SAND PITS THAT TRAP OTHER BUGS.
THEY DIG PITS IN THE SHAPE OF AN UPSIDE-DOWN CONE AND SIT WAITING AT THE BOTTOM. THE SAND CONE IS FRAGILE AND WHEN OTHER BUGS GET TOO CLOSE...
IT COLLAPSES.

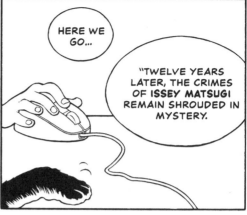

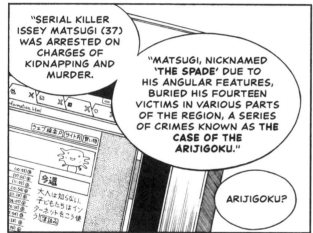

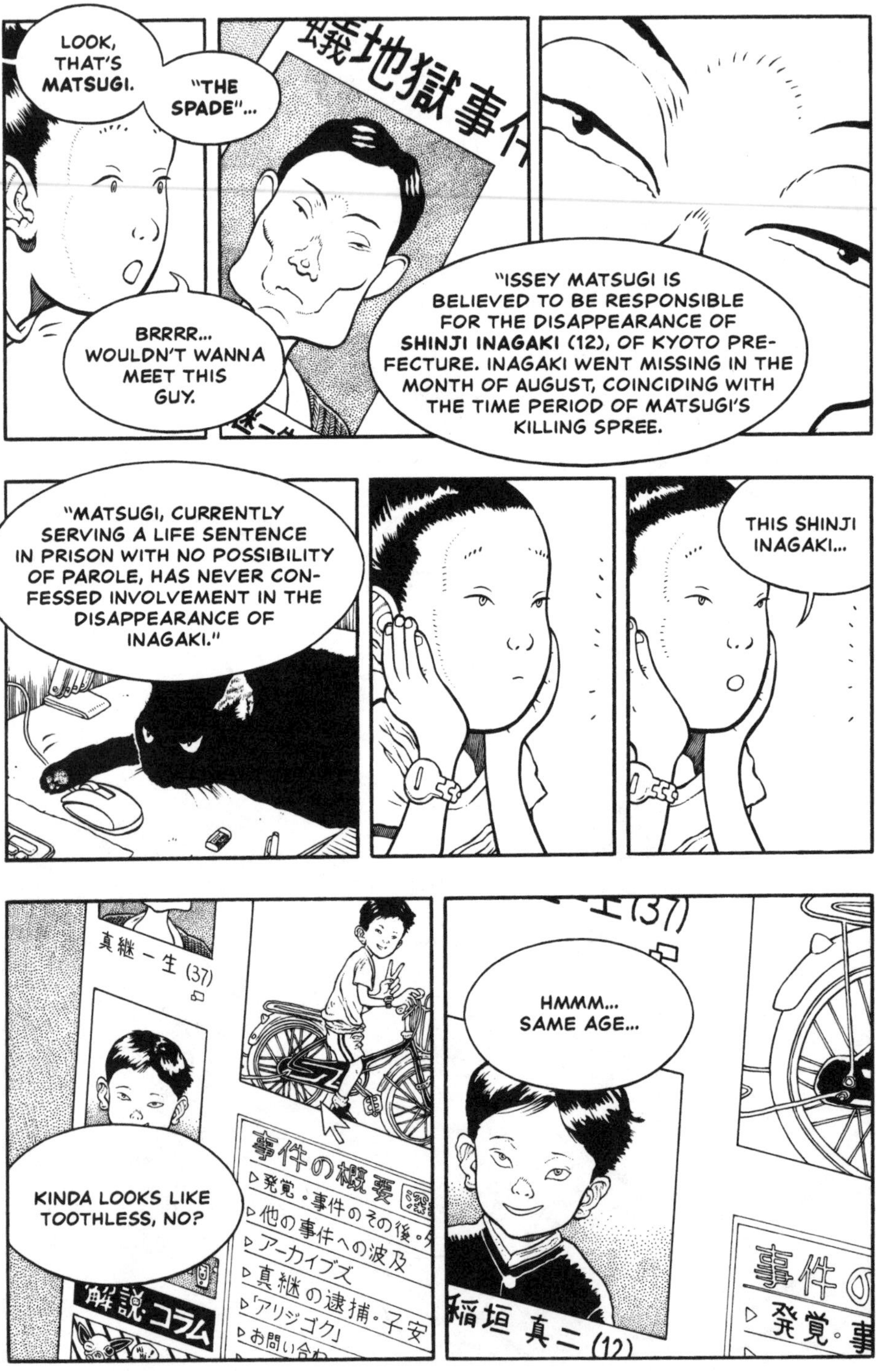
LOOK, THAT'S MATSUGI.
"THE SPADE"...
BRRRR... WOULDN'T WANNA MEET THIS GUY.
"ISSEY MATSUGI IS BELIEVED TO BE RESPONSIBLE FOR THE DISAPPEARANCE OF SHINJI INAGAKI (12), OF KYOTO PRE-FECTURE. INAGAKI WENT MISSING IN THE MONTH OF AUGUST, COINCIDING WITH THE TIME PERIOD OF MATSUGI'S KILLING SPREE.
"MATSUGI, CURRENTLY SERVING A LIFE SENTENCE IN PRISON WITH NO POSSIBILITY OF PAROLE, HAS NEVER CON-FESSED INVOLVEMENT IN THE DISAPPEARANCE OF INAGAKI."
THIS SHINJI INAGAKI...
真継一生 (37)
事件の概要
アーカイブズ
「アリジゴク」
解説・コラム
KINDA LOOKS LIKE TOOTHLESS, NO?
HMMM... SAME AGE...
稲垣 真二 (12)

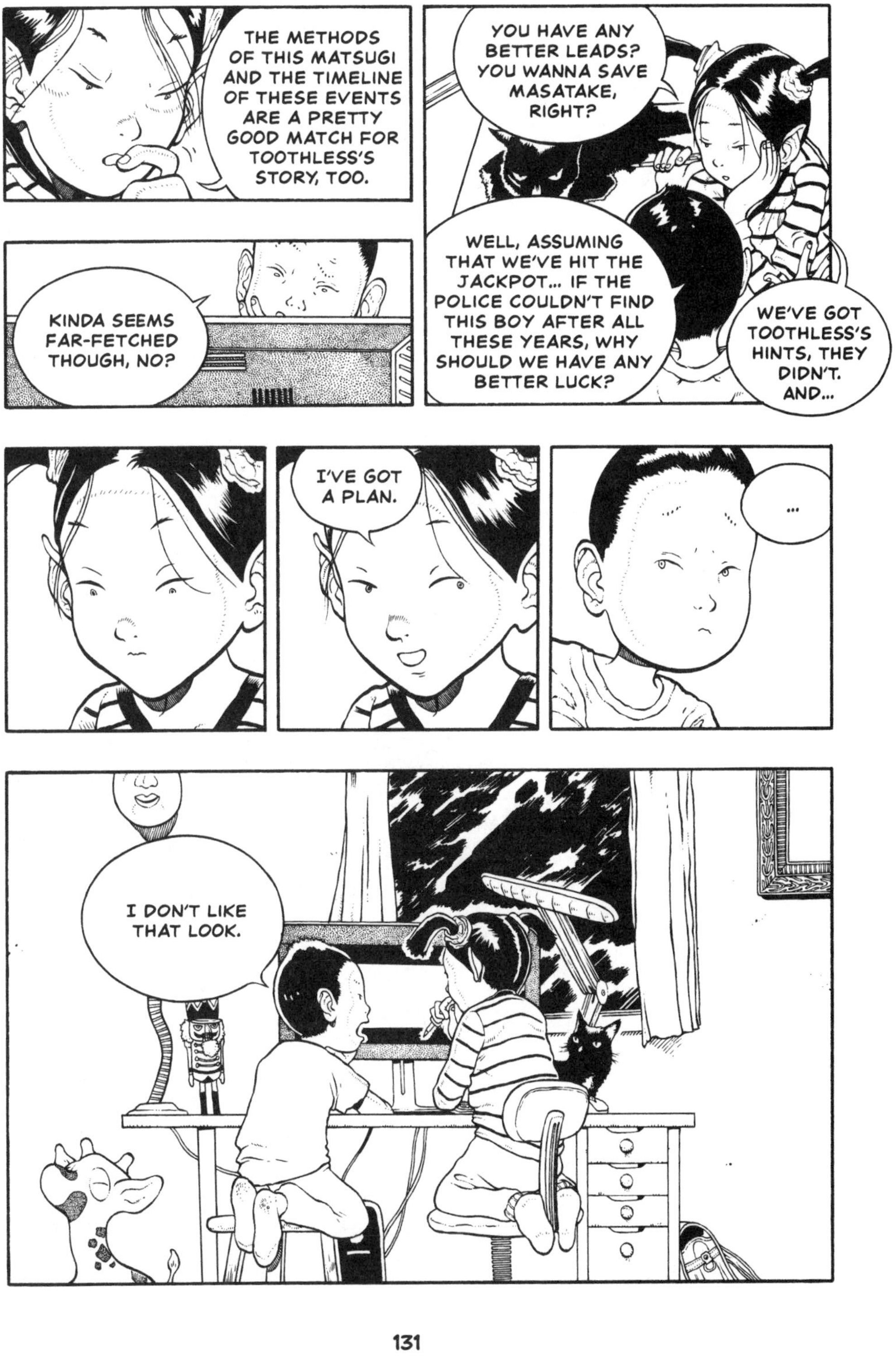
THE METHODS OF THIS MATSUGI AND THE TIMELINE OF THESE EVENTS ARE A PRETTY GOOD MATCH FOR TOOTHLESS'S STORY, TOO.
KINDA SEEMS FAR-FETCHED THOUGH, NO?
YOU HAVE ANY BETTER LEADS? YOU WANNA SAVE MASATAKE, RIGHT?
WELL, ASSUMING THAT WE'VE HIT THE JACKPOT... IF THE POLICE COULDN'T FIND THIS BOY AFTER ALL THESE YEARS, WHY SHOULD WE HAVE ANY BETTER LUCK?
WE'VE GOT TOOTHLESS'S HINTS, THEY DIDN'T. AND...
I'VE GOT A PLAN.
...
I DON'T LIKE THAT LOOK.

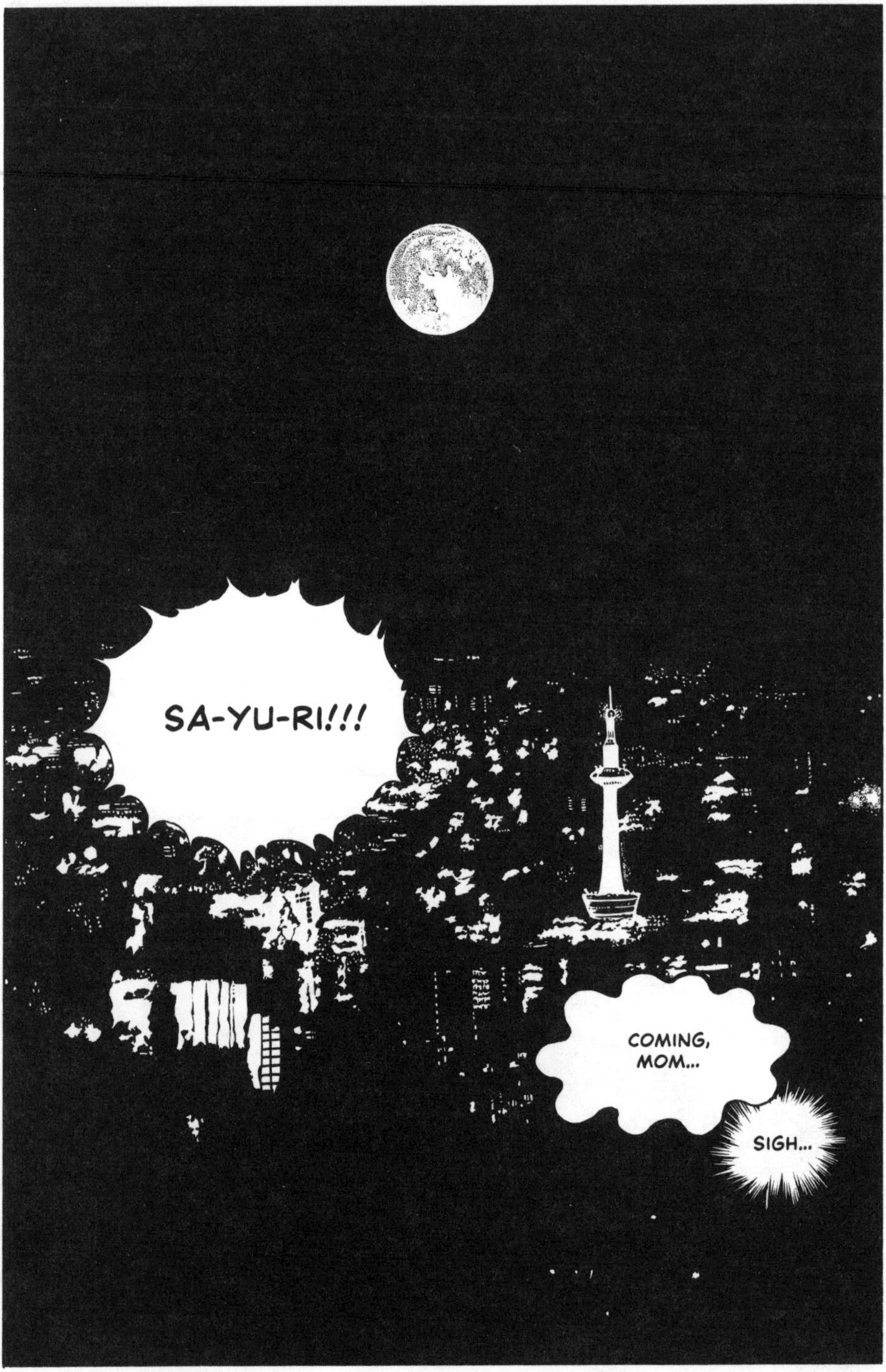
SA-YU-RI!!!
COMING, MOM...
SIGH...

Chapter 6:
Cling! Clang!

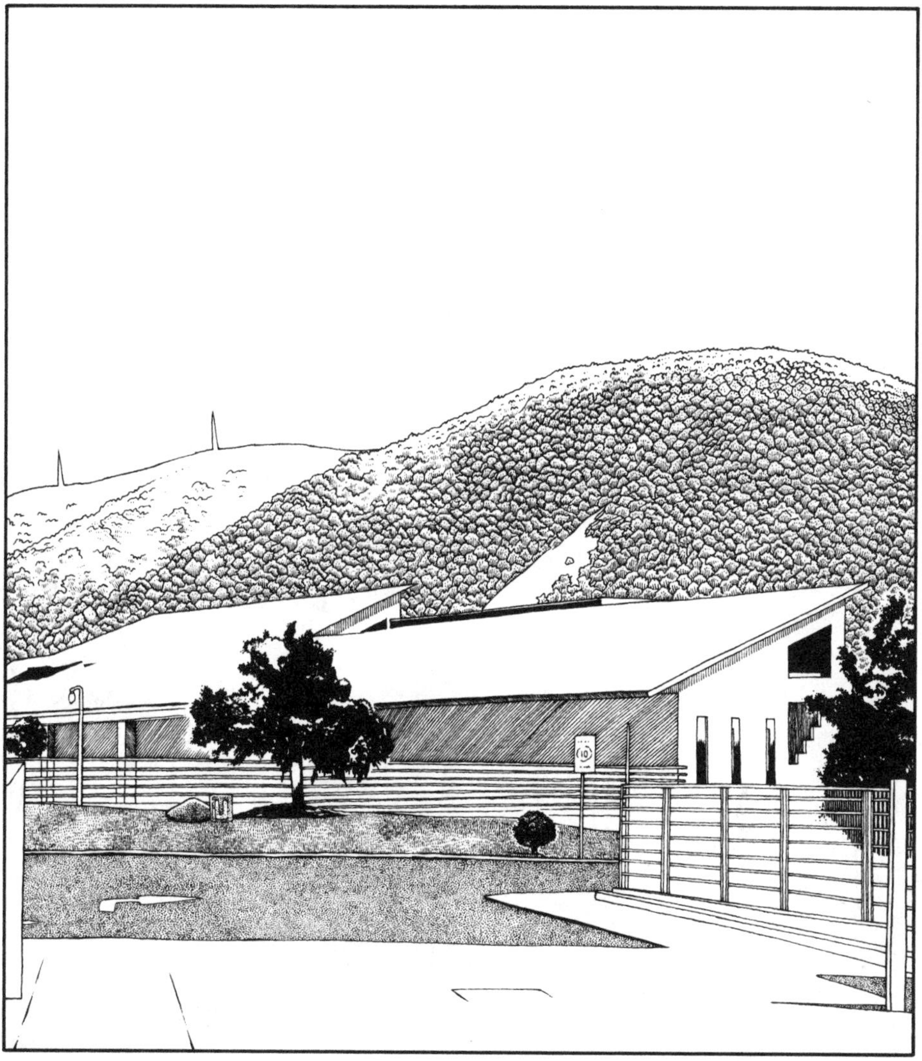

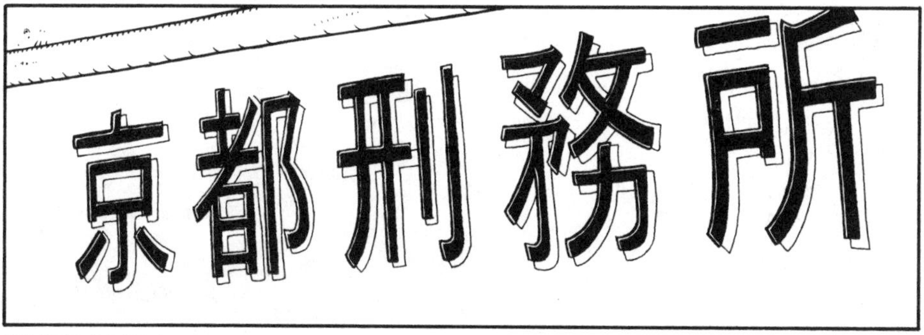
京都刑務所

*KYOTO PRISON

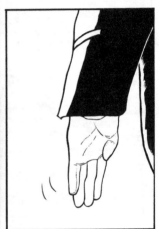

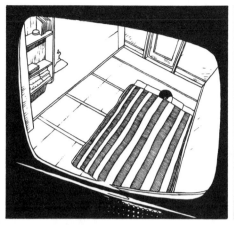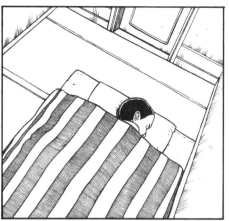

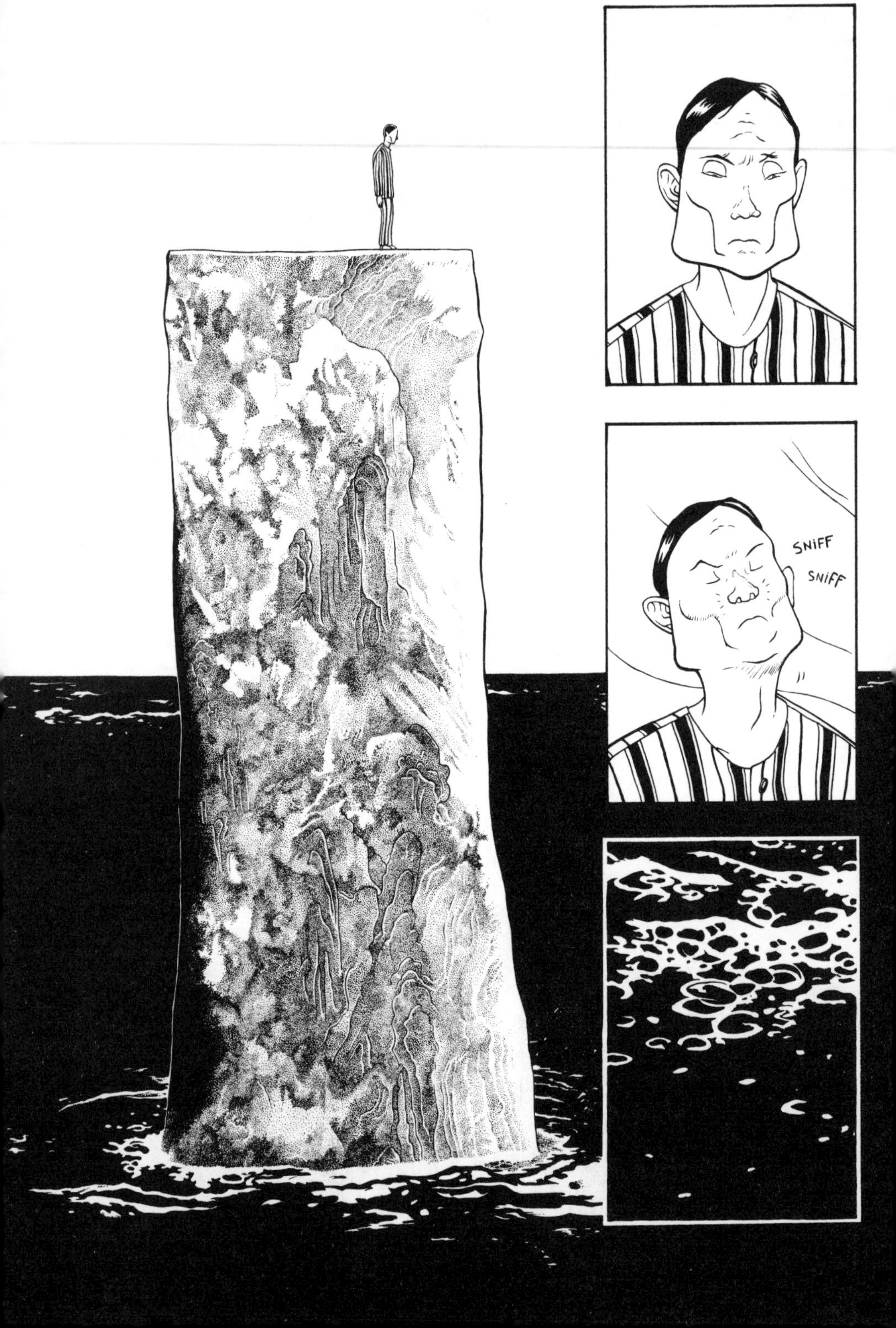
SNIFF
SNIFF

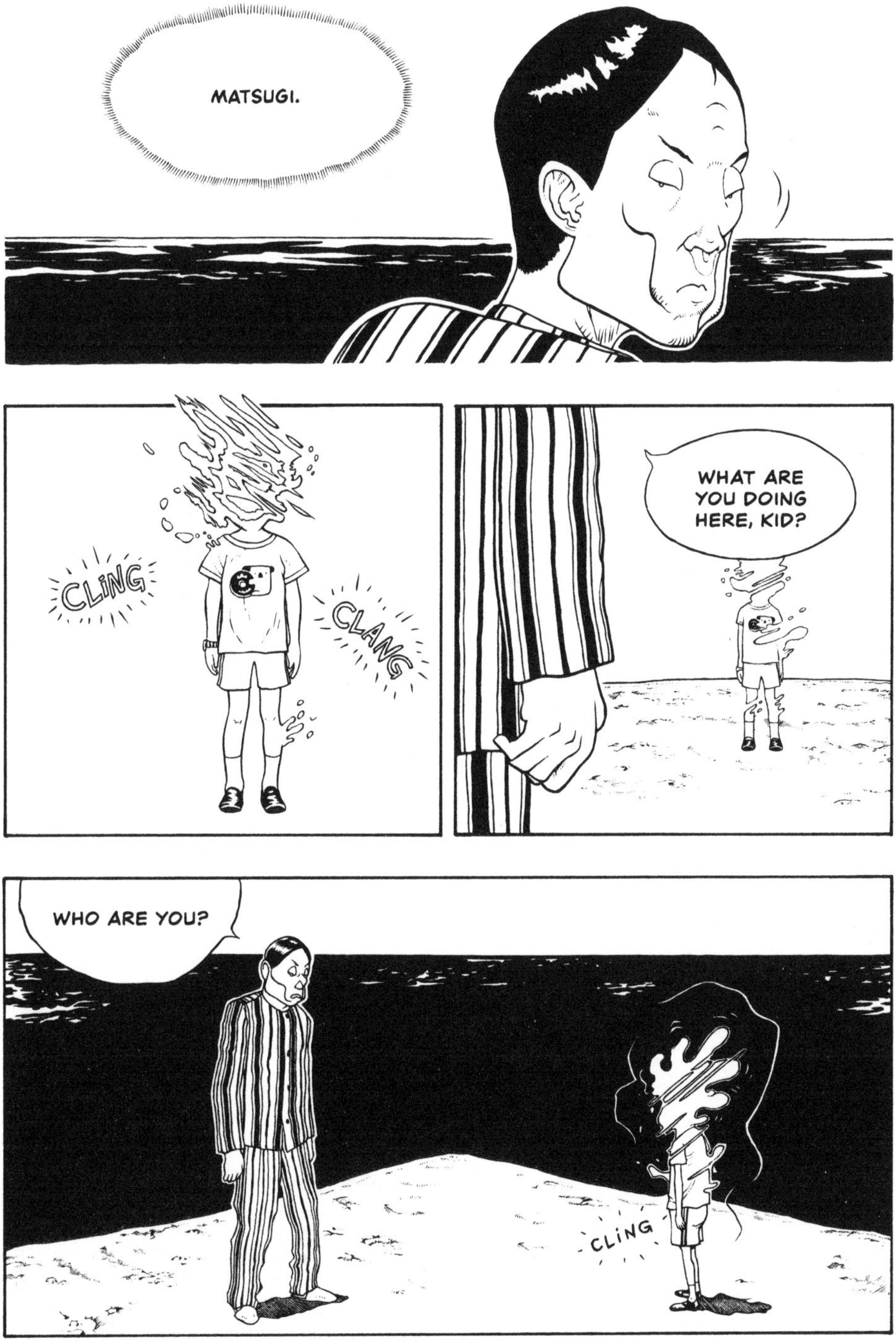
MATSUGI.
CLING
CLANG
WHAT ARE YOU DOING HERE, KID?
WHO ARE YOU?
CLING

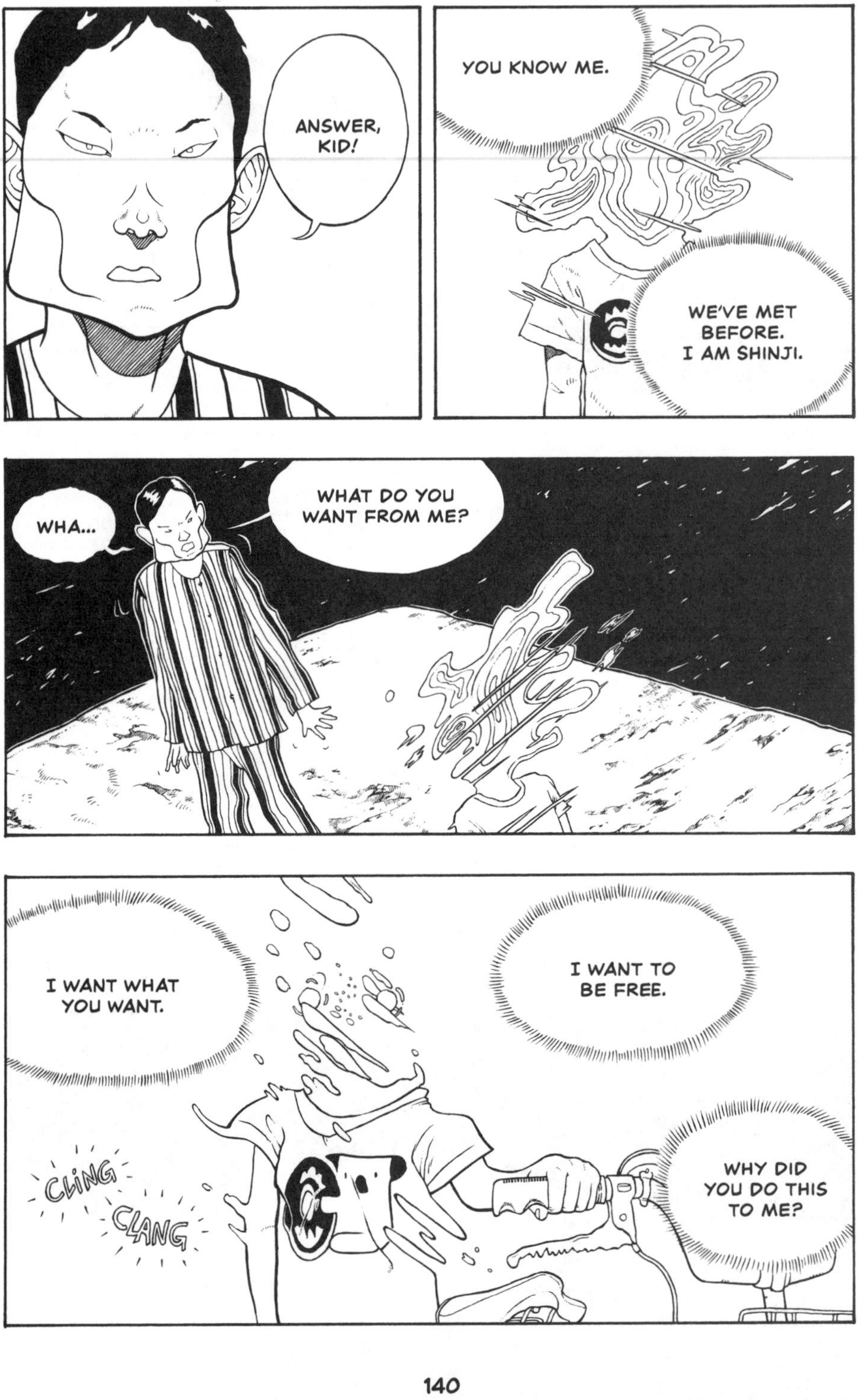
ANSWER, KID!
YOU KNOW ME.
WE'VE MET BEFORE. I AM SHINJI.
WHA...
WHAT DO YOU WANT FROM ME?
I WANT WHAT YOU WANT.
I WANT TO BE FREE.
CLING
CLANG
WHY DID YOU DO THIS TO ME?

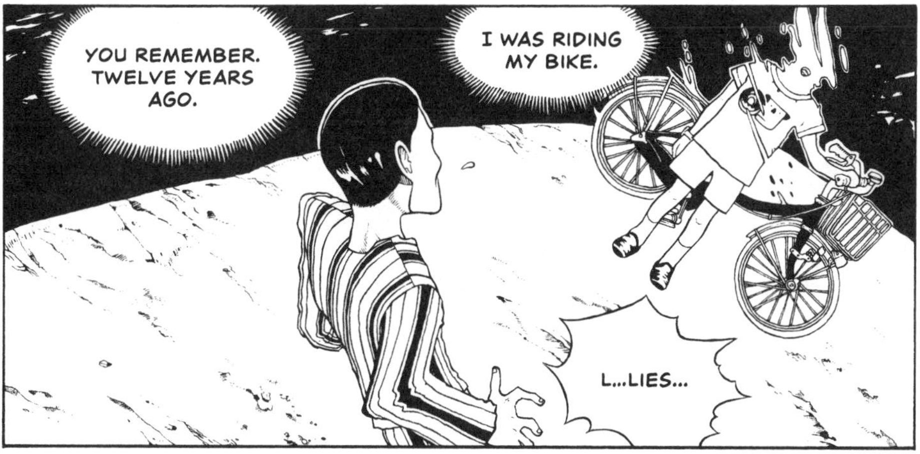
YOU REMEMBER. TWELVE YEARS AGO.
I WAS RIDING MY BIKE.
L...LIES...

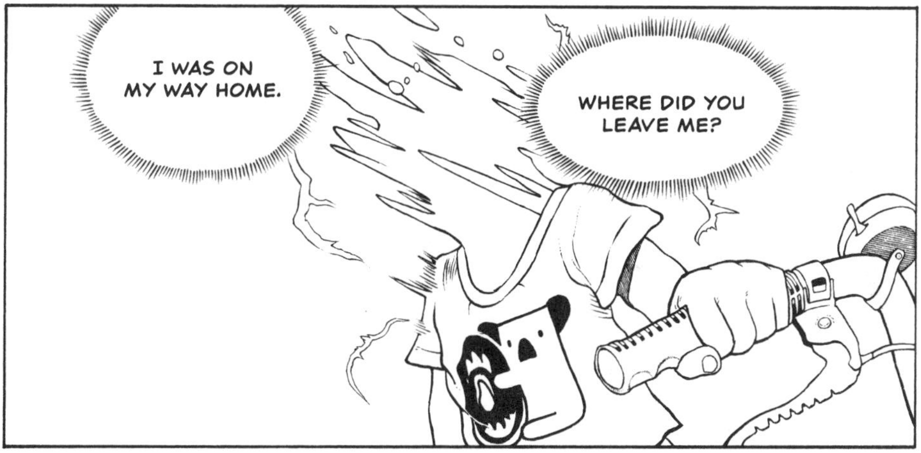
I WAS ON MY WAY HOME.
WHERE DID YOU LEAVE ME?

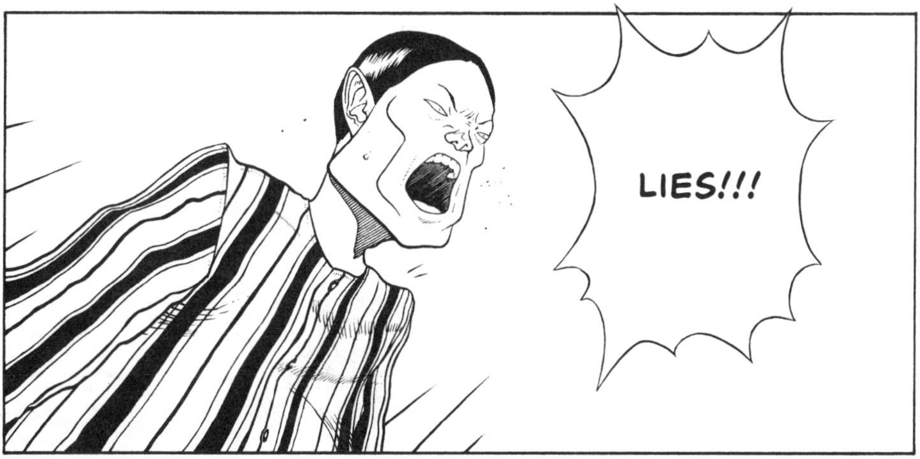
LIES!!!

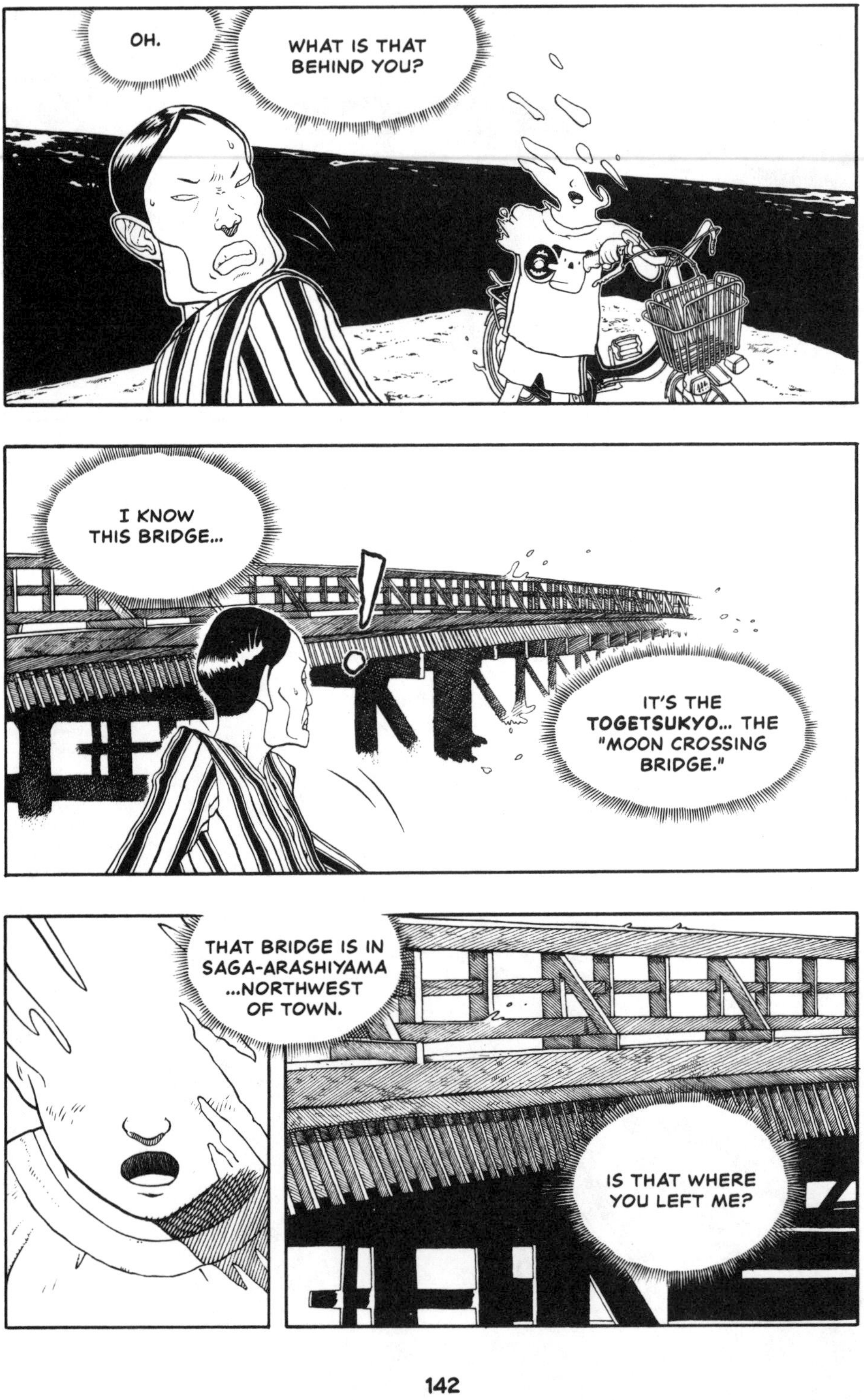
OH.
WHAT IS THAT BEHIND YOU?
I KNOW THIS BRIDGE...
IT'S THE TOGETSUKYO... THE "MOON CROSSING BRIDGE."
THAT BRIDGE IS IN SAGA-ARASHIYAMA ...NORTHWEST OF TOWN.
IS THAT WHERE YOU LEFT ME?

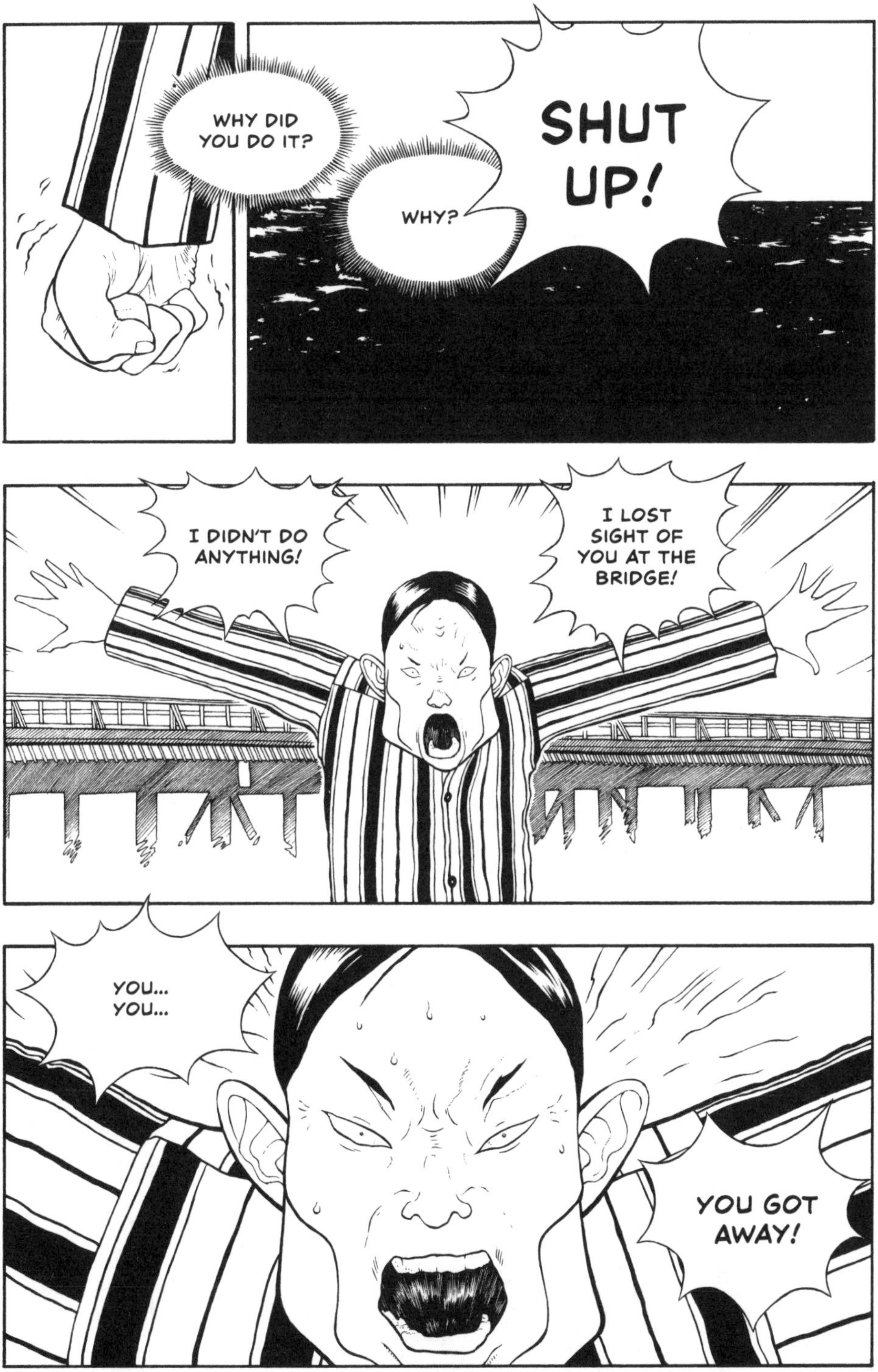
WHY DID YOU DO IT?
WHY?
SHUT UP!
I DIDN'T DO ANYTHING!
I LOST SIGHT OF YOU AT THE BRIDGE!
YOU... YOU...
YOU GOT AWAY!

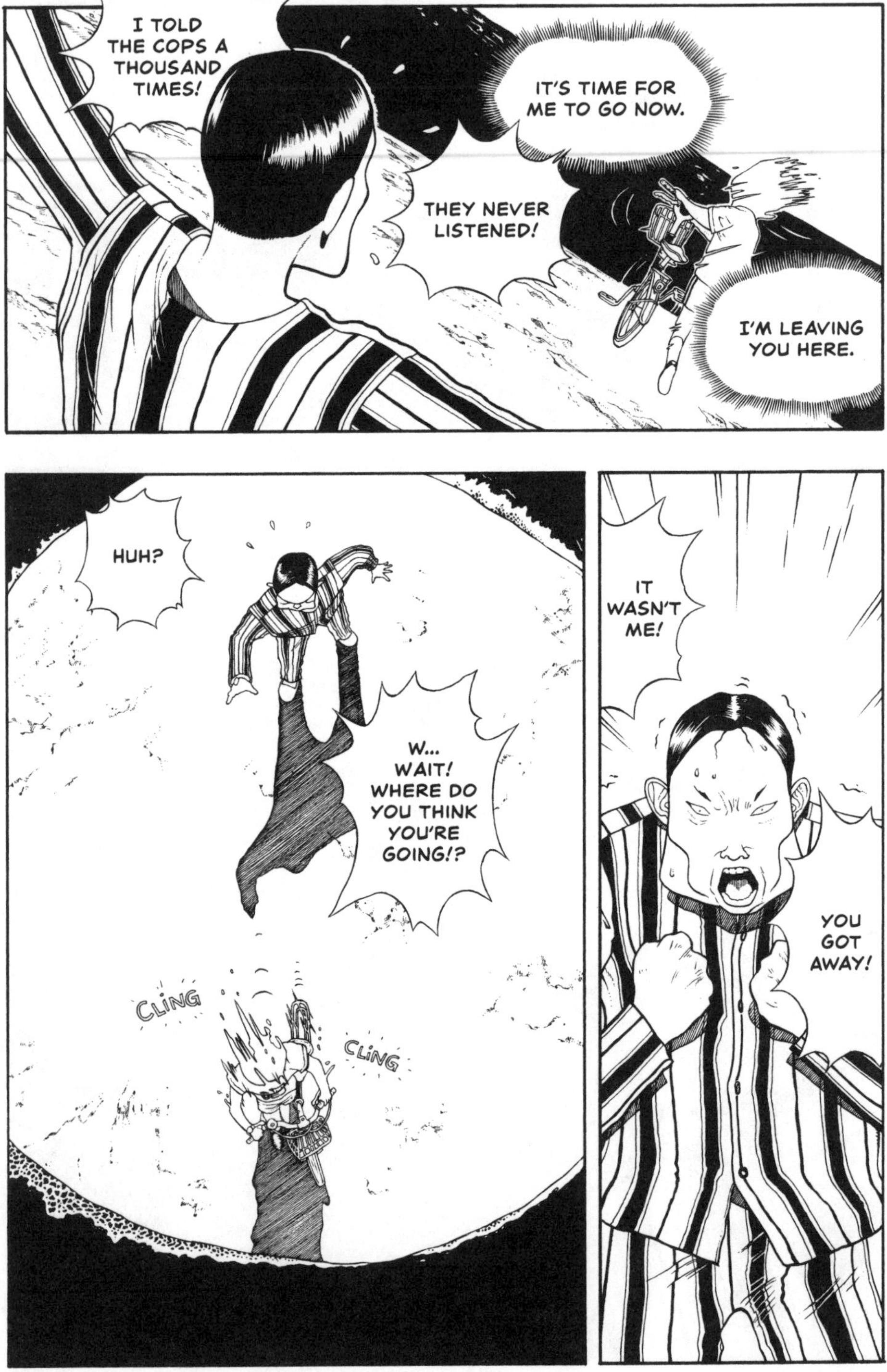
I TOLD THE COPS A THOUSAND TIMES!
THEY NEVER LISTENED!
IT'S TIME FOR ME TO GO NOW.
I'M LEAVING YOU HERE.
HUH?
W... WAIT! WHERE DO YOU THINK YOU'RE GOING!?
CLING
CLING
IT WASN'T ME!
YOU GOT AWAY!

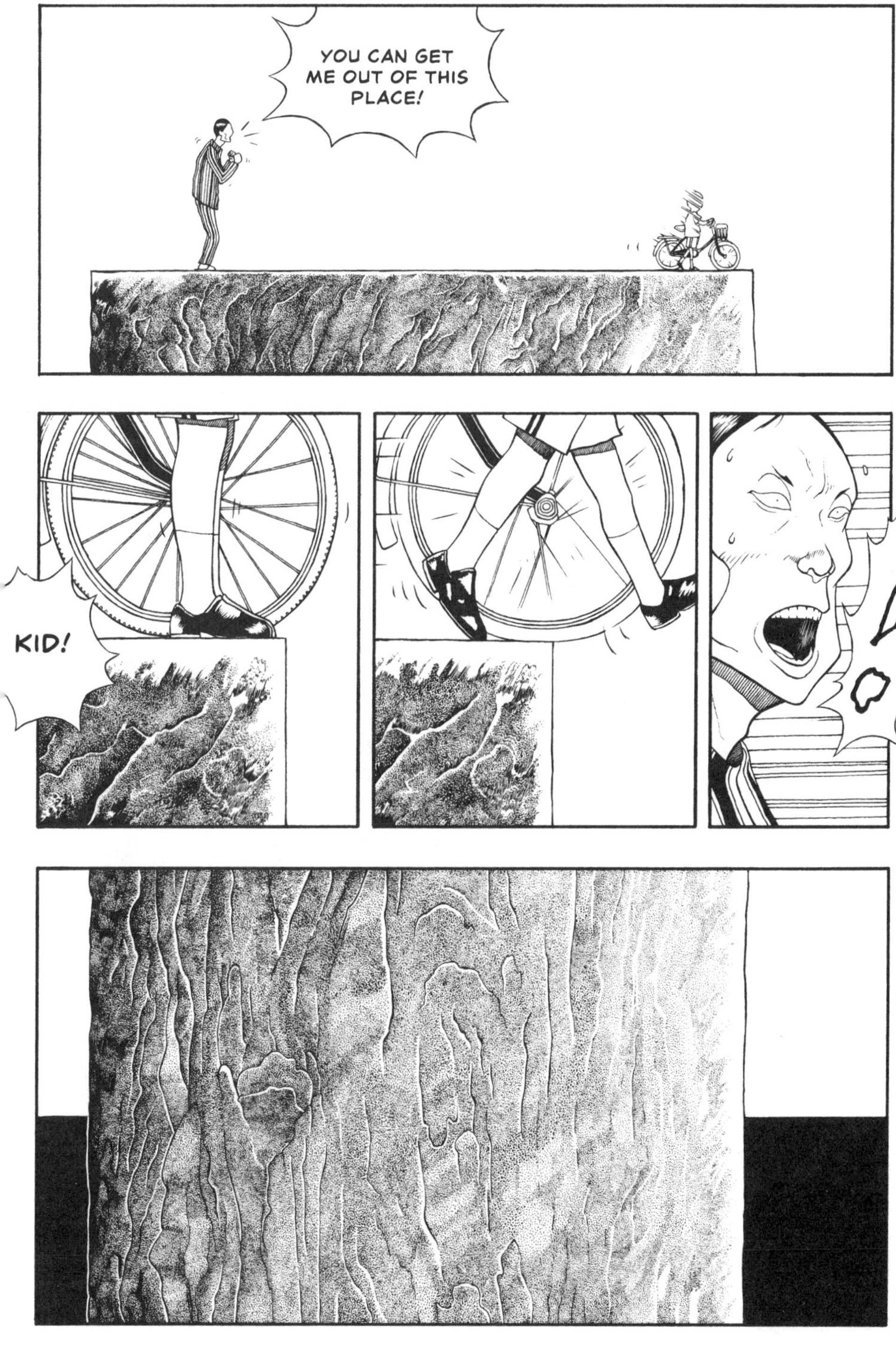
YOU CAN GET ME OUT OF THIS PLACE!
KID!

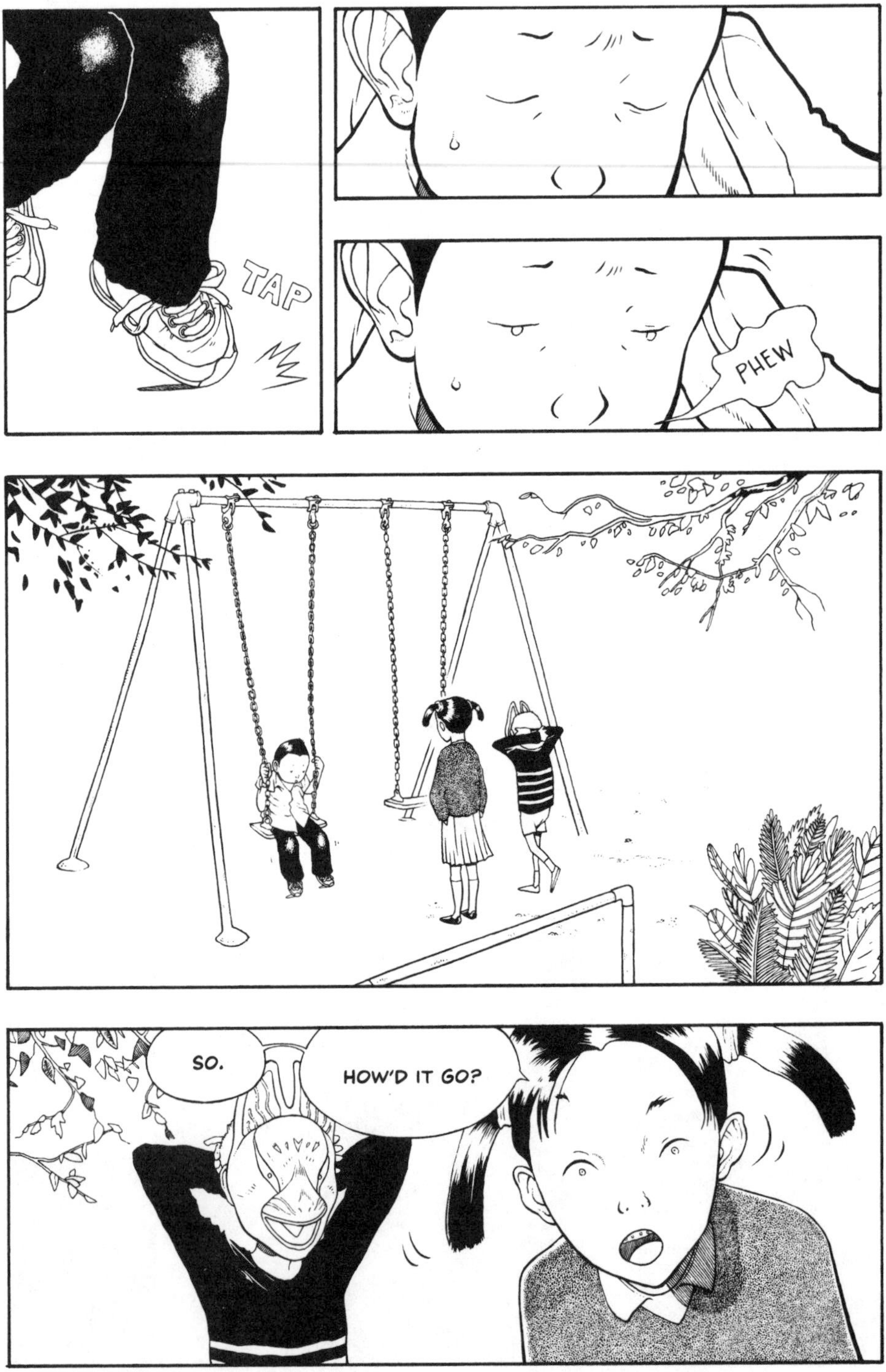
TAP
PHEW
SO.
HOW'D IT GO?

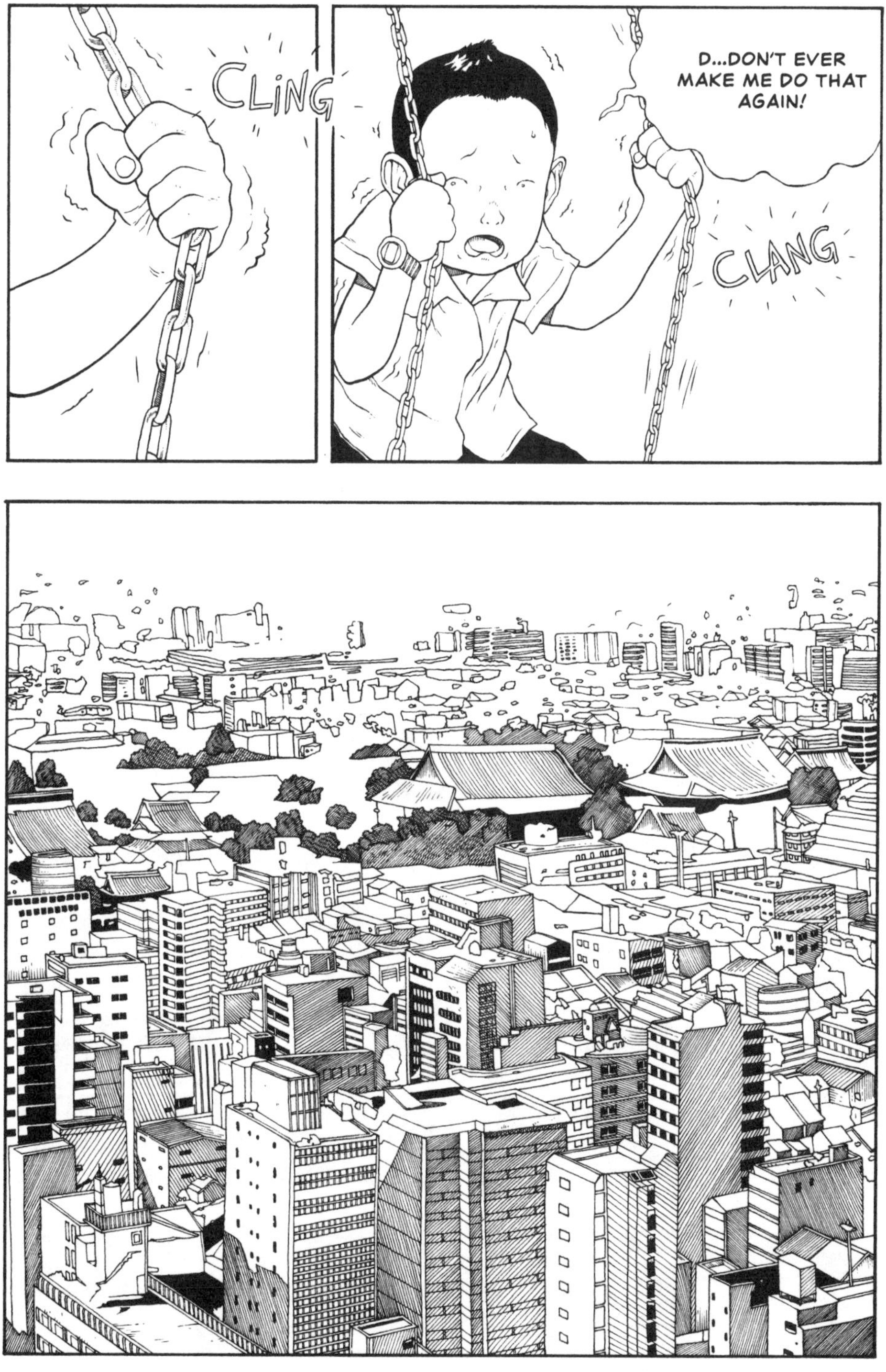
CLING
D...DON'T EVER MAKE ME DO THAT AGAIN!
CLANG

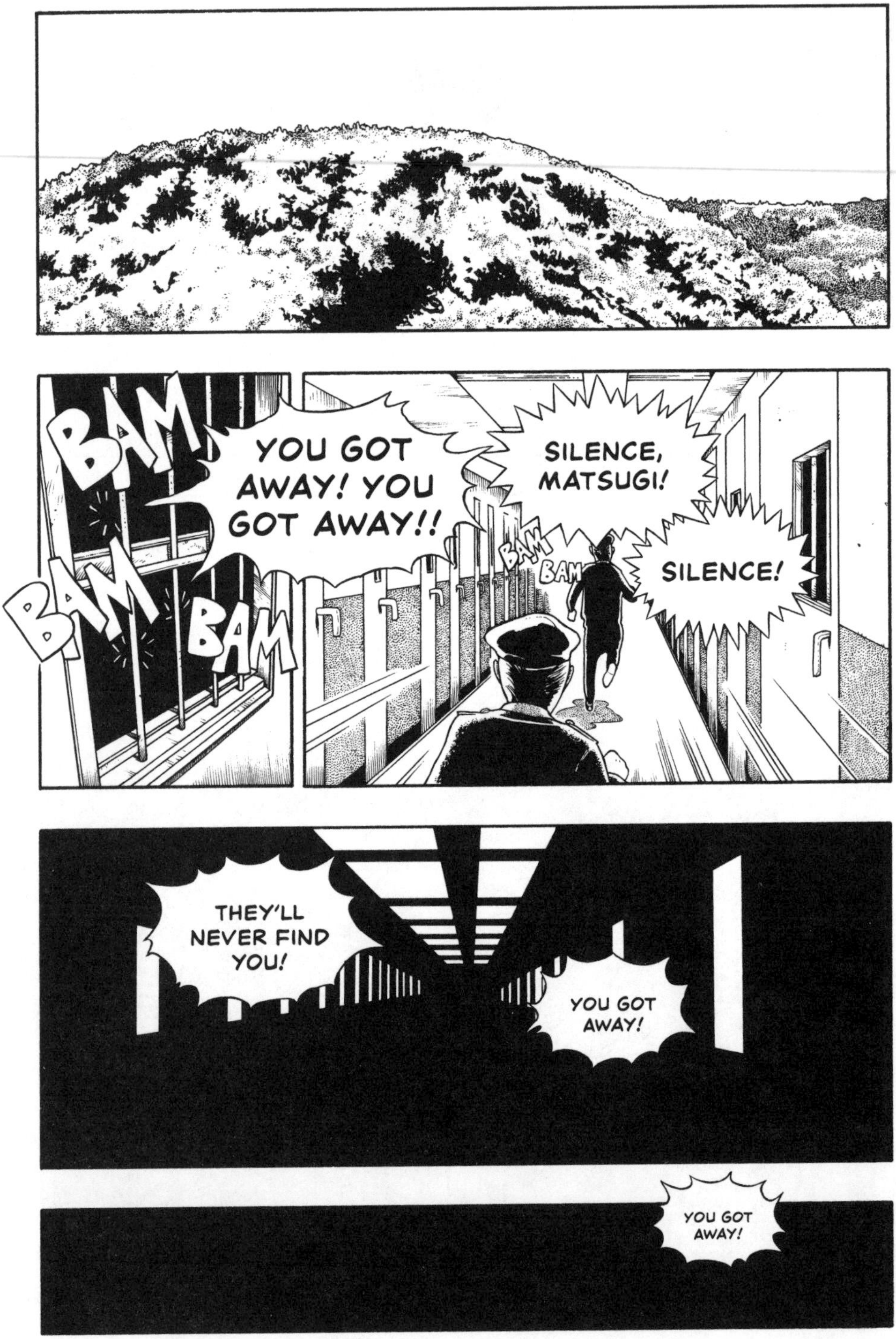
BAM
BAM
BAM
YOU GOT AWAY! YOU GOT AWAY!!
BAM
BAM
SILENCE, MATSUGI!
SILENCE!
THEY'LL NEVER FIND YOU!
YOU GOT AWAY!
YOU GOT AWAY!

Chapter 7:
The Body

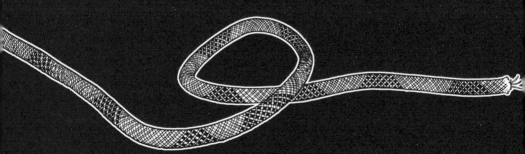

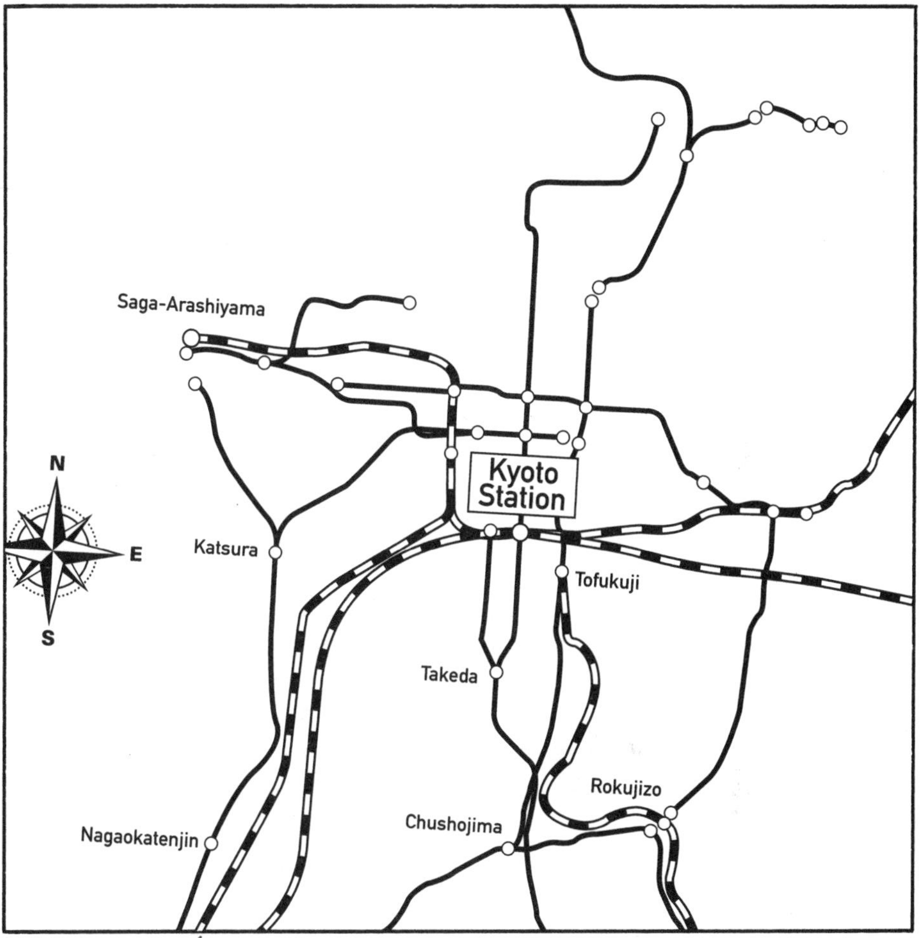
Saga-Arashiyama
Katsura
Nagaokatenjin
Kyoto Station
Tofukuji
Takeda
Chushojima
Rokujizo
N
E
S

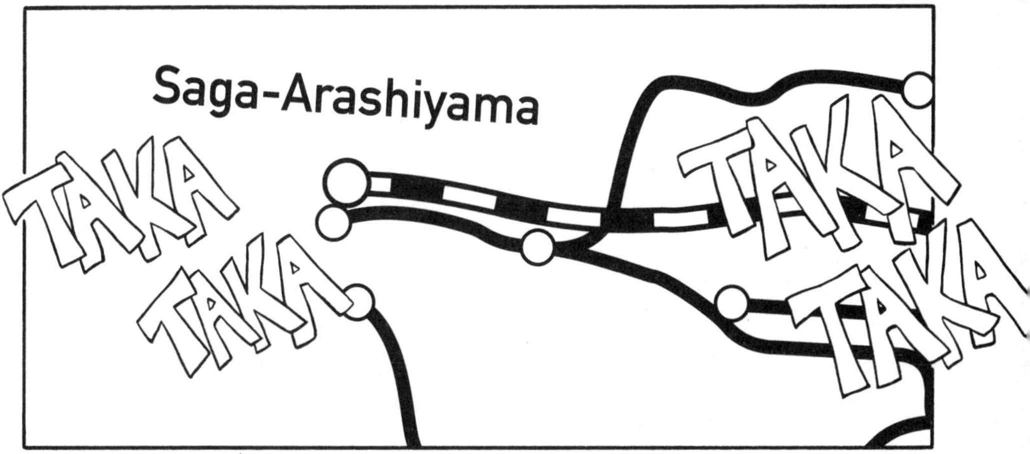
Saga-Arashiyama
TAKA
TAKA
TAKA
TAKA

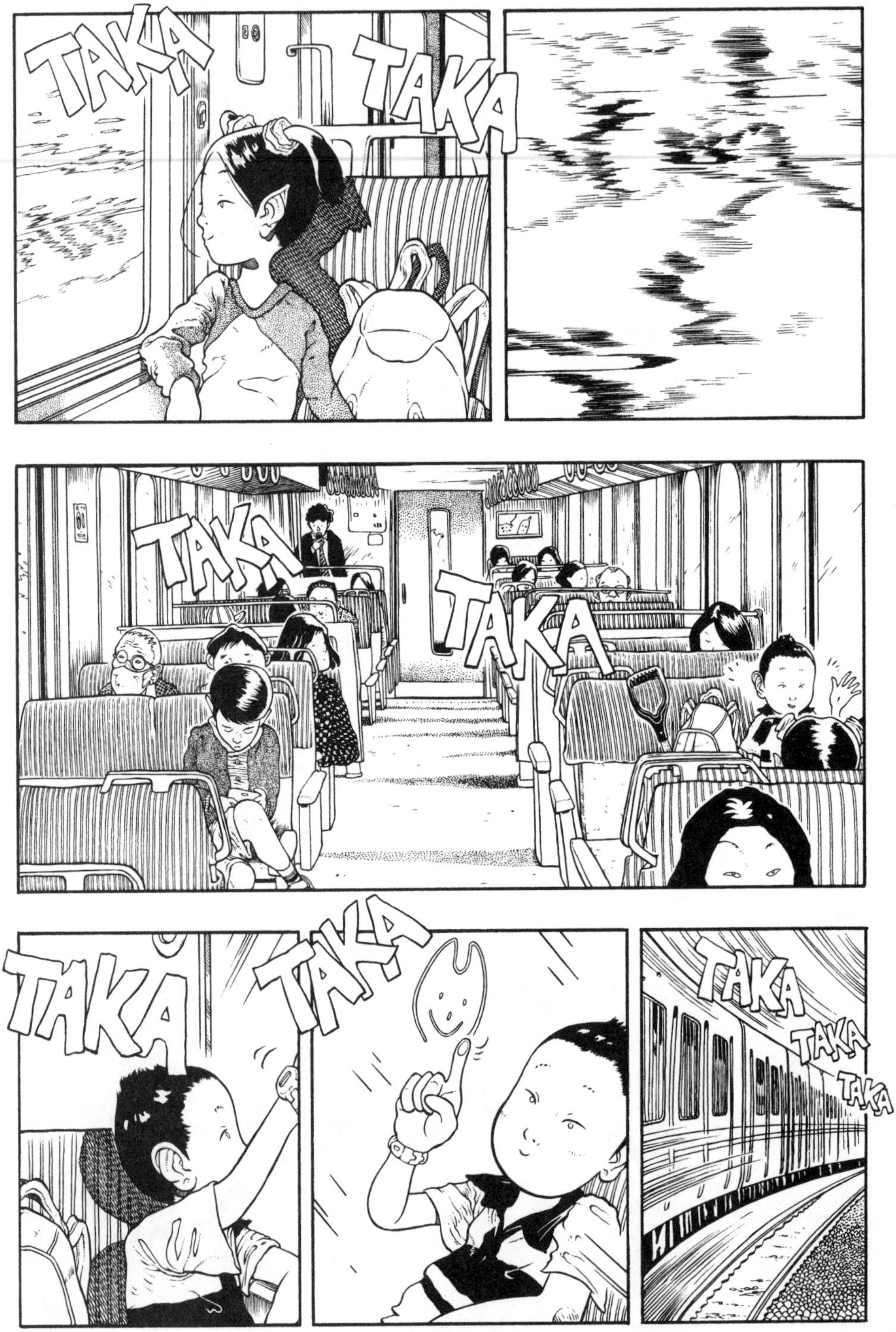
TAKA
TAKA
TAKA
TAKA
TAKA
TAKA
TAKA
TAKA
TAKA

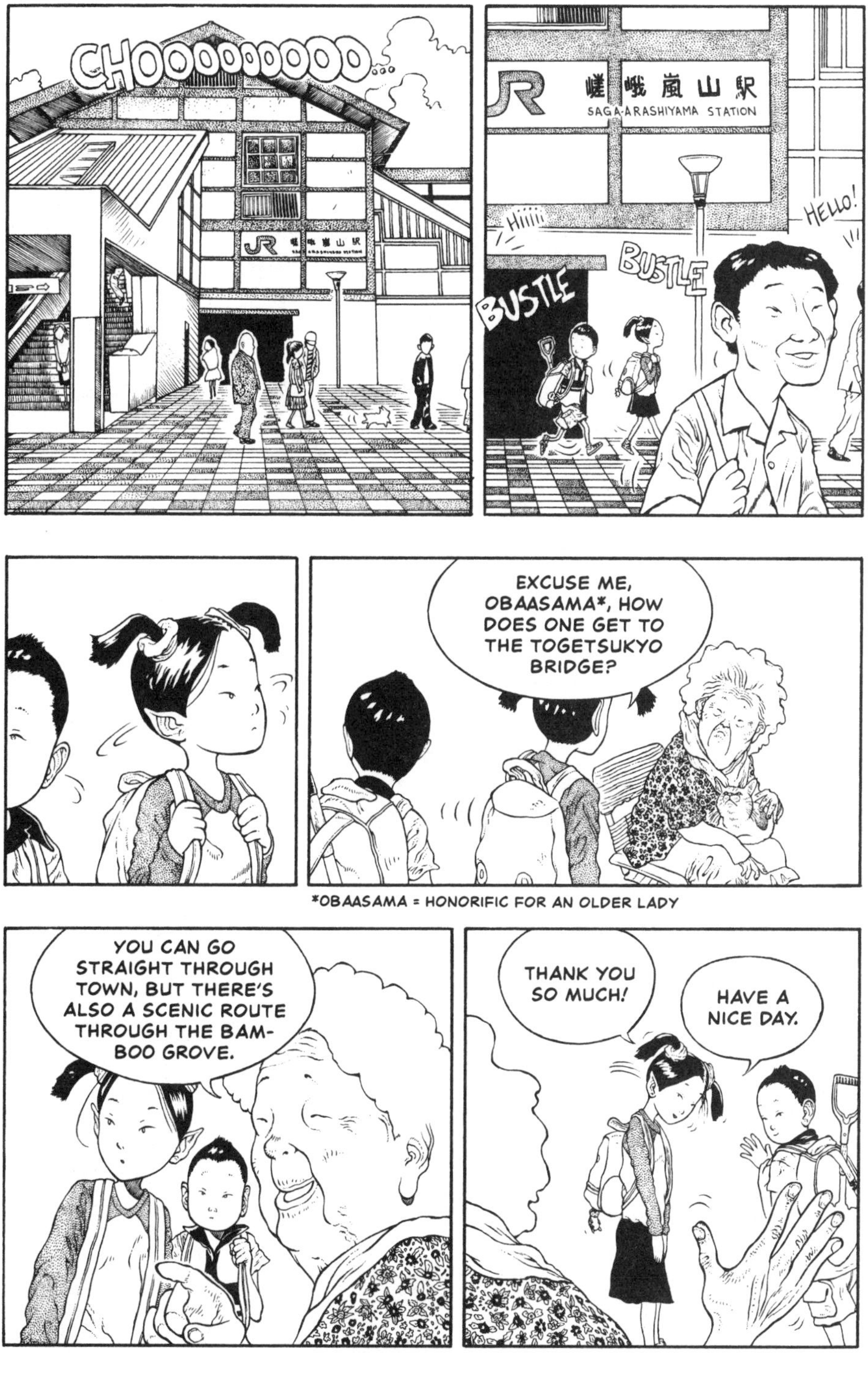
CHOOOOOOOOO...
嵯峨嵐山駅
SAGA-ARASHIYAMA STATION
Hiiiii
HELLO!
BUSTLE
BUSTLE
EXCUSE ME, OBAASAMA*, HOW DOES ONE GET TO THE TOGETSUKYO BRIDGE?
*OBAASAMA = HONORIFIC FOR AN OLDER LADY
YOU CAN GO STRAIGHT THROUGH TOWN, BUT THERE'S ALSO A SCENIC ROUTE THROUGH THE BAMBOO GROVE.
THANK YOU SO MUCH!
HAVE A NICE DAY.

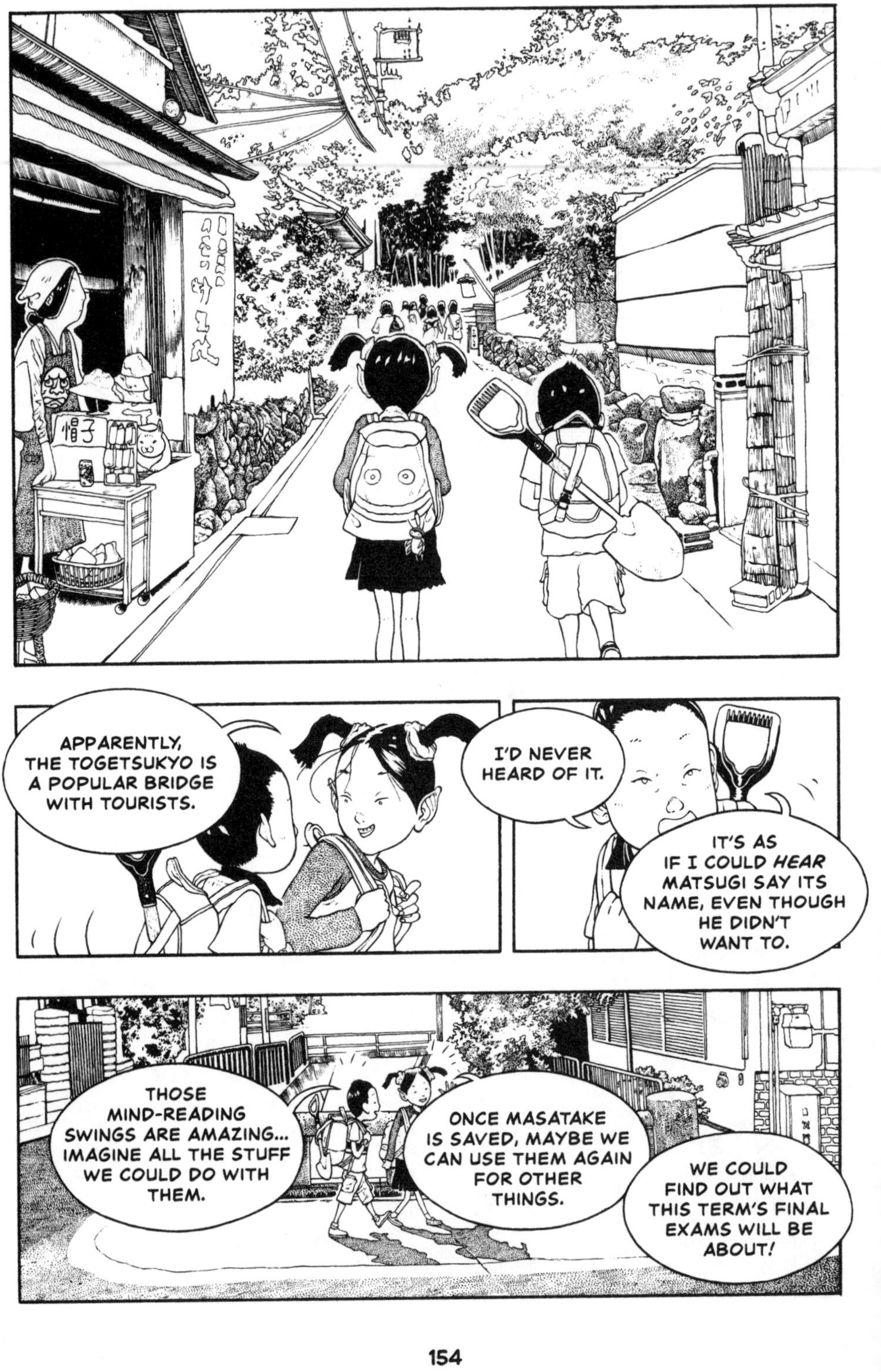
帽子
APPARENTLY, THE TOGETSUKYO IS A POPULAR BRIDGE WITH TOURISTS.
I'D NEVER HEARD OF IT.
IT'S AS IF I COULD *HEAR* MATSUGI SAY ITS NAME, EVEN THOUGH HE DIDN'T WANT TO.
THOSE MIND-READING SWINGS ARE AMAZING... IMAGINE ALL THE STUFF WE COULD DO WITH THEM.
ONCE MASATAKE IS SAVED, MAYBE WE CAN USE THEM AGAIN FOR OTHER THINGS.
WE COULD FIND OUT WHAT THIS TERM'S FINAL EXAMS WILL BE ABOUT!

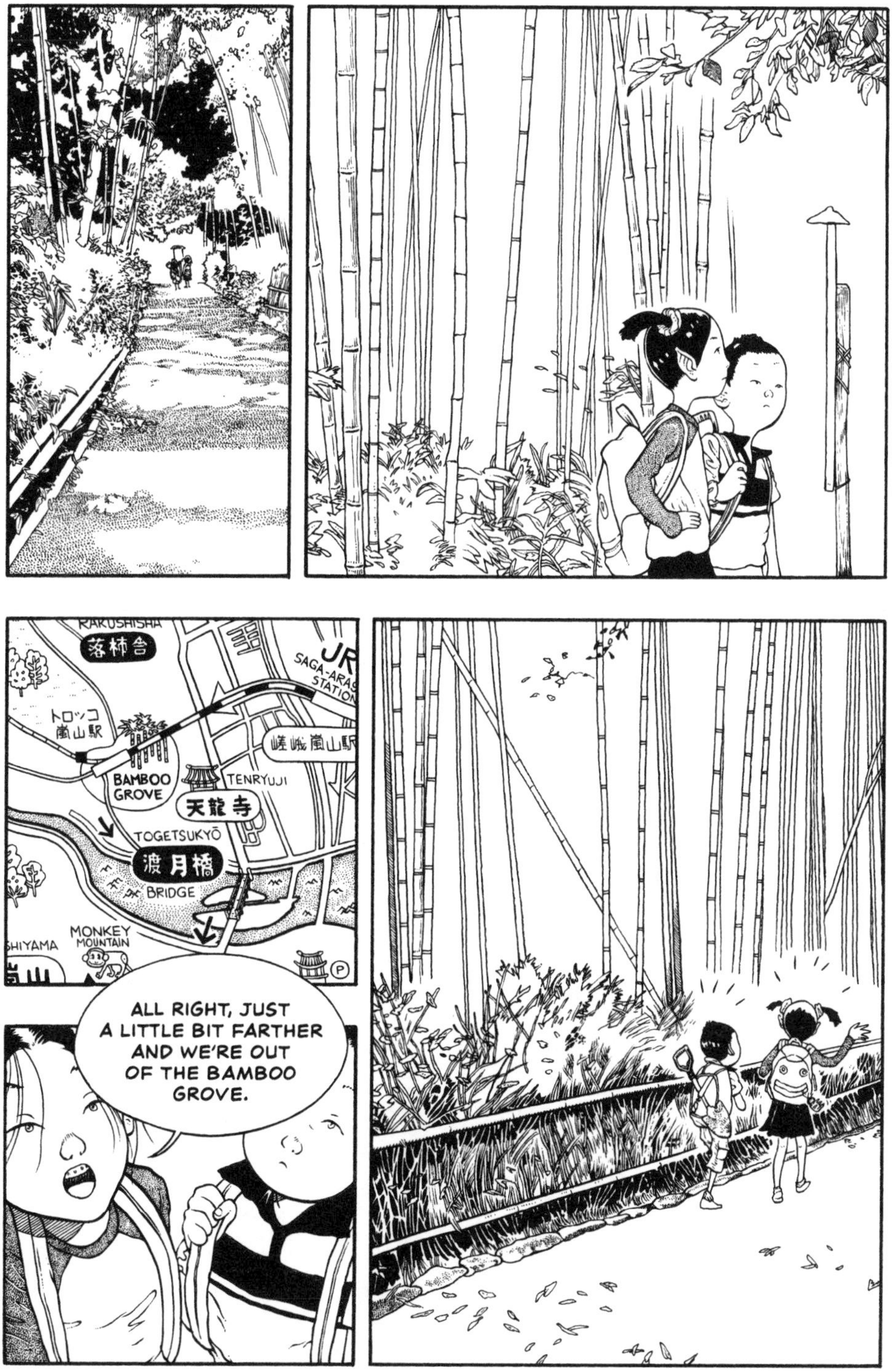
RAKUSHISHA
落柿舎
JR
SAGA-ARAS
STATION
トロッコ
嵐山駅
嵯峨嵐山駅
BAMBOO GROVE
TENRYUJI
天龍寺
TOGETSUKYŌ
渡月橋
BRIDGE
MONKEY
MOUNTAIN
SHIYAMA
ALL RIGHT, JUST A LITTLE BIT FARTHER AND WE'RE OUT OF THE BAMBOO GROVE.

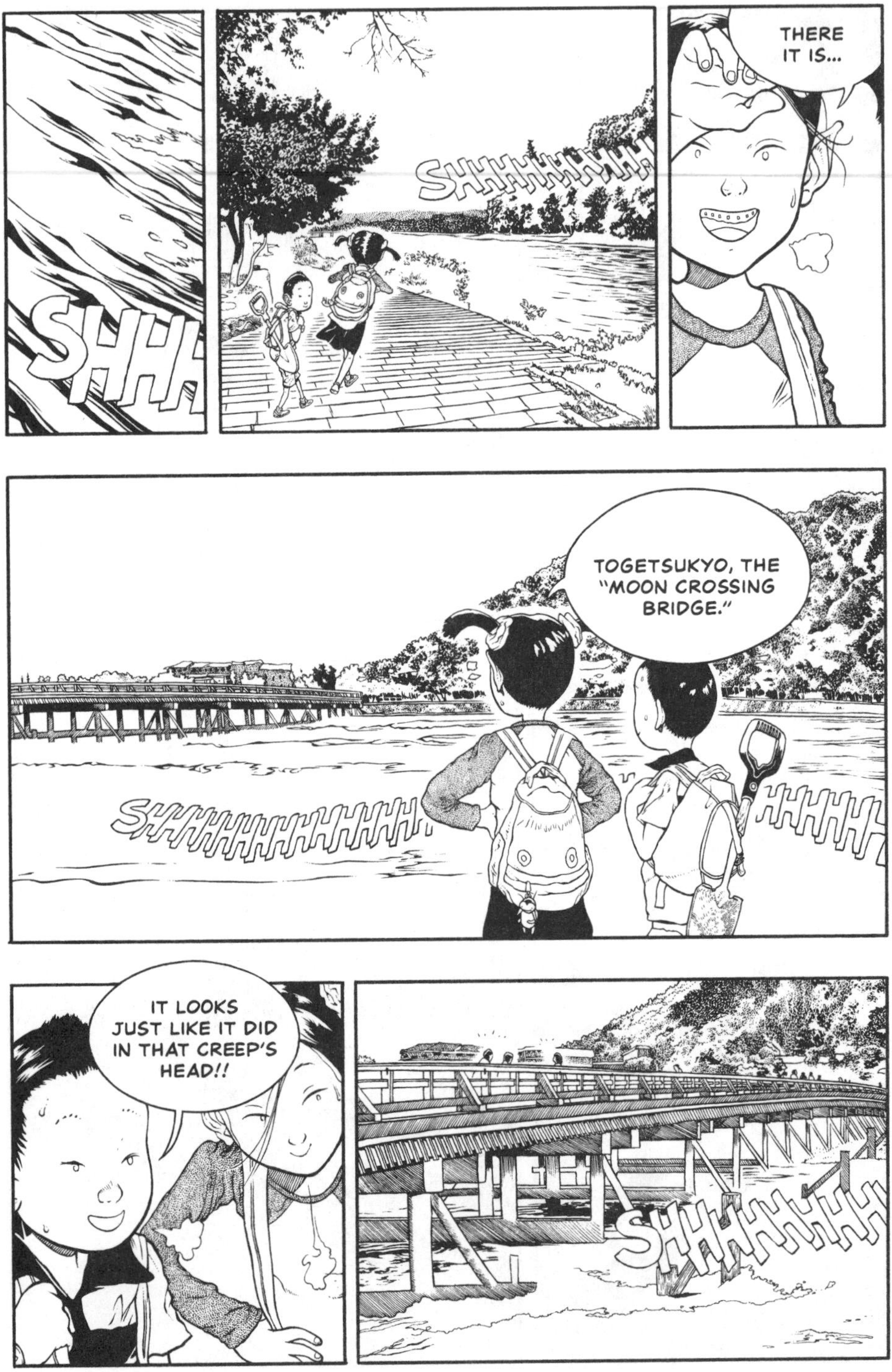
SHHH
SHHHHHHHHH
THERE IT IS...
TOGETSUKYO, THE "MOON CROSSING BRIDGE."
SHHHHHHHHHHHHHHHHHHHH
IT LOOKS JUST LIKE IT DID IN THAT CREEP'S HEAD!!
SHHHHHHHH

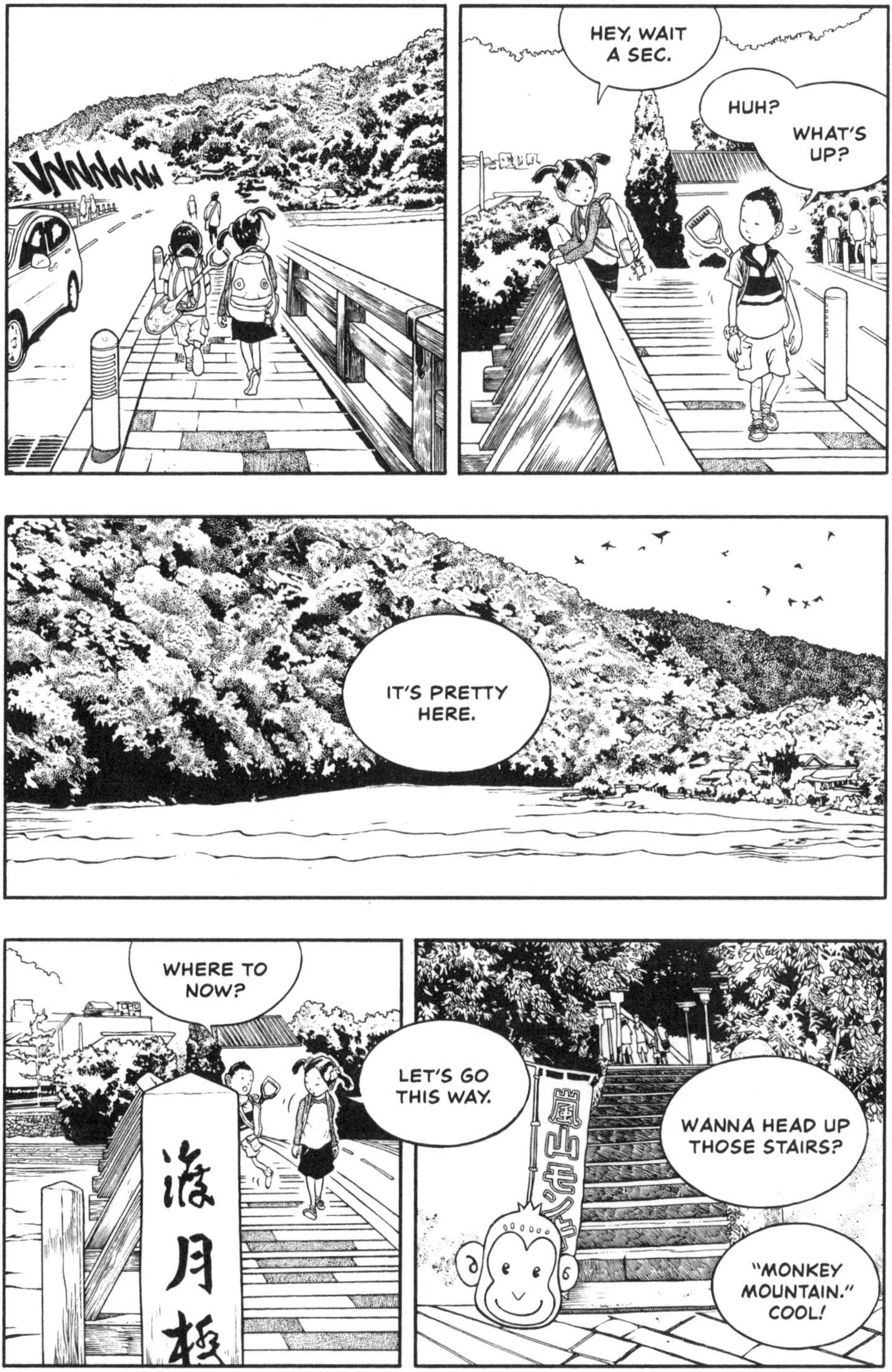
VNNNNNN
HEY, WAIT A SEC.
HUH?
WHAT'S UP?
IT'S PRETTY HERE.
WHERE TO NOW?
LET'S GO THIS WAY.
渡月橋
WANNA HEAD UP THOSE STAIRS?
"MONKEY MOUNTAIN." COOL!

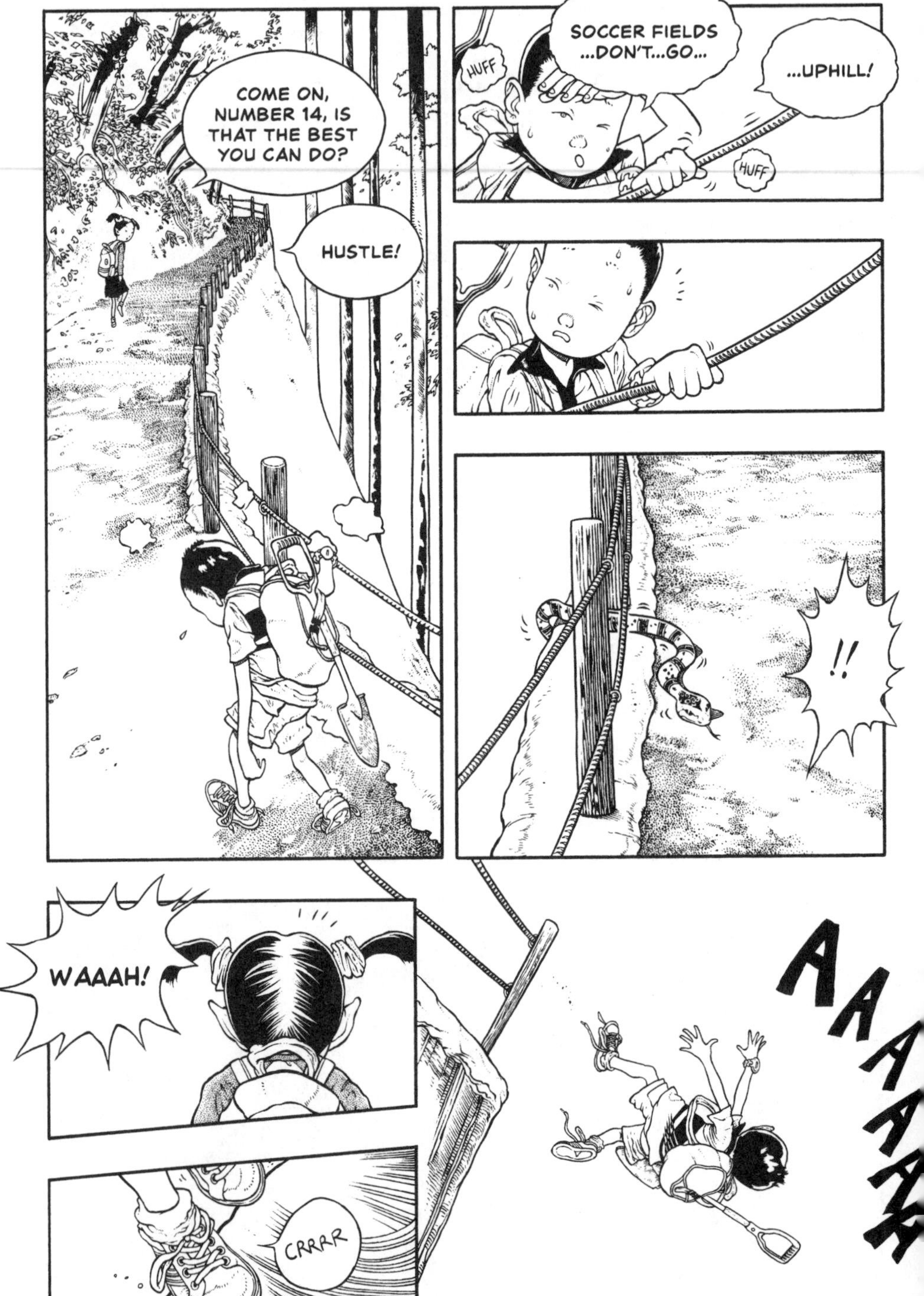
COME ON, NUMBER 14, IS THAT THE BEST YOU CAN DO?
HUSTLE!
HUFF
SOCCER FIELDS ...DON'T...GO...
...UPHILL!
HUFF
!!
WAAAH!
CRRRR
AAAAAAA

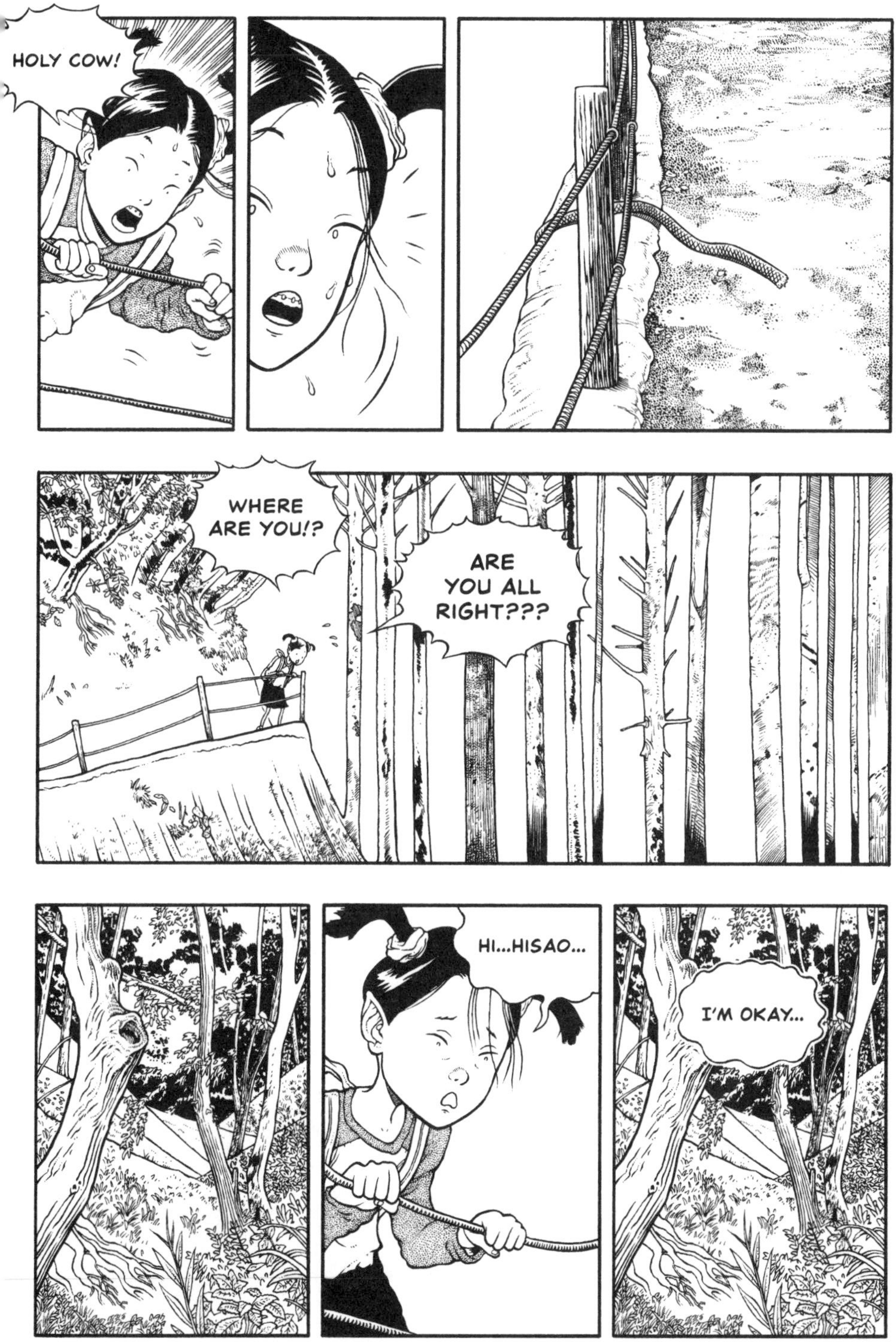
HOLY COW!
WHERE ARE YOU!?
ARE YOU ALL RIGHT???
HI...HISAO...
I'M OKAY...

UGHHH...

I'M ALL RIGHT, JUST A FEW SCRATCHES.

HOLD ON! I'M COMING DOWN TO GET YOU.

HANG IN THERE!

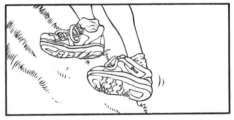

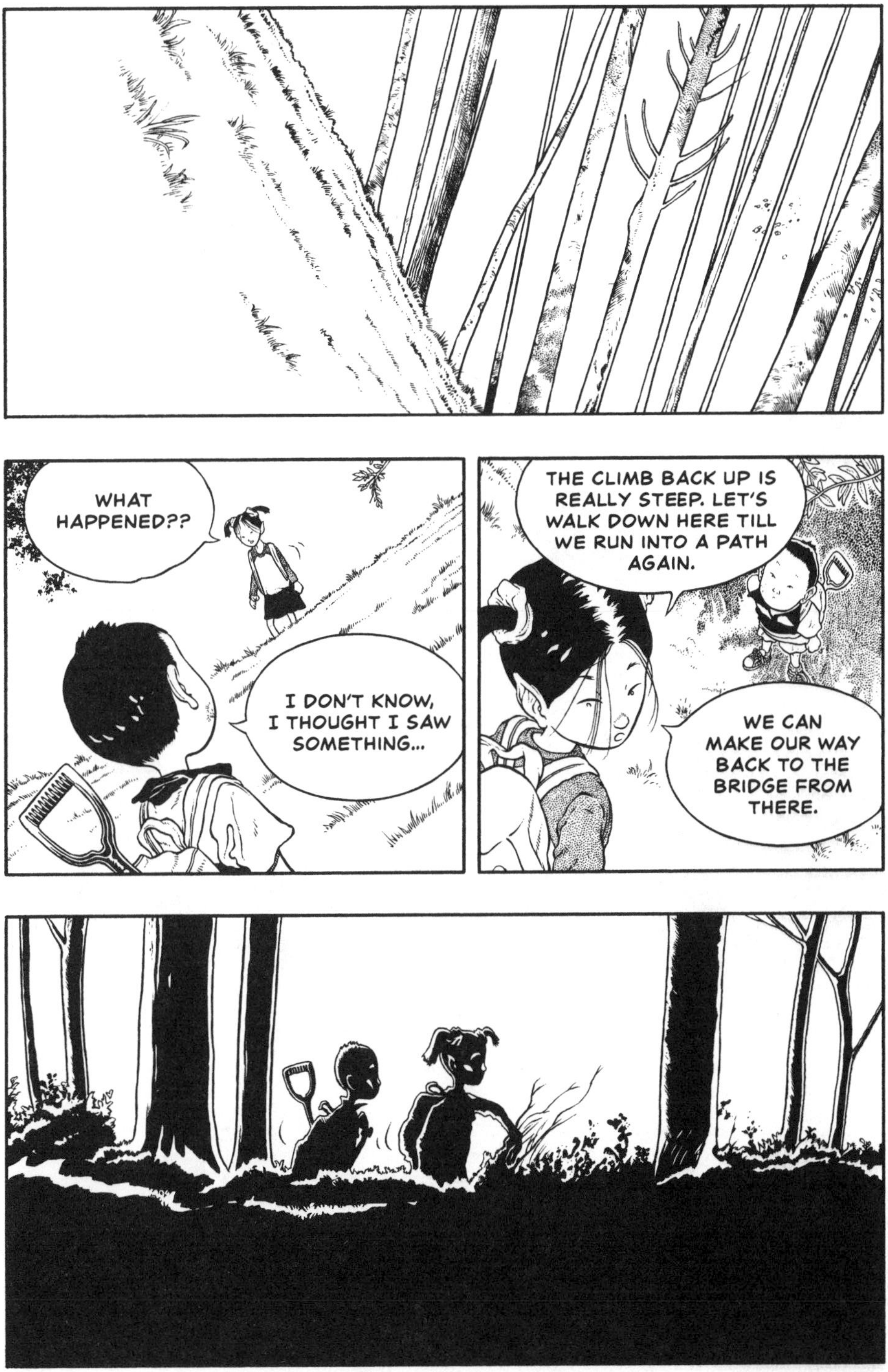
WHAT HAPPENED??
I DON'T KNOW, I THOUGHT I SAW SOMETHING...
THE CLIMB BACK UP IS REALLY STEEP. LET'S WALK DOWN HERE TILL WE RUN INTO A PATH AGAIN.
WE CAN MAKE OUR WAY BACK TO THE BRIDGE FROM THERE.

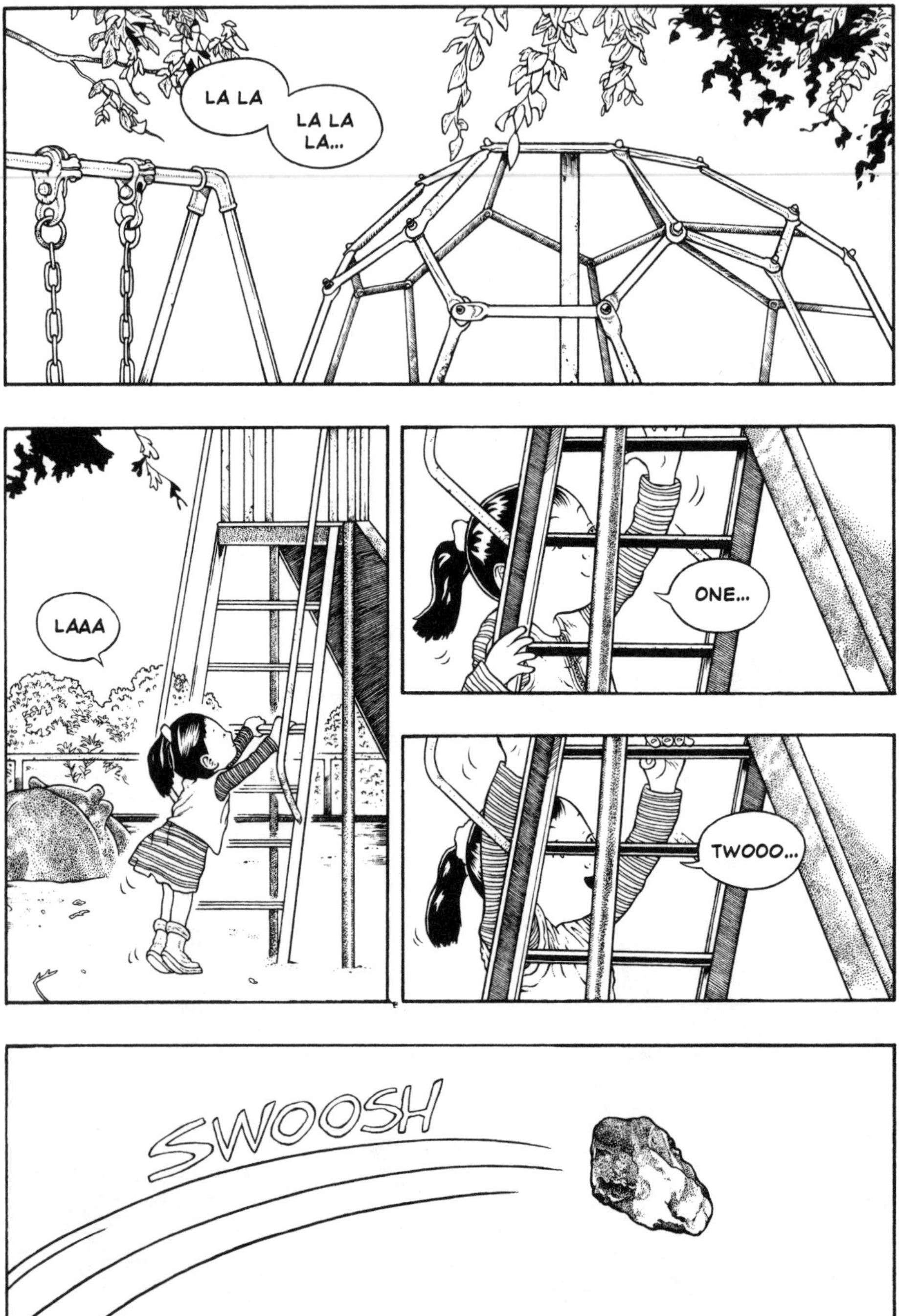
LA LA
LA LA LA...
LAAA
ONE...
TWOOO...
SWOOSH

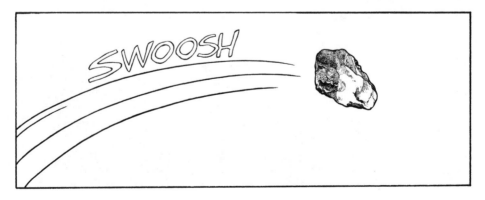

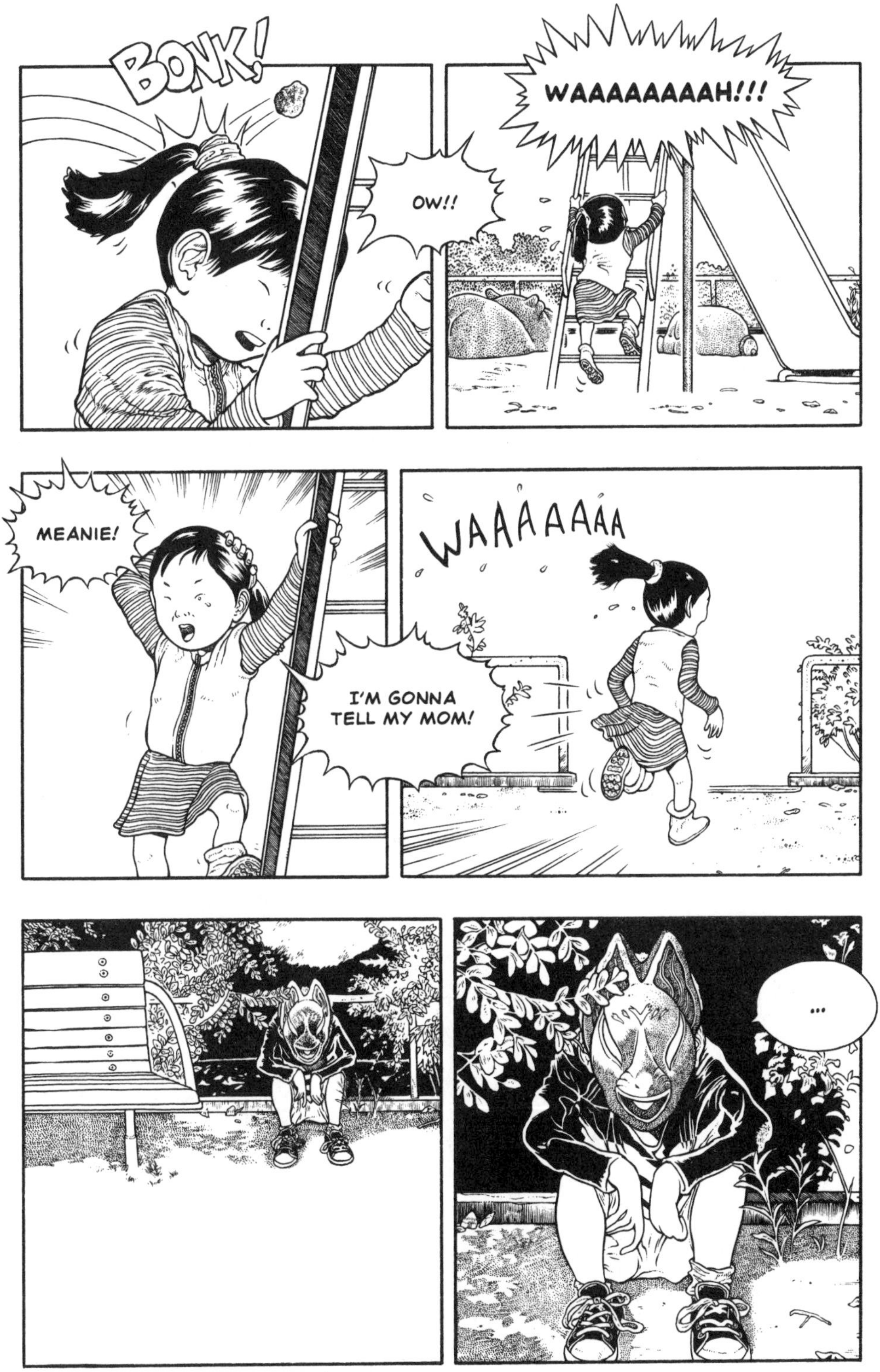
BONK!
OW!!
WAAAAAAAAH!!!
MEANIE!
I'M GONNA TELL MY MOM!
WAAAAAAA
...

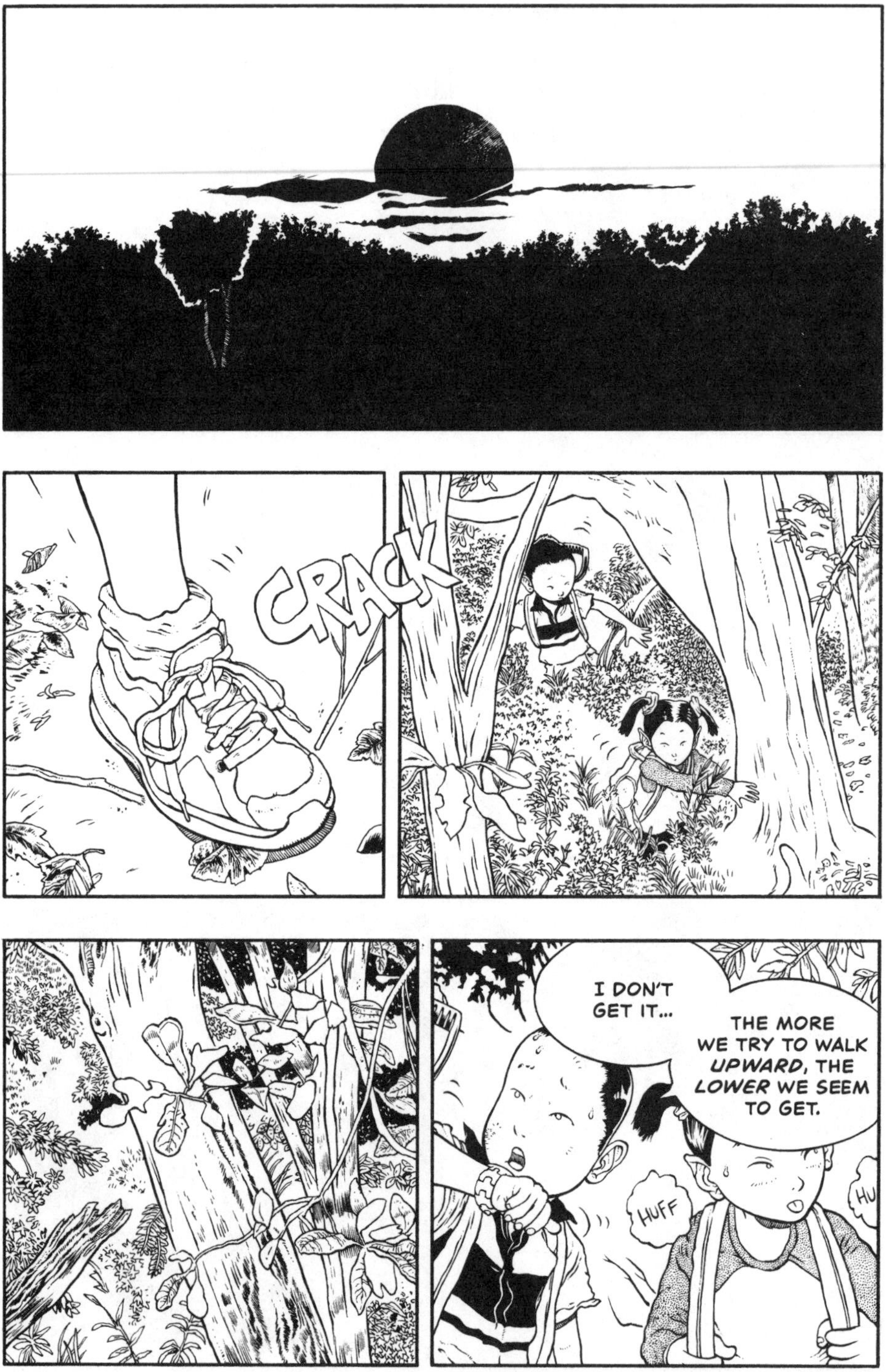
CRACK
I DON'T GET IT...
THE MORE WE TRY TO WALK *UPWARD*, THE *LOWER* WE SEEM TO GET.
HUFF

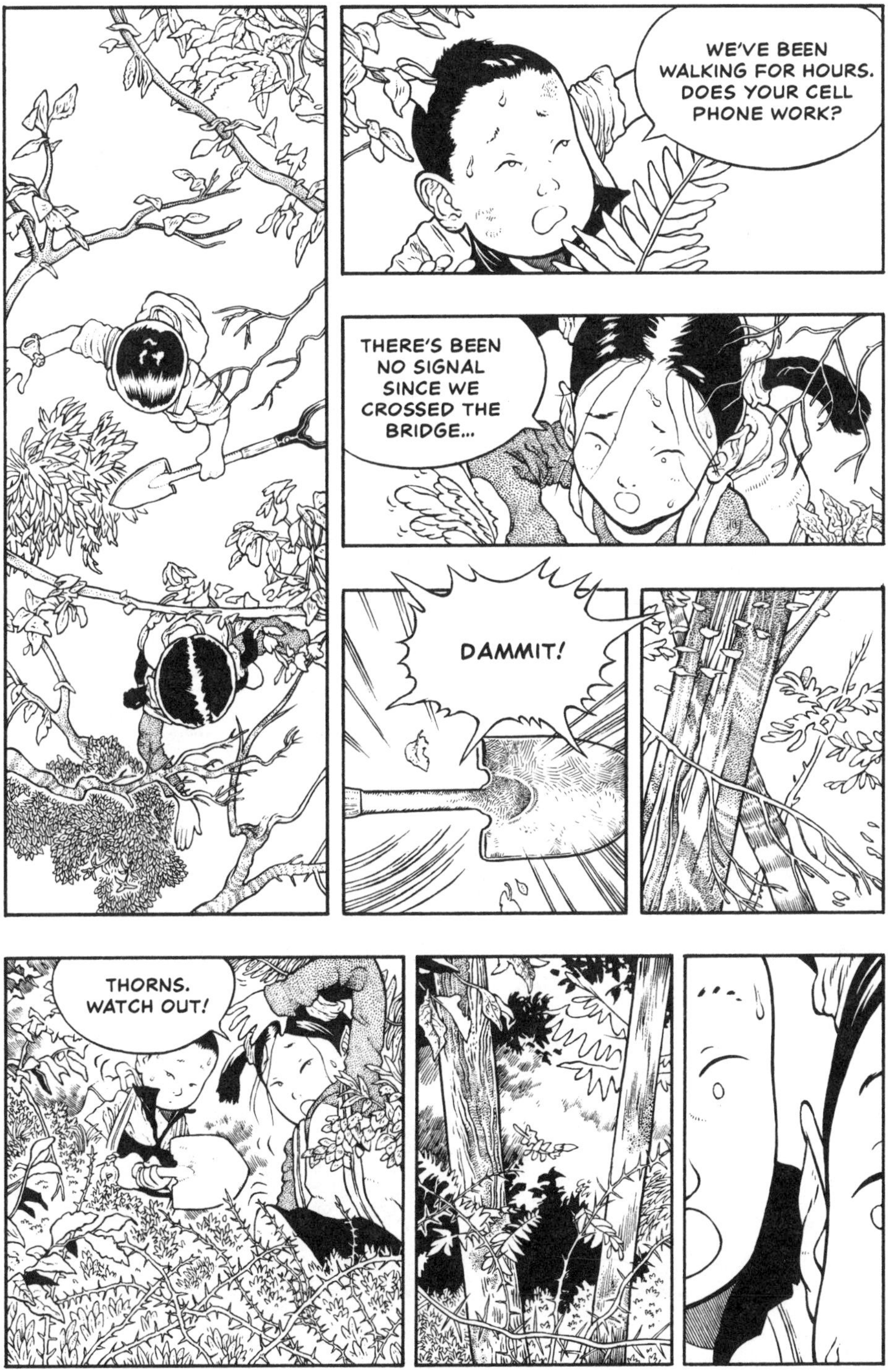
WE'VE BEEN WALKING FOR HOURS. DOES YOUR CELL PHONE WORK?
THERE'S BEEN NO SIGNAL SINCE WE CROSSED THE BRIDGE...
DAMMIT!
THORNS. WATCH OUT!
...

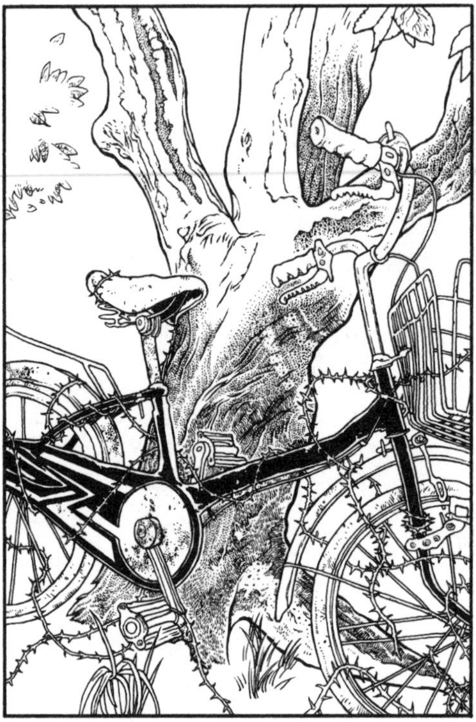

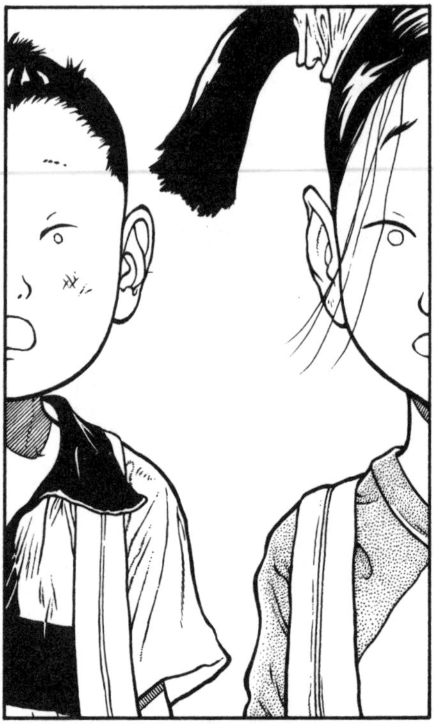

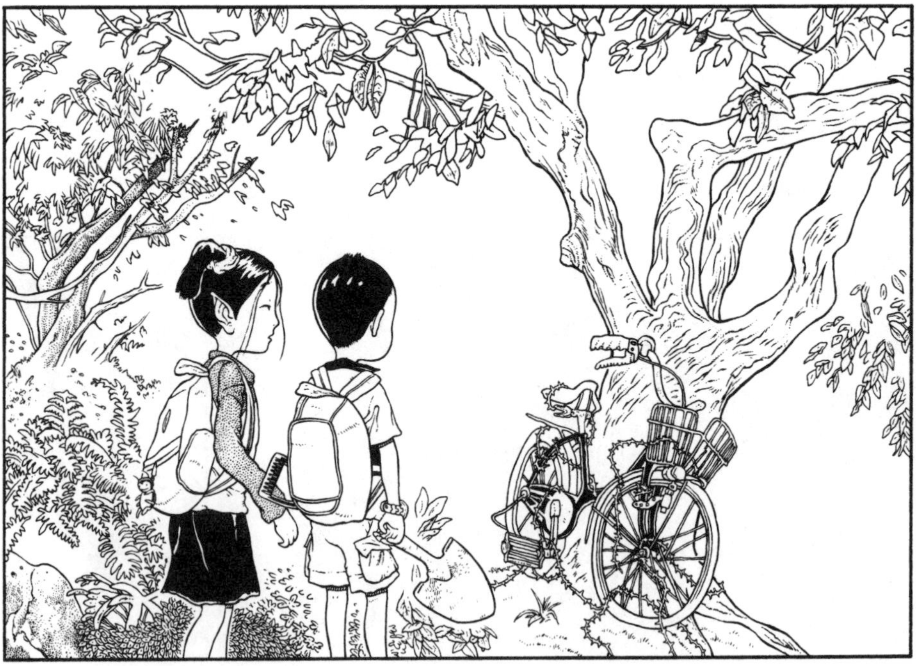

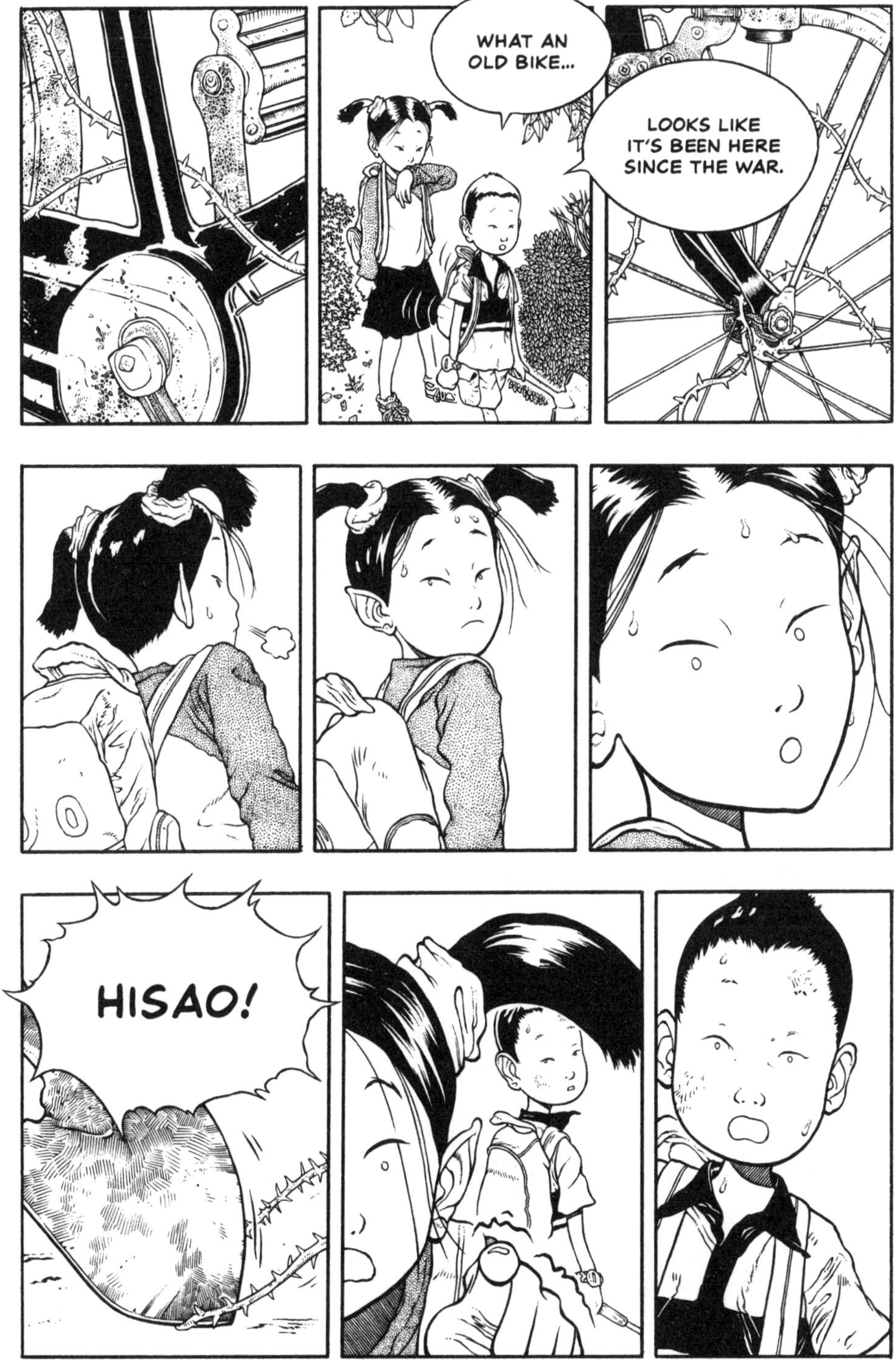
WHAT AN OLD BIKE...
LOOKS LIKE IT'S BEEN HERE SINCE THE WAR.
HISAO!

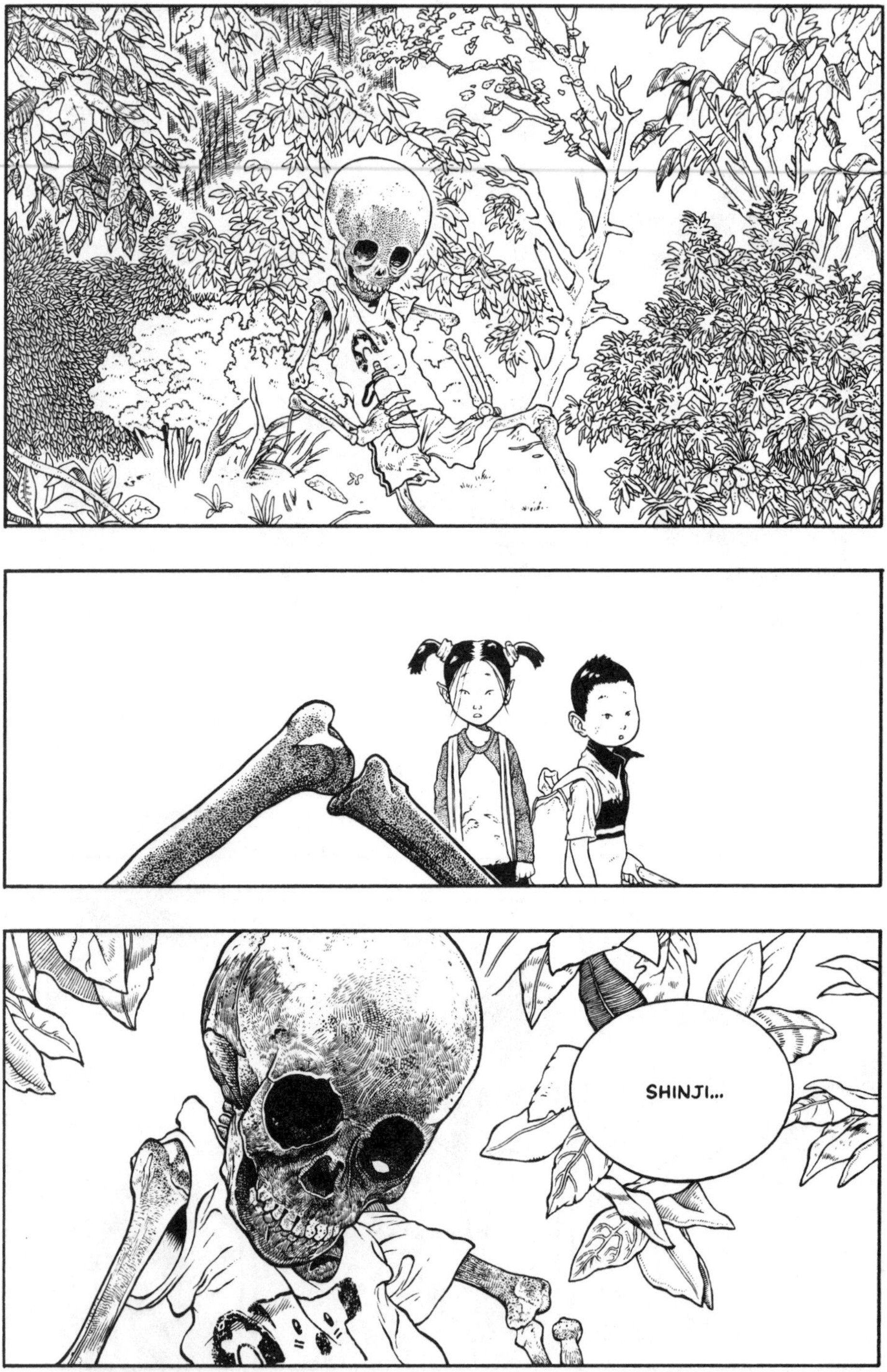
SHINJI...

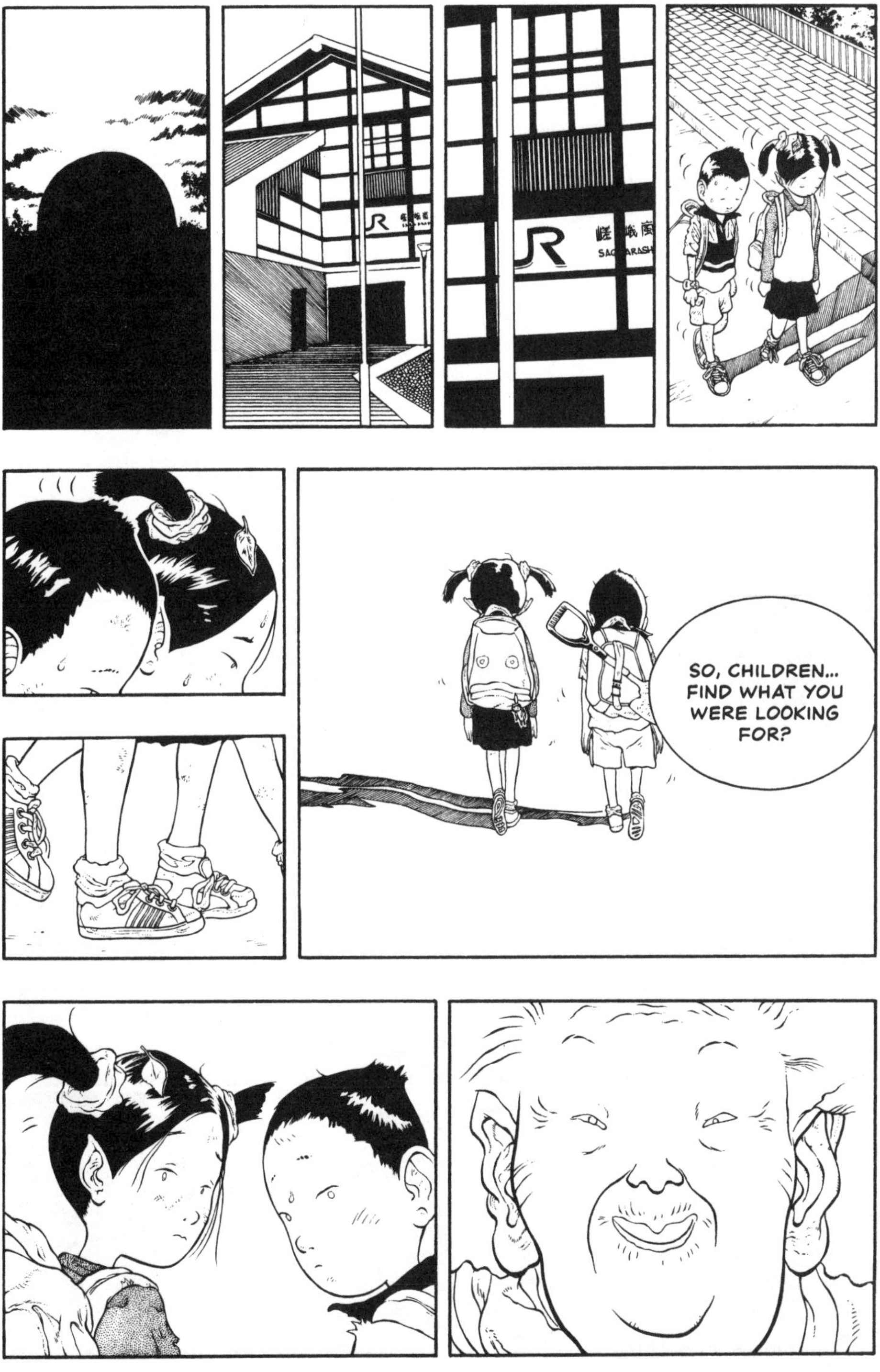
SO, CHILDREN... FIND WHAT YOU WERE LOOKING FOR?

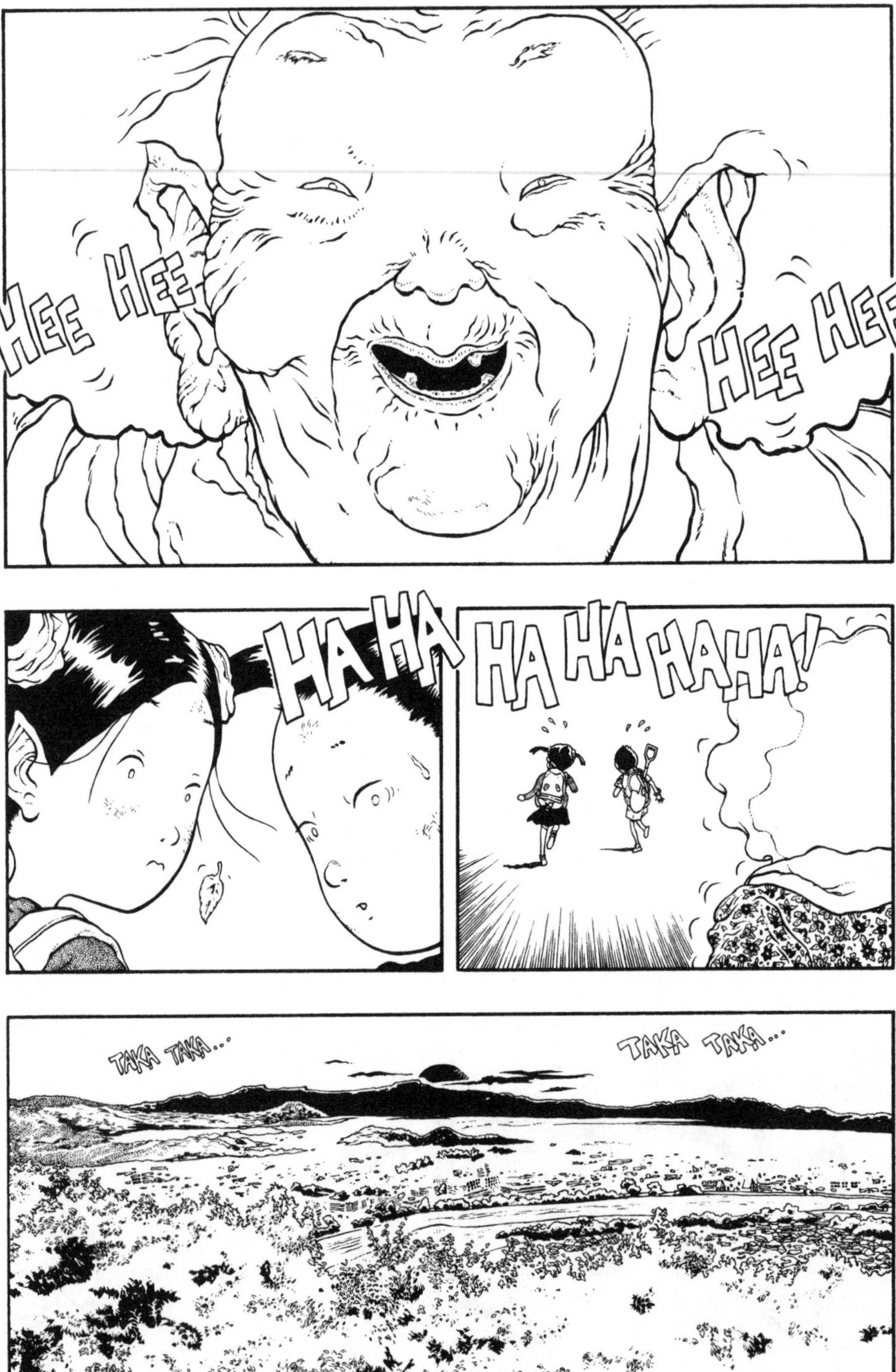
HEE HEE
HEE HEE
HA HA
HA HA HAHA!
TAKA TAKA...
TAKA TAKA...

Chapter 8:
Hisao's Dream

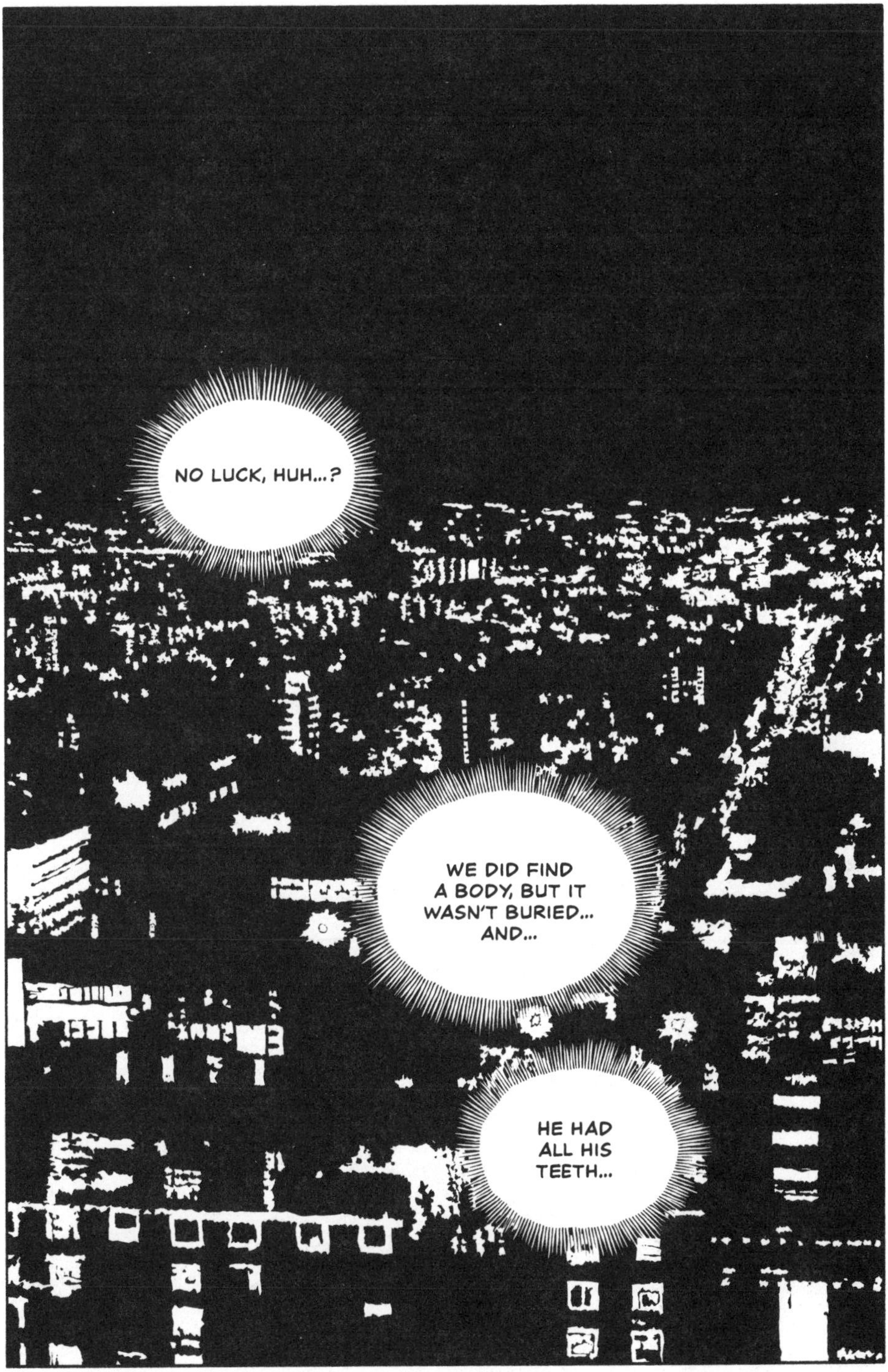
NO LUCK, HUH...?
WE DID FIND A BODY, BUT IT WASN'T BURIED... AND...
HE HAD ALL HIS TEETH...

THAT BOY...
HE MUST HAVE HAD
AN ACCIDENT. OR
GOTTEN LOST IN
THE FOREST.

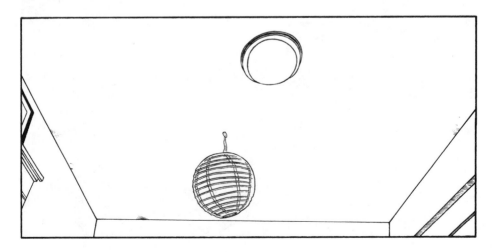

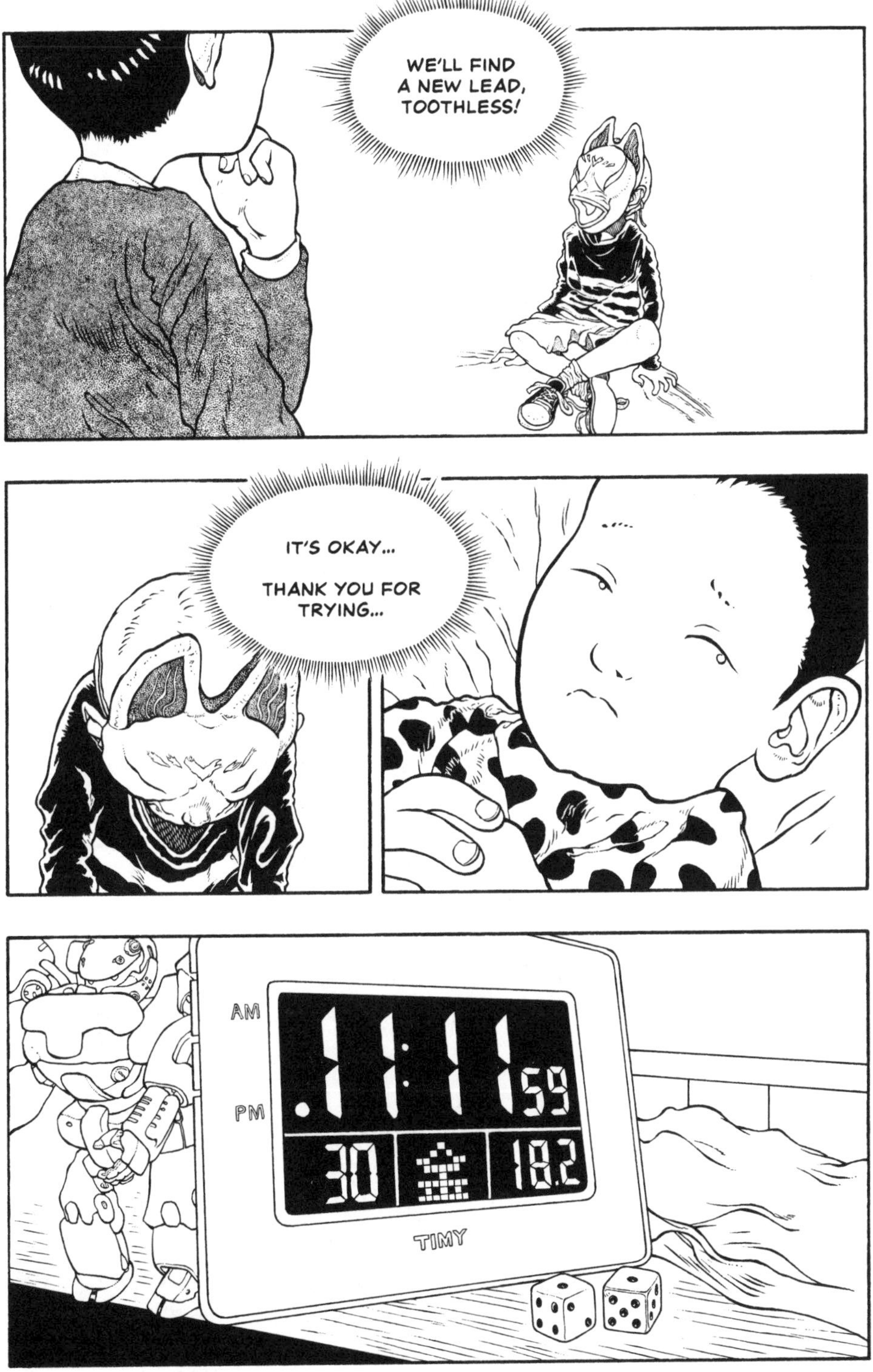
WE'LL FIND A NEW LEAD, TOOTHLESS!
IT'S OKAY...
THANK YOU FOR TRYING...
AM
PM
11:11 59
30
18.2
TIMY

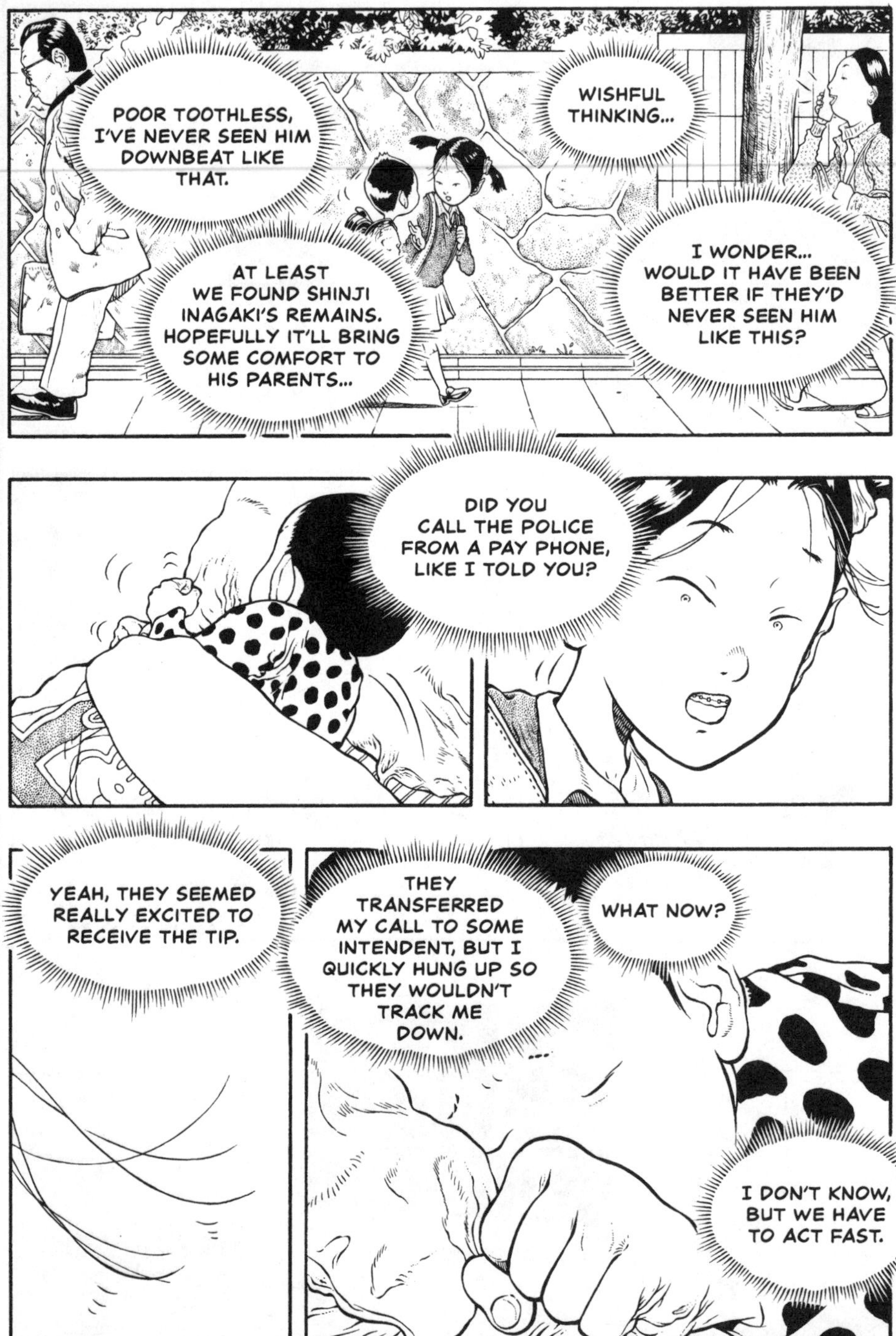
POOR TOOTHLESS, I'VE NEVER SEEN HIM DOWNBEAT LIKE THAT.
WISHFUL THINKING...
AT LEAST WE FOUND SHINJI INAGAKI'S REMAINS. HOPEFULLY IT'LL BRING SOME COMFORT TO HIS PARENTS...
I WONDER... WOULD IT HAVE BEEN BETTER IF THEY'D NEVER SEEN HIM LIKE THIS?
DID YOU CALL THE POLICE FROM A PAY PHONE, LIKE I TOLD YOU?
YEAH, THEY SEEMED REALLY EXCITED TO RECEIVE THE TIP.
THEY TRANSFERRED MY CALL TO SOME INTENDENT, BUT I QUICKLY HUNG UP SO THEY WOULDN'T TRACK ME DOWN.
WHAT NOW?
...
I DON'T KNOW, BUT WE HAVE TO ACT FAST.

MASATAKE'S LIFE IS IN DANGER. HIS BODY MIGHT NOT HOLD ON MUCH LONGER.
IF ONLY TOOTHLESS KNEW MORE!...

[redacted]

[redacted]

[redacted]

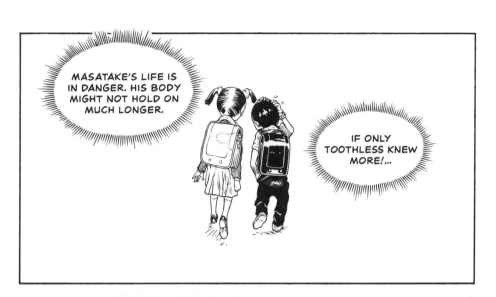

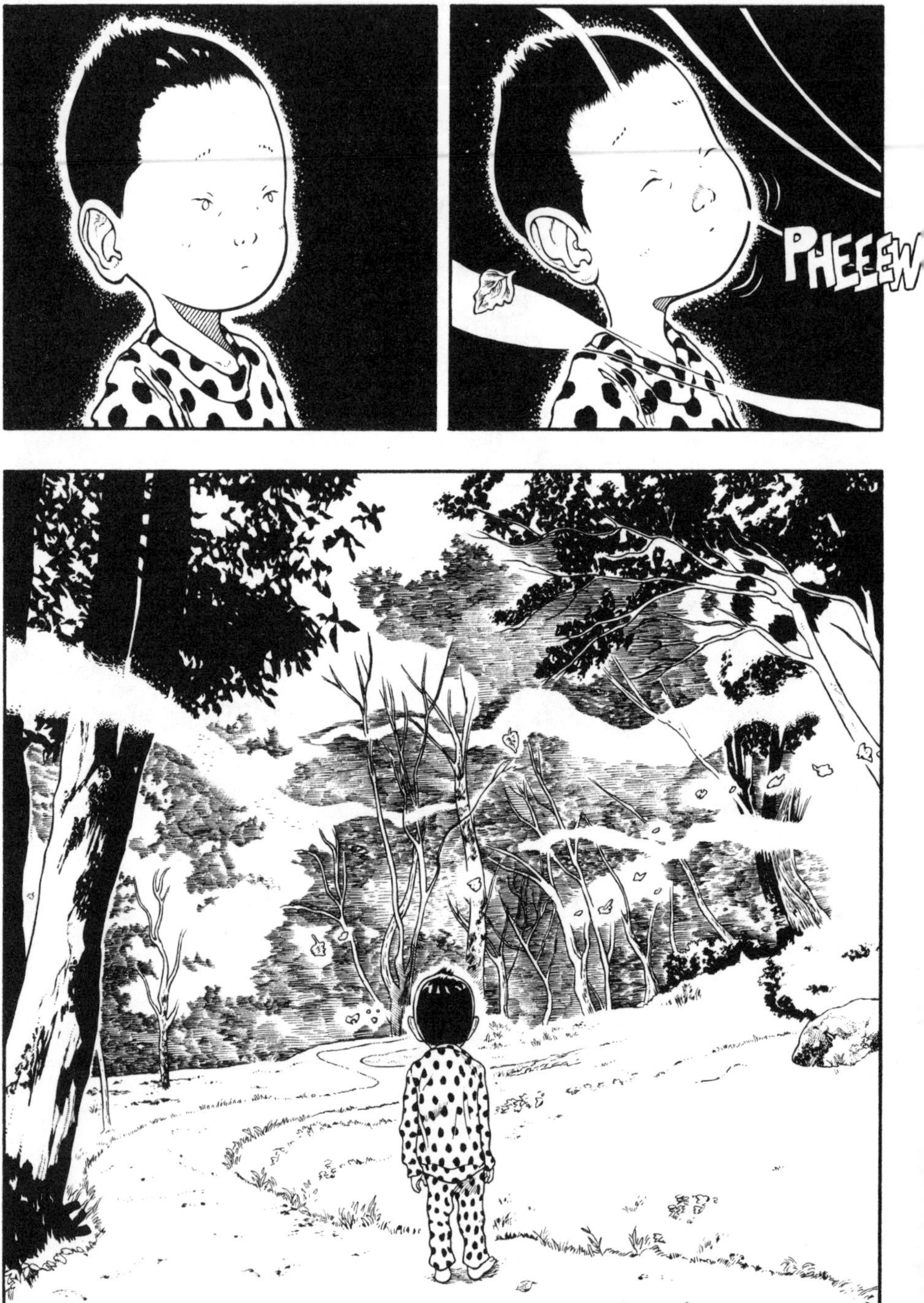
PHEEEW

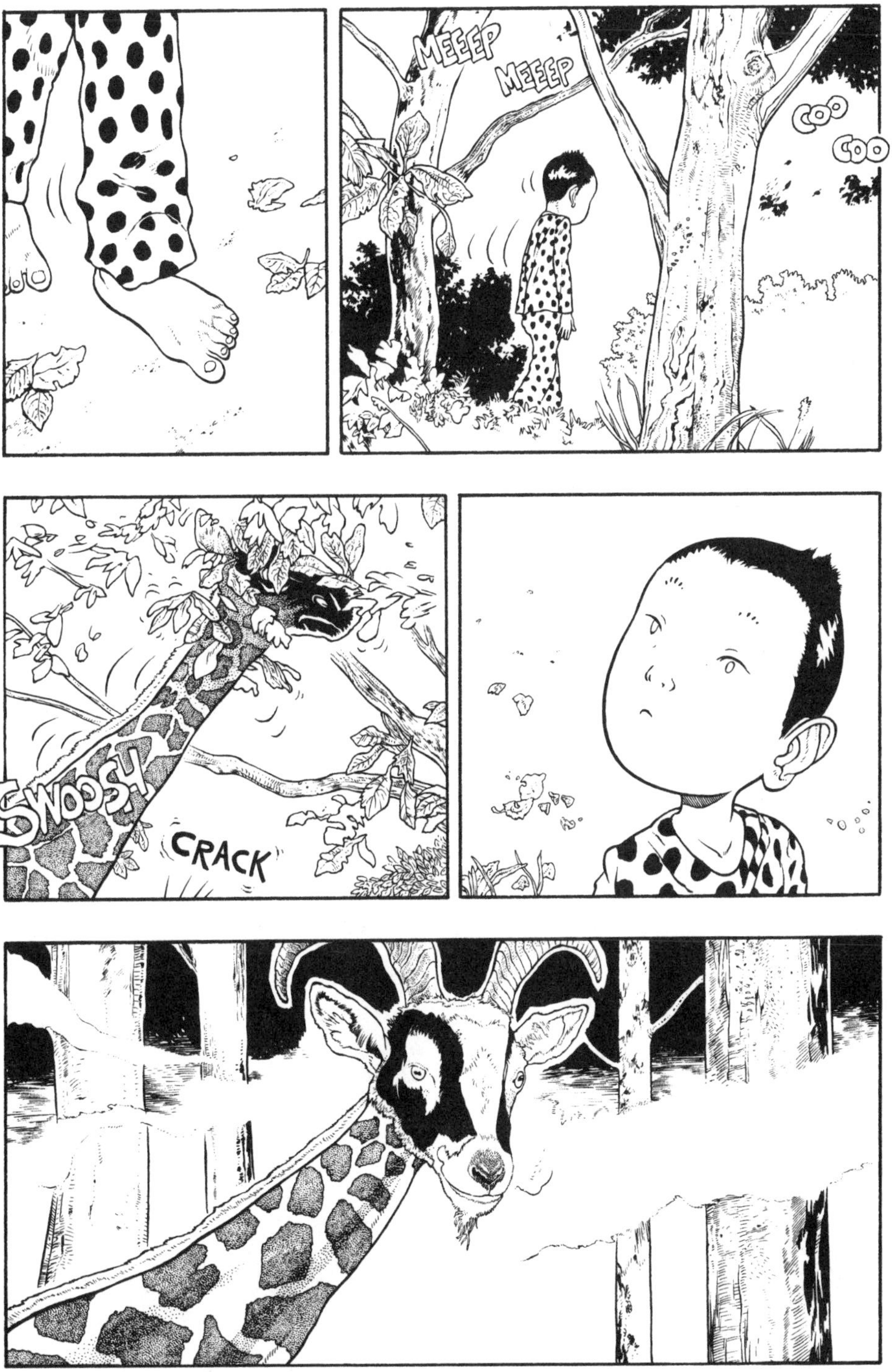
MEEEP
MEEEP
COO
COO
SWOOSH
CRACK

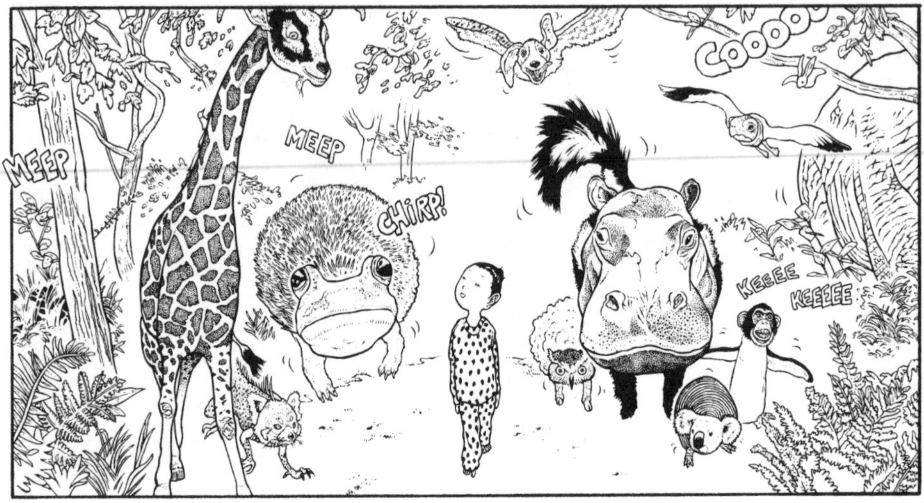
MEEP
MEEP
CHIRP!
COOOO
KEEEE
KEEEEE

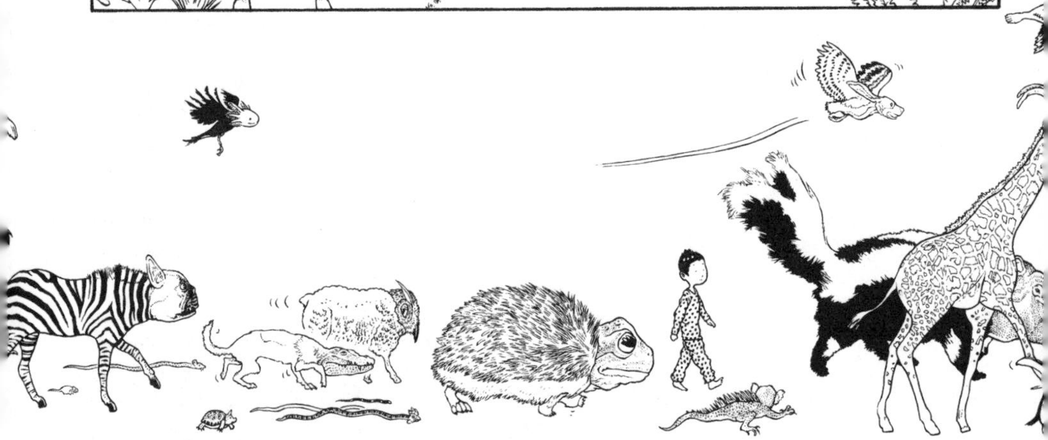

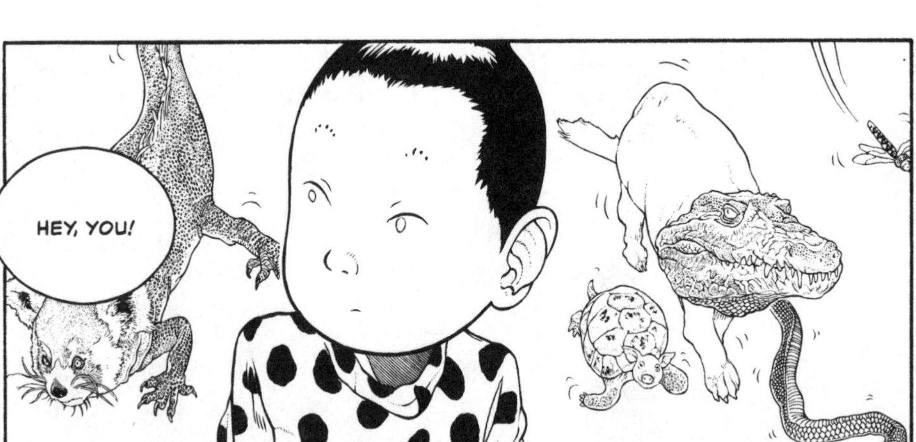
HEY, YOU!

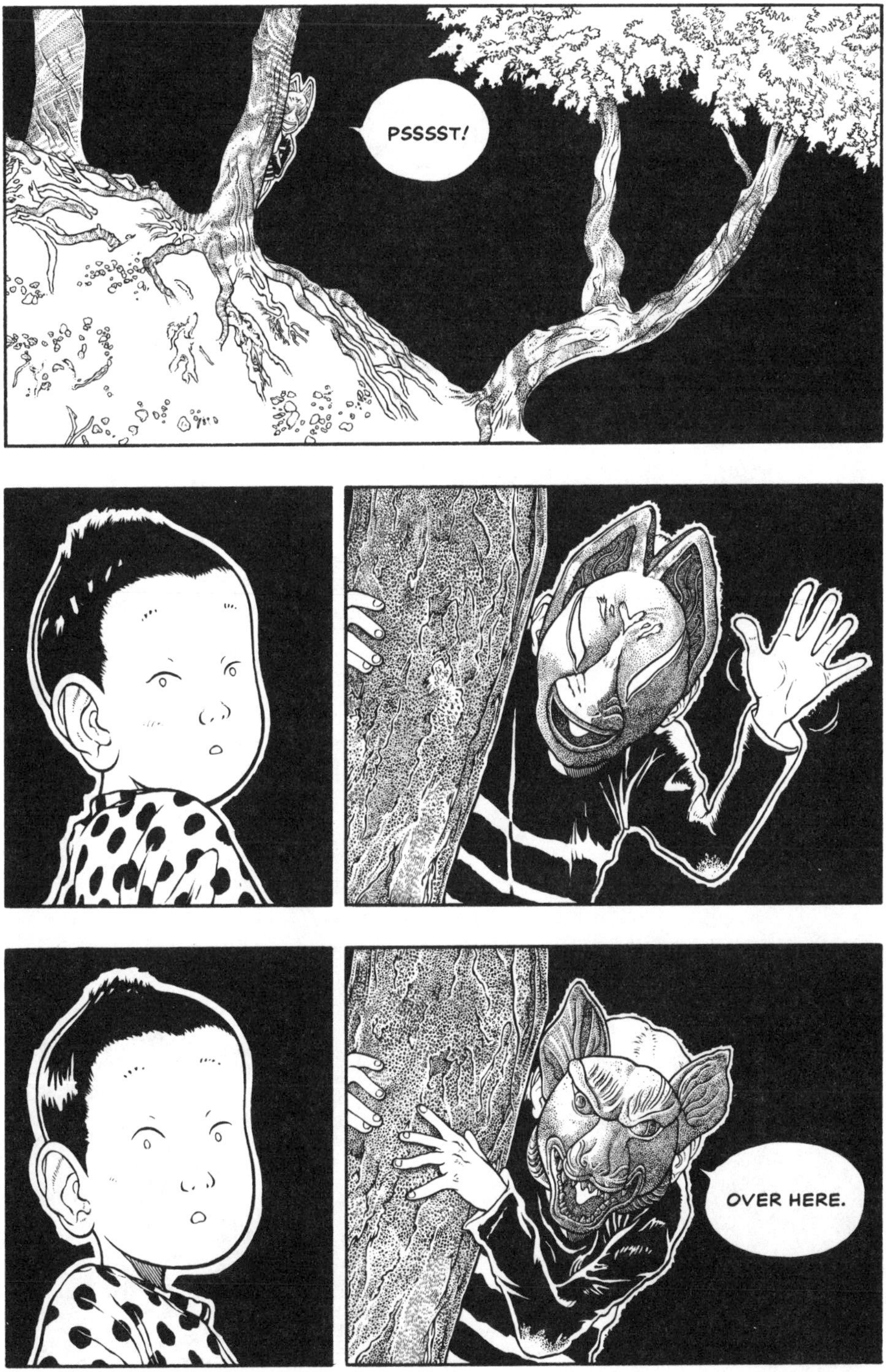
PSSSST!
OVER HERE.

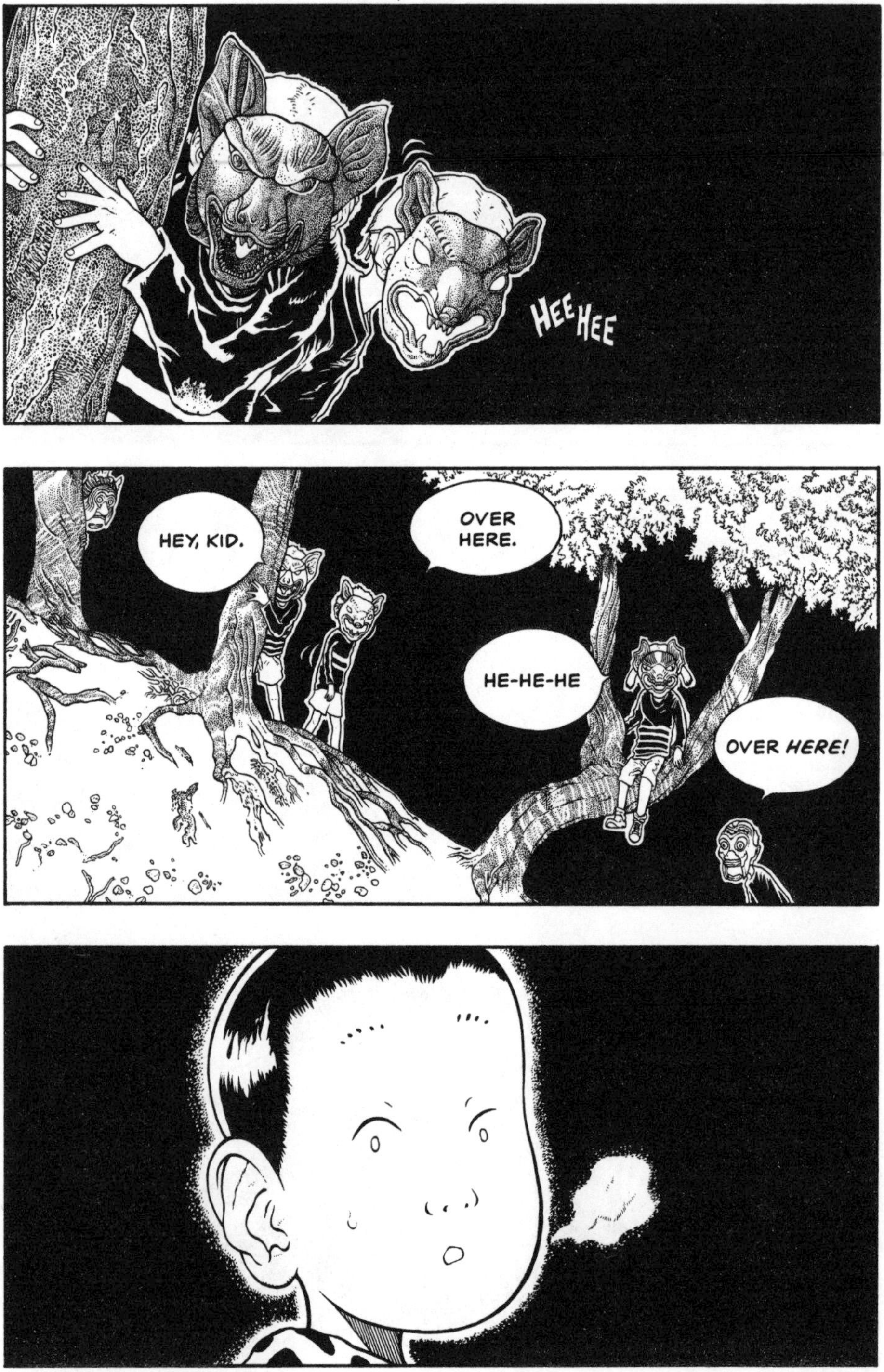
HEE HEE
HEY, KID.
OVER HERE.
HE-HE-HE
OVER *HERE!*

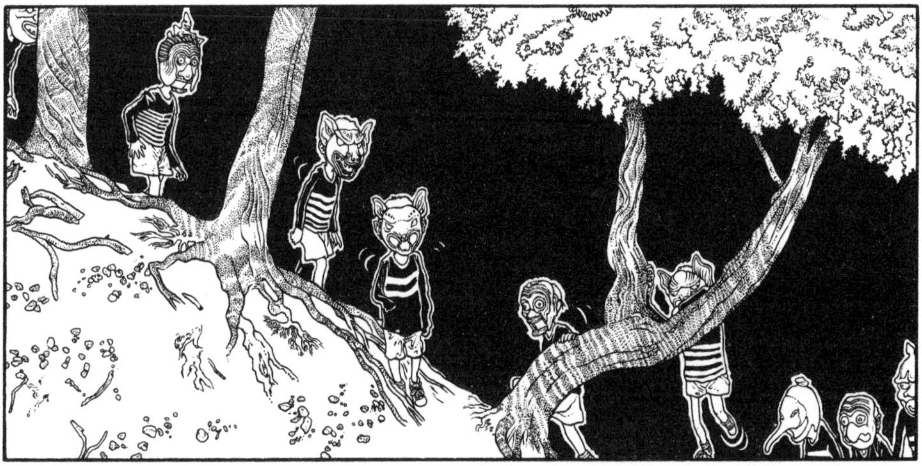

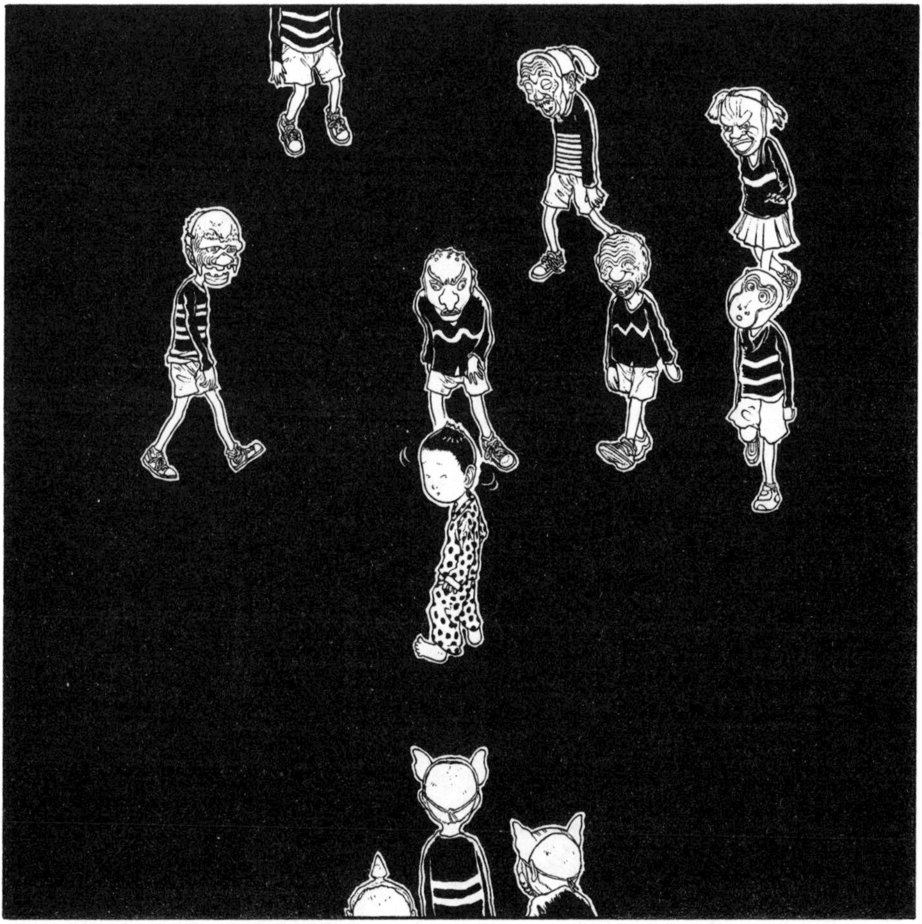

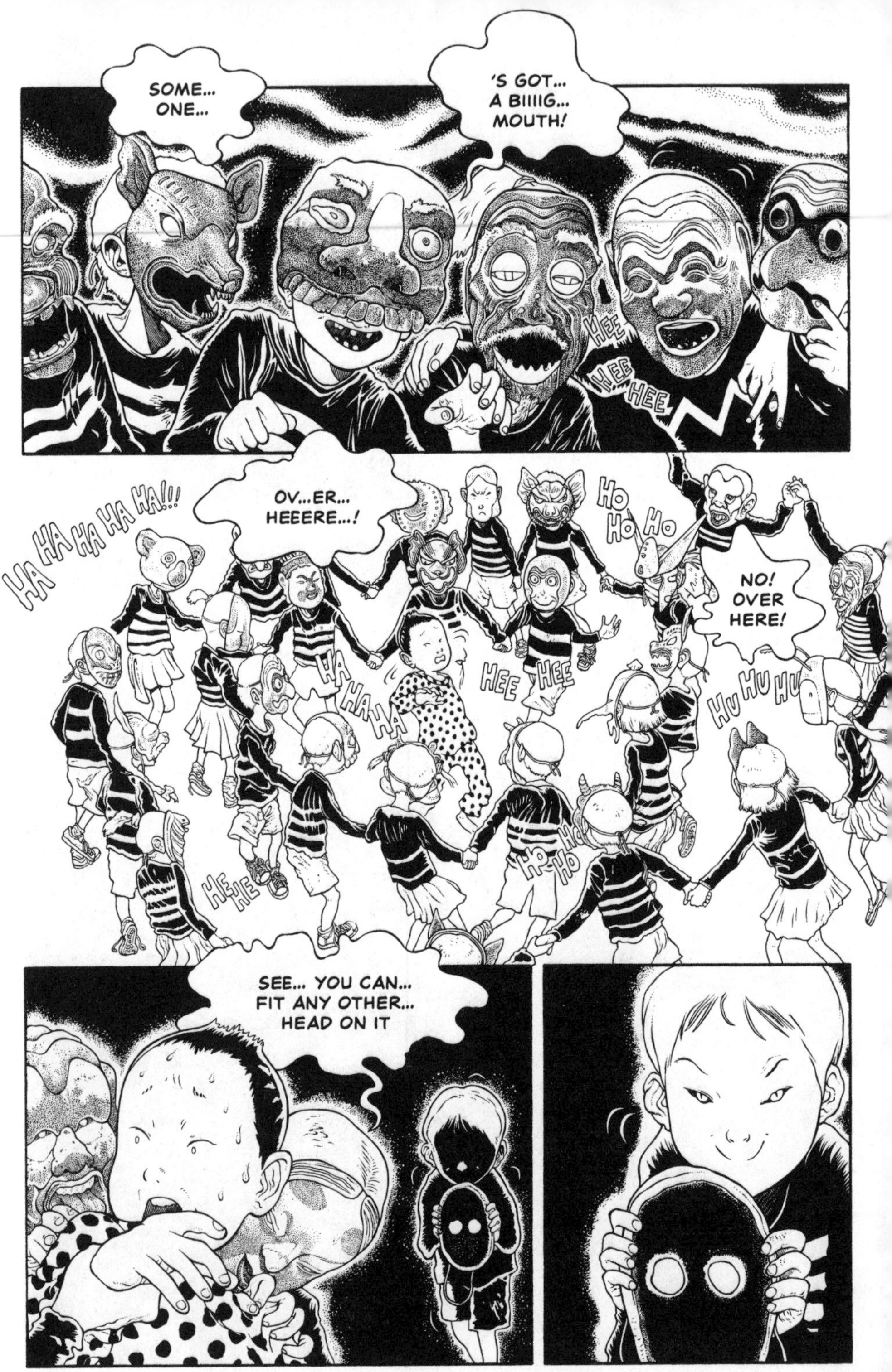
SOME... ONE...
'S GOT... A BIIIG... MOUTH!
HEE HEE HEE
HA HA HA HA HA HA!!!
OV...ER... HEEERE...!
HO HO HO
NO! OVER HERE!
HA HA HA
HEE HEE
HU HU HU
HE HE
HO HO HO
SEE... YOU CAN... FIT ANY OTHER... HEAD ON IT

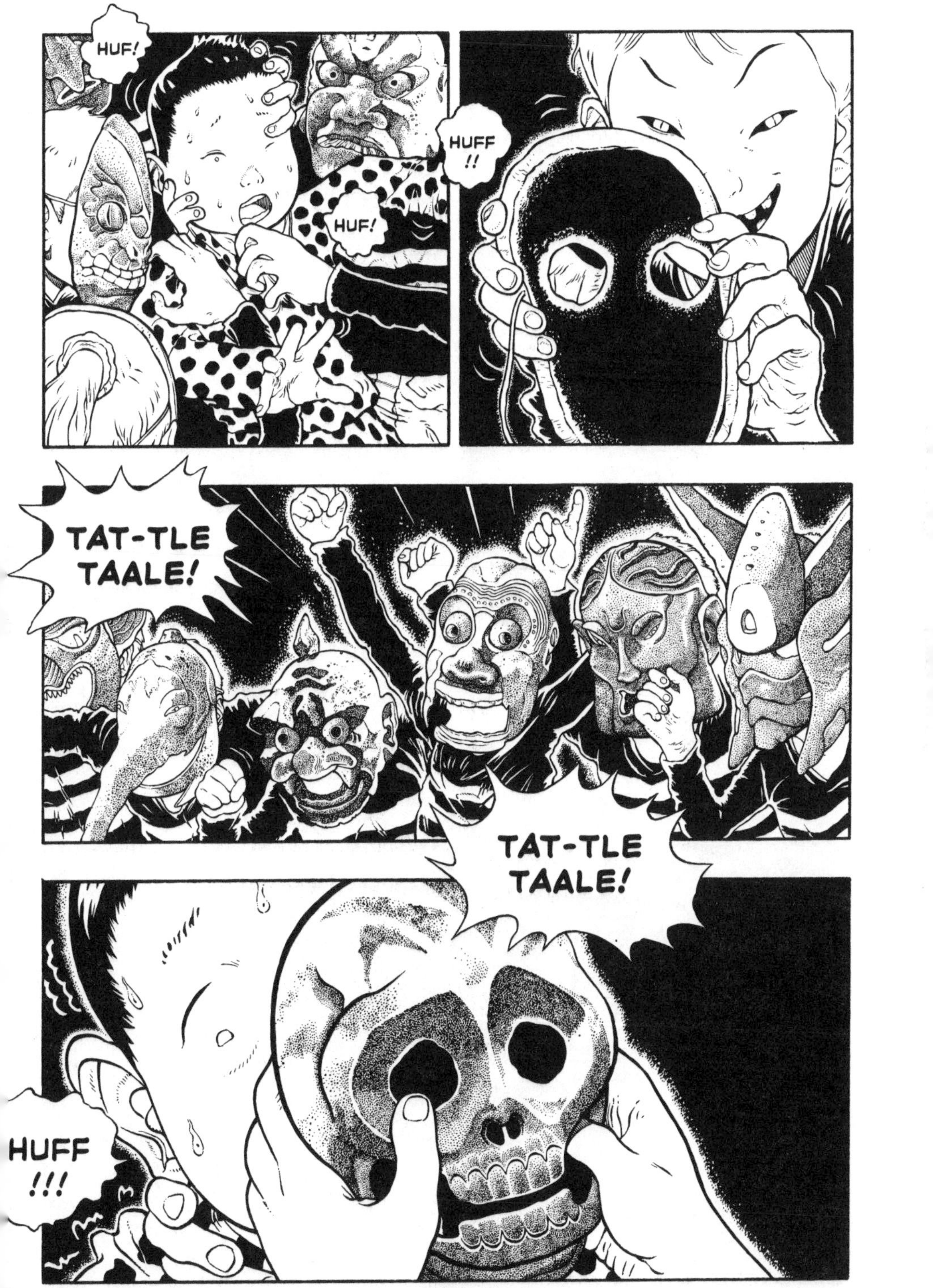
HUF!
HUFF !!
HUF!
TAT-TLE TAALE!
TAT-TLE TAALE!
HUFF !!!

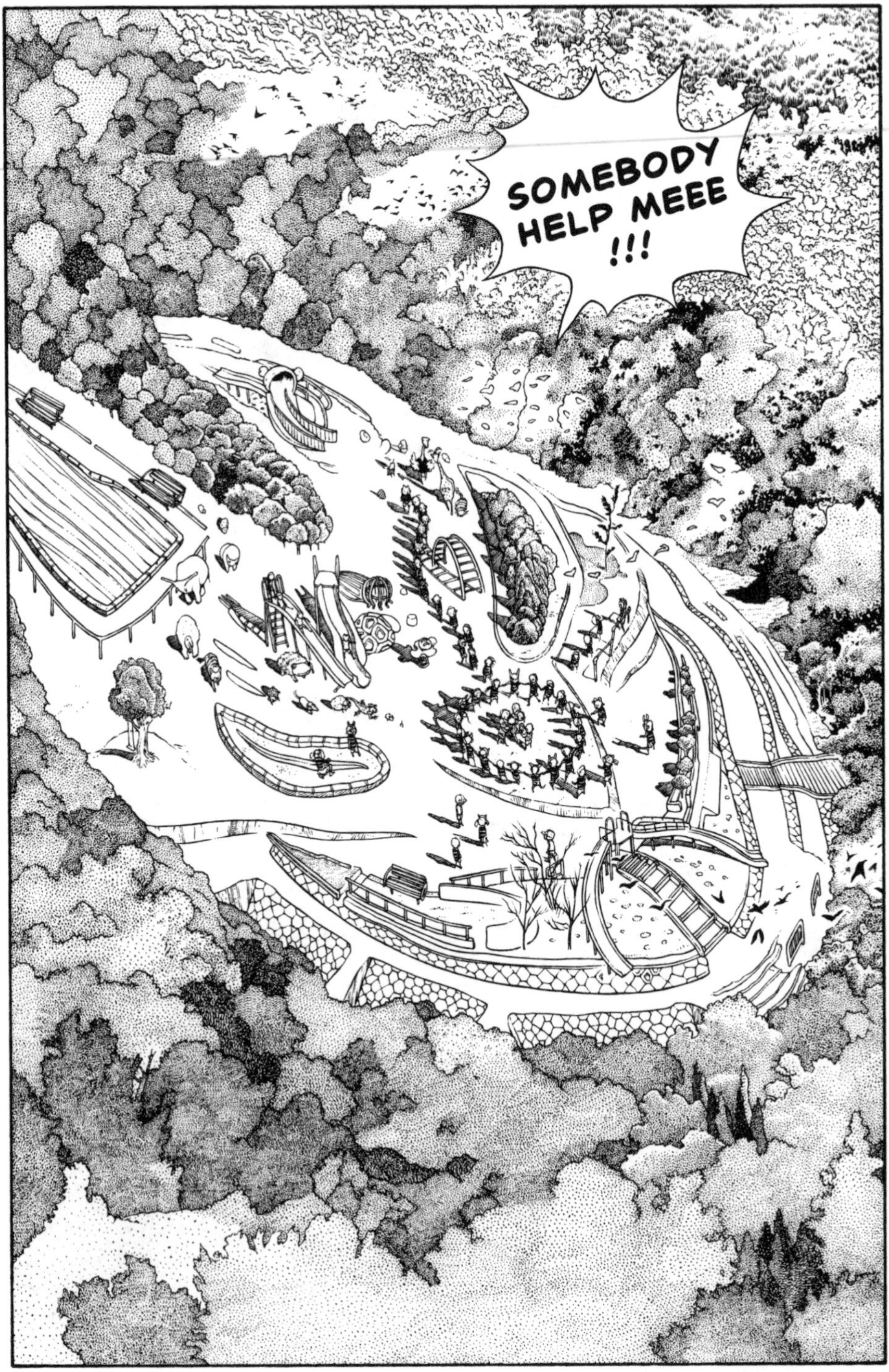
SOMEBODY HELP MEEE !!!

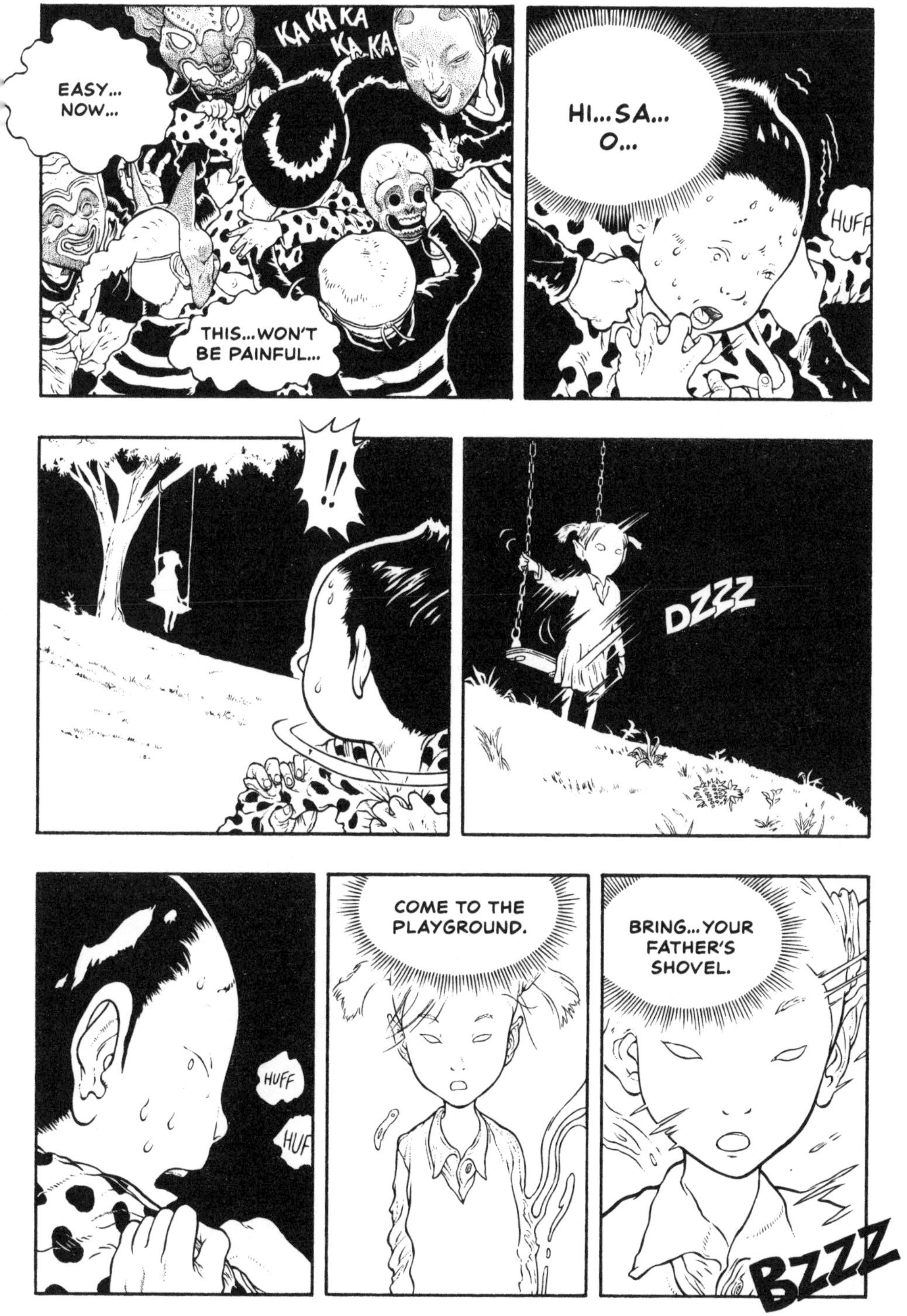
EASY... NOW...
KA KA KA KA KA.
THIS...WON'T BE PAINFUL...
HI...SA... O...
HUFF
!!
DZZZ
HUFF
HUF
COME TO THE PLAYGROUND.
BRING...YOUR FATHER'S SHOVEL.
BZZZ

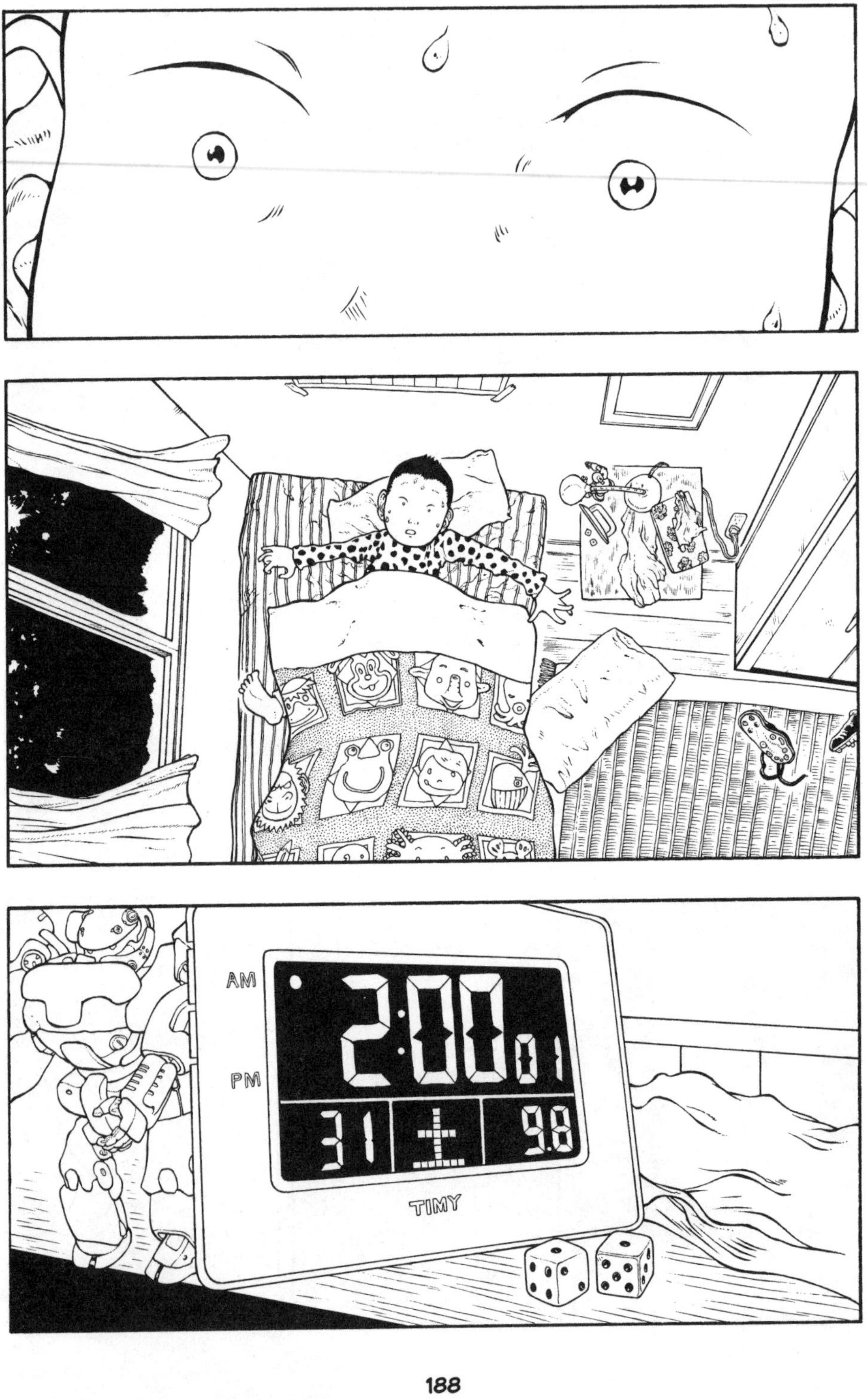
AM
PM
2:00 01
31 土 9.8
TIMY

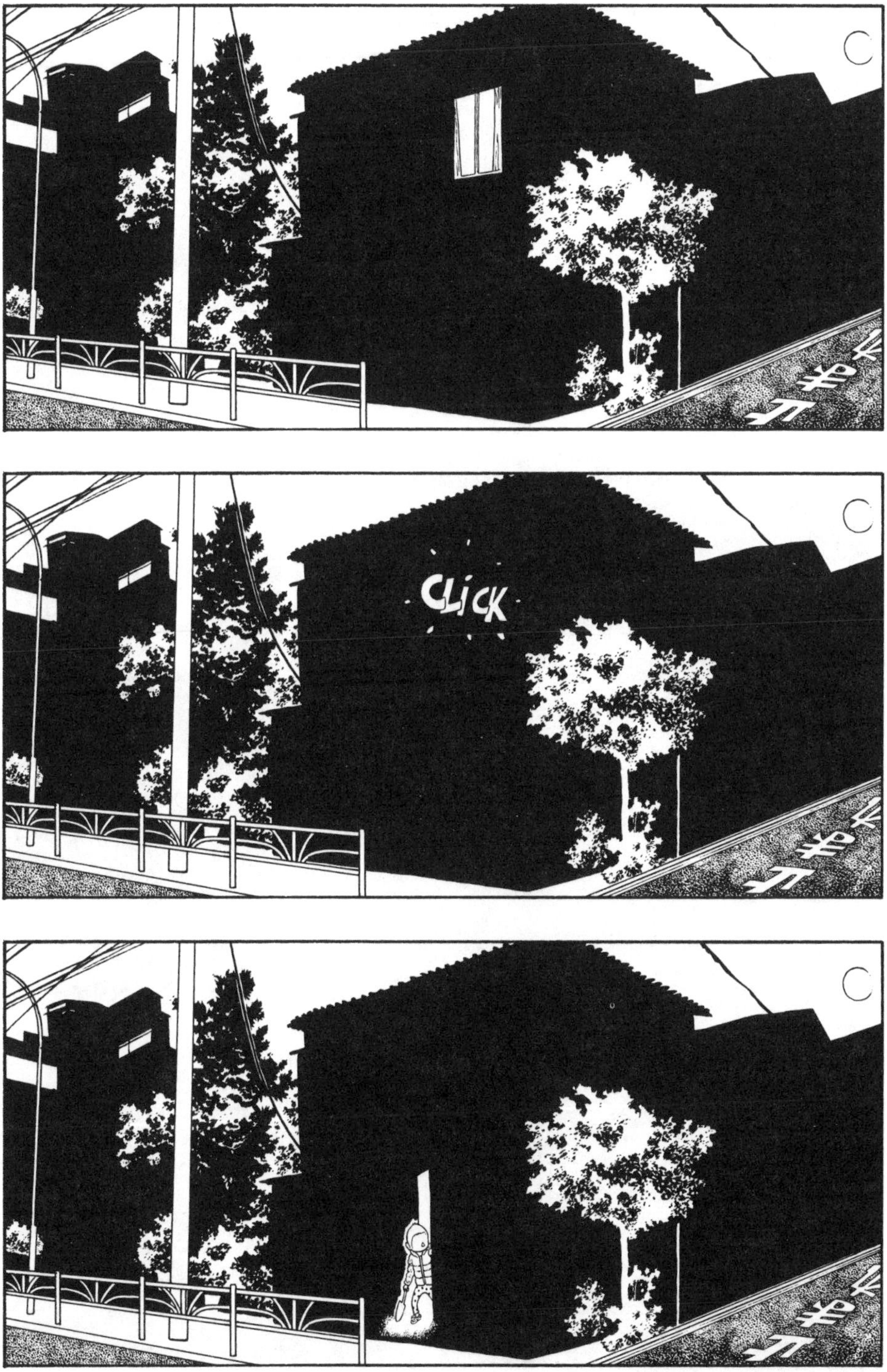
CLICK

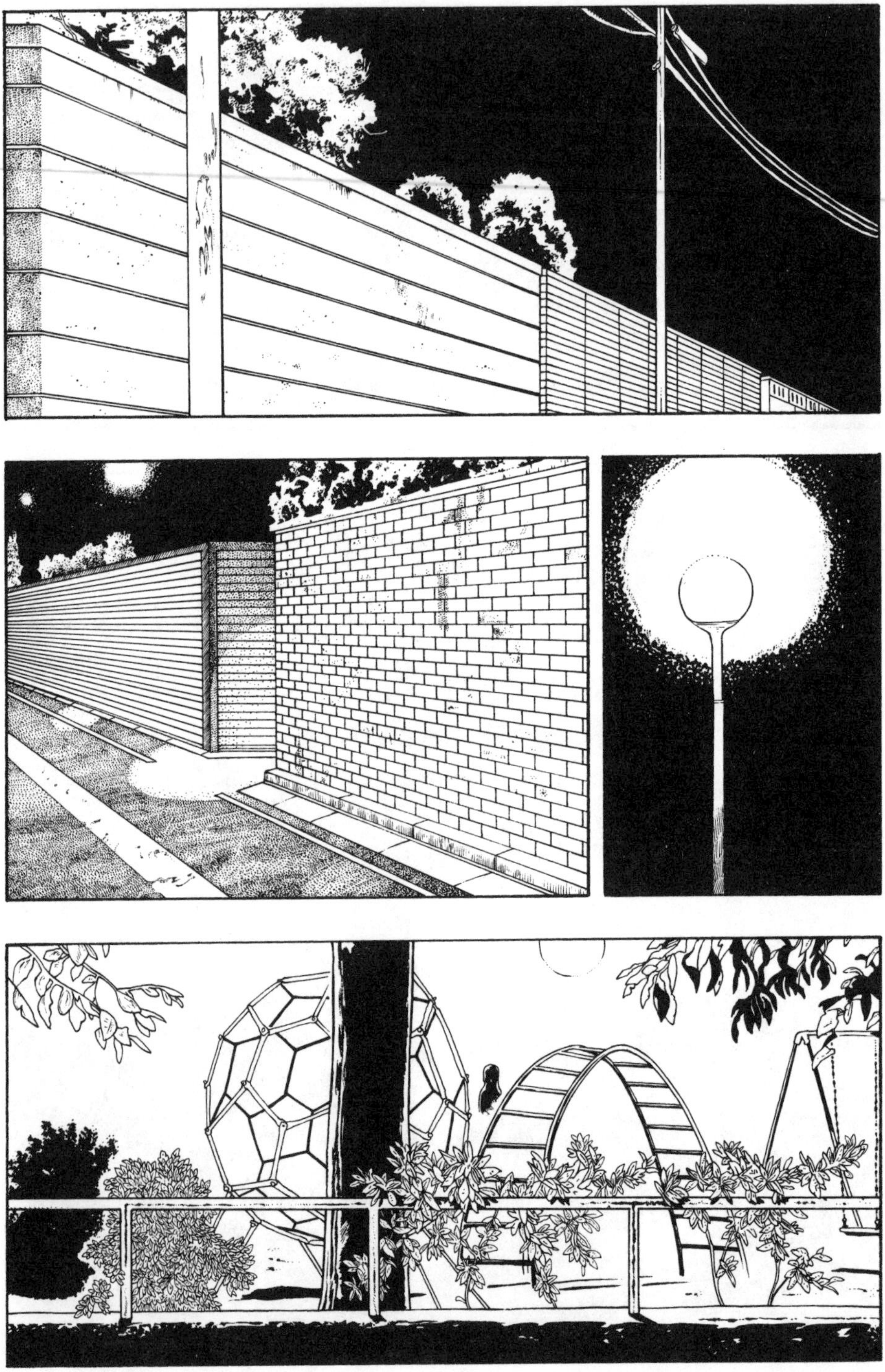

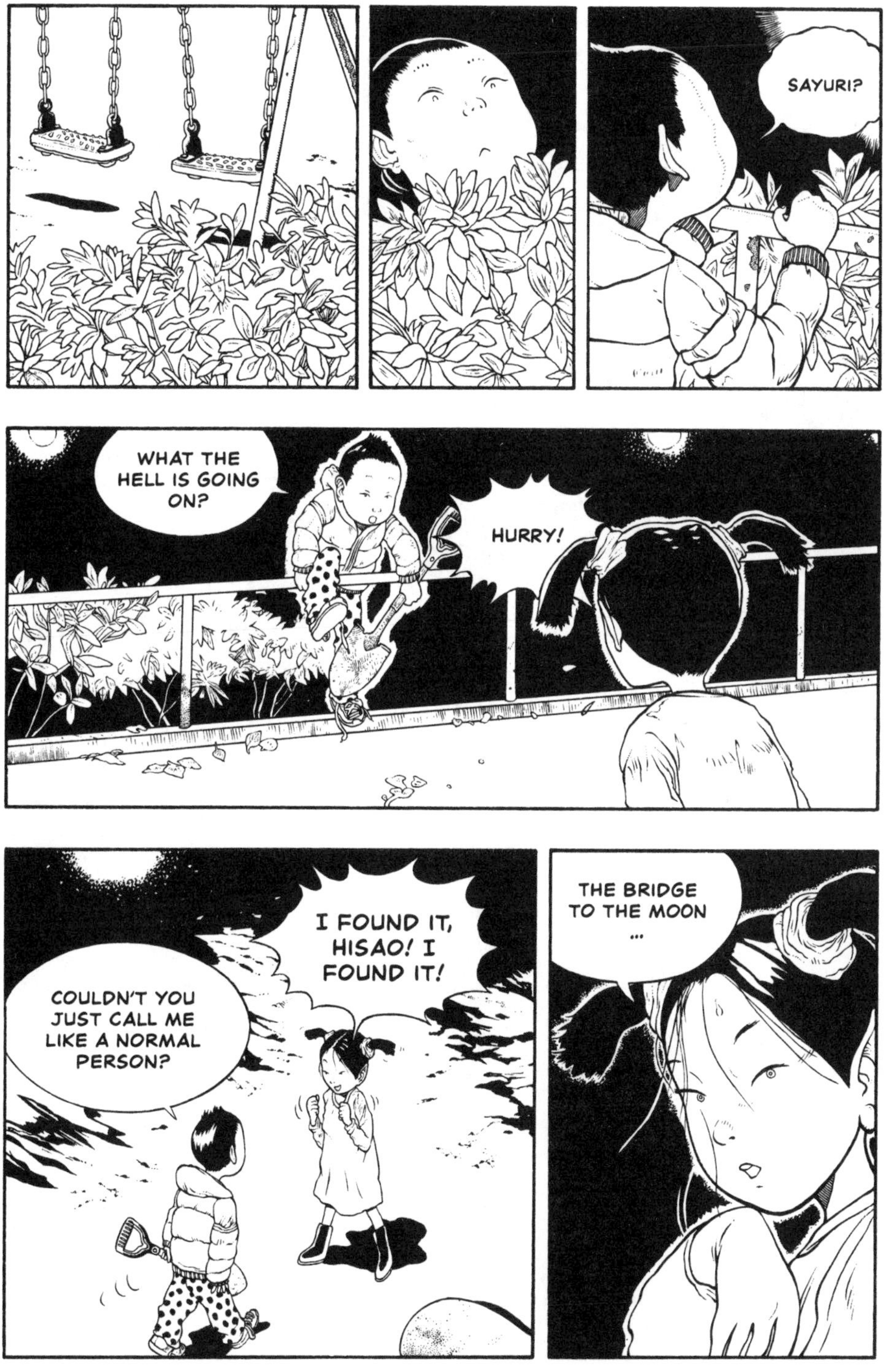
SAYURI?
WHAT THE HELL IS GOING ON?
HURRY!
I FOUND IT, HISAO! I FOUND IT!
COULDN'T YOU JUST CALL ME LIKE A NORMAL PERSON?
THE BRIDGE TO THE MOON ...

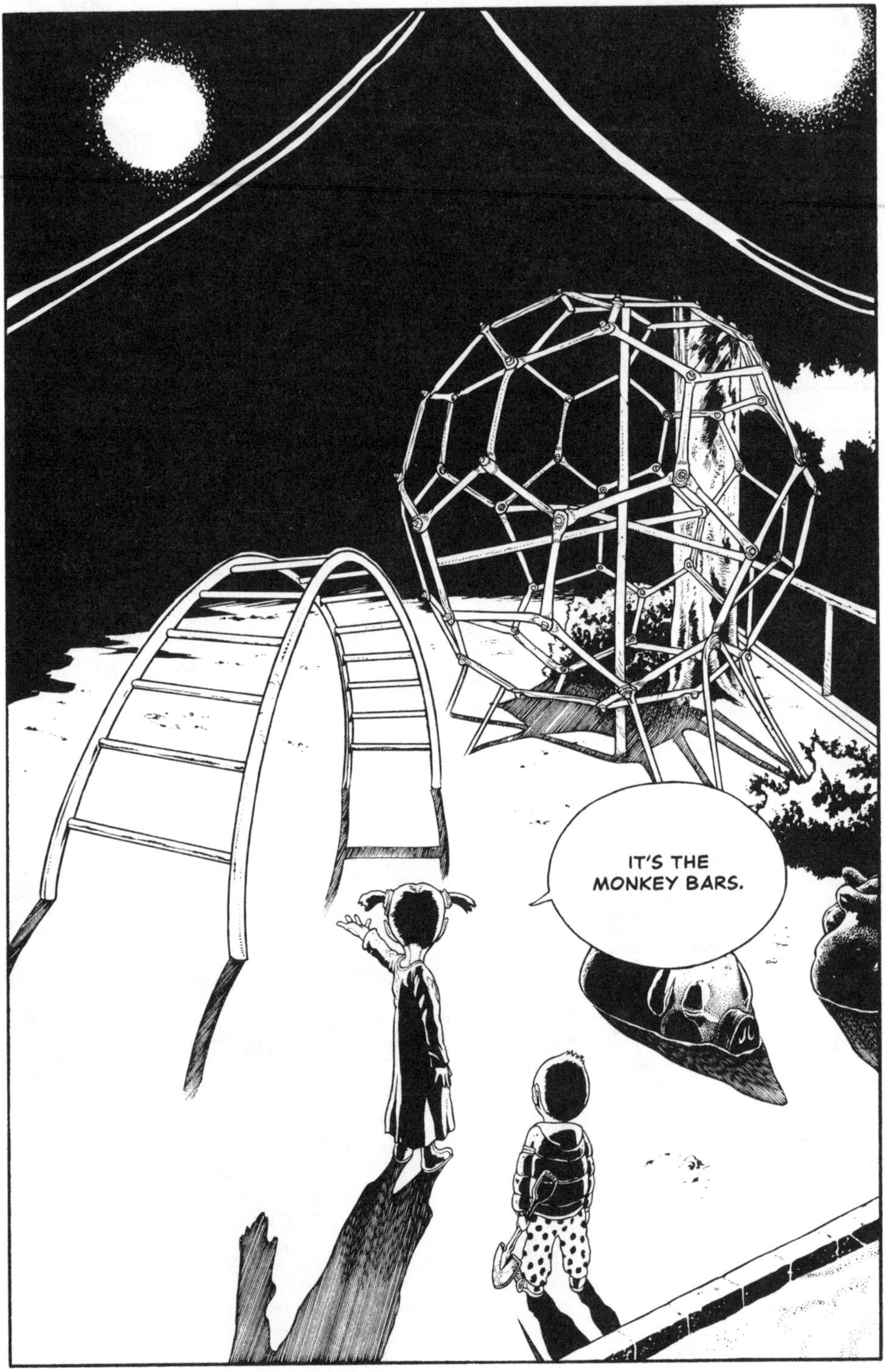
IT'S THE MONKEY BARS.

Chapter 9:
Sayuri's Dream

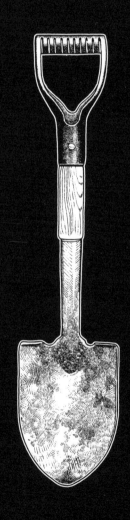

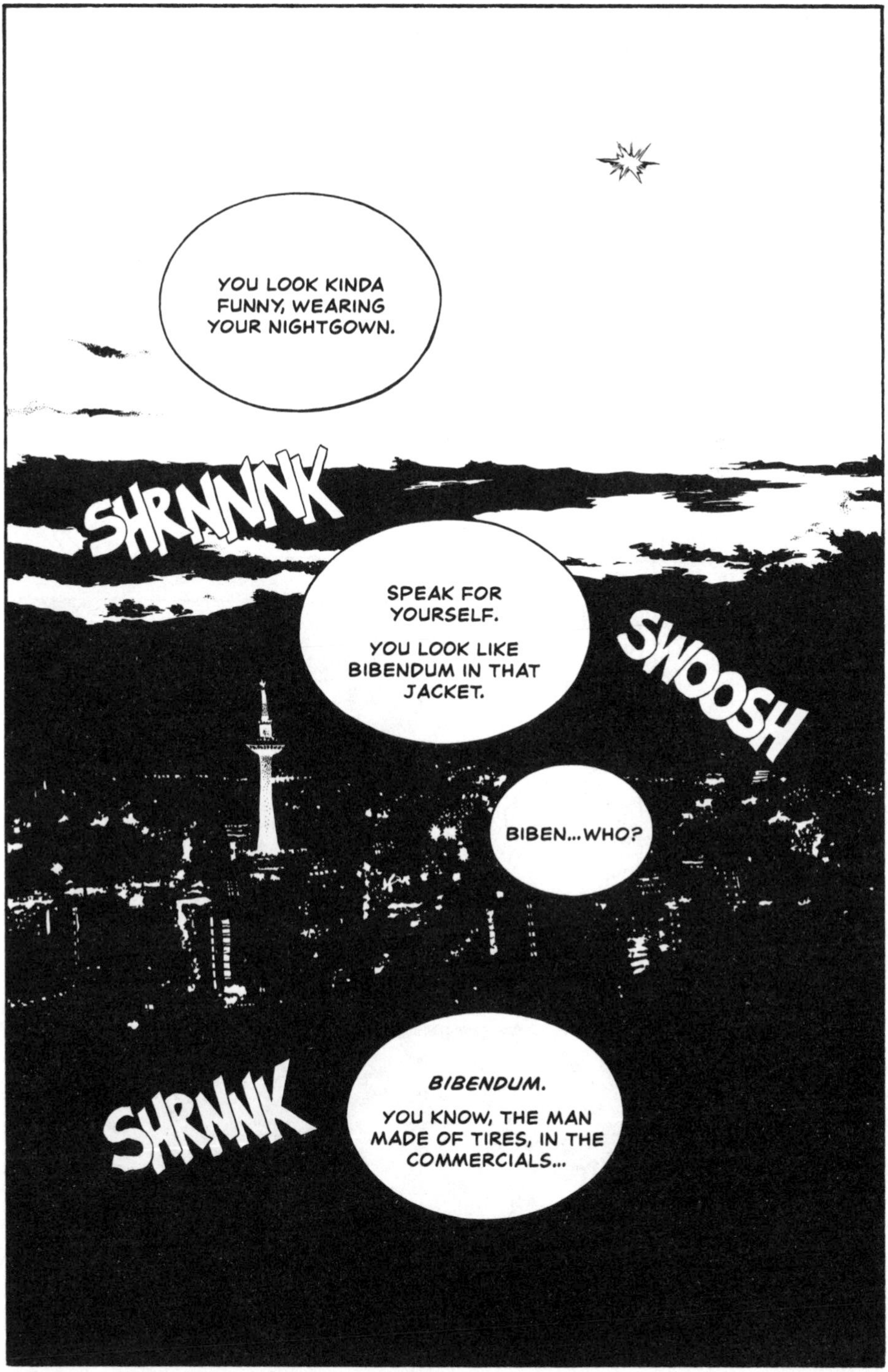
YOU LOOK KINDA FUNNY, WEARING YOUR NIGHTGOWN.
SHRNNNK
SPEAK FOR YOURSELF.
YOU LOOK LIKE BIBENDUM IN THAT JACKET.
SWOOSH
BIBEN...WHO?
SHRNNK
BIBENDUM.
YOU KNOW, THE MAN MADE OF TIRES, IN THE COMMERCIALS...

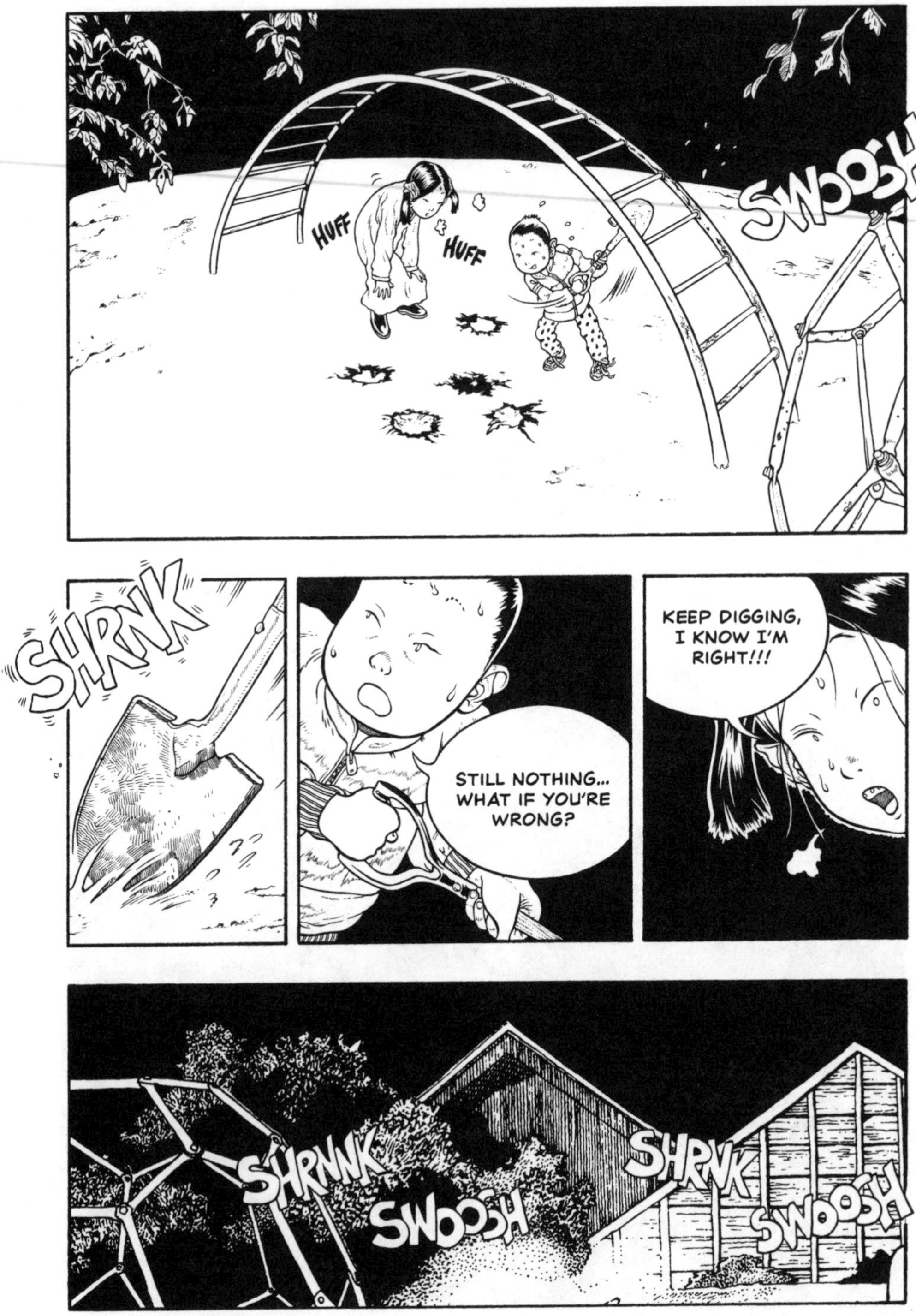
HUFF
HUFF
SWOOSH
SHRNK
STILL NOTHING... WHAT IF YOU'RE WRONG?
KEEP DIGGING, I KNOW I'M RIGHT!!!
SHRNNK
SWOOSH
SHRNK
SWOOSH

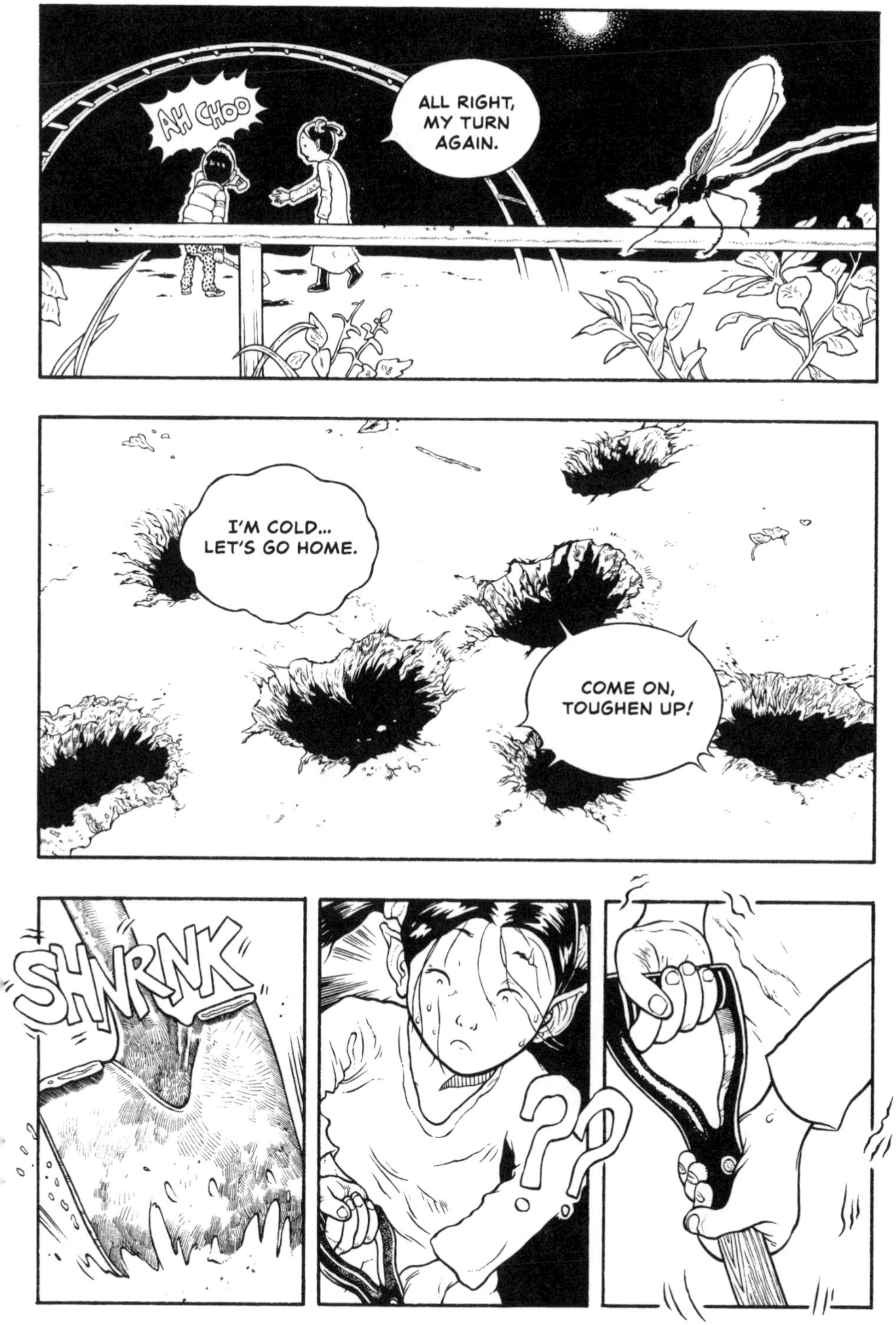
AH CHOO
ALL RIGHT, MY TURN AGAIN.
I'M COLD... LET'S GO HOME.
COME ON, TOUGHEN UP!
SHNRNK
??

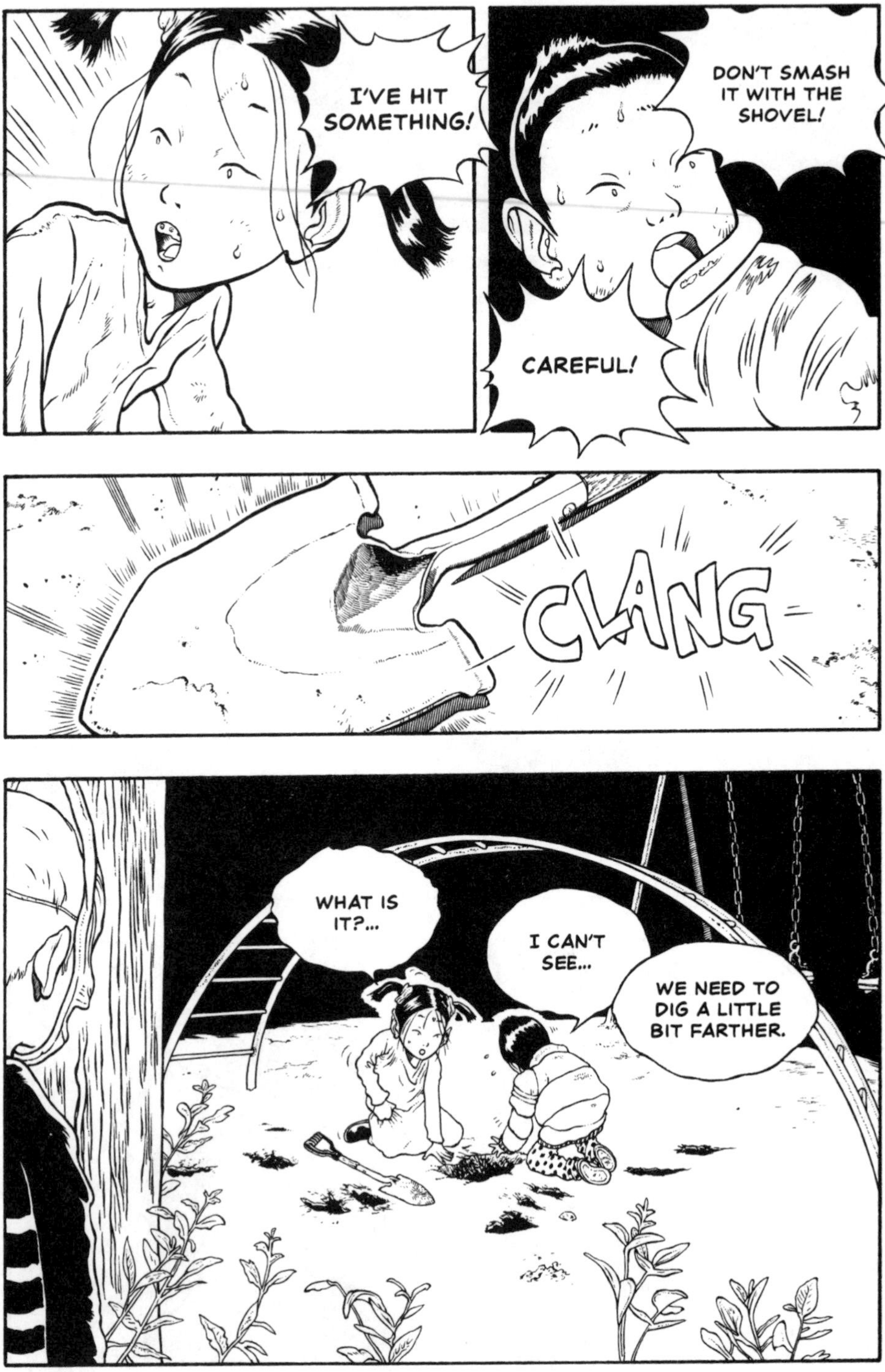
I'VE HIT SOMETHING!
DON'T SMASH IT WITH THE SHOVEL!
CAREFUL!
CLANG
WHAT IS IT?...
I CAN'T SEE...
WE NEED TO DIG A LITTLE BIT FARTHER.

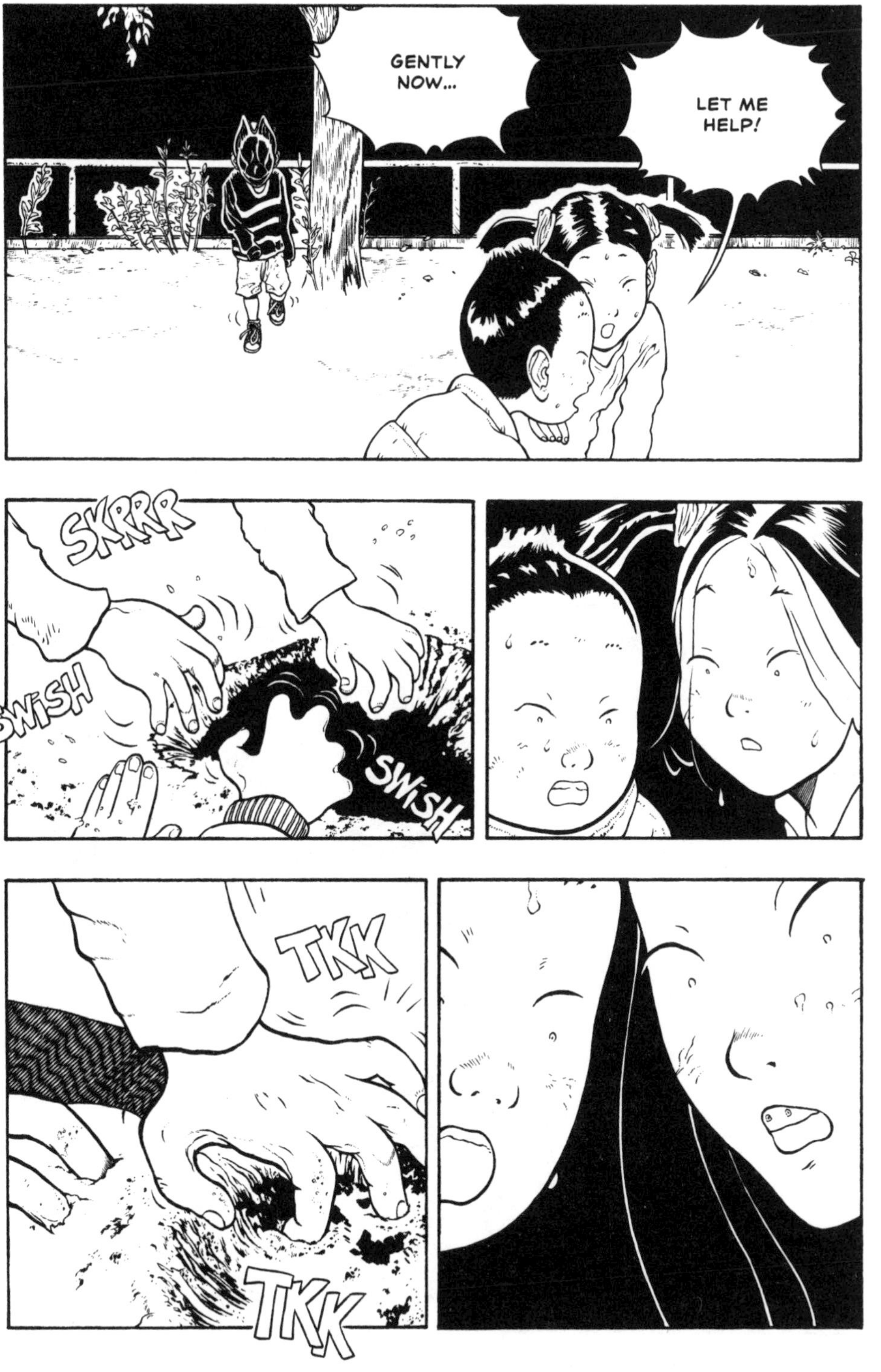
GENTLY NOW...
LET ME HELP!
SKRRR
SWISH
SWISH
TKK
TKK

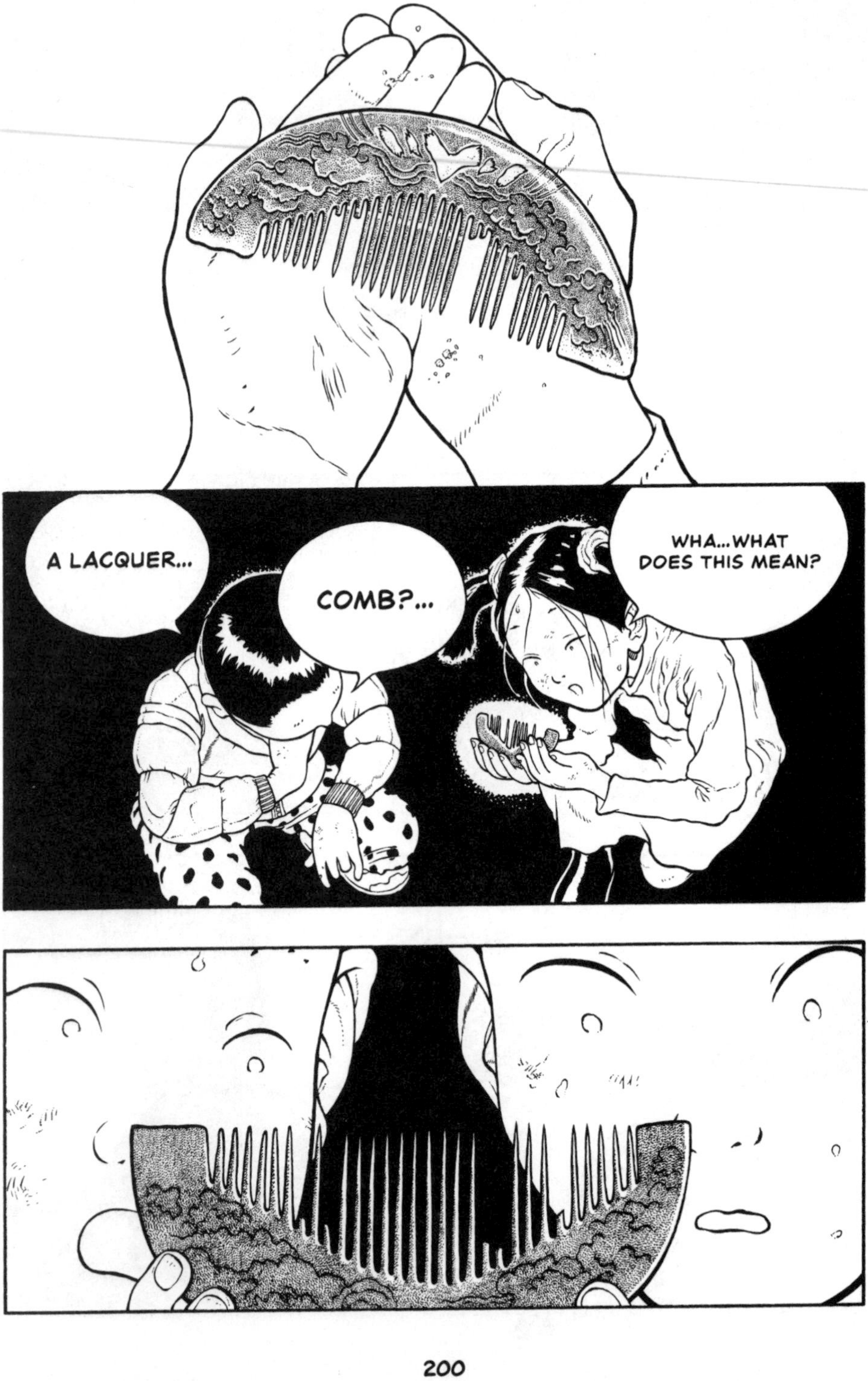
A LACQUER...
COMB?...
WHA...WHAT DOES THIS MEAN?

TOOTH...
LESS

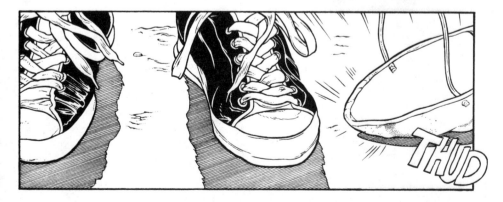

THUD

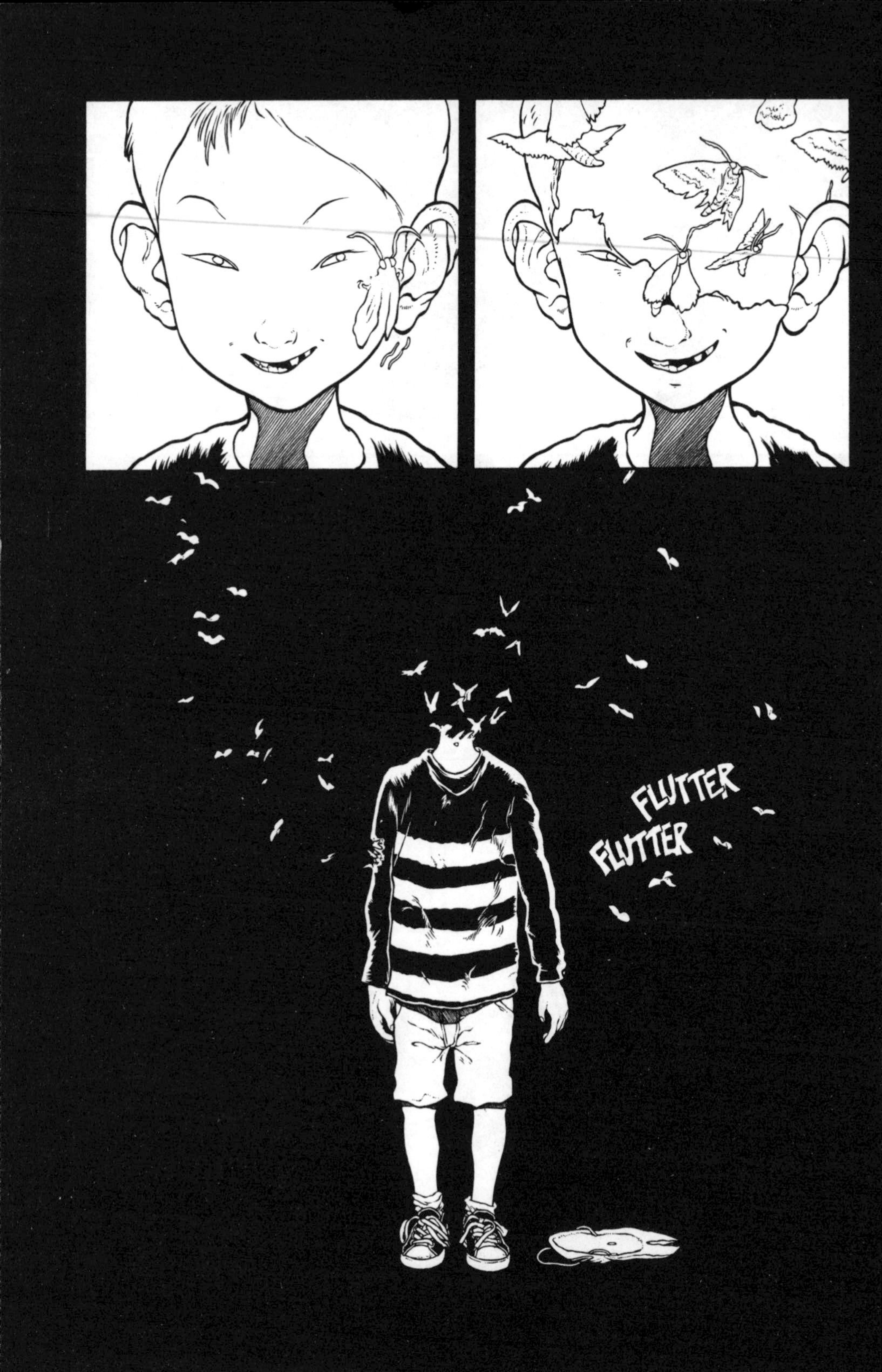
FLUTTER
FLUTTER

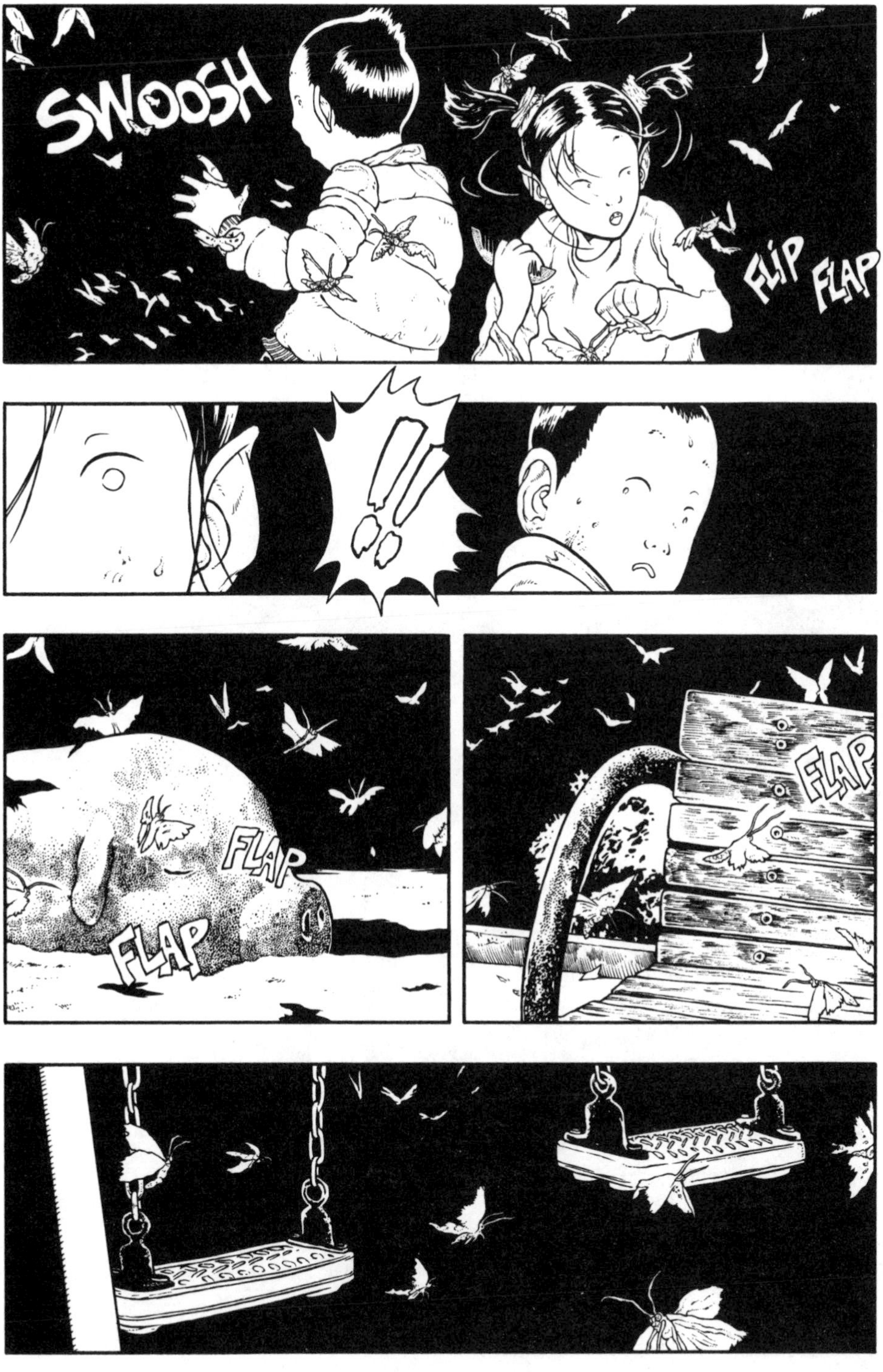
SWOOSH
FLIP
FLAP
!!
FLAP
FLAP
FLAP

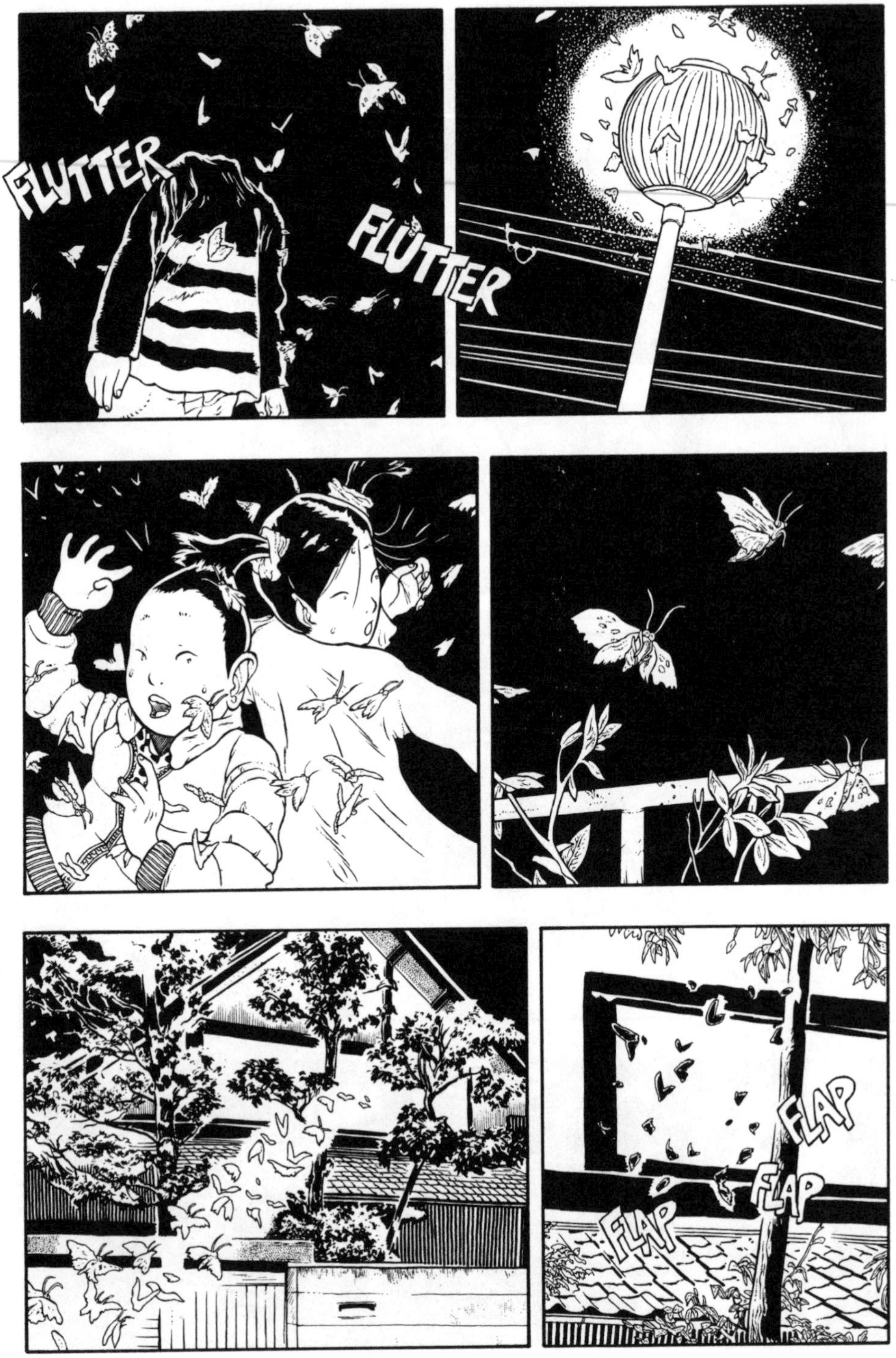
FLUTTER
FLUTTER
FLAP
FLAP
FLAP

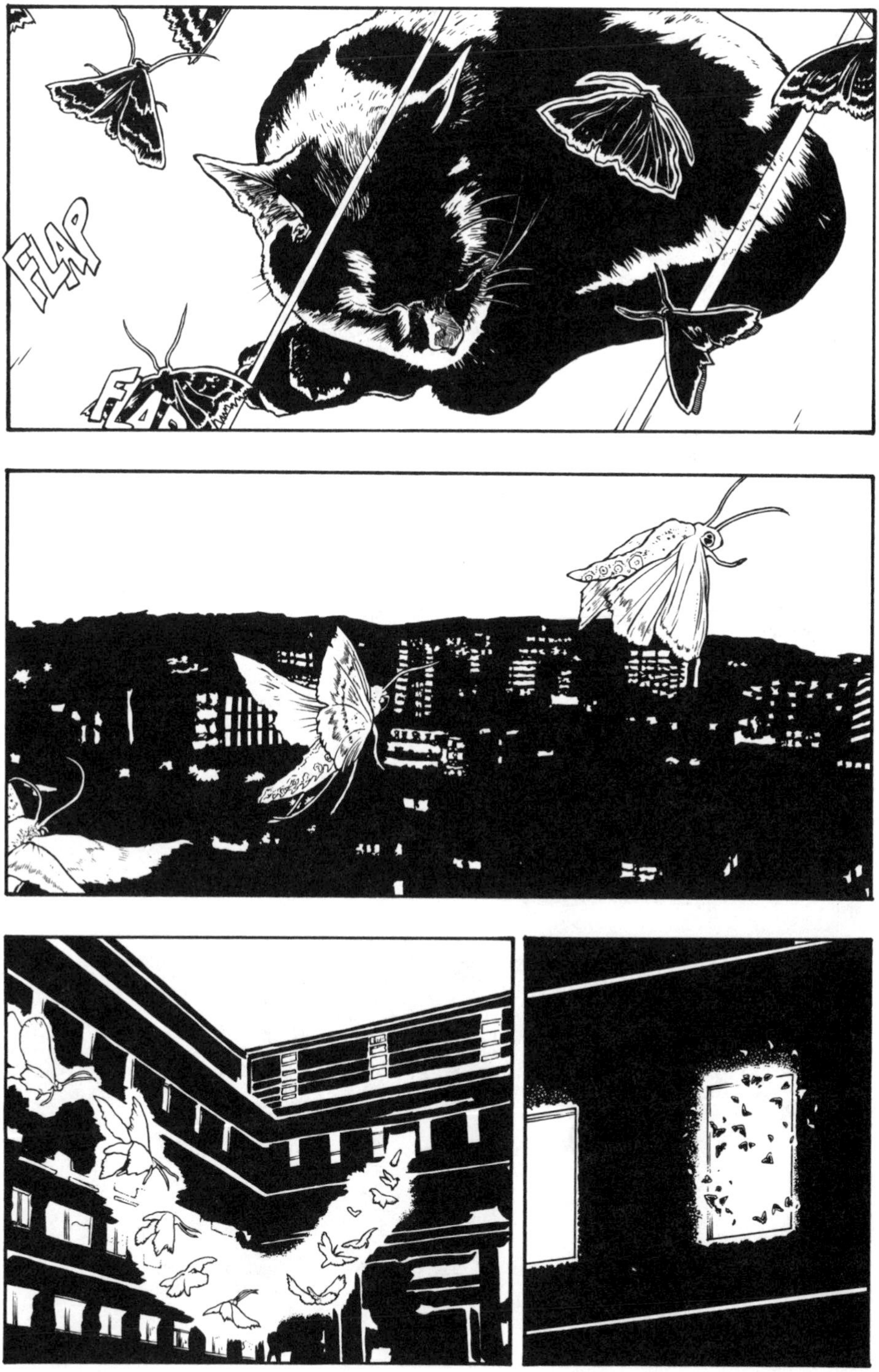
FLAP

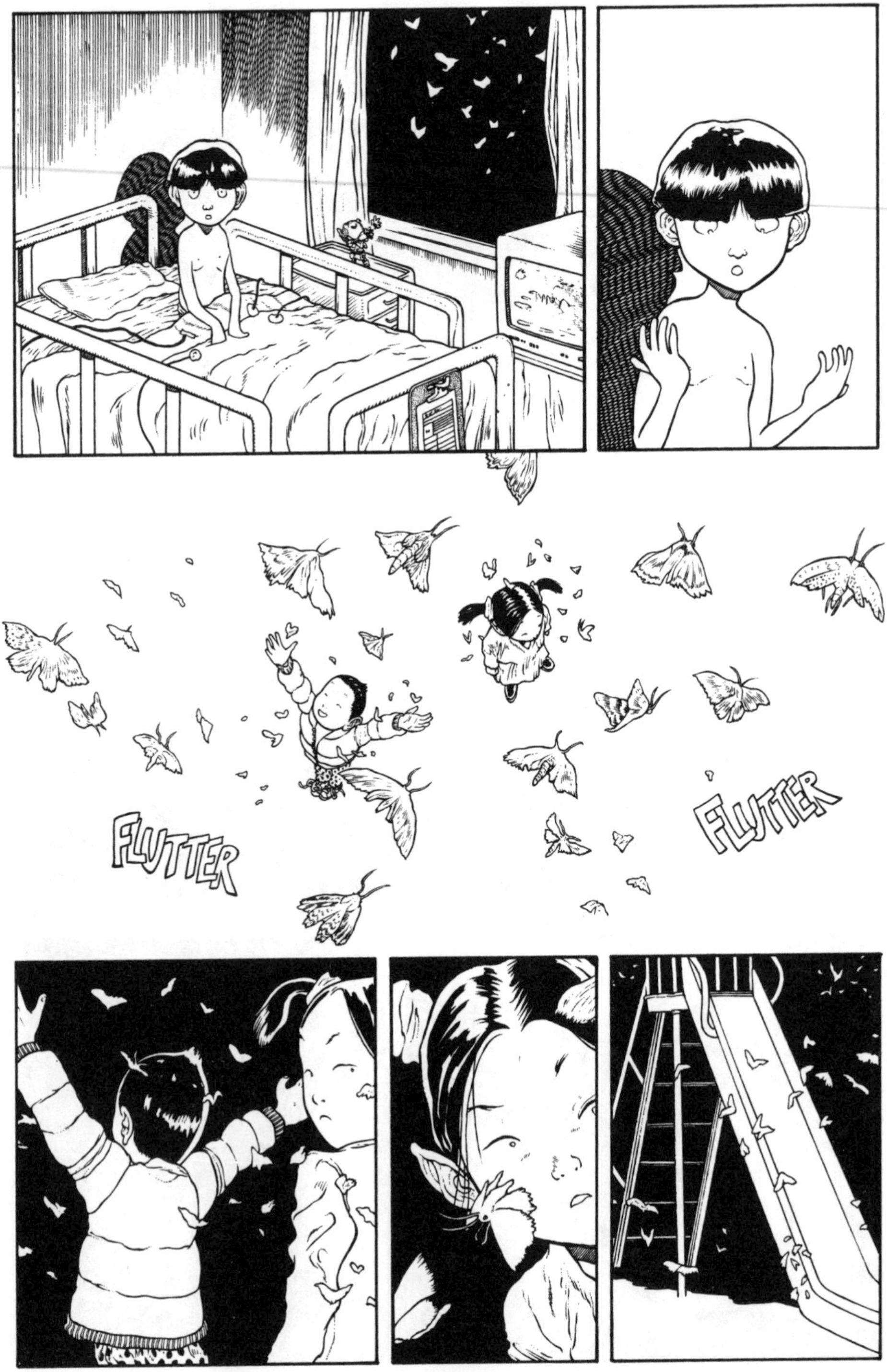
FLUTTER
FLUTTER

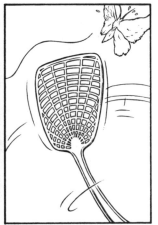

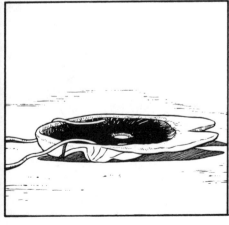

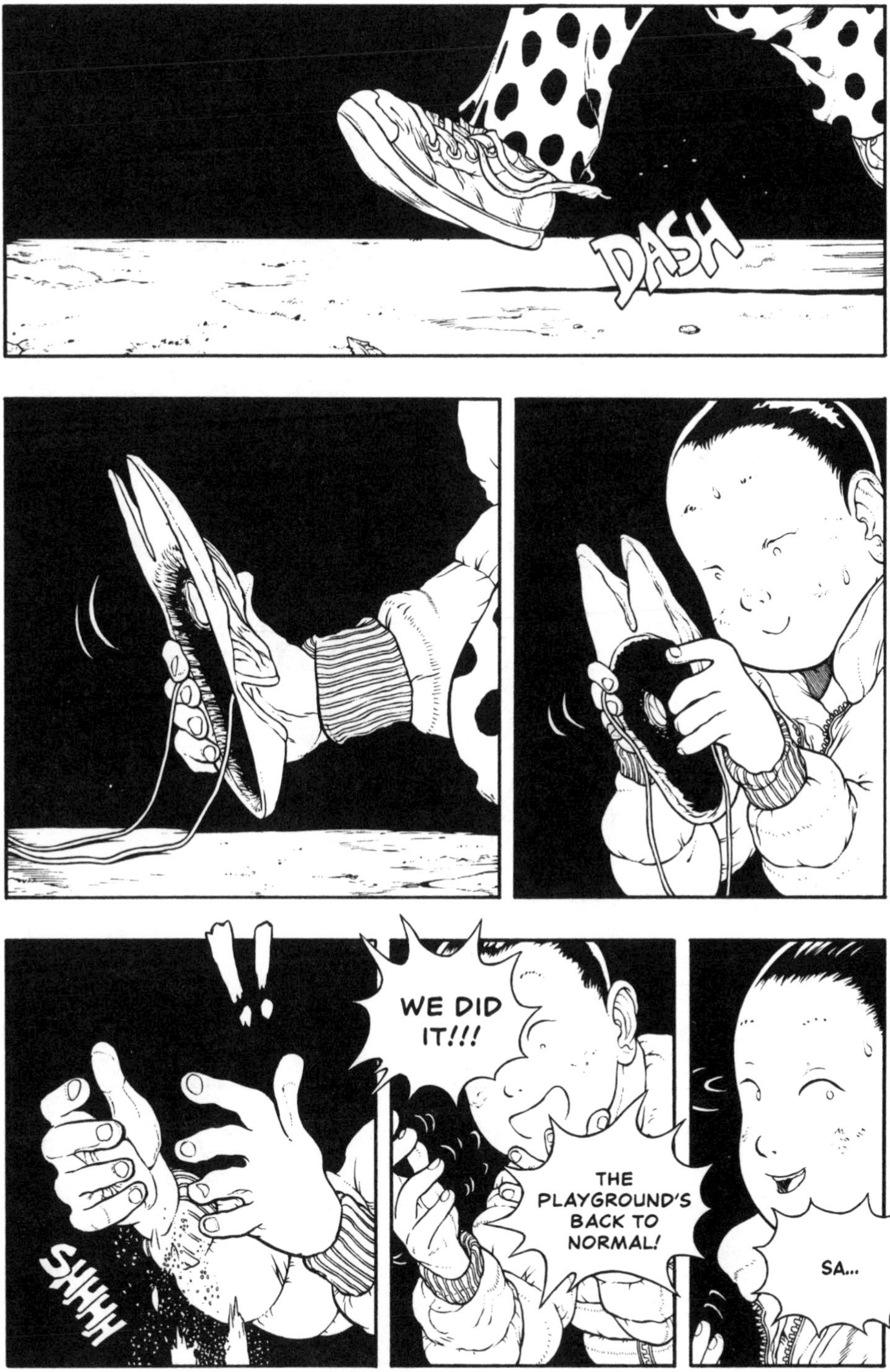
DASH
!!
SHHHH
WE DID IT!!!
THE PLAYGROUND'S BACK TO NORMAL!
SA...

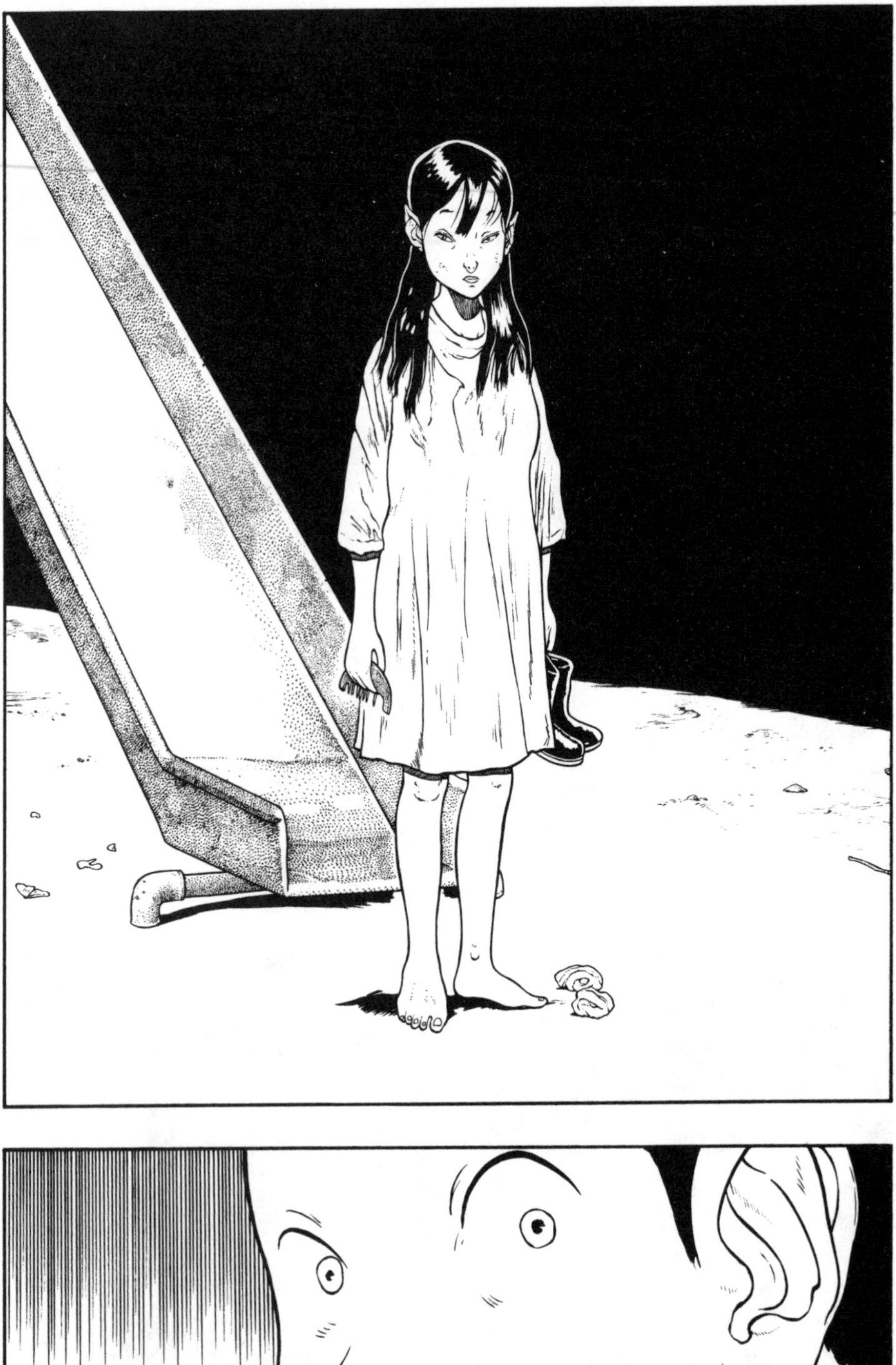

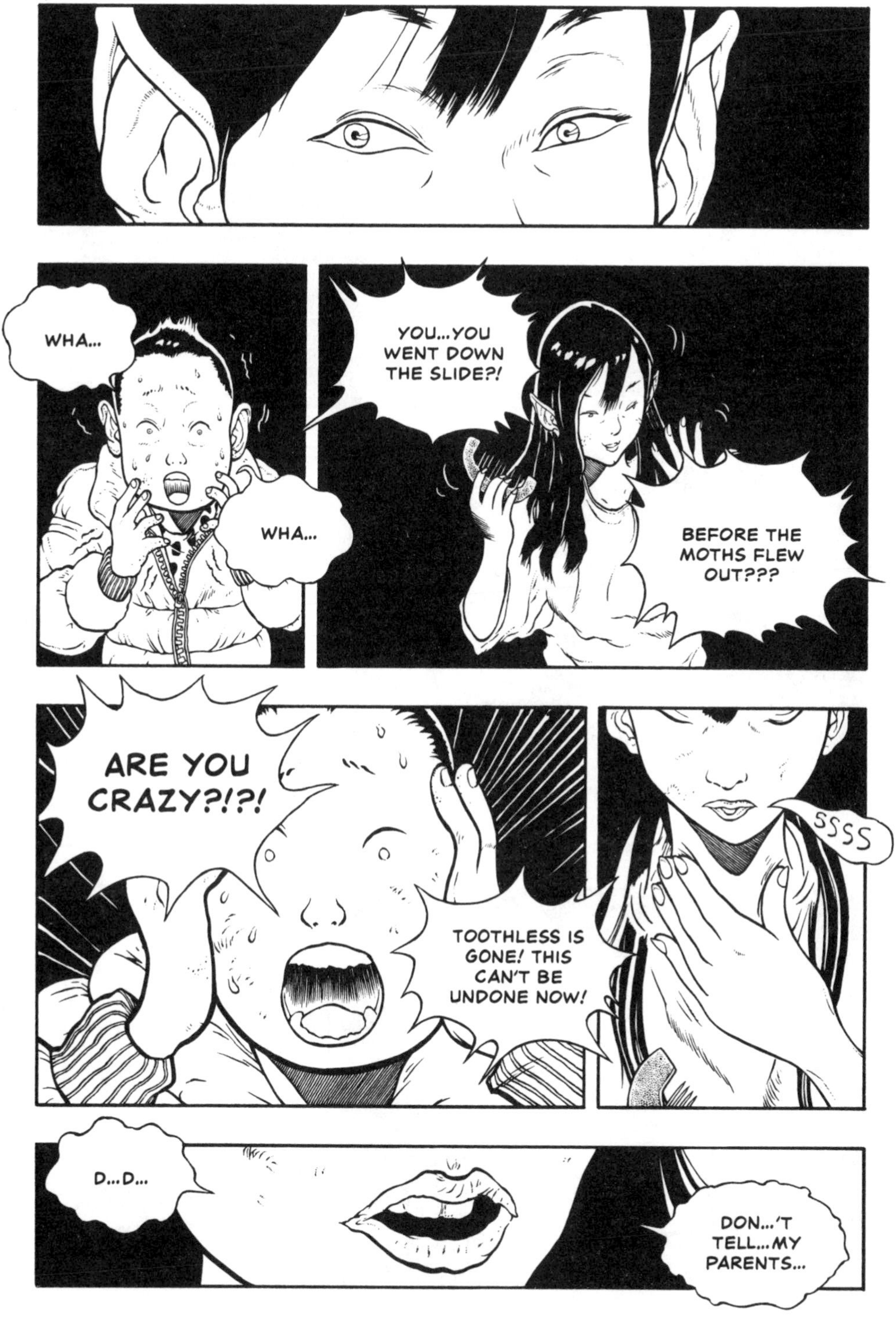
WHA...
YOU...YOU WENT DOWN THE SLIDE?!
WHA...
BEFORE THE MOTHS FLEW OUT???
ARE YOU CRAZY?!?!
TOOTHLESS IS GONE! THIS CAN'T BE UNDONE NOW!
SSSS
D...D...
DON...'T TELL...MY PARENTS...

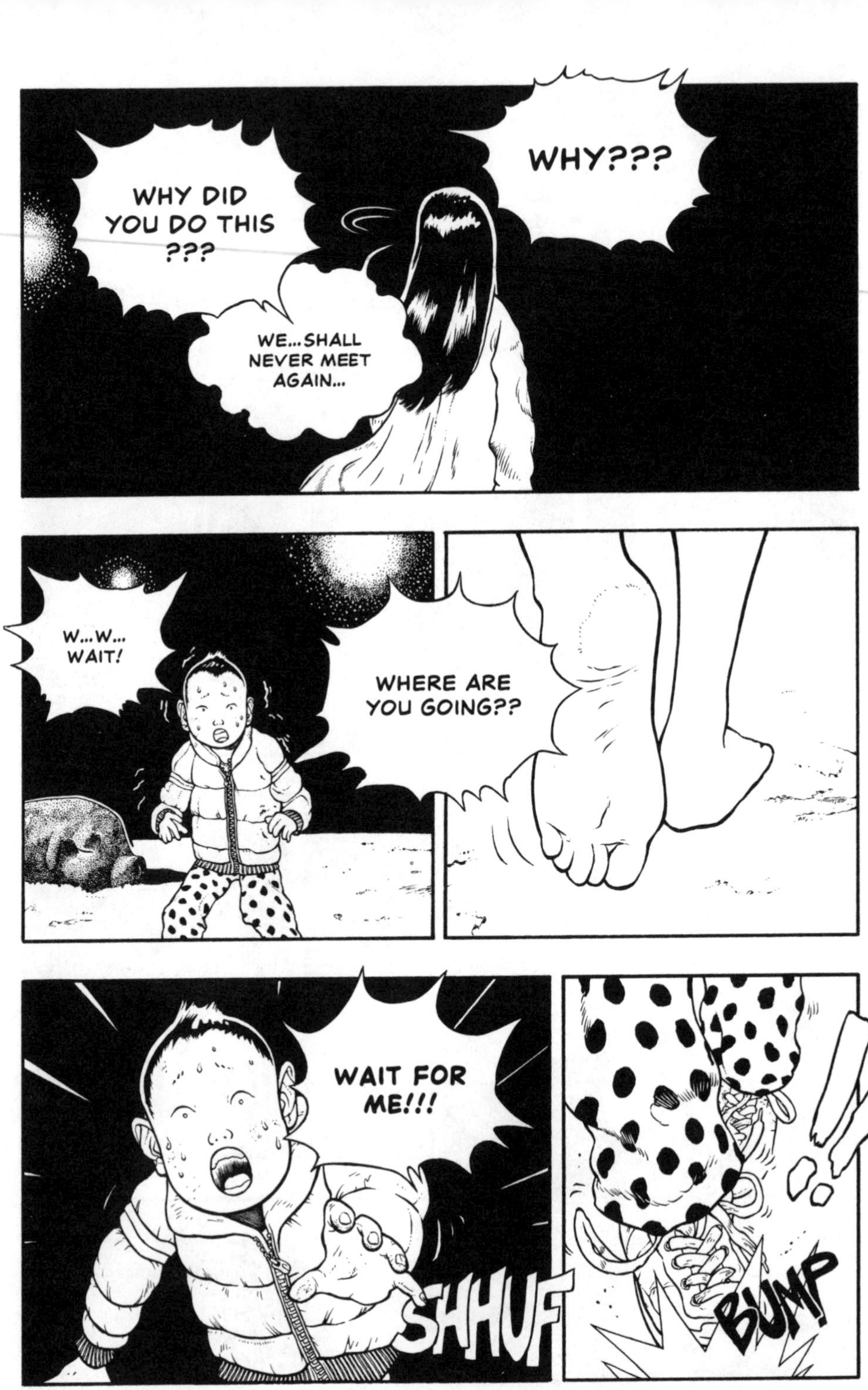
WHY DID YOU DO THIS ???
WHY???
WE...SHALL NEVER MEET AGAIN...
W...W... WAIT!
WHERE ARE YOU GOING??
WAIT FOR ME!!!
SHHUF
!!
BUMP

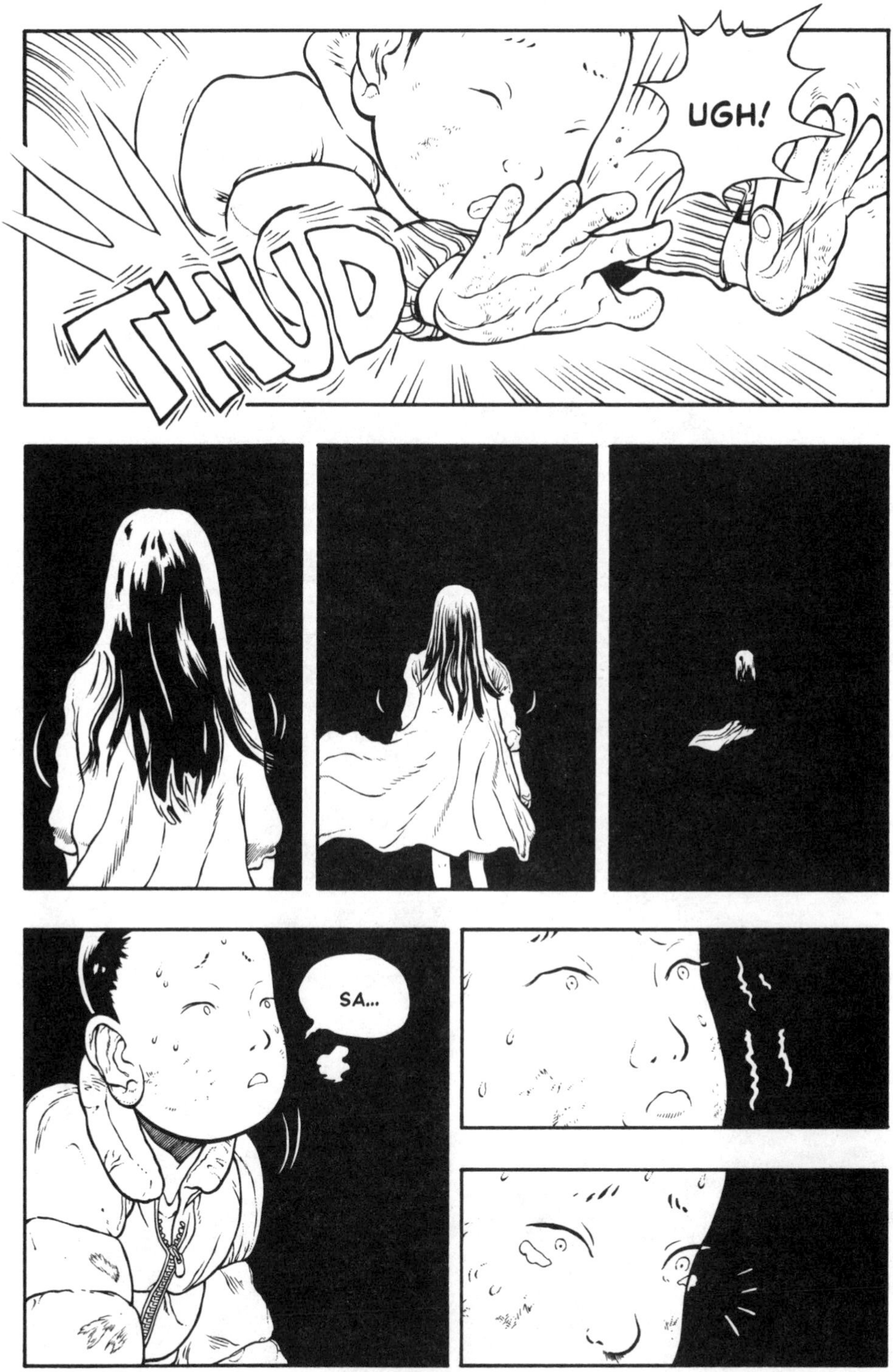
UGH!
THUD
SA...

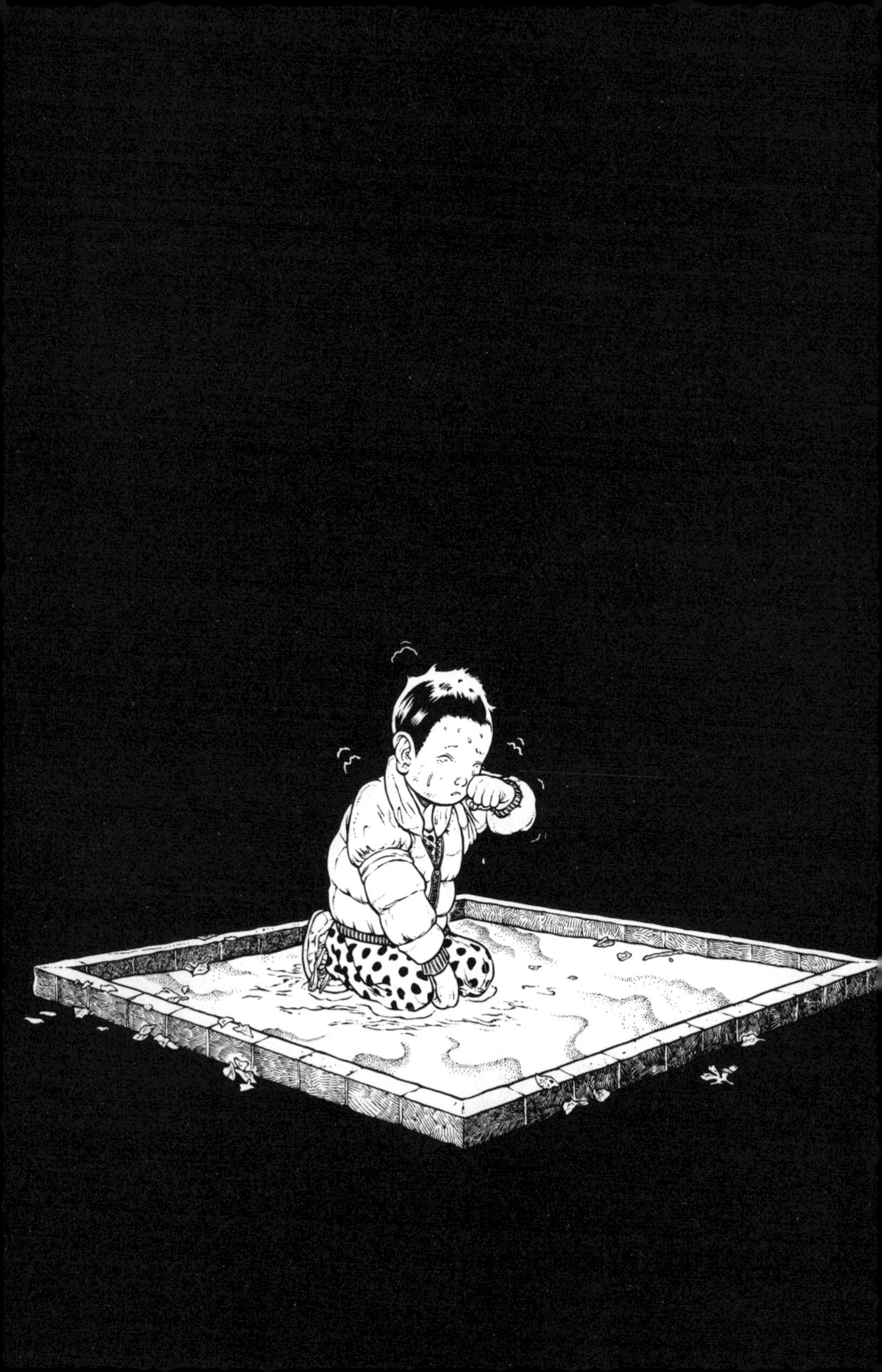

Epilogue:
Fast Forward

FIFTY YEARS LATER...

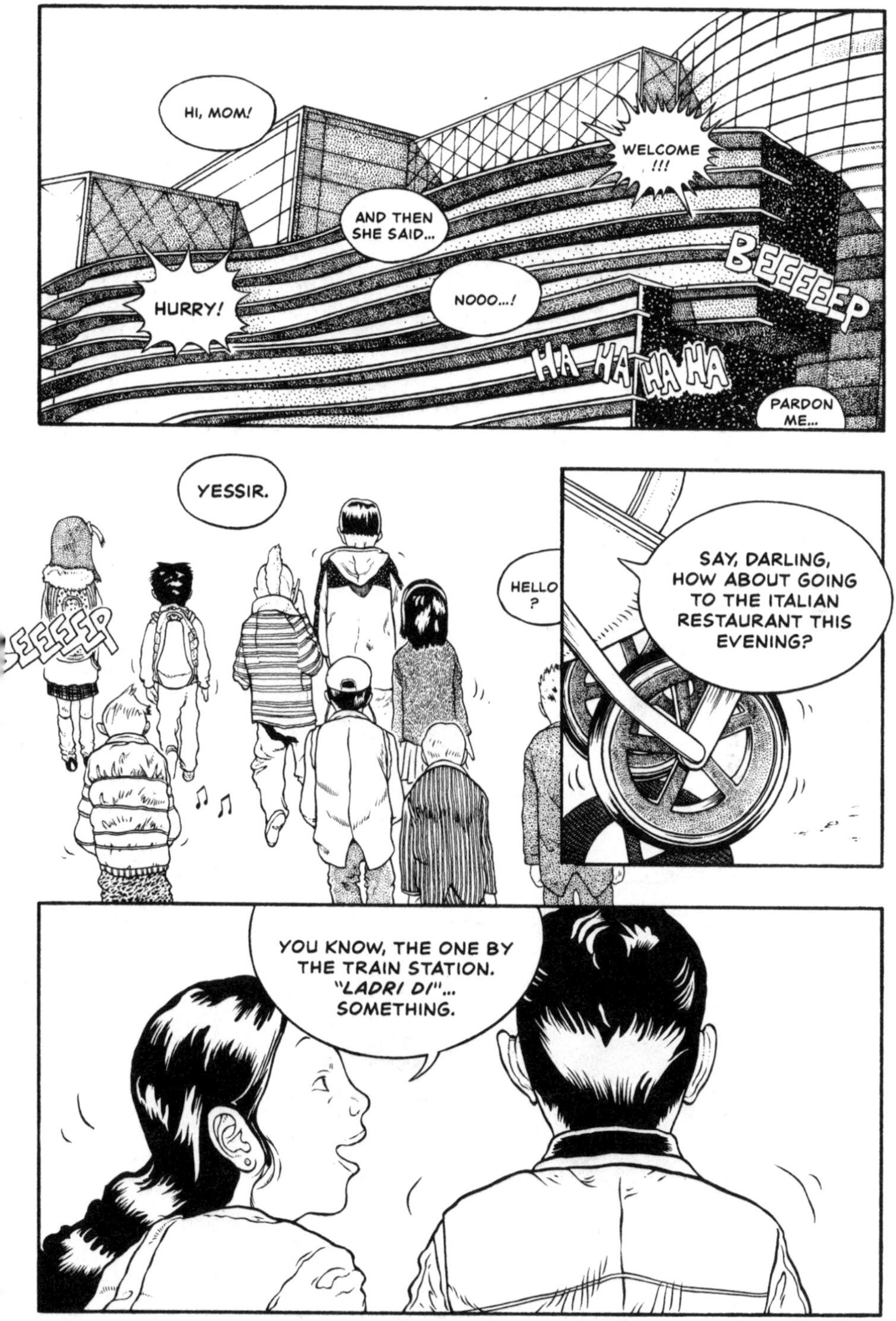
HI, MOM!
WELCOME !!!
AND THEN SHE SAID...
HURRY!
NOOO...!
BEEEEEP
HA HA HA HA
PARDON ME...
YESSIR.
HELLO ?
SAY, DARLING, HOW ABOUT GOING TO THE ITALIAN RESTAURANT THIS EVENING?
YOU KNOW, THE ONE BY THE TRAIN STATION. *"LADRI DI"*... SOMETHING.

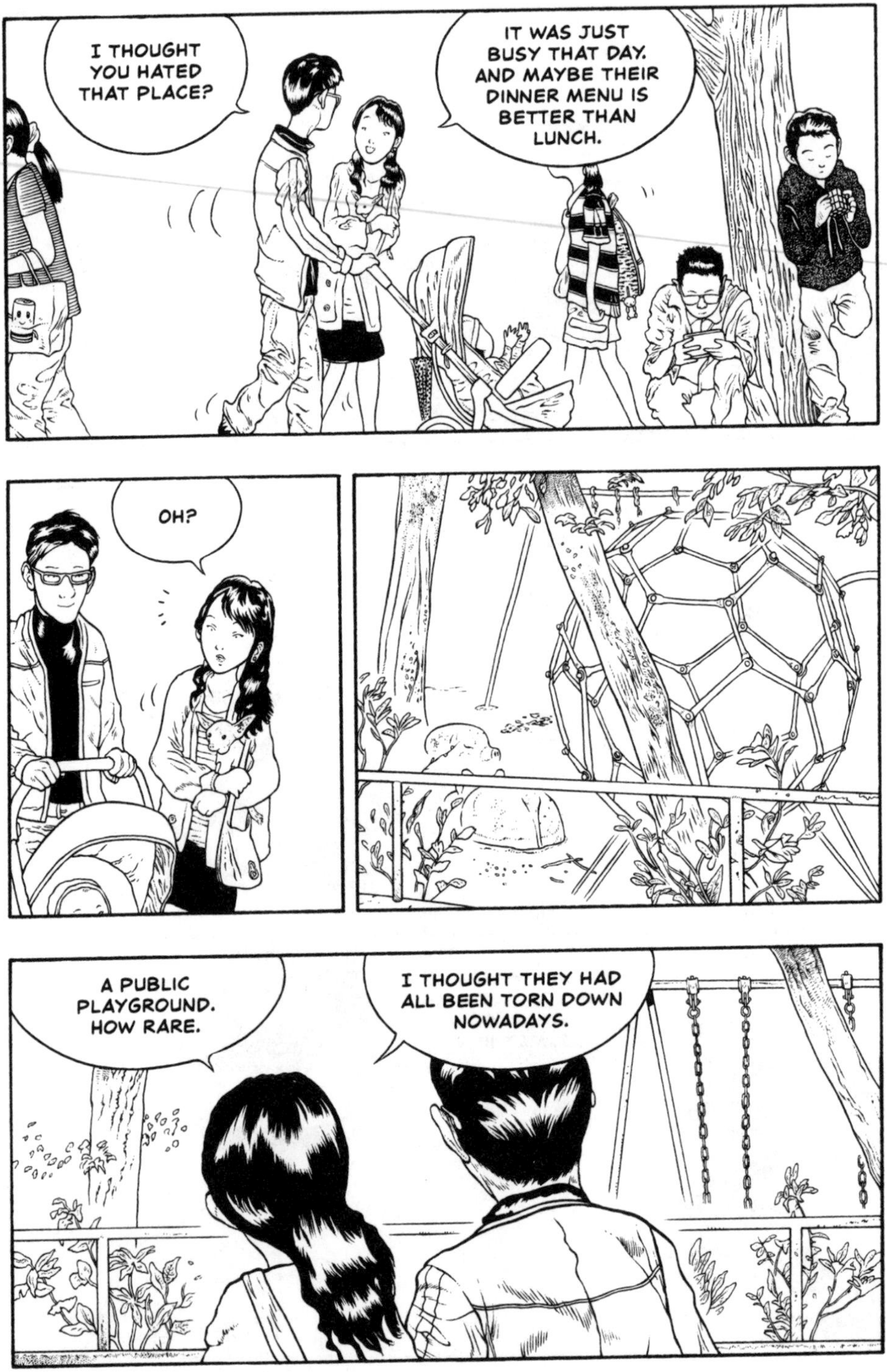
I THOUGHT YOU HATED THAT PLACE?
IT WAS JUST BUSY THAT DAY. AND MAYBE THEIR DINNER MENU IS BETTER THAN LUNCH.
OH?
A PUBLIC PLAYGROUND. HOW RARE.
I THOUGHT THEY HAD ALL BEEN TORN DOWN NOWADAYS.

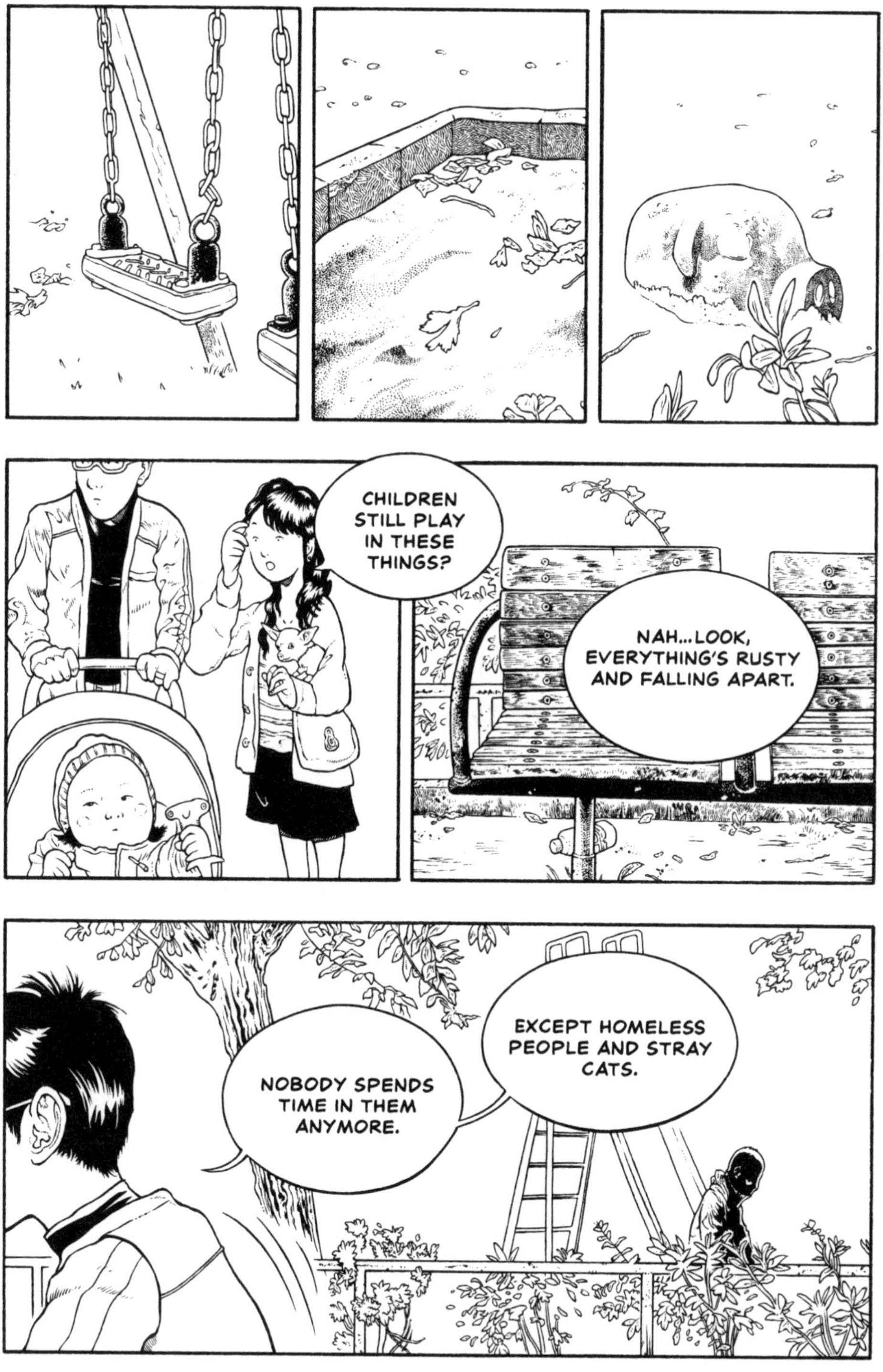
CHILDREN STILL PLAY IN THESE THINGS?
NAH...LOOK, EVERYTHING'S RUSTY AND FALLING APART.
NOBODY SPENDS TIME IN THEM ANYMORE.
EXCEPT HOMELESS PEOPLE AND STRAY CATS.

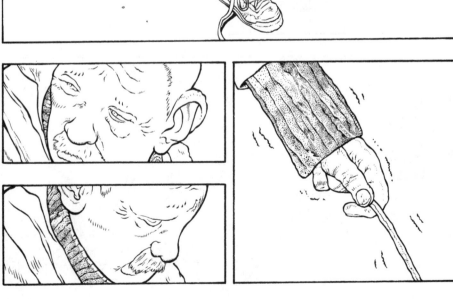

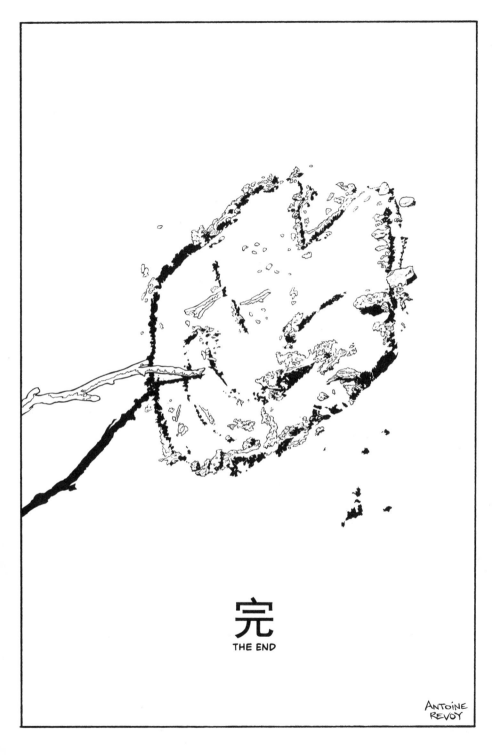

完
THE END

ANTOINE
REVOY

Special thanks to:

Sophie and Sébastien Revoy; Jonathan, Jérémy, Julia, N⋯nd
Patrick Trane; Maurice Audinet; Sven Cosnuau; Julien ⋯al
Martin; Robert Cichostepski; Baptiste Auric; Guillaume ⋯er,
Amaia, and Antoine de Mena; Amélie Guiraud; Fred Lynch⋯nald
Lynch; Sonny Liew; R Kikuo Johnson; Joe McKendry; Jas⋯lef
Brown; JooHee Yoon; Nick and Monica Jainschigg; Lars ⋯c
Telfort; Melissa Ferreira; Cédric Sapien; Rebecca Paiva; Er⋯s
Takashi Tsunashima; Kenzo Yoneno; Cutter Hutton; Elli⋯
Courtney; Robert Mathewson; T. Michael Tracy; Patrick Har⋯to;
Emi Okamoto; Hiromi Hatano; NCAD; the Revoy, Morel, N⋯
Darji, Karl, Larson, Leonard, Thomas, Byrd, Hirano, and K⋯
Toshio Suzuki; Hirohiko Araki; Hitoshi Iwaaki; New Order⋯
First Second staff; Kiara Valdez; Andrew Arnold; Mark Sie⋯
students; the house pe(s)ts; and Kelly Murphy.

First Second

New York

Copyright © 20voy

Published by Faring Brook Press,
First Second ishing Holdings Limited Partnership
a division of HY 10010
175 Fifth Aver

Library of Cumber: 2017946144
ISBN: 978-1

Our books in bulk for promotional, educational,
or businesst your local bookseller or the Macmillan
Corporates Department at (800) 221-7945 ext. 5442
or by e-macialMarkets@macmillan.com.

FIRST

EDITION

First edio and Molly Johanson
Book des of America
Printed

10 9 8 7

BY A
WE LI